THE WITCHES' REDE: BOOK 2

POSSESSION

JEWEL E. LEONARD

DAZZLEINK PRESS

POSSESSION

A DazzleInk Press Book / published by arrangement with the author.

Paperback ISBN: 978-1948399029
Ebook ISBN: 978-1948399036

PRINTED IN THE UNITED STATES OF AMERICA

10 9 8 7 6 5 4 3 2

Cover photography and design by Scott M. Leonard.
Interior text design by Jewel E. Leonard.

This is a work of fiction. Names, characters, places, and incidents either are the product of the author's imagination or are used fictitiously, and any resemblance to actual persons, living or dead, business establishments, events, or locales is entirely coincidental.

The publisher does not have any control over and does not assume any responsibility for author content on social media, nor for author or third-party websites or their content.

If you purchased this book without a cover, you should be aware that this book is stolen property. It was reported as "unsold and destroyed" to the publisher, and neither the author nor the publisher has received any payment for this "stripped book" in its g-string, or anyplace else.

"Who's in charge of the 'Pack,' Miss Chesterfield?" He overenunciated her name so she knew he didn't believe it was really hers.

It was silent for a long time before she muttered, "I am."

"Preposterous!" Liam said through his laughter.

"Ask any of them. I'm Pack leader."

"Well I don't presume I could ask Esquivar, de la Cloche, Kartchner, Schieffelin, or ... Prescott. Could I?"

Alexis scowled, and she lowered her head. "Not unless you know someone who can talk to ghosts."

Liam groaned. "Who's missing from the group?"

"Nobody."

Liar. She was a good liar, granted, but a liar nonetheless; she wasn't head of the Pack and neither were any of the other people he'd listed. "Where were you on September tenth?"

After several moments, Alexis lifted her gaze and met his head-on. She cleared her throat. With a nearly imperceptive shake of her head, she answered, "I was at Church."

"I highly doubt you have ever been to church. Leastly on a Monday."

"I'm offended!" she countered. "I've been baptized and everything."

"Well you're hardly following the Bible's teachings, given what you've already provided in your testimony."

"I don't see how that's the least bit relevant to this investigation. Besides. A lot of folks are Sunday Christians ... as if going to pray one day makes up for all their sins and lack of prayer for the other six. I'm sure your type does the same. If you were godly all days, what's the need to go to confessional on your day of rest?"

"The semantics of religion is not my concern."

She smirked. "Then remember as much the next time you claim someone doesn't seem like a churchgoer."

"Miss! Chesterfield!"

"And if you insist on trying to pin this on me, why don't you stop by the church yourself and talk to the people there. Maybe actually investigate? I'm sure they'll confirm my whereabouts when the Tiff blew."

The Witches' Rede series by Jewel E. Leonard:

ALIGHT
PROPHECY
COVEN

Forthcoming:

ROUT

Other books

RAYS OF SUNSHINE

"Who's in charge of the 'Pack,' Miss Chesterfield?" He overenunciated her name so she knew he didn't believe it was really hers.

It was silent for a long time before she muttered, "I am."

"Preposterous!" Liam said through his laughter.

"Ask any of them. I'm Pack leader."

"Well I don't presume I could ask Esquivar, de la Cloche, Kartchner, Schieffelin, or ... Prescott. Could I?"

Alexis scowled, and she lowered her head. "Not unless you know someone who can talk to ghosts."

Liam groaned. "Who's missing from the group?"

"Nobody."

Liar. She was a good liar, granted, but a liar nonetheless; she wasn't head of the Pack and neither were any of the other people he'd listed. "Where were you on September tenth?"

After several moments, Alexis lifted her gaze and met his head-on. She cleared her throat. With a nearly imperceptive shake of her head, she answered, "I was at Church."

"I highly doubt you have ever been to church. Leastly on a Monday."

"I'm offended!" she countered. "I've been baptized and everything."

"Well you're hardly following the Bible's teachings, given what you've already provided in your testimony."

"I don't see how that's the least bit relevant to this investigation. Besides. A lot of folks are Sunday Christians ... as if going to pray one day makes up for all their sins and lack of prayer for the other six. I'm sure your type does the same. If you were godly all days, what's the need to go to confessional on your day of rest?"

"The semantics of religion is not my concern."

She smirked. "Then remember as much the next time you claim someone doesn't seem like a churchgoer."

"Miss! Chesterfield!"

"And if you insist on trying to pin this on me, why don't you stop by the church yourself and talk to the people there. Maybe actually investigate? I'm sure they'll confirm my whereabouts when the Tiff blew."

The Witches' Rede series by Jewel E. Leonard:

ALIGHT

PROPHECY

COVEN

Forthcoming:

ROUT

Other books

RAYS OF SUNSHINE

DEDICATION

My husband gets this one:
For without him, the handwritten version of this book would literally be in a landfill somewhere rather than typed on the computer, and the digital version would be in the great computer recycle bin in the sky. He invested as much time in this project as I did; the parts that make you laugh and the parts that gross you out are all here as a result of his unwavering devotion to me and my projects, his passion for the work we do together, and his sexy as hell creative genius.
I love you, Scott.

..... $5 00
..... 3 00
..... 1 75

... 1 25
... 2 25

eet.

ing to
or read
yping
de bar
silly
dy is
't

HERO SLOWLY RECOVERING.

Mayve McKinna is reported to be slowly convalescing from her injuries and is now able to walk across her room with the assistance of an attendant. While the effect of her dismemberment is gradually being overcome, the wound on her leg is still very painful, and the patient requires the most careful nursing and constant attention. Alan MacTavish states optimism for her recovery but thinks it will be several weeks, perhaps all winter, before she is able to return to her Redington home.

It was McKinna who, observing the MacTavish grandchildren being taken into a grain elevator by bandits, rushed into the building and at the imminent peril of her own life rescued the children. She was caught in the terrible fire that consumed the building later that evening. MacTavish decided that this act of bravery should not pass unrewarded, permitting her to recover with his family here in Tucson.

Statements have been made regarding the demise of alleged bandit Eskevar Fransisco, who is now purported to be the architect of this deplorable offense.

A NEW YORK DETECTIVE'S STORY.

Detective skill is not frequently invoked to solve matters outside of the profession. The better class of secret agents decline such cases, but "snide and sneak detectives" are delighted to have the handling of all such. Even stories of supernatural persuasion appeal to these less than reliable agents.

The case about to be narrated, while not in the regular line, eventually led up to legitimate detective work performed by one of Pinkerton's agents. The lady, whose husband was a commercial traveler for a *ree New York house, was in a highly ideed it was owing spirit that she was

---

VOLCANIC DISTURBA

A dispatch from Batavia, Ja of the 27th, says: "Terrifi heard yesterday from the vo Krakatoa. They were audibl karato, on the Island of Java. As the volcano fell as far as Cheribou, flashes proceeding from it were visible Batavia. Stones fell in showers on Se which was in total darkness throughout th night. Batavia was nearly so, all gas lig having been extinguished during the nig Communication with Anjier was stopp and it is feared a great calamity occurred. Several bridges between An and Serang were destroyed, the riv having overflowed because of the rush the sea inland."

A dispatch of the 30th says the loss of li by the volcanic eruptions in the Mala Archipelago is now placed at the appallin number of 75,000. A mountain range disappeared entirely in the sea and a number of islands with all the villages thereon suffered a like fate. The catastrophe seems to be the zenith visitation of what will go down in history as a calamitous year.

A dispatch from Batavia says the condition of the Strait of Sunda is dangerous to navigation. A new island has arisen therein and the coast line is altered. The government is preparing to obtain new soundings of the strait. Sixteen volcanoes have appeared between the site where the Island of Krakatoa formerly stood and Sibisie Island. A portion of Bantam is an ashy desert. Cattle are starving and the population is in despair. Soengepan volcano has split in five portions. Seven hundred and four bodies of victims of the disaster were buried in the district Tanara, and 300 in the coast village Kramat.

SPONTANEOUS COMBUSTION.

are investigatin Margaret

CHAPTER 1

 trickle of whispers followed the cowboy in black as he paced the aisle of the Southern Pacific train. Rafaele Forino had been disinclined to sleep thus far on his trip, nor had he been able to sit still for more than a quarter hour at a time. His mind was at a full gallop, his anxiety eating him alive.

Ironically, his appetite hadn't suffered. On the contrary, he thought it possible he would return to his intended with an additional half-person's worth of weight in his gut and imagined he would need to visit a tailor soon after his arrival in San Diego—that is, if his trousers even made it that far. Rafaele wondered if there was a tailor aboard the train; for all his mother's talents with a sewing needle, he didn't know a thing about sewing anything that wasn't classified a flesh wound.

On to better and far more attractive topics: *Maeve.*

Lovely Maeve. Intoxicating Maeve.

Rafaele's beloved but broken Miss MacKenna, his little Irish spitfire with the big heart and even bigger spirit: the very driving force behind this trip.

Thoughts of the young woman succeeded in drowning out the other passengers as well as the train's rhythmic clacking over its tracks.

When Rafaele thought about Maeve, little else existed, and nothing else mattered.

That included the train conductor who was attempting to stare Rafaele down from a solid half foot closer to the ground.

"Sir?" said the conductor to Rafaele. He leaned forward and said more assertively, "Excuse me. Sir!"

Rafaele blinked several times, his vivid daydream of Maeve dissipating. *Goodbye, my love.*

"I'm sure you have perfectly valid reasons for wearing down the aisle rug, but you're making the other passengers anxious."

"Oh," Rafaele replied, half-dazed. That was the first word he'd spoken on the train that wasn't in some way related to food. "My apologies?"

"You seem lost," said the conductor. "I hate to be presumptuous, but I've seen that look many times before. You could benefit from a drink. Why don't you spend some time in the dining car?"

Rafaele watched the passing landscape out the window, long shadows leaning the direction of the train's travel. "A drink? At this hour?"

The conductor smiled, stretching to clap him on the shoulder. "It's a bit early I suppose, but morning light doesn't stop the heart from missing her."

Rafaele was surprised, having convinced himself he hid his longing better. "Yea. I suppose I could pay a visit to the dining car." He followed the conductor, leaving relieved sighs in his wake. They were deliberately loud sounds that left him wondering if it wasn't too late to upgrade out of the combines. The point of this trip wasn't to waste money, however, which was why he'd opted for cargo-class travel arrangements. It was too bad for the rest of them. The trip would be over soon; just not soon enough.

The conductor seated Rafaele and had another train employee fetch him some port. "Is there anything else I can get you?"

Rafaele considered the offer. It was too late to fetch Maeve; perhaps he'd acted rashly in leaving her behind in Arizona Territory. So instead, he requested some paper and a pen, fully expecting he would get neither.

He was brought both.

After planning his words carefully, he opened his letter:

MY DEAREST MAYV.

Rafaele focused on the paper. First, at his shamefully shaky handwriting —he'd never perfected his penmanship after the loss of his dominant hand and when he didn't write much, his handwriting suffered greatly for it—and then at the daunting blank page.

He felt so much for this young woman—bad as well as good—and at such extremes that he couldn't put any of his emotions onto paper.

He sighed; perhaps he could borrow someone else's words where his own lacked. Rafaele dipped into his war bag and retrieved the single book he'd chosen to take on his travels. While packing, he'd waffled between *Two, by Tricks* and *The Adolescent*. Knowing he'd be spending a great deal of his free time writing to Maeve, he opted for inspiration.

Flipping through the book of sonnets for words he couldn't conjure, himself, Rafaele hoped she wouldn't recognize those of a playwright.

SHALL I COMPARE THEE TO A SUMMER'S DAY?
THOU ART MORE LOVELY AND MORE TEMPERATE

"No," Rafaele reprimanded himself under his breath. There was a chance Maeve may not have known whose words they were, but she'd doubt they were his. Never in his life had he used 'thee' and 'thou' outside of prayer. Besides: there was little about her that was temperate.

On top of that, she deserved better. He scratched the lines out, thinking this wouldn't be the most aesthetically pleasing love letter in the annals of written romantic overtures.

What if he rephrased the sonnet? Pleased with that idea, he wrote:

YOU ARE LIKE A SUMMER'S DAY,
BUT MORE BEAUTIFUL AND

Rafaele groaned. "This is awful." He scratched out those lines as well and reviewed the original sonnet. Though there were applicable lines in it, it still lacked accurate sentiment. He continued flipping through the book until he found another possibility. This, he paraphrased immediately:

THERE WILL BE NOTHING TO STAND IN THE WAY OF OUR NUPTIALS
UPON MY RETURN TO YOU.

He couldn't think of a single rhyme for nuptials and scratched those lines out with more vigor than the previous, ripping the paper. *Why is it so hard to write how I feel?* He'd been able to tell her to her face—he had, in fact, immense difficulty in shutting up regarding everything he loved about her. Yet when putting words to the page, the thoughts were jammed into his pen. Rafaele studied the steel nib, trying to will his emotions through it.

Still nothing.

"Excuse me, sir? Would you care for a meal to accompany this drink?" The attendant set a glass at Rafaele's elbow.

"God, yes. Please." Rafaele sighed. If he was eating, he couldn't write, and he considered any excuse to avoid the activity a true act of mercy.

The attendant offered him a menu. "I'll give you a chance to review our selections."

Rafaele nodded, setting down the contemptible pen. "Thanks." He accepted the menu and studied it. What a strange thing to be so desperate to do anything other than writing a love letter that he'd eat several meals' worth of food although he wasn't hungry.

Stranger yet: to be famished and nauseated all at once. Rafaele loathed being away from Maeve. His love sickness was bad enough in her presence but to be away from her made it far worse. What would he have done if Judge Pinney's sentence had been carried out?

He knew what he would've done; his stomach lurched. The melancholy was wooing him again while his fiancée couldn't intervene.

The menu. Read the menu, Wolf. After skimming it, Rafaele made a quick decision and ordered coffee, puree of split peas soup, spring lamb hash with poached egg, and a serving of filberts, hoping a full belly might effectively chase his gloom away. Hunger always had a way of making him mad.

All he had left to do was wait. He grabbed his pen without thinking and scrawled in his worst penmanship ever:

TI AMO. TI VOGLIO BENE. TI VOGLIO MOLTO BENE. TI ADORO. SEI TUTTO PER ME. SENZA DI TE NON POSSO PIÙ VIVERE. SONO INNAMORATA DI TE. SPOSAMI. HO BISOGNO DI TE. TI DESIDERO. TI VOGLIO BACIARE. SENZA DI TE LA VITA NON HA PIÙ SENSO. MI MANCHI, MI MANCHI TANTO.

He found his elusive words; they were hiding in another language.

The path descended from the summit, delivering two horseback riders from colors of early daybreak into the valley's pre-dawn gloom. It would be another hour yet before sunlight reached the town hidden within, which suited the twin riders' agenda.

Approaching the bottom of a steep grade, the Hopi women reached the San Pedro River on Redington's western outskirts. The river was a waterless gulch with the current drought, dry and cracked. Once stately mesquite trees lining it were now grey and lifeless, as if death, itself, inhabited the basin.

Their horses grew restless.

Perhaps the equines were simply tired; it had been a long trip.

Moencopi sighed. The elder twin always did have trouble understanding animals, as her sister made no hesitation in reminding her.

Kököle prompted her that their rides needed something to drink.

The pair dismounted and Moencopi walked into the river to kneel among the cracking reeds. Whispering in an ancient tongue, she traced the sharp cracks in the dried mud before raising her hands. From cloudless skies, a few drops fell—enough to moisten the ground. Her gaze turned skyward and without further incantations, she returned to her feet and left the riverbed.

From upstream, as if a massive spigot opened, a swell of churning water rushed through the ravine. The river flowed, and the two horses drank their fill.

As the women returned to their saddles and continued into town, cracks in the riverbed reappeared, water draining away to nothingness.

They left in their wake a parched wash and plants wilting beneath the harsh sun.

Town, as it were, was comprised of eighteen buildings, excluding homes built in the sprawl east of Redington's small business district. Its population couldn't have exceeded a hundred.

The pair of riders circled Redington's cul-de-sac, taking note of the locations of its boarding house, marshal's office, livery, and the solitary saloon and brothel. The younger sister insisted they stop briefly at the saloon.

Seconds after Kököle emerged from the building, brilliant orange flames leapt from the backroom door. Acrid, black smoke billowed from the few open windows upstairs; the remainder darkened quickly, allowing for the briefest glimpse of slender fingers hastily scratching for the latches and freedom.

As desperate screams pierced the air, a handful of lucky souls made it out through the batwing doors and into the street. With a brilliant flash against the powder blue sky and an ear-ringing pop, the walls of the Tiff and Tawny blew outward.

The inferno that consumed the last standing timbers would leave few survivors.

❧

She was alone. Though Maeve MacKenna spent months with nothing but the local wildlife to keep her company, it was now she was lonesome.

Rafaele had been gone less than a week and Maeve felt his absence despite vowing to him she wouldn't suffer while he was away.

The MacTavishes went about household business as usual, inviting their honored guest to make herself comfortable; Maeve, however, was unwilling to be informal there.

She was, at least, willing to admire their furniture and décor, thinking she would not be opposed to a life of such opulence. Where she would get such things was the operative question, but Maeve couldn't help where her mind wandered.

As she dragged her fingertips along relief wall paper of intricate blue scrollwork, she daydreamed of a world in which she neither teetered nor wobbled on a prosthetic limb still too new to be forgotten. There was a world she was with Rafaele, a more advanced and human-looking arm draped over the cherry wood back of a sofa, smiling at his wife with the come-hither expression she'd grown to love.

Tha' world, thought Maeve, *would be wonderful*. It would be quiet evenings bathed in the light of a fireplace, dreaming of travels beyond borders just for the sake of going, and then the unparalleled joys of that first step into their home upon their return. Rafaele would carry her over the threshold every homecoming; of course he would.

That world included lavish dinner parties, waltzes, masques and high teas—perhaps with Queen Victoria herself. Other girls would fall all over Rafaele and he wouldn't even notice them, so enamored of the woman on his arm, the one he called wife. The befreckled, red-haired American without a trace of her Irish brogue.

That American bride would be the envy of all the men, and she would delight in their attention, politely declining dances and calling cards from anyone who wasn't her husband Rafaele.

Mrs. Forino.

Although he'd promised it and she was wearing that promise around her finger, Maeve laughed. *Mrs. Forino*.

It was silly.

In what world could any of those outlandish things be reality? They were but the foolish dreams of a lovesick child.

Tea with Queen Victoria: tha' only happens for important people. People with proper breedin' or those who've given of themselves enough to be significant to the world. Maeve sighed, gazing at an oil painting hanging over the fireplace. Speaking of monarchs: she recognized the subject as Mary Stuart and it was a wildly flattering depiction of her. The lower right corner of the portrait was initialed with *A.M.*

Alan MacTavish had a lovely, well-appointed home and Maeve's envy surprised her. The MacKennas had been by no means poor. They were old money with generations behind it and Colin had ... well, she wasn't sure *what* he'd done to keep or expand on their fortune. It hadn't mattered to her as a child but now—now that she had nobody to ask—she was curious.

Ashling, Colin, and their only child, Maeve, had lived comfortably in a modest cottage on one of Ireland's green pastures. As Maeve understood, they could've afforded a small castle had Colin decided it.

Rather than living lavishly, he'd funneled all their money into Maeve's dowry; an odd daughter would require a high deposit for an even halfway decent and wholly normal husband.

Some of that dowry went toward the costs of fleeing to America. The rest of that dowry went toward a group of bandits that robbed their train as it arrived in Tucson.

Even if Rafaele had gotten his hands on any of it as leader of Shadow Wolf Pack, certainly it was all spent long before they re-encountered each other. Probably on the ladies with whom she shared the upper floor of the Tiff and Tawny. Maeve sighed; there were still some aspects of Rafaele and his history about which she couldn't reconcile.

It wasn't exactly as though Maeve's background was without dark corners; like the fact that her first time with Rafaele was not her first time ever. Or the fact that it hadn't been on their wedding night and it had taken little effort on his part to coerce her to do it. Or that she tried hiding her magical abilities from the world—and, at first, from him.

The less she said about her association with Death, the better.

As she stepped into the parlor, Maeve gave thought to how she was walking and lost her footing. A sharp pain shot through what remained of her right leg, originating from where it was seated in her prosthesis. There was even a cramp in that foot which she quickly dismissed. *Tha' foot is gone*, she reprimanded herself, as if the sensation had been deliberate.

Maeve lowered herself onto the nearest piece of furniture: a chaise lounge with the darkest wood she'd ever seen and pristine white brocade cushions. Her heart thumped in her chest as she hiked her skirts to inspect the fake limb, a lump blocking her swallowing reflex. She detested having it and having to look at it. As far as she noticed, her knee was seated properly in the sleeve attached to the replacement leg; she assumed the complicated mechanism allowing her ankle its natural range of motion was functioning as designed. Why had she nearly fallen, then? Already, Maeve was taking for granted her ability to walk and inspecting her leg made her feel immeasurably worse than she could've imagined.

She was broken.

Should Rafaele change his mind about marrying her, she couldn't imagine any other man would have her.

Maeve set her jaw; even though she trusted Rafaele, she still worried he might fail her. After all, accidents happened, and death came easily to those traveling the desert.

She rose, feeling the cloak of drowsiness drawing her heavy lids downward. Maeve slowly made her way back to her room in MacTavish's home to retire for a nap—or perhaps for the remainder of the day.

⤜❀⤛

"Miss MacKenna?" Gaylene's voice peeped from the other side of the bedroom door.

Maeve shook her head in an attempt to clear the fog that gathered there during her nap. She was stunned at still being drowsy; after a full night's sleep, she'd napped much of the following morning and afternoon. Rubbing at her eyes, she groaned, "What's the matter with me?"

Gaylene peeped again: "Miss MacKenna?" She rapped three times on the door.

"Aye," she replied, unable to stifle a big yawn. It was if she hadn't slept a wink.

"'You'—?" The young girl replied. "'You' what, Miss MacKenna?"

"Yes," Maeve snapped, deciding then and there she would break herself of using 'aye.' It'd caused her such grief over the past year. "*Yes*, Miss MacTavish?"

"We're having dinner. Please, won't you join us?"

As if her stomach itself heard the invitation, it growled; not in the way that indicated she was hungry but rather that it was a bit perturbed.

"I'll be down shortly, Miss MacTavish," Maeve said. "Thank ye." She sat in bed, listening to the sounds of Gaylene retreating, thumping down the narrow staircase more the way a child might as opposed to a young lady. Then she listened as Gaylene discussed their houseguest's current condition with the other MacTavishes downstairs.

Maeve dragged herself out of bed, loath to dress for what remained of the day but doing so anyway for propriety's sake. While she put on fresh clothes, she considered things.

The MacTavishes were nice, overly grateful for what she'd done for them—as well they should've been.

It was nice living in so lavish a home. There were no drunkards to toss, no smoke-choked air in which to suffocate. No unwelcome advances of filthy men, no sounds of naughty behavior coming from rooms surrounding hers.

So why wasn't she happy?

I don't know these people. Normally this would be of no consequence to Maeve, but presently she had little desire to be around strangers. Actually, all she desired was hibernation. She blinked through her bleariness, thinking she might be falling ill with something. Hopefully it wouldn't kill her.

Maeve scowled, forcing her undergarment appropriately cinched. It was unpleasant, and she worried she would snap off the doorknob she'd used as leverage for her laces, but she certainly couldn't get into her outerwear without it. And of course she couldn't leave the room in her undergarments alone.

Getting downstairs was difficult; without assistance, she stumbled several times. On the bright side—because Maeve was determined to find one—nobody saw her struggles, so she avoided humiliation.

When she appeared in the archway leading into the dining room, Maeve was greeted like an old friend. She couldn't muster the enthusiasm to greet them in kind although she appreciated their hospitality. It lifted her spirits, at least, if not her waning energy level.

Hobard MacTavish held Maeve's chair for her and she delicately settled into it.

At no more than fourteen or fifteen years old, he sported a healthy mop of curly, sandy blonde hair. An attractive boy with striking blue eyes, he was a bit gangling despite the baby fat lingering in his cheeks. It wasn't outlandish to believe he would grow into a handsome man; not her type, but one who wouldn't struggle in taking himself an enthusiastic bride— between his appearance and inheritance.

Presently, she caught the boy staring unabashedly at her breasts. She was reminded that her cyclical excess was a little more excessive than usual.

Nonetheless, she wondered why nobody taught Hobard it wasn't polite to stare and that he shouldn't do so, or at least to be discreet when he couldn't resist.

To his right sat his younger sister Gaylene, portrait of an angel on Earth: pale blue eyes and impeccably styled white-blonde ringlets. This girl, at maybe twelve-years-old, led every meal in prayer for which Maeve had been present.

Gaylene had developed a terrible case of idolatry regarding Maeve and she was in no way shy about sharing her feelings. Maeve knew she should've been honored to have someone hold her in such high esteem—because few people did—but considering her history with other children, it made her anxious. She disliked the idea of this girl getting so attached to her.

She didn't want Gaylene hurt—or worse. In addition, it was plumb difficult for Maeve to associate with a child; that was among numerous reasons she thought she'd make a terrible mother.

Even though Gaylene was well-spoken and well-read, Maeve still saw her as a young child, and one who couldn't resist condescending explanations of words Maeve was unfamiliar with.

Though Maeve tried to keep the girl at a distance, Gaylene had been stubborn, sticking nearby and rarely leaving Maeve alone when she was at home, actively engaging her in conversation for most of their waking hours. The child was smart, adventurous, and nosy to the point of being obnoxious.

Just like her idol.

At the head of the table sat Alan MacTavish. Maeve guessed he was around seventy or eighty years old—but she was no good at pin-pointing ages of people much older than she. Case in point: she once brushed off Milton's advances thinking he was several decades her elder when he was scarcely even one.

Any case, Mr. MacTavish was a feeble old man who dressed sharply and kept well-groomed, literally wearing his wealth. For what his hair lacked in color, it made up for in mass. She guessed he'd been blonde in his youth like both his grandchildren.

Maeve cleared her throat. "Thank ye for havin' me."

"Think nothing of it," Mr. MacTavish greeted her. "We can't have you starving."

"I'm hardly starvin'," muttered Maeve.

Gaylene asked, "Are you well? You miss Mr. Forino, don't you?"

No. Aye. It would be more accurate to say she was too sleepy to miss the handsome Italian and his insatiable carnal appetite. *Tomorrow*, she vowed, *I'll miss him tomorrow.* "I've ... been through a lot," said Maeve. "'N' I'm still adaptin'."

Mr. MacTavish gave her a pained smile. "Of course you are. An injury like that will take a long time to recover from. Even with a marvel like your prosthesis, I'm amazed you're wandering about already. My old friend Grossmith received a pin leg following the taking of Sebastopol, and even upon his death he rarely walked with it ... Let alone well. I do believe you're remarkable."

The children's expressions indicated that was an oft repeated tale MacTavish was eager to dust off and present to fresh ears.

Maeve wanted to thank him for the reminder she didn't need but turned her attention, instead, to the table.

Unsurprisingly, the MacTavishes had an impressive spread of food at their dining room table and—she assumed—a talented chef at their disposal. Though Maeve ate little of what she'd been offered, she was jealous. They had such wealth and they got to enjoy it, unlike her family.

Mr. MacTavish continued to engage Maeve in conversation throughout the meal. She replied to be polite and even turned some of the questions back on him. In general, she didn't care and was trying to get through the meal without offending anyone.

As the dishes were cleared away by the maids, Hobard invited Maeve for an unchaperoned walk. If she hadn't experienced otherwise, she might have assumed his intentions were pure. To that point, she didn't know of a single man who didn't have ulterior motives.

She declined politely.

Gaylene asked her to join in a spirited discussion of Mary Shelley's *Frankenstein*. Having read the book previously, Maeve considered participating until Gaylene's boasts of having a rare second edition copy put her off the conversation. She declined that, as well—a little less politely.

While Maeve prepared to retire for the evening after a long, hard day of sleeping, the household was interrupted by a series of quiet taps at the front door.

Maeve was too tired to even hope Rafaele had already returned or changed his mind about going before he'd had the chance to board a westbound train.

It was the next best thing to Rafaele: Milton Price and Edison Stilwell. She surprised even herself for her enthusiasm in greeting them.

Mr. MacTavish's frosted eyebrows flew upward as he watched Maeve embrace Edison, then Milton in turn before mocking a kiss on both his rosy cheeks.

"Mr. Forino mustn't appreciate how freely you give your affection to other men," noted Mr. MacTavish.

"Oh, he doesn't mind it," Maeve fibbed. "These are me friends, after all. Me affections toward them are—are—" She poked at the air with her index finger as she hunted for the word in English.

Milton and Edison chimed in with it: "Platonic?"

"Oh." She didn't expect it would be so similar to *Gaeilge*.

"Please excuse us, Mr. MacTavish. We wish to take an audience with Miss MacKenna." Edison tilted his head, white hair falling sideways with it. In comparison to MacTavish, Edison's 'old' was likely twenty years younger than Maeve used to think of him.

Mr. MacTavish gestured to their right. "Have use of my parlor."

Edison, Milton, and Maeve went to MacTavish's parlor, where the old man afforded them privacy. Maeve assumed, however, he or a staff member was standing outside the door and eavesdropping. She wouldn't have blamed him; that she was holding private conversation with two men her senior must've given the wrong impression.

"How have you b-been, Ducky?" Milton said.

"I'm well," Maeve replied without thinking. Upon further consideration, she said, "No I amn't. I'm plumb exhausted, Milt. I slept like the dead last night, 'n' slept most of today, afterward."

Milton and Edison glanced at each other. "Are they still giving you morphine?" said Edison.

"What—?" She didn't understand initially. "Oh—uh … No." She shook her head. "No, not for a while now. I amn't exactly … feelin' meself, as it were."

She knew she wasn't exactly looking herself, either. Whether they didn't notice the bloat or were too kind to mention it, neither ventured any comment on the topic.

Edison cleared his throat. "Have you heard from Wolf?"

Maeve found the strength to chuckle. "No, but he just left. It's not been long enough for him to even think about missin' me."

Milton shook his head. "If I know F-Forino, he misses you."

"That's sweet of ye to say."

"It's true," insisted Milton. "I think he misses you if you're nuh-not in his arms."

Maeve regarded her lap, her face warming in a flush.

"So tell me," Edison changed the subject, "how's your leg treating you? I thought we might make sure it's working properly, seeing as we're here."

"I, uh …" Maeve shrugged and choked on her phlegm.

"Miss MacKenna," Edison pressed, "if something's wrong, please be honest so we can fix it."

"There's no problem with the machinery. The problem's with me."

Milton frowned. "In what way?"

Maeve demonstrated, first by struggling to stand from her spot on the chaise lounge and then by wobbling several steps forward.

Milton rushed to her side, supporting her with a gentle grasp under her right elbow. "L-l-let's inspect that l-leg. With such struggles, it must be the prosthesis at fuh-fault."

They sat her back down and Maeve rearranged her skirts to give Milton and Edison access to the limb. Her face was so hot, she was certain it could spark a fire.

"Huh." Milton got on his knees, bowing as if supplicating at her feet. "Interesting." He fiddled with the ankle joint, manipulating it before rotating the foot in its socket.

"There doesn't suh-seem to be a problem. Can you see anything, Stilwell?" Milton straightened.

Edison took longer to get into a halfway decent position from which to inspect his mechanics, several of his joints cracking loudly in protest. "We old men aren't meant to kneel," he griped and studied the false leg. "I must say, you outdid yourself with this sculpt."

Milton tilted his head in a shy acknowledgment.

"Trying to match the beauty of its recipient, I wonder? Or to endear yourself further to Wolf?"

Milton chuckled. "You caught me."

"Nothing appears out of order." Glancing at Milton and waving his right hand, Edison said, "Help me up, if you would."

"W-would you walk for us again?" Milton asked Maeve while he helped Edison to his feet, the motion accompanied by more loud pops.

She heaved a dramatic sigh. "Must I?"

"Please?" said Edison.

So Maeve took another step.

"I b-beg your p-pardon, but luh-lift your skirt," Milton requested, his cheeks going pink. He blurted, "So we can see what the mechanics are duh-doing."

Reluctantly, Maeve pulled up her skirts and took several difficult, stiff steps.

"You're over-thinking it," Milton decided. "The more you focus on the prosthesis and w-walking with it, the more difficult it will be for you."

"Tha' seems backward."

"Why d-don't we step outside for a walk?" Milton nodded toward the door. "The fresh air will do you good."

"I shouldn't," said Maeve. "I mustn't—"

Edison and Milton both held her hands and led her to the front of MacTavish's home.

She wandered out into the street for the first time since the explosion in the granary, her face upturned beneath a bizarre sky. "It's—" She struggled for the words. "Why's it look so strange?" Maeve cried.

Milton and Edison exchanged glances.

"You don't know?" Milton asked.

Maeve glared at him. "No! I don't!"

Milton recoiled at her response; she was disproportionately upset about the orange and purple sunset. The cotton puff clouds were blue rather than white and the risen moon was—of all colors—bright green.

"Ducky," Edison said slowly. "A volcano erupted off the coast of Java."

He might as well have been talking about some spot on another planet for all she knew of Java or its coastline. *A volcano erupted.*

She was stunned, for several minutes milling the street aimlessly, staring at the sky, trying to wrap her brain around the whole thing, trying to figure out why she felt responsible for it.

"When did this happen?" she gasped.

Milton pouted. "L-last month, the ... twenty-sixth."

And there it was.

Tha' night at the railyards. A month ago. Dear Lord, a month later 'n' it still looks like this? How much worse was it thirty days ago?

How out of control had her fury been? With all that rage and fear consuming her, could it have been possible she did it? Did magic even work that way?

No. It doesn't.

Because if it did, that made her responsible. And if she were responsible, she would've had a three-fold price to pay.

Maeve swallowed hard. "Did people—were there ..."

"It's bad," Edison said, bobbing his head morosely. "A disaster, I'm afraid, the likes of which may never be seen or heard of again." He cleared his throat. "Our pity and sympathies won't change what nature's dealt."

Nature. Ha. "Why'd ye bring me out here?"

They exchanged glances. It was Edison to slowly admit, "You were distracted, and now you walk without difficulty. It mustn't be the replacement leg."

"I told ye as much!"

"F-for now," Milton interjected with a soft voice, "we really should sh-show you how the prosthetic limb functions, and you should learn to fix it yourself. Don't you agree, Ed?"

Edison looked confused as Milton pulled him aside for a quick word in the ear.

"Yes, yes, you should," Edison hastily agreed.

"Excuse me, but when would I need to fix it?" The first reason Maeve asked was the assumption it could never break, followed immediately by her unwillingness to believe she would outlive the only people who knew how it worked.

Milton cleared his throat. "Luck favors the prepared."

And so Milton and Edison proceeded to share with Maeve the finer points of their handiwork.

Her stare may have been focused on what they were doing, but her mind was elsewhere.

She missed the Tiff and Tawny. She missed the excitement, the companionship, the income—although she had no use for it presently. The more she thought, the more she realized she likely wouldn't need the money upon Rafaele's return, either. She guessed he wouldn't be the type to let his little woman contribute to his finances.

Why does tha' bother me?

Why did everything bother her lately? She readily assumed her temperament had to do with her leg and wondered how long before that improved —if it ever would.

Maeve sighed.

"I understand it's a lot of information," Milton apologized. "I just want to prepare you in case something g-goes wrong and we're not available to help. After all, you're fully capable when the machinery works. Without it, lame."

She nodded.

"We'll kuh-keep working on this together little b-bit by little bit, so you're not overwhelmed."

Suspecting they caught her daydreaming, Maeve smiled sheepishly. "Thank ye, Milton."

"The only thing you need to remember is to not pay that leg any mind," said Edison. "The more you focus on it, the more difficulty you'll have using it."

"I'll try tha'," Maeve said. "It may take me a while, though. It's … quite the adjustment."

"I've little d-doubt," responded Milton. "We watched Rafaele struggle with his arm."

Edison elbowed Milton in his side with a sharp glare.

Maeve frowned. "What?"

"It's not our place to discuss any of that business," Edison replied. "If Forino hasn't already told you, I'm sure he will if you ask." Under her glower, he said, "We're going to retire for the evening at the Palace Hotel. We'll stay in town a few more days to continue working with you."

Maeve wasn't excited for that although she was otherwise thrilled for their visit. "Thank ye both."

"I'm g-g-glad you're on the mend," Milton told her with a brief hug.

"Take it easy, Ducky." Edison hugged her next. "And remember: don't overthink it."

Naturally, that was just what she did as she followed the two men to the front door; she stumbled, and Milton caught her before she fell.

CHAPTER 2

t took a little over a week following Edison's and Milton's departure for Maeve to wear out her welcome with the MacTavish family.

The household staff was far less pleasant when tending her; even when she politely declined their services, she was aware she burdened them with her mere presence. And their behavior grew worse when the family wasn't around. They knew she was nothing more than a brothel barmaid and while they were servants, themselves, they still outranked her. She withdrew from what little of the family's activities she participated in and sought solace in solitary pursuits.

Fearful the unearthly sunset was aftermath from something she'd been responsible for in her inexperience and negligence, Maeve was desperate to gain control over her powers. These fears took precedence over the logic of postponing magical attempts until she returned to Redington even though her powders and potions remained abandoned in her room at the Tiff and Tawny.

She needed some control, at least; at best, full. Such things, however, were a pipe dream.

And so, when the MacTavishes left for their regular Sunday morning outing, Maeve finally had the time and privacy to train.

She wondered what Rafaele would think if she practiced her craft and honed her talents into sharp, easily accessible skill. Judging by how excited he got over her gifts and strengths, she guessed it might please him. These were far more pleasant thoughts than thinking of how her temper bested her, a volcano erupted, and she'd destroyed so much land, killing so many innocent people.

For those reasons among others, she sat on the mattress in her room during one of her more lucid moments—they were coming fewer and farther between—and gazed at the candelabrum. When its candles declined to promptly light themselves from her sheer force of will, Maeve grew frustrated. She stalked to it, snatching the candle tree from the bedside table. "Why will ye not light?" she snapped at it.

The stubborn candles were refusing to ignite just to spite her. She was sure of it.

"Oh. So *this* is the way ye wanna be?" She glared harder at their mocking, pristine wicks.

Perhaps the problem was that they hadn't been broken in yet and she could only magically light ones which were worn. What did Maeve know? She'd rarely done this sort of thing before.

Yes, she learned at an early age to heat water to make bathing tolerable, but that had been necessity. She'd taught herself to conjure fire using direct touch around the time she came to Redington. Another necessity, as raw gecko meat hadn't been toothsome.

There also was the fireball she'd created to save Rafaele's life, and what she'd done in the granary to save her own. Necessity, both.

If it was, indeed, necessity, then nothing she could do would make the candles seated in the candelabrum ignite short of rubbing them between her fingertips, which was better than not having magic at all. She could always use matches which she didn't have at her disposal.

Maeve rationalized, however, that a strong enough desire for something to happen would turn a 'want' into a 'need.' The obstinate—and thus far unlit—candles disagreed.

She set the candelabrum down and tried a different approach.

"Fine, then." Maeve turned her back on them. "I don't even want ye to light." She glanced over her shoulder.

Still nothing. Psychological tricks on inanimate objects apparently didn't work either.

She exhaled and sat on the bed, fatigued for minimal effort, and entirely done with the pigheaded candles.

With the bedroom window open, Maeve heard the MacTavishes returning from their outing. There were more than the usual voices—several families'-worth of chatter—as some of the neighbors must've joined them on their return walk. She hoisted herself off the bed and hobbled to the windowsill where she watched as the adults lagged behind Hobard, Gaylene, and her friends. Hobard was the sole boy among them and didn't mind the company he kept, flashing interested smiles at a few around him.

In response to his smiles, one folded her parasol, and another tucked her little hat under her right arm. Yet another dropped both her gloves, which Hobard dutifully retrieved from the ground. They were all flirting and obvious signals, though Maeve was unfamiliar with specifics.

"It was terrifying," Gaylene was saying to the cluster of young girls who spared her any attention. "Absolutely horrible. It was dark and dusty and the man who tied us up told us he was going to take all of Grandfather's money and kill us."

Her friends fanned themselves frantically with white-gloved hands. "I would have fainted dead away," one of them declared. "How did you not positively die of fright?"

Gaylene beamed, glancing at her brother. "Hobard was so brave. He reminded me of God's almighty presence and we prayed together. We prayed for ourselves and we prayed for the bad man that he might have a change of heart."

Yea? Maeve snorted. *So did I.* God seemed disinclined to listen to any of their prayers. She turned her attention to her skirts; though she couldn't see the prosthetic shin through them, she needn't see it to be conscious of its presence. *That* had been the result of her prayers.

"Miss MacKenna," Gaylene shouted, waving at her from the street.

Maeve waved back before taking a big step away from the window, embarrassed to have been caught eavesdropping.

She continued to listen once she was out of sight.

"That's the lady who rescued us," said Gaylene to her friends.

Maeve smiled. *She called me a lady.*

"But of course it was all due to God's glory and our prayers."

Maeve's smile faltered.

"And then? As soon as we were saved, the building went up in flames."

Hobard punctuated his sister's statement with an approximation of the explosion and loud gasps of surprise filled the air.

"It's true. God smote the bad man who was there. Miss MacKenna was caught in the explosion and injured. It's why she's living with us now."

That sounded sickeningly permanent. What little remained of Maeve's smile fell away.

"Gayl, if … if she was sent there to rescue you, why wouldn't God have protected her, too?" one of the girls asked.

It was an excellent question.

Gaylene dropped her voice in reply and Maeve strained to hear it.

"Well, Miss MacKenna *is* a nice woman but … she's lain with a man and they're not married. In fact, she sinned with him in her bedroom in our house."

Maeve's mouth fell open and she clapped a hand over it.

"It happened a lot. I kept count."

A chorus of *ooohs* came from Gaylene's friends, followed by individual comments:

"The scandal."

"Shame on her."

"How dreadful."

"It's disgusting."

"Not to mention disrespectful!"

"Obviously," Gaylene interrupted, "she needed to experience what awaits her if she continues her sinful ways. To be in that building when it exploded must've been like being in—well, *you* know—surrounded by all that fire. But I doubt such things concern her. You'll notice she didn't even come to church today. She never has, and we ask every Sunday."

Maeve gasped, mouthing, *No, ye have not!* Until that moment, it didn't even occur to her where they went those mornings.

"How ungrateful," one of the girls chirped. "What kind of woman doesn't attend church?"

"*You* know what kind," Gaylene replied.

There was a long silence, followed by a lot of giggling.

Another girl commented, "You're so naughty, Gaylene!"

"I'm just being honest. God wants it that way."

Maeve heard the front door swing open and shut, the girls' laughter staying out front. She sidled to the window to see that Gaylene and her friends hadn't followed Hobard and the adults inside. She stepped away again and held her breath.

"So tell us about the handsome gentleman you met on the street yesterday," one of the girls asked.

"Oh," Gaylene sighed. "Well, he's older and clearly wealthy. He was handsome and tall, with wonderful dark hair. He had a light accent and oh, his eyes were just for me. When we spoke, it was like I was the only girl for miles around."

Maeve smiled. That reminded her of a man she knew in Redington.

"You're so lucky. Do you suppose he'll call?"

Gaylene tittered. "He promised he would when Grampa and Hobard are away. If he kisses my hand I think I might die."

Maeve's jaw dropped. *The little hypocrite! Judgin' me so harshly when she's but a child entertainin' strange men—invitin' him to her house purposefully without a chaperone? How dare she?*

"You'll have to tell us everything."

"Don't be silly," Gaylene replied. "A lady never kisses and tells."

No, Maeve fumed, *a lady just kisses 'n' tells other women's stories!*

Gaylene concluded, "I'd best go inside now."

"See you next Sunday!" the group called to her.

Maeve heard the front door open once more, followed by the voices of Gaylene's friends dispersing down the street.

Gaylene was thumping her way down the hall and Maeve swallowed a groan; her desire to talk to the girl went from little to nonexistent. And why should she talk to the girl who compromised her reputation?

Maeve's nose itched.

Why, exactly, was she staying with the MacTavishes anymore? Yes, she had risked life—not to mention limb—for Gaylene and Hobard.

Oh, how she longed to sneeze.

It was odd she regained consciousness in one of their bedrooms and nobody said a word about it. She'd never asked to stay; it was almost as though someone did that on her behalf. She doubted Mr. MacTavish offered it out of the kindness of his heart.

Maeve's eyes were stinging.

"Miss MacKenna? It's a lovely day outside." Gaylene let herself into Maeve's room without knocking. "Would you walk with me to the park? There's a concert at the bandstand starting in an hour."

"I—" Maeve inhaled sharply.

"Miss MacKenna?"

Maeve sneezed so hard it hurt her ribs and she cried out.

Gaylene gasped, stumbling back against the wall, wide-eyed gaze locked across the room.

"… Miss MacTavish?" Maeve asked.

When Gaylene didn't answer, Maeve turned to see what had stolen the girl's attention.

The defiant candles in the candelabrum—not to mention every other candle in the room—had ignited when least opportune. Their flames were full, whipping around and standing well off their wicks. The shelves above them were already covered in soot and the candles were burning so swiftly wax poured from them, down the candle holders and onto the floor in long stalactites. "*Rinne tú margairlí cránach de, Maeve,*" she muttered.

Gaylene didn't hide her horror—which, after everything Maeve had done for them, was far more hurtful than it should've been. Because of the girl's reaction, Maeve couldn't even celebrate her inadvertent triumph over fire.

"Do not ye be scared," she implored. "I won't hurt ye, I promise."

Gaylene said nothing, her expression unchanged.

"Please—can I trust ye'll keep this secret? I'll clean it meself—"

With a shriek, the girl fled Maeve's company, knocking over a standing candleholder in the process. Wax from the tall pillar candle splashed across the floor and carpet, followed by a brief flare-up on the rug. Maeve rushed to extinguish the flames as Gaylene thundered down the stairs with continued screaming.

"*Damnú!* That's a big 'no,' then."

Gaylene's shrill voice echoed throughout the home: "This demon woman unleashed the fires of hell at the granary and now she's doing it here, too!"

Of *course* Gaylene told them.

Maeve exhaled when Gaylene's assertions were met with healthy laughter from the other members of the household. She pinched out the flames with her fingertips as Gaylene's story grew taller and included claims of Maeve speaking in tongues and placing hexes on their home. Maeve supposed the speaking-in-tongues part of that wasn't a fabrication but a mere stretching of the truth.

Gaylene was told to stop fabricating intrigue and smartly reminded, "God doesn't abide gossips!"

When she carried on regardless, several sets of feet hit the staircase.

First in the doorway was Hobard, followed by Gaylene and Mr. MacTavish.

The flames were gone but their damage remained.

"What happened here?" Mr. MacTavish bellowed.

"I—it was—it's not what it must look like—" Maeve stumbled over her words, withering beneath his disapproving stare. She'd seen judgmental stares like his from her mother every time she had the audacity to be her magical self. In her mother's case, the glower was always paired with '*You disgust me, little demon.*' Suddenly she was a nine-year-old again.

Maeve didn't need such reminders but there they were: eyebrows pinched downward, lips curled into a sneer and not an ounce of kindness in the eyes behind tiny round spectacles. She was reassured Mr. MacTavish wouldn't kick her out for fear of appearing ungrateful to the townsfolk; nonetheless, she would've been overjoyed to walk out that second, except she had no way of getting back to Redington.

"I'm so sorry," whispered Maeve as Mr. MacTavish turned away. "I'll do me best to clean it—"

"Don't worry," he snapped. "I'll have the help do that." He waved at Hobard and Gaylene to follow him. "What plague has been set upon my house?"

Maeve sighed, dropping onto the mattress. The granary was no hell compared to this.

As if Maeve wasn't trouble enough for the MacTavishes, two women appeared at the front door asking for her the following morning.

Maeve had no idea who they were, or how they knew who she was and where to find her. She had countless questions but was too scared to ask so she made a pathetic attempt at hiding halfway up the staircase.

One of the pair of Native Americans—beautiful if not out-of-place in a perfectly westernized purple gown—introduced herself to the servants: "My name's Sarah. This is my sister, Rachel." She motioned to the other woman, dressed in traditional Native American trappings accessorized with a spectacularly sour expression. "We're here from the Hopitushínumu tribe to take care of Miss MacKenna."

The servants wrinkled their noses at each other before turning unimpressed glances on Maeve, who was more confused than anyone else. She shrugged at them as Mr. MacTavish joined them in the foyer.

The sister—Rachel—wearing a simple black dress with rough, hand-stitched seams and a thick black band around her waist, came forward, white deerskin moccasin boots shuffling against the wood floor. "An old friend, Rafaele Forino, sent for us to care for Miss MacKenna in his absence."

Mr. MacTavish's head tilted to the ceiling. Yet rather than turning the women away, he addressed his servants through clenched teeth: "Missus Gerber? Mr. McCann? Please help make our guests comfortable."

Maeve wondered what Rafaele did to make Mr. MacTavish behave so submissively, but she had no doubt he'd done something.

Missus Gerber, a portly woman who stuffed herself into a corset likely too small for someone as waiflike as Maeve, directed the guests down the main hall, grumbling behind them, "Filthy savages. What a mess I'm going to have to clean once they leave."

Mr. McCann, who'd proven the silent, indifferent type, didn't care to hide his opinion of their situation as he accompanied Mrs. Gerber in front of Maeve. "This household is going to hell … first the heathen red-haired demon—" he tossed a glance over his shoulder at her and she stopped midstride. "—and now this."

Maeve bit her tongue and swallowed her anger as she took tea in the parlor with the new guests, both attractively stouter than she but taller only by an inch or two. The ticking of the grandfather clock and the ever-present gentle whirring of her ankle provided background music to uncomfortable lack of conversation.

Maeve guessed the Hopi women were twins. Their facial features, complexion, hair, and eye color were identical. Where the woman in the socially acceptable gown appeared completely at home in the opulent parlor as she sat and sipped her tea with a pinkie up, the other hadn't sat since entering the room and occupied the lull in conversation by looking over MacTavish's belongings. Presently, she studied a framed collection of butterfly wings.

Maeve picked one of her plethora of questions to start with when she feared the silence would suffocate her: "Me apologies, but what were yer names again? I'm terrible forgetful these days."

"Sarah," said the Native in the simple black dress. She nodded at her sister in the purple gown sitting on the divan. "And Rachel."

Eyes narrowing, Maeve selected her second question: "Is it a cultural thing tha' ye switched yer names in the last few minutes?"

The women gaped at each other.

"Yer *real* names, please." Maeve rose from her seat. "Or I can have Mr. MacTavish remove ye from his home." She had little doubt he'd happily oblige the request. Maybe he'd please everybody and remove her, as well.

The original Rachel glowered at Sarah-then-Rachel.

"Moencopi Redbird," the maiden in traditional attire introduced herself. "And my sister, Kököle."

That certainly seemed far more believable than Rachel and Sarah. But since they'd already lied to her once, what was to stop them from continuing?

Moencopi continued, "I believe you know our younger brother, Tithu."

"Oh." Maeve blinked. "Aye—Yes—I do." She didn't think often of the strange boy in Shadow Wolf Pack who'd connected with her in the most eerie way the day the Pack kidnapped her. "How—exactly—did ye say ye knew Mr. Forino again?"

Kököle cleared her throat. "Wolf has been an honorary member of our clan—our family—for many years."

Moencopi cast a narrow-eyed glance at her sister. "And some of us know him very well."

Maeve couldn't swallow her scowl.

"Wolfie sent for us shortly after your ..." Kököle hesitated. "Your injury."

"I don't understand why," Maeve replied through clenched teeth.

Moencopi peered outside the parlor. She stepped back into the room and lowered her voice. "Wolf did not trust Mr. MacTavish to provide for you as promised. Having experienced such a warm reception, I do not blame your intended for his assessment."

Though she didn't say as much, Maeve couldn't fault Mr. MacTavish his reaction to the strange women materializing willy-nilly on his doorstep.

"Why did ye give fake names?"

Moencopi explained, "Kökö fell back on Christian names because they make people outside the tribe a little more comfortable with us."

"'N' ... Ye find people actually believe those names are rightfully yers?"

"If they do not, they never say it. You are the first," Moencopi replied.

With a warm smile, Kököle commented, "Wolfie warned us you wouldn't be fooled."

Maeve didn't appreciate Kököle's familiarity with her fiancé. It was all she could do to maintain her temper. "I'm glad I didn't disappoint. Though it may have been harder if ye hadn't mixed yer names up." She studied the brocade pattern in her top skirt. Without raising her head, she muttered, "I'm eager to get back to the Tiff 'n' Tawny. I feel I've spent several lifetimes here."

Moencopi and Kököle exchanged glances. Kököle sighed as if having lost a silent argument and said, "Miss MacKenna ... There was an explosion. I'm so sorry to tell you, but the Tiff and Tawny was destroyed."

"What?" Maeve whispered.

"Most everyone escaped with minor injuries, but a couple people were still missing when we left. Despite our efforts, one body was recovered, and ... she did not appear to have had the blessing of a swift death."

Maeve swallowed around the words, "A body? Was it—"

Kököle attempted to answer. "Miss—"

"Burke. *Caitlin.*" Maeve squeezed her eyes shut and covered her face; her chest ached. Her home was destroyed, her few remaining belongings undoubtedly gone. And with them, her closest friend. "Oh, Caitlin."

"We're so sorry," replied Kököle. "But ... How could you know?"

"Because," Maeve said with a defeated sigh, "who else would it have been?"

"If it is of any consolation, the marshal began investigating the explosion within a few hours," Moencopi said.

Kököle added, "He sent away for help from the East Coast."

"I don't understand," Maeve cried. "Who would do such things?"

Moencopi regarded her with what she interpreted as an accusatory expression.

Maeve yelped, "Well it wasn't me!"

Her mind jumped to the granary, which she had been responsible for. Nobody knew it'd been her fault except for Rafaele, and she trusted he hadn't told anyone—if he'd even been aware of the truth when he sent for these women. He could've done that before she woke to find herself in MacTavish's home, missing the better half of her right leg.

"We're not blaming you," said Kököle. "We meant ... perhaps you know who may have done it or who had motive."

Maeve shook her head. "The only person I think would've done somethin' so awful is—was—Francisco Esquivar."

"I'm sorry," Kököle said. "'Was?'"

Selecting her words with care, Maeve answered, "Esquivar perished in the granary, in the fire tha' almost claimed me life, as well."

Someone mentioned an ongoing search for Francisco's remains among the rubble of the granary. Maeve wanted to tell them they were wasting their time and effort, but she didn't need for anyone to realize she'd been so thorough with dispatching him that there wasn't even enough of his soul left to haunt the grounds.

Her thoughts drifted back to Caitlin.

"Please excuse me," Maeve said, standing. "I need to go lie down." When Kököle jumped to Maeve's aid, Maeve shooed her away. "I will go by meself. Thank ye." Retreating to her bedroom, she hoped the two liars would be gone by morning. Then she could go back to figuring out how to get herself back to Redington and finding a place to stay in Rafaele's—and the Tiff and Tawny's—absence.

Gaylene's continued shrill complaints about the candle incident and talk of hellfire and brimstone roused Maeve from pleasant dreams.

Nobody offered her breakfast. She dozed again, sleeping off and on past lunch, for which nobody fetched her. She woke famished and nauseated; the purposeful oversight of her needs adding fuel to her fire.

The two Native women's voices in the neighboring bedroom penetrated their shared wall. Knowing they were still there further upset her—so much that she barely refrained from pitching the wax-encrusted candelabrum across the room.

Since nobody acknowledged her presence, Maeve thought that was as good a time as any to figure out her escape. She sneaked around the room to dress herself, peering out from a bedroom door left slightly ajar. The hallway was unoccupied.

Maeve slipped out, hoping the rustling of her skirts and her footfalls with their abnormal gait would go unnoticed. It proved a real challenge to concentrate on tiptoeing as Milton and Edison instructed: without over-thinking how she used the prosthesis.

At the bottom of the staircase, a winded Maeve glanced back to the second story. The door to the room in which Moencopi and Kököle had slept was still closed.

Maeve inhaled deeply through her mouth without a noise. The front door of the house was across the hall—sweet freedom, within her reach.

She took a single step as someone knocked.

"Coming," sang Gaylene. Judging by her tone, she must've assumed it was her handsome stranger calling.

Maeve had no chance to escape. *Mac soith*!

Upon seeing Maeve standing across the hall from the front door, Gaylene froze. They regarded each other in strained silence, and another series of knocks followed.

"Oh, go answer it already," snapped Maeve. "I amn't gonna turn ye into a toad but tha' fact matters to ye none."

Gaylene's wide-eyed stare grew more terrified.

"Fine," Maeve huffed. "I'll get it." She stalked to the door, yanking it open.

"Howdy, ma'am." Alexis greeted Maeve with a wide smile and a tip of her dusty cowboy hat. "Just the fair filly I came to see."

Maeve clutched the door; it was all she could do to keep from flinging herself at Alexis and crushing her in a hug. "Miss Chesterfield. How lovely to see ye."

Alexis extended her right hand. "Put 'er there."

Maeve accepted her hand and, in a heartbeat, the two women shared an embrace.

"How're you recovering, Miss MacKenna?"

"I—" Maeve pulled back from the hug, glancing at Gaylene who was having no qualms watching their reunion. *Who knows what she's thinkin'?* "Let's take a walk. Care to join me?" With a hard gaze, she pressed, "Please."

Alexis glanced at the girl. "Trouble in paradise?"

"Ye might say as much."

Alexis held Maeve by the elbow like a gentleman would and escorted her from MacTavish's house. Gaylene slammed the door after them.

"Lovely girl," Alexis sneered.

"Ye have *no* idea." Maeve walked with her as far as the next house before stopping. "Ye gotta help me."

Alexis blinked. "I beg your pardon?"

"Please get me outta here!"

"I don't ... I don't understand. You want to leave this lap of luxury?"

"Yes."

"Yes?" Alexis gawked at her.

"What part of 'yes,' exactly, are ye not gettin'?"

"Where did 'aye' go? It was actually kinda cute. And seriously, why are you so desperate to leave?"

"Where do I start?" replied Maeve. "These two crazy women arrived yesterday claimin' Rafaele sent them to help me."

"Kököle and Moencopi?"

"Ye gathered tha' based off me callin' them crazy?"

Alexis smirked. "No. What tipped me off was that they came following Raf's request. I was with him when he sent the telegram." She paused. "So ... you didn't hit it off with them?"

Maeve wasn't certain what she meant and shrugged.

"Don't be that way. I know those two, and Raf trusts them."

"Maybe so, but Raf isn't here. 'N' they showed up out of the blue—" Maeve thought briefly. "He trusted Esquivar enough to keep in the Pack."

Alexis cleared her throat. "That's beside the point." She paused. "Isn't Kököle gorgeous?"

Maeve had, indeed, noticed Kököle's beauty; it was hard to miss. She could likely have charmed the Devil himself with looks like hers. Nonetheless she replied with a frown, "They're identical."

"They may look similar," Alexis said with a laugh, "but they're very different people, believe me. And personality can be really attractive, or real deterring. I'm sure you of all people agree."

She bristled. "Regardless, I get the distinct feelin' tha' neither of them is leavin' any time soon."

"And that's enough to get you to flee such opulence?"

"The MacTavishes don't like me 'n' I'm obviously imposin', even when I'm goin' out of me way to ... *not*. The boy makes me uncomfortable, the girl's terrified of me, 'n' ... it shouldn't hurt me feelings, but it does."

"You're too sweet for your own good."

Maeve didn't acknowledge Alexis's assessment, glancing away. "They said the Tiff is destroyed."

"It is. I'm so sorry."

"'N' Cait ...?" She held out hope the liars had lied about that, too.

"Gone with it." Alexis put a hand on Maeve's shoulder. "I'm sure this is hard for you."

Maeve felt doubly awful—not just for what happened but because her fabricated distrust of the twins had no legs on which to stand. They weren't lying, at least not about that. "I want to be there. I need to help with the recovery effort."

"Wolf made us promise to keep you here. To ..." Alexis swiped her hat from her head, dusting it off with several sharp swats. "What were his words? Oh. Yes. To keep you out of trouble while he's away."

That should've infuriated Maeve, especially lately when everything angered her. Yet she smiled. "How sweet."

"Surely you can understand my misgivings about going against his request in removing you from the premises. I'd be breaking my promise to my honorary brother."

"What trouble would I be to help in Redington? I won't hurt meself, 'n' it'll make me feel like I'm contributin' again. Right now, I'm ... Useless. It's terrible. I hate it. Please, will ye save me from this misery?"

Biting her lip, Alexis slipped the hat back onto her head and replied, "We leave first thing in the morning, Miss MacKenna, and may Wolf have mercy on my soul."

"Please … call me Maeve."

"What? Really?"

"Yes. Really."

"Thanks." Alexis's smile turned impish. "Mrs. Forino."

CHAPTER 3

 aeve was awake before dawn the next morning, bleary-eyed, but abuzz with excitement. She put together what few things were hers and dressed in what few things weren't hers: the plainest travel outfit in the wardrobe. At least the old work boots were rightfully hers and she shrugged off her guilt as she pulled on the one she wore, wiggling her left foot to manipulate the ten-dollar gold eagle until it settled beneath her big toe where it was most comfortable. After a brief debate, she slid her athame into the boot alongside her ankle, taking care not to nick her stocking with its blade. Should she need it in an emergency, it wouldn't be as convenient as storing it in her right boot where she used to.

Fully dressed, she settled at the window of her bedroom, waiting for the sun to rise following an unusual yellow glow in the cloudless sky and holding her breath as she sat vigil.

When dawn came, it was beautiful though bizarre, filled with nearly the whole spectrum of colors. For how long would the sky bear its scars from last month's eruption?

She heard the twins rummaging in their room and wondered if

they commonly woke so early. Had Maeve not been so put off by them, she imagined she had a great many things about their culture she wanted to learn. She was fine with never knowing anything about them if it meant they parted ways later that morning when Alexis stole her away.

Maeve's stomach growled and she became awash with nausea; she needed breakfast but vowed to wait until after she was out from under MacTavish's roof. Perhaps they could stop by the bakery Rafaele had when they visited Tucson to see *HMS Pinafore*.

She was drowsy, hoping that maybe getting on the way would help wake her. "Where are ye, Alexis?" Maeve whispered, bouncing in her spot. "C'mon."

A half hour after sunrise, just as Maeve feared Alexis wasn't coming, the brunette arrived.

Alexis helped Maeve move her few belongings onto the saddlebags of a horse she swore she was borrowing from a local friend. She shifted from foot to foot and kept glancing around them, which left Maeve skeptical the horse was, in fact, borrowed.

Maeve had, herself, stolen horses before—what was another to her growing list of offenses?

At least she hadn't killed anybody.

Oh. Wait.

Alexis stroked her horse's flank. "So, um … You ever actually figure out how to ride?"

Maeve's eyebrows darted skyward.

"Wolf told me," Alexis said with a wink.

"Of course he did. Why wouldn't he?" replied Maeve.

"Don't worry. We'll work together and take it slow."

"Thank ye. I appreciate it. It's about time I learnt to ride, anyway." While Maeve was eager to get back to Redington, the rush was really in getting away from Tucson.

Moencopi and Kököle exited the house, thanking MacTavish for his hospitality. He returned a strained 'you're welcome,' which was more than he'd given to Maeve upon her departure.

She turned to Alexis, wild-eyed.

"They're a package deal, I'm afraid," whispered Alexis. "And they made a promise to Wolfie they're less willing to go back on than I am. You're gonna be hard-pressed to lose them."

Maeve groaned. Every time she faced a reminder they'd been sent by Rafaele, it turned her stomach. She wasn't even sure what bothered her most: that the women had opened their relationship under false pretenses; that she'd judged them impulsively and harshly, which was out of her character; that Kököle seemed so close to her fiancé it bordered on possible intimacy; that Alexis seemed to currently be in the same boat with Kököle as Rafaele had been; and the last nagging thought—the worst of them all by far —was that Maeve didn't trust them for no other reason than they were Natives. She was disgusted with herself.

"I suggest you find a way to get on with them because they're staying with you until your fiancé returns—whether or not you like it. So you might as well just like it."

When one of the Hopi women noticed Maeve eyeing them, she offered a chipper, "*Ha'u!*"

Despite both being dressed in their Native style, Maeve guessed it was Kököle due to her long, straight locks. The other still wore her hair in elaborate knots behind each ear, as Moencopi had yesterday. She also offered her sister a disapproving frown following the greeting, further supporting Maeve's suspicions on which woman was which.

Maybe they would go away if Maeve ignored them. And so, she pretended they weren't there.

After going through some basic horse commands with Maeve, Alexis offered to assist her onto her probably-stolen mount. Maeve refused her help, insisting she could do it herself, so Alexis settled on her own ride and watched with mirth as the Irish woman attempted to steady herself in a sidesaddle position.

Alexis muttered with a little roll of her eyes and shake of her head, "Bleedin' *knew* it."

Following her second slide off the saddle to the packed dirt below, Maeve relented to riding as Alexis and both Native women were: with a single leg on either side of the saddle horn. As the warmth of mortification cooled, she straightened her skirts and bustle to sit as nicely as they would, and glanced at Alexis, awaiting further commands.

By then, Alexis failed in not laughing aloud.

The four women set off following the rough start. They stopped on the outskirts of Tucson to break their fast before getting back on their way. Alexis had to repeat her lesson for Maeve but at least the redhead readily welcomed assistance in settling on her mount without even trying to ride sidesaddle.

They made camp upon entering Tanque Verde. Maeve said nothing to anyone, skipping dinner and going right to sleep. Moencopi, Kököle, and Alexis had their late meal around a small campfire; each offered a whispered comment about Maeve and her unpleasant demeanor.

Moencopi excused herself to sleep with a Hopi phrase to Kököle.

Alexis raised her eyebrows at Kököle. "What'd she say?"

Kököle smirked. "She told me not to do anything she wouldn't do, so clearly I'm going to: *You*." Her gaze slid purposefully toward Alexis's tent. "You haven't visited the reservation for a while. You've been missed." She held out her hand, palm down—either hunting for a hand to hold or for her own to have a kiss placed upon it. "May I join you?"

Alexis considered the opportunity; not because there was anything to consider, but because Moencopi clearly didn't approve of such things. She'd made it no secret she thought it a shame her sister was of this persuasion.

And Maeve. Maeve would—what *would* she do? Doubtful she'd understand it. She likely wouldn't even recognize what she was seeing if she walked in on them. Alexis asked herself, "I'm sitting here still considering this because *why?*"

Giggling, Kököle followed Alexis into her tent.

"I'm so used to seeing you dressed like every other gal around," Alexis remarked, as they settled on the lambskin rug. "This is becoming on you." She trailed her fingertips along the front of Kököle's manta.

"It's a lot more comfortable than a corset, I admit, but I don't enjoy the looks I get while wearing it in town. People are such bigots."

Alexis leaned in, pressing her lips to Kököle's. After a few moments, she pulled back enough to say, "You might enjoy the looks you get while you're out of it."

"What say you we trade tomorrow?"

"The idea's laughable," replied Alexis around another kiss.

"I don't—" Kököle covered Alexis's hand to stop her from sliding the lone strap from her shoulder. "Shh—"

Alexis frowned.

There was the sound of fabric rustling, followed by uneven footfalls in loose dirt. Then retching.

Blood drained from Alexis's face and her stomach tumbled at the noise; though an otherwise sturdy woman, to be exposed in any way to vomiting always threatened her constitution. Against her better judgment, she jumped to her feet and pulled back the tent flap enough to peer out into the night. She glanced at Kököle and hissed, "It's Maeve."

Kököle beckoned for Alexis with a whispered, "She'll be fine."

"Are you sure we shouldn't help? She sounds pretty ill."

"Yes, I'm sure. She's a big girl. Now come back here and finish what you started."

Alexis sighed, casting a lingering glance at Maeve where she hunched over a few yards from their tent, breathing labored and loud between quiet groans. She secured the flap with a frown. "OK." But her heart was no longer in it.

Alexis was first to wake, preparing their breakfast in silence and beginning to dismantle their modest encampment as the other ladies emerged from their slumbers.

Maeve was still under the weather, and Moencopi left no question she was displeased with her sister's nocturnal activities; thus, breakfast around the campfire was without conversation.

After another review of horsemanship, they went on to finish the second half of the journey to Redington. Following lunch, Maeve demanded her privacy.

"I'll lead," she insisted. "Whistle if I start goin' the wrong way."

With a sigh, Alexis consented, and she and the twins kept a respectable distance behind Maeve.

Moencopi asked quietly, "Is Miss MacKenna always this way?"

"From what I've seen of her, she takes a while to warm up to people." After a pause, Alexis added, "She's sweet but distressed, and I've no doubt she misses Wolf more than the rest of us. Poor girl's been through an awful lot lately."

"We are aware of that," quipped Moencopi.

"I'm just saying, don't judge her until she's had the chance to get comfortable with you. Wolf wouldn't fall in love with a miserable woman." Alexis straightened in her saddle; she'd been pitching that sentiment a lot recently.

"I honestly did not think he would ever fall in love. I will have to see it before I believe it."

"Believe it," Alexis said, adding under her breath, "the poor boy is head-over-heels."

There was no point in arguing it, so they fell silent.

Roughly a mile down the path, Kököle broke the silence: "Miss MacKenna's in the family way."

"Whoa!" Alexis's horse mistook her exclamation as command and stopped appropriately. She adjusted her posture, white-knuckling the reins while staring at Kököle.

"What?" Moencopi snapped.

Matter-of-factly, Kököle said, "She's with child."

Moencopi asked, "How do you know?"

"How don't *you*?" Kököle countered.

"… Kökö, are you sure?" said Alexis. "You're not basing this on what I saw last night. She could've had any number of reasons to be sick—"

"I'm quite sure. It's …" She thought out loud, "How, exactly to explain this to a mortal? You might say I have a sixth sense for these things."

"Well, then." Alexis nudged her horse to trot before they lost sight of the pregnant woman. "Way to go, Raf. Oh!" She smacked both hands atop her thighs, her face breaking into an irrepressible smile. "Oh, he's gonna be so happy!"

Moencopi asked, "Is she aware?"

Kököle frowned. "You're asking after Miss MacKenna? That's tough to say. Outwardly, it doesn't seem so, but I wouldn't be surprised if she's in denial. Or doing her best to hide it from everyone. How do you tell one from the other without being inside her head?"

"We are going to have to take especial care with her," Moencopi noted. "Now we are charged with her well-being, as well as that of her child."

Alexis groaned. "Maeve's sure to be thrilled."

"Why?" said Kököle.

"Besides being distrustful of you? She's convinced she doesn't need help. She doesn't want it. And she's as stubborn as Wolf, maybe even more. So—and trust me on this—good luck getting her to accept it. You saw how she was with the riding lessons."

"My dearest sister will win her over, of that I am certain," said Moencopi.

With a knowing smile at Kököle, Alexis replied, "I've no doubt. Hopefully it'll help our cause."

❧✦☙

"Dare I ask what happened with those who didn't survive?" Maeve said when Redington appeared on the horizon.

Alexis replied quietly, "You don't want to discuss that."

"Yes, I do. I'm tryin' to prepare meself."

Alexis replied, "They were buried. What was left of them, I mean."

Maeve glanced at her. Alexis turned away and so Maeve prompted Moencopi and Kököle for clarification. They did as Alexis did.

"'N' … Caitlin?"

"Buried," said Alexis. "She was the first identified. Did you wanna pay your respects?"

Maeve shook her head. "No. Thank ye," she replied, her voice weak. "It's too soon."

"If it helps, there was a nice little ceremony for her. One of her—" Alexis faltered. "—patrons set aside some money for her. He made sure there was enough for a marker."

"Oh," breathed Maeve, "good lord."

"It's only wood but it's better than what she would've got—"

"No. Tha'." Maeve pointed ahead. She hadn't prepared herself for seeing the saloon.

The Tiff and Tawny was nothing but unrecognizable charred wood all jumbled in a big, blackened pile. A nauseating combination of scents hung in the air: musky, sweet, putrid, like leather being tanned over flame with overtones of something metallic. There were a few of Redington's residents still combing through the mess as sunset was upon them and every so often, somebody coughed, choked, and gagged. Maeve pressed the back of her hand to her lips to repress her rising bile.

She didn't recognize any of the people working and wondered what they were searching for. Anything of worth that belonged to someone who was no longer around to use it? They weren't likely to find any survivors by this point. Were they still attempting to recover bodies for proper burial?

A chill swept across Maeve. "Something's here."

Alexis and Moencopi exchanged wary glances with Kököle.

"Mrs. Forino," Alexis said, ignoring the glares she got in response, "we've had a long day and we're already losing daylight. Why don't we rest now? We can start fresh in the morning. We'll work together ... however you're willing to accept our help. Come stay with me." She turned to Kököle and Moencopi. "All of you. Please."

"Alexis ... Are ye sure? I've imposed enough on someone already in recent weeks. I couldn't."

"It's no imposition. You're soon to be my sister-in-law. Ish. I insist."

Maeve sighed. "OK."

It was dark by the time they reached Alexis's home, and Maeve wanted nothing more than to get some rest. Alexis obliged happily, putting her in the unoccupied room nearest the front door.

Maeve sat on the edge of the bed and grabbed a cloth to brush the dust off her prosthetic leg; with the amount of filth she'd gathered on the trip, the moving components would need oiling.

She picked at her ankle joint's cracks with the tip of her athame to dig out the pebbles wedged in them, cursing each little rock as it popped loose: *To hell with ye.*

Alexis came in with Maeve's luggage and after a quick glance at the proceedings, looked elsewhere. "So tell me, Miss MacKenna ..." She set the luggage down. "What happened in the granary? Wolf refused to talk about it."

"He didn't tell you?" She assumed he had. Didn't he tell Alexis everything?

"No. It seemed like he wanted to, but it wasn't his experience to share."

"It wasn't." Maeve shrugged, thumping her right foot on the floor and brushing her hands on her skirt. She would need to work on being at least a little more graceful with that leg.

In the ensuing silence, Maeve heard Kököle and Moencopi preparing for dinner over the gentle whirring of her ankle as she rotated it aimlessly.

"I apologize if I'm overstepping my bounds, but I want to hear about it. I only saw the Tucson sky light up in the explosion. That's all I know."

Maeve took a deep breath. "I don't remember details. Mostly I remember …" She exhaled. "I remember unbridled fury. Esquivar was sayin' these awful, terrible things about Rafaele. 'N' I … I knew he was lyin'. If he was goin' to shoot me all along, why did he not just kill me first?"

"The little turd was fond of torturing others."

"He shot me."

"He shot at you?" Alexis gasped.

"No. He *shot me*. In me leg." Maeve motioned at her right shin and resumed what loosely passed as maintenance on it, dripping oil from a small can into its crevices.

"Is … That how—how you …" Alexis wrung her hand in the air. "—lost it?"

Maeve shook her head. "No. It was crushed beneath a wood beam. That's how Rafaele 'n' Tithu found me, accordin' to stories I'm told. I don't remember it, meself. Probably for the best tha' I don't." She paused. "Esquivar said Rafaele doesn't love me. There were other things, I think—I can't remember—'n' I … I lost me temper, completely lost all me self-control. It was the same as when I saved Raf from de la Cloche, but … on a global scale. All me anger came out as this white-hot rage. I guess the granary was the right material to explode once a single spark was introduced. The thing is, I didn't mean to kill him."

Alexis tipped her head back with a groan. "After all that, you didn't want him dead? Are you serious?"

"No. I … I wanted him to cease to exist. So … I vanished him. When I was done with tha' man, there wasn't a trace of him left." A smile spread across Maeve's face as she savored her memories. "No skin, nor hair, or teeth. I reaped his soul, too." Killing Francisco brought with it a sense of power she'd never allowed herself to experience.

Alexis took a large step away from Maeve but said nothing.

The reaction sobered her. What sort of horrid creature could conjure fire and destruction on such a global scale, and rain it upon on a helpless soul? What sort of wretched beast relished such things? *Me. I did. I do.*

"There wasn't enough left of him to haunt anyone." Maeve caught Alexis's gaze. "I made sure of it. If he was tha' horrible in life, just imagine how he could be in his ... after-times."

Alexis stiffened. With an equally stiff laugh and several blinks, she said, "It's not as if ghosts can hurt people."

"Are ye so sure of tha'?"

"*You* are?"

Maeve nodded. "Yes. I see ghosts. I talk with them, too."

Alexis stared in silence, her jaw slacked.

"Raf doesn't know."

With a nervous little giggle, Alexis said, "Aw, already keeping secrets from each other?"

"The topic didn't ever come up. We discussed other things. Me control of fire. 'N' then ..." Maeve smiled in recollection, her cheeks going rosy. "There was a change of subject."

"Yuck."

Maeve smiled more, despite herself. Or rather, despite them both. "They look—to me—like fog."

Alexis cocked her head. "Ghosts?"

"Yes. Some, I hear clear. Others have faint voices; not even the hint of a whisper. Mostly they don't remember who they were before they died. They don't remember bein' a man or woman. The one I shared a room with at the Tiff 'n' Tawny used to be a woman. 'Least I hope so; I dressed in its presence near to every day."

"If they don't remember being male or female, do they notice if we are?"

"Mr. McLaury did. But he was special."

"Special? How so?"

"He had features. He remembered he was a man. He remembered how, 'n' when he died. He was present 'n' aware in ways I've not ever seen in a ghost."

"Where is this fellow? Can I see him?"

"He was in the Tombstone jail, 'n' I doubt it. He commented I was remarkable because nobody else ever noticed him." Maeve paused. "Sometimes I can feel them, too."

"You *feel* them? Excuse me?" she yelped.

"Cold spots. There was one at the Tiff 'n' Tawny today. 'N' it was different from what I knew was there before ... It was ..." She closed her eyes and took a long breath. "New."

"Do you know why ghosts become ghosts?"

Maeve shook her head. "No. Nothin' beyond the usual belief tha' ghosts are people with unfinished business."

"Have you ever asked them?"

"No."

The grandfather clock in the hall chimed ten.

"If you'll excuse me, Miss MacKenna, I should check on the other ladies ... Perhaps even help them get settled."

Maeve stood. "Allow me to help—"

Alexis cut off Maeve with a sharp wave of her arm. "I'll have none of it. Stay here; relax. Read those books Wolf left you. I promise you, he *will* inquire about them upon his return. I imagine you wouldn't wish to disappoint him."

Maeve glowered at her. "Ye sneaky, under-handed woman."

With a grand flourish, Alexis backed out of the bedroom.

After a few minutes, Maeve stood. Awash with dizziness, she braced herself against the hardwood bookcase to her right. The room around her went white fleetingly before her eyesight returned and she blinked hard, widening her eyes. It didn't take much for Maeve to decide she in no way cared for the sensation and hoped to never experience it again. Taking a deep breath, she collapsed onto her bed with a long sigh.

CHAPTER 4

 afaele dropped from his horse with a heavy thump and a loud exhalation. The mission was a sight for sore eyes; moreover, a relief for his sore rump. This had decidedly been the road less taken, with most Californians who traveled the state opting to do so via other means.

He rubbed his horse's face before approaching a portion of the building, experiencing a sense of reverence accompanied by a stronger sense of loss.

What once was a spiritual gem was now dilapidated in the portions that weren't in utter ruin. A great hand must've come down from on high that the walls of the church were nothing but rubble amid dirt. Rafaele's soul ached for it.

If there had been any residents of Mission San Juan Capistrano, Rafaele was sure they hadn't been by in quite some time. Still, trespassing made him uncomfortable.

"Hello?" he called out. "Anybody home?"

His voice echoed off deteriorating adobe walls, and a flock of slender birds with pointed wings scattered into flight at the disturbance, several flying toward him and scarcely missing his head.

Dio mio! Basta!" Rafaele dropped to his knees, covering his head with his hands until the birds settled.

Amid their squeaks and guttural grating sounds that raised his skin into gooseflesh, a meek voice responded, "Hello? Do you need help?"

Rafaele raised his head but didn't shift his hands much. "No." He tried to steady his shaky voice. "I'm OK."

"Are you sure?"

"Yea." He stood slowly. "I'm just making my way to San Diego."

"Well, young man, welcome. I'm Father Mut. I offer rooms for rent at a rate of ten dollars for two months."

"Oh," Rafaele chuckled, "I—I'm not staying long. I have a business meeting to attend in a few days but I wanted to sightsee since I was passing by." He deliberately made no mention of having heard the mission was haunted and he was there to make contact, not as if he'd ever been able to. The witches flocked to him—three had, anyway—but, with a few exceptions, other paranormals generally didn't.

"Is this why you were on your knees?"

Rafaele ran his right hand through his curls. "No. I, uh … I've got a bit of a—" God, he didn't want to admit to having a fear—any fear, for that matter, but especially not this. He laughed at his own expense. "I don't much care for birds."

"What a shame," said Father Mut. "Some consider the migration of the swallows a spiritual affair. Or a magical one, if you will."

It's a disgusting affair. He extended his hand. "Rafaele Forino. Pleased to meet you, Padre."

The priest accepted Rafaele's hand with both of his and held it briefly.

"May I ask what happened here? I imagine this was once a stunning bit of architecture. And now—" He gestured toward the building.

"Oh, yes," Father Mut replied with a hefty sigh. "Come." He led Rafaele through dense brush. "This was the Great Stone Church."

Overhead covers were missing from the colonnades in the part of the mission that was in greatest disrepair.

Rafaele's heart crumbled. The grounds were littered with enormous mounds of debris. Even the newer adobe walls were already deteriorating, and the roof was all but non-existent.

"This is the result of a sizeable earthquake combined with years of neglect. Smallpox ravaged the community and those who didn't die moved away."

A sizeable earthquake.

Rafaele swallowed. California was paradise when compared to every place he'd been on this continent. It was all too easy to forget even paradise had its faults.

"What year was this built?"

"1776."

It was over a hundred years old; Rafaele took solace in its condition considering its age. He dared to hope he'd wear so well by 107.

A newly built home with modern techniques and sturdier materials would certainly fare better on unpredictable ground than an ancient building comprised of mud brick. *Wouldn't it?*

Too late for cold feet, Wolf. You owe this to her.

Boy, did he ever.

"You're weary," assessed Father Mut. "Please join me for dinner at least. It's quiet here; nobody will disturb us."

Rafaele exhaled. "I'm a bit peckish." If by peckish he meant ravenous.

As Father Mut led Rafaele through the mission, he offered an assortment of luxuries. "Do you smoke?" He held out a cigarette.

Rafaele accepted it with an absent nod.

"Do you need a light?"

"No, thanks. I've got one." He made no motion to fish it out of his pack while gazing at the decaying walls around them. Rafaele wondered why he was being subjected to so many ruins lately, further wondering if it was a sign from God, and if he should've been concerned.

The priest might have answers. He opened his mouth but hesitated. Where did spirituality become superstition? *Probably better to not ask.*

"Mr. Forino?" Father Mut cast him a sideways glance. "Is there something you wish to get off your chest?"

Oh ... only everything. "I could use Confession but ..." he hadn't enough time for acts of penance to absolve him of his guilt.

Father Mut prompted, "But?"

Rafaele smiled wickedly. "You've seen my face, Padre, and I've already given you my name."

"You must've really misbehaved," chuckled Father Mut.

"What can I say? I'm a man in love."

The priest craned his neck to look at Rafaele. "Love? Where is your wife?"

"Oh—I'm not married." He stopped midstride. "Hopefully soon, though!"

"It would be my honor to officiate."

"Well … there may be some difficulty with that." *Some. A lot.* Did the volume of problems matter?

All it took was one to stop a wedding.

Father Mut frowned. "How so?"

Rafaele sighed, pressing a fist to his lower back and stretching. When would the soreness of the trip go away? "She's not Italian."

"And she's not Catholic?"

"Uh …" In theory, being Irish, she should've been but somehow due to her nature, he guessed otherwise.

"Has she been baptized?"

Rafaele dropped his gaze. It wasn't that he hadn't given it consideration; he feared he wouldn't be able to reconcile his religious beliefs with hers—or her lack of them. Certainly, he wasn't the best Catholic there was—maybe even among the worst of them—but the worst religious person had to be better than an atheous one.

He'd seen nothing of her behavior that led him to believe she was religious—especially Catholic. Maeve was a witch; he knew that much.

In all the time they'd spent together, he never pursued the topic. Had she learned her Craft from someone? Did witches have some sort of religious order?

They were nothing but monsters in fairytales as far as everyone was concerned—including him, once upon a time. And the first he'd met still practiced their Hopi beliefs, so that wouldn't answer his question.

"I … don't know if she's been baptized."

It was silent for a while before the priest continued walking without him. He glanced back at Rafaele, indifferent. "Well then, young man? You best remedy that."

Maeve was in such poor shape that she was unable to return to the remnants of the Tiff and Tawny for two days. She scarcely touched the food she was offered by the overly attentive twins and drank as little, opting to sleep while Alexis was continuously coming and going.

On the third day following her return to Redington, Maeve got a second wind. Though she was grumpy, she was alert and had regained her appetite.

She dressed herself in the borrowed gown from MacTavish's family. It was plain and inexpensive when compared to what Gaylene wore but for Redington, it was still nicer than Maeve preferred, especially when she knew it would likely get ruined.

It was much too nice to wear while mucking around, and it certainly wasn't designed for such activities with its more delicate fabric. The purpose was for a lady to sit around in it and blend into her surroundings. Maeve had never been good at such things.

And, she realized, if she ruined this gown, she had no other clothing to her name. Surely her wardrobe hadn't survived the blaze.

She tucked her hair into a snood and left her earrings on the bureau before emerging from the bedroom.

Maeve hadn't paid attention to her surroundings upon her arrival and had confined herself to her room in the days since, so this made for the first real opportunity she'd had to investigate Alexis's home; she expected the same kinds of trappings she assumed she'd see at Rafaele's home and was wrong on both counts.

The décor Alexis owned revealed she had some money—ill-gotten or otherwise—to her name, and she either had good taste or borrowed a friend's.

Milton, Maeve assumed.

Alexis had richly detailed dark wood furniture that shined hints of red where light hit it. There were a few floral paintings on the walls—including one with Milton's signature on it—and plenty of porcelain trinkets in the China cabinet.

Maeve found the three women seated at the dining room table—Alexis donning her usual shirt, trousers and dust-covered cowboy hat, Moencopi in her traditional manta and Kököle in a beautiful gown far nicer than most anything Maeve owned—or used to own, like the red dress Rafaele helped himself to tearing apart the night they consummated their relationship. She choked on a twinge of jealousy followed by deep feelings of loss. It wasn't just Caitlyn, or a place to live.

What few things she had with her from Ireland: all gone.

She had nothing.

Her stomach didn't care about her sadness and griped loudly of being neglected.

"Care to join us?" Kököle addressed Maeve. "There's plenty of breakfast to go around."

Maeve, in turn, regarded Alexis. "Thank ye. I probably should." She attempted to help herself to the spread, but Alexis shooed her into a chair.

"I'll get that. You've served people enough, and you'll exhaust yourself later working at what's left of the Tiff."

She sighed but remained seated as Alexis overfilled her plate and brought it to her, followed by the teapot.

Maeve ate more than her weight in scones, drowning them with the entire contents of a teapot before declaring, "I'm goin' to the Tiff 'n' Tawny." She excused herself before anyone argued it.

"Will nothing stop that little hellion once she sets her mind to something?" Alexis scowled, shooting eye-darts after Maeve.

The sisters exchanged somber glances.

"There … *is* something that would keep Miss MacKenna indoors," said Moencopi.

Kököle frowned. "Do we dare stoop to that? Isn't it a bit extreme?"

"You're not gonna tie her to the bed." Alexis cast a pointed look toward Kököle. "Are you?"

Kököle smiled sweetly.

Moencopi cleared her throat. "I can make it rain."

"Well sure Maeve looks delicate, but she's no milksop. Why would a little rain keep her inside?"

Moencopi and Kököle exchanged glances. It was Moencopi to reply, "We should let Maeve explain that, herself."

"Well," said Alexis slowly, "let's give her the chance to do what's right by her before taking any extreme measures. I don't wanna intervene, otherwise."

"We should be keeping our eyes on her," Kököle said as she stood. "Be sure she's keeping out of trouble."

"Yea," Alexis muttered, "good luck with that."

Maeve tried staying out of trouble but still got roped into an obnoxious conversation about the saloon with the town marshal.

She asserted, "It wasn't Francisco. Can ye not trust me?"

"How can you be so sure of that?" Cummings replied. "You weren't here."

"Because: He's dead."

"He could've survived; they haven't found his body in the granary yet."

"They won't. Ever."

"How, exactly, did *you* survive such a blaze, Ducky? I'm told the explosion of the granary put that of the TnT to shame."

Maeve shrugged helplessly. Somehow rumors of witchcraft at the granary had transformed to standard every-day arson while she was at the MacTavish home and she chose her words now with care. "I guess ... I must be lucky?" *I'm one lucky ducky*, she thought bitterly.

"My dear little girl, you have a remarkable way of getting into the middle of things."

She couldn't respond, and it was for that reason Maeve was grateful when Alexis approached, followed closely by the Hopi women.

"... As do you two," the marshal addressed Kököle and Moencopi wryly. "You've returned. Color me stunned."

Kököle, seemingly undeterred by his chilly welcome, greeted him jovially, "It's such a pleasure to see you again, Marshal Cummings."

The flicker of a smile on Maeve's face crossed her features and vanished too quickly for anybody to notice.

"You both fled the town so swiftly I never got the chance to talk with you," the marshal replied, his gaze flickering between the twins.

"Actually," Alexis interrupted, "they're here to help Miss MacKenna recover her belongings."

Cummings sighed, his narrowed eyes softening as he turned to Maeve.

"S'pose I'll permit it if that's the case." He waved toward the remains of the saloon. "Knock yourself out, Ducky. Holler if you find a body, will ya?"

Maeve glowered. "Of course." In the event she had reason to holler, she prayed the words wouldn't be propelled by vomit. She glanced at Alexis. "I could certainly use some extra hands. This is—" She turned her gaze to the destruction. "It's ... Overwhelmin'."

"I'd be perfectly happy to comb through the wreckage on your behalf," said Alexis. "Go home and rest a bit. Eight, maybe nine months?"

Moencopi hushed her.

"What's tha' supposed to mean?" Maeve snapped. "What's tha' look for?"

"Uh? What look?" Alexis batted her lashes and put on a smile.

"That's only makin' me more suspicious!"

"I'd be happy to help you for as long as you need—and want. That's all I meant." With a quick glance at the twins, she added, "We'll all help. Won't we, ladies?"

"Of course." Kököle responded, confusion scrawled across her face. "Any friend of Alexis or Wolf is a friend of mine."

"'N' what's *tha'* look for?" cried Maeve at Kököle.

"Nothing."

"I don't believe ye."

Kököle yelped, "This is the way I always look."

"Ye're keepin' secrets," said Maeve. "All of ye."

Kököle chuckled. "No more than you are."

There'd be no winning this conversation, so Maeve turned her attention to the ruins. "May as well start here, I guess."

She kneeled and combed through blackened chunks of wood and beams; bits of stone and broken glass; a veritable obstacle course of splinters and shards itching to weasel their ways into her skin.

She moved things aside with care, lifting lighter fragments only to discover more beneath them: layers of destruction. Revealing each brought with it the same stomach-churning mix of anticipation and fear about what she'd uncover next.

It appeared she'd never reach the foundation of the saloon. Maybe it didn't exist, nor did the dirt beneath it. All that was left at the site was rubble.

Maeve's desperation mounted.

While sifting through the remains, she lost herself in thought.

She feared the other facet of her personality—the one forged in the events in Tucson, Aibheaeg—and what it represented.

Deep down, Aibheaeg was the person she constantly hid under a façade of Not-Really-Maeve; the person she truly was all this time making herself out to be human rather than the other way around.

An unholy demon in ladies' clothing.

She shifted in her spot, struggling to reposition a large beam—what must've been part of the second-story balcony. It took a few jerks before it moved and snagged the hem of her dress, taking with it a length of thread. She bit off the thread and adjusted the snag; likely it'd go unnoticed.

For how long did she insist to others she was proper? How often did she struggle to behave as she'd been taught a woman should?

'N' how often did I fail because I couldn't keep up the charade?

Am I really the harpy Máthair always said I was?

Of course she was.

The more she considered it, the more Maeve wondered if her insistence upon being ladylike was her mother talking and not her desire at all. In retrospect, she was happiest when Rafaele showed her it was so much more enjoyable to throw propriety to the wind.

With her thoughts resolving to a single clear impression, Maeve realized why it was so important she find something there among the wreckage.

The Tiff and Tawny was the only place she'd felt normal; neither monster nor lady, not in some dangerous adventure alongside Rafaele. That of course wasn't a horrible thing; in fact, she enjoyed it tremendously. But those adventures were also where this other Maeve—Aibheaeg —emerged.

For that reason, she wanted to go back to her time at the saloon. Things were simpler there, safer and saner. The magical time before she changed.

And it was home.

She needed something physical from this place to ground her.

Maeve plucked a few small, dirt-encrusted blocks from the ground. Still hunched over, she wiped the dust from them to reveal several white rectangles and a couple smaller black ones. Monroe's piano keys: now nothing more than ivory and ebony debris.

She set the keys down and brushed a few more scraps to the side, catching glimmers in the filth. Gingerly, she took them from their surroundings.

"Brothel tokens." Maeve held them in her open palm, staring at them. "I got these for tips all the time."

Glances were exchanged and Kököle offered her hand. "Do you need to sit?"

"I was offended when I first started gettin' them because I assumed—"

"They wanted to take you upstairs?" Alexis guessed.

"Yes." Maeve acknowledged Alexis. "The tokens were useless to me. I certainly wasn't gonna use them." She added hastily, "No offense."

Alexis smirked. "None taken. And believe me, I've heard worse."

"I used to give them to Joplin. To this day, I dunno if he ever used them." Maeve bit her lip. "I'd give these to Milt, I guess, but after Esquivar killed Sabine, I doubt he'd want them."

"He is a man," commented Moencopi. "I am sure he would."

"You don't know Milton," Alexis said. "Not like I do." Nodding at Maeve, she augmented, "Not like we do."

"So what do I do with them? The ladies still need work, I suppose, 'n' I'm sure the tokens aren't completely worthless." After a long pause: "Do ye suppose they'll rebuild?"

"A town is nothing without its brothel," Kököle said.

Moencopi added, "Wood buildings burn down all the time and are rebuilt as often. This would not be the first."

"I don't think it's in Smith's nature to give in so easily," said Alexis. "I'm sure a new Tiff and Tawny is in short order." She frowned into the distance. "Tawny will need a few replacement ladies though." Her gaze turned to Kököle and Moencopi; both reacted with glares. She addressed Maeve. "I'll take those if you don't want them, Miss MacKenna."

Maeve said, "OK," and handed the tokens to her.

"Wow. Hey, thanks!"

"Ye saved me from torment at MacTavish's," said Maeve, resuming her task as the interlude had gotten a bit uncomfortable for her taste. "It's the least I could do in return."

Maeve spotted something familiar sticking partially out from beneath a beam: a single milky white breast, maroon nipple, the sharp curve of a waist going into a hip.

"Oh!" she gasped, struggling to grab it and pull it out from underneath the half-charred beam.

The painting that formerly decorated the upstairs hall was scarcely recognizable even after she tried cleaning it of the caked-on soot. Maeve didn't recognize who the subject was, but she knew the painter well, and his signature was in the missing portion of the painting.

The artwork—and artwork it was even if of scandalous nature—was destroyed. She dropped it to the right of her feet and stared at it with the sinking sensation in her gut that accompanied a painful realization. Maeve glanced around herself; first at the immediate disaster area, and then the buildings of Redington still standing.

This wasn't her home. Not anymore.

Not without Rafaele or the Tiff and Tawny.

Not without a job or her belongings.

Not without Caitlyn.

Her breath turned ragged, fire rising from her chest to her cheeks and eyes. She didn't want to cry so she focused on returning to her work, stepping over a jagged piece of wood jutting from the rubble. Part of someone's bed? No, those all had metal frames. It could've been remnants of a mirror.

Her foot caught a board and she fell, a sharp pain jolting through her right hand. She raised it and squeezed it into a fist, the heat of blood oozing between her knuckles.

Maeve was back on her feet as quickly as she fell, a pair of dark hands on her right sleeve, a pair of pale hands on her left.

She was a mess, her hair down and wind-blown, skirts torn with threads trailing. And, of course, the injury to her palm. She opened her fist to wipe away some of the blood, uncovering a puncture wound already healing, welts forming where blood had been.

"Are you OK Miss MacKenna?" called Kököle from beyond the worst of the ruins.

Alexis added quietly, "If you're stumbling and need to rest, please do."

"We've been at this for hours," Maeve replied stiffly, yanking her arms from their grips. She snatched her snood from Moencopi. "'N' ye think a little slip is gonna keep me from continuin'? I amn't stoppin' 'til we're done."

Out of the corner of her eye, Maeve caught a young boy walking along the boardwalk who'd stopped to watch them. She caught his gaze and held it briefly before he ducked his head and ran off.

"We are sorry to upset you," said Moencopi.

Alexis muttered similar sentiments.

Maeve dismissed the apologies with a scoff. They couldn't have meant it. After all, they knew Rafaele had an encumbrance like hers. Shouldn't they have realized someone with a missing limb was no less capable than a complete person?

"I didn't fall because of me leg. It was me dress tha' tripped me." She pointed at the tear in her skirts, hoping to prove a point. Looking at Alexis, she added, "Count yer blessings tha' ye're better dressed for this." She glanced at Moencopi long enough for her to understand she was being addressed. "Ye too ... Rachel, or whatev—"

"I am called Moenc—"

"I don't care!" Maeve turned to Kököle. "'N' ye: other girl ... better keep to the edge of things in tha' gown if ye don't wanna get stuck."

Kököle's lips dipped and she inhaled through her nostrils, her eyes glistening as she blinked furiously.

Maeve felt terrible but was unwilling to apologize. Her voice considerably softer, she explained, "Ye don't wanna ruin yer dress or hurt yerself too ... um ..." She searched for a name. "Sarah?"

"My name's Kököle, Miss MacKenna."

"Right." Maeve cleared her throat. "That's enough time we've wasted. We oughtta get back to work—"

"And you ought to tend that injury." Alexis pointed at the ground where Maeve landed, her blood splattered across the charred wood.

"I really don't—"

"Oh *hell*," groaned Alexis, her gaze trained behind Maeve.

Maeve turned to see Marshal Cummings several yards away.

He waved at them. "Find any bodies?"

Maeve glared. "How can he be so heartless? These were our friends."

"He's a man," answered Alexis through clenched teeth. "They're all that way, I'm afraid." She called back to the marshal, "No, sorry, no bodies here."

"Well ... I'm sorry to interrupt, but I need to speak with the Ladies Redbird." He looked between the two. "I've been more than patient with you two."

Alexis regarded Kököle and Moencopi. "You'd better comply; Shadow Wolf and his Pack don't need more trouble."

"But Miss MacKenna needs us," Kököle protested.

"I've got this," said Alexis. "Don't worry."

Kököle and Moencopi left the remnants of the saloon accompanied by Marshal Cummings.

"Well, shit, guess it's just you and me, girlie. You sure you're OK there? That's an awful lot of blood to have brushed off as nothing."

Maeve sneered at the crude language and got to her knees to resume sifting. "But it *was* nothin'." She paused, peering over her shoulder to watch the women being escorted away by the marshal. "They're Pack members, too?" How she detested them! That they were members of Rafaele's band of misfits merely made things worse.

"Yes. Though this is the first time … well, second … they've come to Redington." Alexis kneeled beside Maeve. "It's been quite handy to have Indian allies. Now gimme your hand."

"It surprises me Rafaele would have them."

"Why?" Alexis glanced at Maeve, her eyes wide.

"… Because of the Comanches?"

Alexis frowned. "What about them? They're well east of here."

"Oh." Maeve realized maybe Rafaele hadn't told Alexis the truth about his arm. Alexis's confusion regarding her mention of the Comanches stunned Maeve. "Yea. Ye're right." Attempting to cover for nearly revealing Rafaele's apparently well-kept secret, Maeve said, "I'm sorry … I've been havin' difficulty keepin' track of me thoughts lately." Which, frighteningly enough, was neither embellishment, nor lie.

"Mmm," replied Alexis. "Gimme your hand, please."

"Alexis?" Maeve said.

She sighed. "Yea?"

"They said wood buildings burn down all the time."

Alexis shrugged. "That's because they do."

"I mean … It's the way they said it. Like …" Maeve exhaled. "I dunno … Like maybe they did this."

Alexis laughed. "Really? Those two? Trust me, they're not the type. They're kind, helpful, and loyal to a fault. Wouldn't hurt a fly!"

Maeve tossed a few bottles to the edge of the rubble where others had already done the same. "That's what people say about me." She paused. "'N' I've killed a couple men."

"OK," said Alexis slowly. "Let's review facts, shall we? De la Cloche was gonna kill Wolf. What were you to do: let the weasel kill a decent man?"

"Well—no—of course not—"

"And Esquivar? He was a turd, not a man. So you haven't killed any ..." She hesitated, then emphasized, "Men."

"Ye're vulgar," remarked Maeve. "'N' real funny."

Alexis cocked her head and replied with a crooked smile, "Thanks. Now seriously, Miss MacKenna: make with the hand."

"Fine." She offered her left hand to Alexis.

"I'm not stupid."

Maeve sighed, presenting her formerly injured hand.

"Oh, my God." Alexis looked between Maeve's hands. "It can't be!"

"But it is."

She met Maeve's gaze wordlessly. After several moments, Alexis's attention shifted to something behind her.

As Maeve turned, Alexis shouted, "Back to stare some more, huh, kid?"

The boy had returned; escorting him was his mother as well as the shopkeeper, who juggled a paper-wrapped bundle.

"Miss MacKenna!" The shopkeeper greeted her. "My son told me you were back in town, and I couldn't believe it." His gaze made a vertical sweep of her body. "They say you ... I mean, your ..." he stammered. "In Tucson—"

"They say you're a foot shorter than when you left," the boy blurted.

"William!" Mr. Bailey snapped, his face flooding red.

Maeve wasn't sure if the story emerged as gossip's victim or if the child, William, was making a cruel joke at her expense.

Though she was inclined to make light of her injuries by referring to them as nothing more than flesh wounds, she opted for a more gracious, "I was injured but I'm doin' better now, thank ye for yer concern."

"And what of the dreadful issue with the law? Is it true you were on trial?"

She wondered how it was any of their business but before Maeve replied, Alexis cast her a sly smile and jumped in: "It was gonna be a hung jury but Mr. Forino blew some holes in their case, so Maeve's free."

Maeve smirked. "'N' in the end, I even got a lovely necklace as a partin' gift."

The Baileys stared blankly.

"So ... the money you gave us for all those things you bought? Turns out it wasn't yours to give?" said the shopkeeper.

She swallowed. "Apparently not?" As if she didn't already know it. "I am so sorry."

"That you got caught?" blurted Mr. Bailey.

Veronica shot her husband eye-daggers, explaining, "The money was confiscated."

Mr. Bailey turned his gaze onto the bundle in his arms. "But considering how you've lost ... well, everything, really ... I wanted to give you—"

Veronica cleared her throat. "Credit, dear, where it's due. Please."

"We—"

"Ahem?"

He sighed. "*She* wanted to give you this."

"No ... it's not appropriate," said Maeve. "I couldn't accept tha'."

"I wanted to get rid of it as we couldn't sell it anyway in light of your death, but Veronica," he spared a glance at his wife, "wouldn't let me. And since you're not dead—thank God!—and it's already to your measurements—"

Maeve looked to Alexis for encouragement. She was no help.

Ultimately, Maeve hadn't paid for any of this, couldn't pay for it now, and the only reason they were giving it to her was because the shopkeep had been harangued by his wife into not throwing it out. "I—don't know—"

Veronica snatched the bundle from his arms and approached Maeve, her voice soft. "Please. I insist. I'm proud of the alterations I did on this, and, besides, you're a good woman. You've been through so much and you deserve to have something you've well more than earned. Take it. Don't insult me."

"Well ..." Maeve sighed, accepting the bundle. "If ye insist. Thank ye for yer kindness, generosity ... 'n' beautiful work."

"I'm sorry I couldn't bring the other gown. It was never modified and still good for sale and since you didn't actually pay for it—I mean—" She lowered her voice. "It was hard enough to convince him to let you have this.

Surely you understand." Veronica bowed away with a small smile and rejoined her husband at his side before Maeve could respond.

Alexis spoke to the package in Maeve's hands: "I get the feeling I'm going to be working in this mess all by my lonesome."

Maeve opened her mouth to reply but Alexis preempted with a smile, "I'm joking! Please. Go. Change into something comfortable. Hey, maybe even take a load off your feet while you do that."

Maeve considered her options before nodding and heading for Alexis's home with a small wave over her shoulder.

Maeve sneered at her reflection in the standing mirror. Never had a corset been so uncomfortable, nor had she needed to adjust the lacing so much prior to putting on her bodice.

In this case, she had to tighten the laces not once but twice before the grey bodice would fit without unsightly gaps at the buttons as it strained over her undergarment.

Yes, the pristine white chemisette and drawers were lovely, the stockings without holes. Her skirts, small bustle, and petticoats were hemmed the appropriate length for Brandon's beer-jugger but that was where Mrs. Bailey's boasting should've ended. Maeve's measurements had been taken properly and the woman had them at her disposal; apparently, she wasn't compelled to use them when altering the corset and bodice for her.

The secondhand boot fit well, though she opted to switch back to her old one given the task ahead.

But with the shorter skirt length of a barmaid's outfit and the dark greys of the dress and boot, the unapologetic white and gold of the prosthesis stood out in stark contrast.

While she was always keenly aware of how incomplete she was at MacTavish's home, their longer gowns hid the monstrosity, making it easier for her to pretend she was normal. And, she contented herself with assuming, it made it easier for others to forget the truth, as well.

There was no doing that here and now. She steeled her nerves and went for the front door, still unsure she was ready to put herself on such display yet. She needed to get over this hurdle, however, so she steeled her nerves to face the world.

When she returned to the Tiff and Tawny site, it seemed the whole world was there; word had spread of Maeve's return to Redington and most of the saloon's regulars, and those in its employ were rummaging throughout the site while awaiting her arrival.

Brandon and Tawny were discussing if anything was salvageable—the obvious answer being no.

Monroe had Booker's ear, talking of relocation. Booker remained silent, focusing first on his fingertips, then the back of his hand, followed by the ground and sky.

About half the soiled doves were in attendance—Maeve's stomach turned realizing the rest were presumed victims—chatting amongst themselves.

Maeve hoped they were there to greet her but figured they came to gawk at the cripple who destroyed part of the Tucson railyards; she was their entertainment.

A circus sideshow performer.

Many of the smiles greeting her turned serious as their gazes flickered south of her face—or bust line, depending on whose gazes they were.

Conversations ceased.

Jia Li and two soiled doves Maeve knew by their working names—Ruby Buttocks and Bristol Prat—cast her pitying looks before hurrying on their way. Monroe patted Maeve wordlessly on the shoulder before leaving with a pout. Booker left without so much as a glance her way. Much to her disbelief, Jethro Byrd did likewise.

There were a great many doleful stares, murmurs of "so sorry," and uncomfortable coughs from patrons who crossed her path.

It wasn't until Maeve settled beside Alexis to resume her work that Brandon and Tawny approached.

"How are you doing, my dear?" said Tawny.

Maeve forced a smile and answered without thinking, "I'm well," which, of course, was complete and total bunkum. *As if Tawny or Brandon care about me woes?*

"Listen, 'Kenna." Brandon cleared his throat, his gaze locked well south of Maeve's face. "In the event we're able to rebuild the saloon—"

"I'm short a few prostitutes," Tawny blurted. "Including an Irish one. Can you imagine the enthusiasm from our regulars if such a favored member of the team was promoted? It would certainly encourage returning business from the men who like you."

Maeve was flattered by the suggestion but didn't consider it a promotion. Hoping it would be the politest way to decline Tawny's offer, she showed off her engagement ring. "Rafaele wouldn't appreciate his fiancée takin' on such employment. I'll be back to wait tables." If, of course, Brandon would have her considering she lacked half her right leg.

"I find it hard to believe Forino actually proposed marriage," Brandon replied. "Though I suppose it's less surprising he chose an Irish woman."

Maeve frowned.

"Any case," Brandon shrugged, "blessings on your union." Under his breath, he added, "Whenever that happens; much luck to you."

Brandon looped his arm with Tawny's, escorting her away. They leaned in close to each other, but Maeve heard their whispers.

"I pity her," said Tawny. "Thank goodness she turned me down; who'd want the services of an invalid whore?"

"Frankly, I doubt she'd be able to keep up at her old job. Bless Forino for disregarding that. Guess he figured he couldn't do much better than a cripple."

Maeve's mouth fell open in a silent gasp. How could anyone be so cruel?

Alexis's voice carried across the site: "I found a tintype."

Maeve recognized the picture frame from afar and scrambled over unrecognizable items to get to her, catching her right foot on debris.

"Oh! You OK?" Alexis yelped as she caught Maeve by the arm.

Maeve composed herself, allowing Alexis to pull her upright. "Yes. I'm … I'm OK." Her next step forward with Alexis clinging to her arm was as shaky as her voice. She sighed, much aggrieved at admitting to herself she wasn't the young woman she used to be. Not yet, anyway. She had every intention of getting back to the way she was—fake leg be damned. "What'd ye find?"

Alexis handed over the tintype. "I thought this might be yours," she explained.

Maeve pressed the tintype of her family to her breast, turning her face toward the sky and blinking away tears; this wasn't worth the stinging agony that accompanied them.

"Miss MacKenna, I'm so sorry. I can't imagine how hard this is for you."

"I'm in yer debt for findin' this. Thank ye so much."

"Think nothing of it; I'm just glad I can help."

"How could this've survived?" The last time she'd seen it had been as she put it back into her cauldron. Her gaze darted from the tintype to Alexis. "Where'd ye find it?"

Alexis made a sour face and pointed at the ground a foot away. "Must've been blown into a chamber pot, if you can believe it."

"No," Maeve cried, spotting a familiar possession. "I put it in there—in me cauldron!"

"A cau—a—oh." She picked it up, passing it to Maeve. "Wow, I didn't realize those were real things. I mean, other than being used for cooking soup or … newts, rabbit eyeballs, toadstools, wart-riddled withered old hands—" she rambled. "Or something. Whatever. Didn't realize your type—I mean, hell, you know what I mean—really used cauldrons outside of fairy-tales …" Alexis sighed in defeat. "God. Forgive my ignorance."

"Ye're plenty forgiven." Maeve dumped the contents of the cauldron out, setting her family's tintype in it carefully. "I'm so blessed; I didn't think I'd recover anythin'."

"So." Alexis cleared her throat. "I'm guessing there's also a broom and a wide-brimmed, tall, pointy black hat of yours buried somewhere in this mess?"

Maeve elected to ignore the question, replying instead: "For what it's worth, I don't do newts 'n' toadstools. I most recently brewed an unused love potion." She smirked. "Bunny eyeballs, however, were the main ingredient."

Alexis blanched.

"I'm only teasin'."

"It's good you're smiling again, Mrs. Forino … even if it's at my expense."

The two women trudged into Alexis's house, homeowner in front and Maeve bringing up the rear. Exhausted, Alexis dropped her gun belt on the kitchen counter beside the back door as Maeve settled into a chair at the table, their bounty from the day set on the floor along the back of the dining room: the cauldron, the tintype of her family, and Caitlyn's favorite gold locket. Maeve's Seth Thomas was behind the cauldron, its case decidedly worse for wear and its mechanism in need of repair—again. And of course, the frightful corset Edison made her; much to her chagrin, that item was pristine.

Alexis made a big to-do about locating the chest Maeve kept under her bed—it was barely recognizable following the explosion and the powders within it were unusable; she would need to start her Book of Shadows anew. It was stupid to drag the chest back from the saloon but she couldn't leave it there; it was still hers.

Maeve closed her eyes for a momentary respite but opened them to find a full meal gracing the table in addition to the previously absent twins. "I fell asleep?" she yawned. "For how long—"

"Do not worry yourself," Moencopi replied with a kind smile. "You needed your rest, so we let you. Please. Eat your fill."

"We should wait for Miss Chesterfield," Maeve suggested.

"She's refreshing herself and won't be but a few minutes," replied Kököle.

"If that." Alexis walked into the dining room and sat in the chair at the head of the table.

Maeve was stunned into silence. Alexis's cowboy hat was nowhere to be seen, her chestnut brown hair loose down her back. She was far from feminine in an exposed brown short corset and white button-down man's shirt beneath it, womanly thighs poured into men's brown trousers neither designed for nor tailored to accommodate her ample curves. No, she wasn't feminine, but she was gorgeous.

Stunning.

Maeve had never felt so inadequate as a woman, not even when comparing herself to Caitlyn and her abundant resources.

Caitlyn had been pretty, to be sure, but Alexis had something else atop her beauty.

She's attractive.

Maeve was vaguely aware of somebody saying, "What?"

She didn't acknowledge it.

"Miss MacKenna?" Alexis asked.

"Aye—" She blinked hard. *Snap out of it.* "Yes?"

"Are you alright? You're staring." She motioned with two fingers toward her mouth. "Have I got something in my teeth?"

Maeve shook her head, wrenching her gaze from Alexis's hourglass figure. *It's not fair.* And what made that thought more disturbing was that she wasn't sure exactly what was unfair about it—nor even to what 'it' referred.

"I'm … fine." Except, of course, for questioning why Rafaele chose her over Alexis, and the crippling lack of self-esteem accompanying this whole wretched line of thought.

None of that was 'fine.'

Maeve turned to picking through her meal in search of items she found least unappealing while forcing herself to keep her stare off Alexis.

After dinner Maeve retreated to the parlor to be alone with her thoughts, but Alexis followed.

"Your silence is concerning," Alexis noted. "I imagine you're the type who freely speaks her mind when something's on it."

What was she to say when she couldn't sort out her feelings on the topic, or when she wasn't sure what, exactly, the topic even was?

Maeve sighed and opted, instead, to study Alexis's curio cabinet; the easiest way to get insight into a person who was essentially a stranger was to see what she collected.

Her gaze settled on an item out of place amongst delicate knick-knacks: a woven basket in which sat an incomplete knitting project. Three needle tips not much larger in circumference than toothpicks protruded from a rich green cloth tube that may have been a sock or glove in progress. How lovely it would be against Alexis's skin tone.

"I didn't know ye knit," blurted Maeve, hoping a change of subject would put her mind away from such odd thoughts.

Alexis turned to Maeve with a pout. "I don't."

"Well then what is this?" She nodded toward the fabric tube in the basket. "Looks like knittin' to me. Or is it crochet?"

"It's knitting. Gram was making me gloves when she passed away."

"Oh—I'm—I'm so sorry."

"Yea well these things happen."

Strained silence and heavy stares that spoke more than words filled the air between them.

Maeve never figured Alexis out, and seeing her as actually womanly did nothing but add jumbled thoughts to the mix.

Her lips pressed into a hard line, Maeve leaned toward Alexis.

Alexis startled and straightened, drawing in a sharp breath and hollering into the neighboring room, "So, now that little sleeping beauty here is awake—" she made a peculiar face at Maeve before pushing by her and returning to the dining room. "How did your little chat with Cummings go?"

Maeve steadied herself and followed.

"Your delightful marshal thinks we blew up the saloon," Moencopi said.

Kököle added, "Just because we came into town on the same day it happened."

Alexis gave Kököle a long kiss on the mouth as if making some sort of point.

Moencopi averted her eyes with a frown etching her otherwise flawless forehead.

"Well," Alexis teased Kököle, taking her hands, "you have to admit it *is* suspect."

"That is beside the point," Moencopi said. "For lack of evidence he let us go … At least until this consulting detective he hired arrives."

Alexis groaned, releasing Kököle with an annoyed flourish. "Wonderful."

"I'm still not sure I understand your legal system," Kököle added, "but aren't we supposed to be innocent until proven guilty?"

Maeve sat and though she wasn't participating in the conversation, she couldn't withhold a loud snort.

"Care to contribute?" said Kököle.

"No," Maeve replied.

After a long pause, Alexis explained, "Mrs. Forino, here, has had her own experience with our legal system."

Maeve glared at her; it wasn't her experience to divulge.

"Still too soon to discuss it," Alexis assumed. To the twins, she added, "I understand it was a horrible experience."

"Ye 'understand' it was a horrible experience?" griped Maeve. "Nothin' about the outcome of me trial would prove without a reasonable doubt tha' it *was* a horrible experience?"

"That's ... a ... perfectly valid point," Alexis said. She glanced at Kököle and Moencopi. "I saved her from being hanged."

Jaws dropped.

Maeve snapped, "It was their fault I was there to begin with." She leaned back in her chair.

"Do realize, Maeve," said Alexis with narrowed eyes, "I will always defend my brother before anyone else. Having said that, the truth of the matter is—I remind you—it was the turd's fault you were there to begin with."

Maeve neither agreed nor disagreed, instead turning her attention to her hands as she folded and unfolded them in her lap. There was nothing more than a faint mark where she'd impaled her palm earlier that day. By morning there'd be no trace of it, just like every injury prior.

Tired of the silence and their stares, she stood. "Excuse me. I'm retirin' for the evenin'."

"Goodnight," the twins said in unison.

"Sleep well, Miss MacKenna," added Alexis. "We'll try not to disturb you."

Maeve nodded and retreated to her borrowed bedroom. She changed into a nightgown, lying in bed for some time, a mild ache in her lower abdomen keeping her conscious. In the dark, she stretched her arm across the bed, reaching for a body she knew she wouldn't find.

She missed Rafaele most at night; when the world was quiet, when breathing and heartbeats slowed. A hard, warm body to press against, to be safe beside.

Her eyes squeezed shut, fending off those contemptible tears, those tiring, wretched tears. The relief of crying was never worth the agony of its accompanying welts.

He would've had comforting words to dull the sting of losing her home. He would make adjusting to the new women in her life less awkward. She wasn't sure how, exactly, but he would.

Really, the only thing that made sense was the physical comfort she found in Rafaele's presence.

Maeve didn't like thinking about it, but their relationship was little more than antagonism wrapped in sex and tied with a satin ribbon of romance that came undone at the first sign of trouble.

Maeve fiddled with the opal ring with the pad of her thumb. She had promised to marry a man she barely knew. It excited her as much as it frightened her.

She vowed when he returned—if he still wanted her—that she would better acquaint herself with him. Maybe first by running her hands over every inch of him and covering his body with kisses.

CHAPTER 5

 aeve hunched over and splashed her face with boiling water from the basin, watching as it dripped off her tinged brown. The dirt of another grueling day came off with little effort, but the fatigue would not wash away so readily.

It turned out Alexis was quite the workhorse and without her there, Moencopi, Kököle, and Maeve had to work harder than usual to compensate for her absence.

For all their diligence, they came home empty-handed. It became apparent there was no reason to return to the ruins except for Maeve's need to not be burdensome; there would be nothing for her to do until they rebuilt. And maybe not even after.

Too tired to empty the basin of its filthy water, Maeve dried her face, dressed in a shift, and retired to bed.

When she exhausted herself failing to fall asleep due to her aching muscles, she sneaked into the hall; the house was quiet, and someone left a lamp burning in the dining room.

"Miss MacKenna," Alexis greeted her with a fleeting glance as she sat alone at the table. "You're still awake."

"We missed ye today."

"I—um … stuff." She rubbed her collarbone through her shirt. "Something." Alexis shook her head. "I had pressing business."

"We figured." Maeve assumed she was off to break some law or other, whereas Moencopi assumed she spoke with the marshal. Kököle hadn't wagered a guess either way.

Maeve turned to leave. At this rate, the cacti out front would be better conversationalists.

"Wait."

The terse statement gave Maeve pause and she glanced at Alexis.

Alexis's cheeks darkened. "Join me."

Maeve swallowed. "What?"

"Please?"

"… Why would ye want me to stay?"

Alexis tucked a hand around the nape of her neck and scratched. She moistened her lips. "I s'pose the least we can do for that man of yours is to get to know each other."

"I just wanted a night cap." With marked hesitation, Maeve sat.

"Figurative?" said Alexis. "Or literal?"

"I want to sleep. But …" Maeve gestured to her forehead. "Me thoughts. They're racin'."

Alexis stood. "There's a tonic for that."

"Oh?"

"Whiskey." She caught Maeve's sour expression. "No? Tequila?"

"No." The thought made her stomach lurch.

"Amaretto?"

Maeve's face lit up. "Ye have it?"

"Of course I do. No offense, but I kept out of the saloon; diluted booze at inflated prices and being surrounded by women I couldn't afford isn't my style."

"OK." Maeve stood. "Tell me where it is 'n' I'll get it."

Alexis put a hand on Maeve's shoulder, gently pushing her back into the seat. "I won't have it; you're my guest. And as I understand it, you should be resting."

"I beg yer pardon?"

She smiled serenely. "You're so tired you can't even sleep. You need your rest. Let's help silence whatever's keeping you awake."

"I don't know those strange women from Adam," Maeve said. "I hardly know ye. All tha' aside, it seems to me somethin' strange is goin' on here. I'd even be inclined to say ye're actin' peculiar."

"Whatever are you talking about?" Alexis's voice was an octave higher than its usual timbre.

Maeve leaned forward, staring hard. "This is yer chance to come clean with me, Miss Chesterfield."

Alexis squeaked, "Wh—what do you want me to say?"

"It's because of me leg, isn't it?"

She exhaled. "Your leg?"

"Yes, me leg. Ye see me as a cripple."

"God no! Believe me, it's anything but. Honestly, I haven't given your leg a thought—except when I had to catch you the other day." She paused. "It didn't even cross my mind then!"

"Then why are ye all treatin' me like I'm an invalid? What's all this 'rest, Maeve,' 'eat, Maeve,' 'do not ye lift tha', Maeve?' I've not ever in me life shied away from hard work. Ye're makin' me feel awful!"

With a sigh, Alexis said, "Look: Kököle, Moencopi, and I were charged by your fiancé to take care of you. It's a responsibility we're taking seriously. The absolute last thing we want is for Wolf to return to a broken woman. An injured woman. A dead woman. So, yea, perhaps we're being overly protective of you, but it's for good reason. Don't be offended by it. Please try to understand. Try, at least, to let us help you. Hell, maybe even slow down a little and make it a tiny bit easier for us to keep our promises to Wolf?"

"I promise nothin'." Maeve swallowed. "I have work to do here, 'n' I amn't restin' 'til it's done."

"Really? Seems you came back empty-handed today." Alexis's gaze flickered away from Maeve's face. "I noticed."

"Just because I didn't find anythin' today doesn't mean there aren't things left to be found."

Groaning, Alexis said, "I knew you wouldn't cooperate. Do you have any idea how perfect you are for Wolf?" She murmured, "And how much you're going to put the poor man out of his mind?"

Maeve sighed. "I'll let ye help so long as ye stop badgerin' me to do stuff. Or … to not do stuff."

"You promise nothing? I promise nothing. Now. I believe I was going to get you a drink?"

"Please?" *Because boy do I need it.*

Alexis disappeared into her kitchen, followed shortly by the sounds of glass clinking against glass.

Maeve listened to the grandfather clock in the hallway ticking away the passing seconds, thinking how each brought her a second closer to finding herself back in her lover's embrace. *Tick.* Seeing his beautiful lips twisting into a devious smile and his eyebrow quirking, sending a flash of excitement through her veins. *Tick.* God how she loved that wicked eyebrow wiggle. *Tick.* Feeling his caress follow the curve of her bare back. *Tick.* Cupping her rear end. *Tick.* Squeezing it and coaxing her closer to him. *Tick.* Claiming her mouth with his. *Tick.* Squeezing his arousal between her thighs. *Tick.*

"My God!" Alexis gasped, both eyebrows near her hairline. "What are you thinking about?"

"I'm sorry?"

"I've been talking to you and you were just staring at the table with this look on your face."

"Was I?" Maeve offered a sheepish smile.

"Fine. Keep your secrets." Alexis poured amaretto into a shot glass for Maeve before crashing into her own chair, legs spread like a man who had ample reason to spread them. She drank straight from the bottle.

Maeve held up the shot glass to inspect it. "This is odd."

"How so?"

"I amn't used to others servin' me alcohol. It's always been the other way around."

"You mean to tell me you worked in a saloon and never partook?"

Maeve shook her head. "I did … I have. Rarely. Besides, yer argument's faulty. I worked in a brothel 'n' didn't participate in *tha'* activity."

"Cryin' shame."

"Seems everyone says so."

Alexis frowned. "Why are you so baffled by it?"

"Why does anyone—everyone—want me bein' a painted lady so badly?"

Alexis shrugged. "It's something to do. Besides: Have you seen yourself?"

"Raf thinks I'm too thin."

"Raf's an idiot," Alexis blurted. She immediately apologized: "I'm tired.

It's the booze talking. I should've just said I disagreed. Truth is, you're gorgeous, and you're not gonna convince me you're oblivious to it. Raf told me your beauty stunned him into silence when you two first met." She chuckled. "I didn't think it was possible to shut him up."

Maeve smiled. "That's what the ladies upstairs said." Her smile faded. "I dunno. I haven't ever given it all tha' much thought I guess. I amn't beautiful or homely. I'm just me." A nice smile, pretty eyes, dainty nose, but underfed, missing half a leg, and with those awful freckles on her shoulders her mother used to tell her resembled lizard scales under proper lighting.

She had a taste of the amaretto, hoping it might drown the painful memories. "Lately, though, Rafaele has me thinkin' otherwise. Like ... maybe I *am* somethin' special."

"Good. He's doing his job."

Maeve commented on the amaretto: "Mmm! This is better than Smith's rotgut."

"Well I should hope the hell *so*! Hey ... You can tell me. What goes into that stuff?"

Maeve finished her shot glass, holding it out to Alexis. "More, please."

Alexis poured Maeve another shot. "You mixed that poison, didn't you?"

"Yes. I did."

"What's in it? Maybe I wanna make my own."

"Alexis?" replied Maeve, before drinking half the contents of the shot glass in one gulp. She exhaled with a hiss. "Ye don't wanna know. I didn't wanna, but I had to learn for me job. Trust me when I tell ye, ye're better off innocent." She finished her drink. "More."

Alexis obliged. "Me? Innocent? That ship sailed with my uncle at the helm."

"More." Maeve then emptied her glass.

"I'm running out." Alexis gave her another refill nonetheless. "Say ... What do you see in Rafaele, anyway?"

"Ye always spoke so high of him. Do not ye see it?" Maeve's thoughts were going fuzzy with the onslaught of alcohol. Across from her, Alexis was wilting over the table.

"I love him like he's my brother." Her statement spread into a barely intelligible soup of words. "You. You love him like he's your lover. I mean, you don't have to talk about it if it's too embarrassing but—" she fluidly shook her head. "—I admit my curiosity."

Maeve snapped, "No. He loves me like a lover."

"Dear God, why are you angry about that?"

"I amn't angry—" Maeve looked at her glass, realizing it was empty. If she was to explain why she felt as she did about Rafaele's sexual prowess, she would need more alcohol.

Anticipating the request, Alexis said in unison with Maeve, "*More.*"

They burst out laughing, and Alexis poured her another.

"*Jyng,*" Alexis said through her laughter. "You owe me a phosphate."

"Wait—what?"

"Oh—never mind." Alexis waved it off with an exaggerated sweep of her arm. "It's—it's a stuper—supter—superstition, nothing. Don't worry about it, it's just this silly thing my family did."

"... OK."

"By-the-way. See this?" Alexis swirled the remaining alcohol in the bottle. "It's mine."

"Well in tha' case, I suppose I should savor this." Maeve took the drink in a single swallow.

"Maybe we ought to review some English vocabulary—"

"Cait used to do tha' with me." She bit a pained smile. "The thing about Raf is tha' he knows what he wants 'n' makes sure he gets it."

"Huh?"

"He touches 'n' kisses me wherever he pleases. He's shown me heaven. But for all me body he's explored, he hasn't afforded me the opportunity to explore his. 'N' I want to." Maeve moaned, "Oh, do I ever want to."

"Well." Alexis cleared her throat, her face going red either in embarrassment or from the liquor. "I clearly didn't have enough of this." She took a couple loud swigs from the bottle before banging it on the table, emptied. "That was more about Raf than I ever cared to know."

"He's given me more than anyone could."

"I'll bet he has," Alexis muttered.

Maeve tittered and flipped her wrist. "Not like tha'. Well ... OK, also like tha'. I mean ... Me parents wanted me to be a midwife. They were prepared to marry me off to the neighbor-boy."

"Did you—were you—I'm sorry? Did they arrange your marriage?"

With exaggerated nodding, Maeve said, "Yes. They were essentially goin' to pay a man to take me. Tell me: how's tha' any different from prostitution?"

She sobered. "It isn't?"

"I sure don't think so. 'N' now tha' I have someone who wasn't paid to wed me ... I—"

Alexis frowned, leaning in and resting her forearms on the table, a few degrees shy of being draped over it. She didn't interrupt.

"I got swept up in me own passion for tha' man. 'N' of course I leapt at the opportunity he gave me with his proposal. But ..."

"Don't tell me you're having second thoughts."

No; by this point, Maeve experienced third and fourth thoughts.

"When we left Éire behind 'n' I knew the arranged marriage was ... no more ... I started fearin' I'd not ever find anyone else who'd want me. 'N' if I did, I worried tha' if he got to know me, he'd come to not want me anymore." *Like Davidson.*

"Seriously?"

"Me ma used to tell me no man would love someone with me temper." *Among other things.*

Alexis said nothing.

"I love Raf. Truly. But ... once I was free of me arranged marriage, I realized I enjoyed bein' alone. Everyone wanted marriage for me more than I did for meself. I wasn't expectin' to fall so hard in love with someone tha' I'd forget I didn't want to be someone's little wife."

"No offense, but you're damn near elfin. You'd need a stepping stool to see over blades of grass. There's hardly a man out there you wouldn't be 'little' next to."

Maeve glowered, slowly continuing, "'N' on top of tha', I feel like things are ... I dunno. At a standstill thanks to me injury. Like I can't be as good as I once was. Slow. Totterin'." She exhaled, "Useless."

"Miss MacKenna, if I may be so bold?"

She was inclined to say 'no.' Instead, Maeve regarded Alexis.

"I've known my share of cripples over the years; I worked a circus. And honey? You aren't one and you can—and should—thank Stilwell and Price for that. Dare I say you've been a bit of an ingrate. 'Least you aren't on a crutch. I mean hell: we can barely keep up with you!"

"Well." Maeve sighed, turning her focus back to the collection from the Tiff and Tawny. "I've come to crave adventure after spendin' so much time by meself. 'N' what I'm gettin' is a man expectin' some sort of domestic bliss. I can't give him what he wants. I'm afeared I'm gonna break his heart."

Alexis guffawed. "You think Raf wants domestic bliss? You're in a town gripped by arson undergoing a murder investigation. Your home was obliterated. What part of all that is dull, exactly?"

"Well—"

"Listen: Raf has an extraordinary way of attracting remarkable things to himself, and you think you're going to be a standard bride to a standard man?"

"Amn't I?"

"What's changed that's causing you worry?"

Maeve sighed. "The Pack's what changed. It's disbanded."

"Maybe so but you can't take the wild from the wolf." Alexis shook her head. "What I meant was … Pack or no, Raf is Raf. He won't stay out of trouble just because Shadow Wolf Pack is gone. And you'll want to be right alongside him for every fuss 'n' fracas."

"Want to be, yes. Allowed to be? Ha!"

"'Ha!' nothing, Miss MacKenna. A good marriage should be an equal partnership … not that I'll ever have it." Alexis turned her attention to her fingers, clicking the tips of her thumbnails together. "Both spouses are meant to be hands-on and involved in exploring life together. Raf must know this if he went through the pains of asking you to marry him considering he wasn't willing to entertain the institution previously."

Maeve smiled crookedly, speaking her thoughts: "In me betrothal to Rafaele, I've a type of freedom I couldn't dream of. He treats me as a person, not just a woman or a possession—he does! Well … Most of the time, anyway." It was equal parts sweet and infuriating how he'd made sure she would be well cared for in his absence.

"He may not be perfect—he's a man, after all—but he's among the few good ones." Alexis smiled. "I owe him a lot, too." A wistful look shimmered in her eyes. "To be honest with you, he's the only man I'd go to the ends of the earth for. And … I'm glad he found himself a good woman. Maybe I'm a little jealous, but I'm no less glad."

Maeve wondered in what way Alexis was jealous but figured it better not to ask.

"So." Alexis cleared her throat and ran her hand through her hair. "You're a witch. What's that like?"

"What an odd question."

Alexis shrugged. "I'm odd. It's not the most offensive thing I've ever been called." She smiled. "Raf warned me you would torch me in my skin if I made you angry enough. I genuinely couldn't tell if he was teasing me."

"I conjure fire— 'n' I don't even do tha' well. I won't torch someone for makin' me angry." *Except tha' was kinda what I did to Esquivar.* "Tha' goes against the Rede."

"The reed?"

"Rede." Maeve clarified, "R-E-D-E. If it harms none, do what ye will," she recited. "Whatever ye do is returned to ye threefold."

"So the Rede is a stricter version of the Golden Rule."

"What's the Golden Rule?"

"Do unto others as you would have them do unto you?"

"Oh. I see the similarities."

After a few moments of silence, Alexis remarked, "That fire thing must be convenient. I imagine your ridiculously fast healing time is, too."

"I suppose they are convenient things." Her expression soured. "Though I can't heal faster than the doctors around here can saw off limbs."

Alexis's face washed white.

Feeling bad for mentioning it, Maeve hastily changed the subject: "The fire thing is especially convenient when certain people have difficulty startin' campfires."

Alexis's laughter erupted in a loud *ha!* and she smacked the table with an open palm. She tottered in her seat as though she would pass out.

Maeve, however, was having difficulty fending off the sleep previously eluding her. "That's the laugh of someone who understands."

"Oh yes. Raf's never been good with those." She straightened in her seat with a deep breath and pointed at Maeve. "His weakness, your strength. How … cosmic. You two are absolutely meant to be together."

With a sigh, Maeve admitted, "We're dreadful mismatched."

Alexis studied Maeve for several moments, her face knotted in deep concentration. "I don't think so. I really don't. Maybe with time, you'll see it the way I do. Although ..."

Maeve slumped forward, resting her elbow on the table and her cheek in her palm. "Although?"

"I'd have taken Wolfie for the type to pursue someone ..." She loosely cupped an imaginary pair of breasts. Ample imaginary breasts. "*You* know." She squeezed the air. With a watery smile, she added, "*Honk, honk.*"

"Well now I feel inadequate," cried Maeve, covering her chest with her arms. Her endowment was a far cry from Alexis's gesture—or her chest size.

"Honey. You have nothing to worry about. I didn't think Raf would ever wanna marry. And he chose you." Alexis paused. "Honest, I believed there wasn't a woman alive who deserved him, but you proved me wrong. Just ... Treat him right, OK? He's so in love with you that you needn't do much to destroy him."

Maeve was having the strongest sense of deja vú. "I could say likewise."

Alexis smiled. "I'd like it if we were friends."

"Really? Even though I'm ... what I am?"

"I don't understand."

"After the stuff with Gaylene, with the MacTavishes ... I couldn't imagine anyone wantin' to be near me, let alone to be me friend. I sometimes find meself wishin' I could turn it off. Me life would be immeasurably easier without all this ... magic stuff."

"But it's who you are. It defines you, and it'd be wrong to deny that part of yourself."

"'N' when the part ye're denyin' turns ye into a pariah?"

"You enjoy what makes you better than everyone else. I know I do."

It took several moments for Maeve to consider Alexis's statement before she decided, "I'd like to be friends, too."

"Good. Listen. It's been a long, exhausting day. I'm going to bed," said Alexis, stifling a yawn. "Do as you want here. Goodnight, Mrs. Forino."

Maeve's cheeks dimpled. "Thank ye. Goodnight, Miss Chesterfield."

Alexis patted Maeve on her shoulder as she staggered out of the dining room, pausing in the hall to let the wall support her for a few moments.

Maeve turned the shot glass over in her hands, her mind at peace.

She woke several hours later without the feeling of time having gone by and raised her head from the table. With a quiet groan, she rubbed her temples with her fingertips. It was still well before sunrise, so Maeve left her seat at the table and dragged her bottle-aching self to bed.

It was going on noon when Maeve woke with a start. She put a hand to her tender chest, her heart racing. The last thing she remembered was sheer terror. Rushing to the bedroom with Rafaele at her side, feeling it was too late for help, and bellowing an unfamiliar word: "uh-*dee*"—whatever that meant.

It was a dream. Oh, Lord. She exhaled.

It's probably not a dream. After all, such vivid dreams seldom were.

Maeve crushed the sheet over her abdomen in a tight fist and delicately repositioned herself in bed. The increasing frequency of pregnancy dreams was making it that much more difficult to deny she was carrying Rafaele's baby.

Not just any baby. A bastard.

Overtaken by queasiness, Maeve grabbed the closest thing she could find in which to heave. As she wiped her mouth afterward, she realized she'd vomited into her cauldron and hoped the god or goddess in charge of such things would forgive something so heinous.

One of these days, I should figure tha' out. Such tasks would prove easier thought than done; her Book of Shadows was good as mulch now.

Ironically, even the Book of Shadows belonging to a witch gifted with fire wasn't immune to flame.

Paper, no matter how magical, still burned.

It was the bad half of Maeve's psyche that sought those answers. The half that erupted a volcano and made people cease to exist. *The half tha'*—Maeve shook her head sternly. *This is who I am. Nothin' 'n' nobody can change tha'. I'm a witch. One who's a little bit inexperienced 'n' has a whole lot of control issues. 'N' maybe a little bad temper.*

Though Maeve's grandmother spoke of magic infrequently, when she did, she emphasized the importance of control. What Maeve needed now was guidance and training.

In any event, until she had those things, she should've limited her use of magic until she had more control over it, until she could be sure what she was doing wouldn't cause more significant issues in the long run. Until she could be sure she wouldn't kill anyone—unintentionally, anyway.

Which would involve usin' it. To learn.

What a miserable quandary.

And so she put it out of her head, taking her time to prepare for the day, though there wasn't much to prepare for since they weren't returning to the Tiff and Tawny's ruins. That was for the best; while Maeve hadn't lacked enthusiasm, her energy remained at a premium.

Maeve struggled into her corset and gown. It scared her how abnormally thick she was for being less than two months into her pregnancy.

Maybe it's twins. Her lower lip trembled.

Maybe it's a whole litter.

Regardless of the pain it brought, she burst into tears.

"Miss MacKenna?"

From the other side of the door, Maeve wasn't sure if that was Kököle or Moencopi: either case, it wasn't Alexis.

"Are you OK?"

"No," sobbed Maeve, her tearducts and cheeks burning with tiny welts. "I amn't."

"May I come in? Maybe I could help."

Maeve nodded.

A few moments later: "Miss MacKenna?"

"Yes, come in," Maeve snapped, agitated for having to repeat words she never actually spoke.

The door popped open, Kököle wide-eyed. "What's the matter? Oh goodness, your face; you must be in agony!"

"I—" Maeve tried to find her words, but they weren't coming. None in English. Neither in Irish.

"Can I help?"

Maeve shook her head, desperate to compose herself.

"Please talk to me." Kököle guided Maeve to her bed, helping her sit. She ran a hand over Maeve's fiery strands in a maternal way.

Maeve glanced at her through scorching, tear-blurred eyes. Kököle's lips were moving. Though she knew nothing of the Hopi and their religion or customs, Maeve felt something familiar in what Kököle was doing. Something akin to the kinds of things Máthair Chríona did to help others in distress. The tears stopped—thank goodness—but her eyes narrowed. "What're ye doin'?"

"I'm trying to calm you. It would do none of us any good if you fainted."

Maeve remarked, "Nobody can be as nice as ye're bein' without havin' somethin' to hide." *Like why ye were just doin' an incantation?*

"We all have our little secrets. But ... Yes. I'm really this nice." Kököle smiled. "Sorry to disappoint."

Maeve dropped her gaze to her hands, clasped tightly in her lap, half hidden by her fluff of skirts. She was shaking.

"I'm going to venture a guess. Correct me if I'm wrong, but ... You're missing your beloved?"

It would've been all too easy to snap, *Of course I do.* And it was true. However, as Maeve was loath to admit her pregnancy to herself, there was no way she would tell anyone else, let alone a stranger.

A *strange* stranger.

Maeve replied, "I've been through a lot lately. I'm still adjustin'. I've a fake leg. No home. 'N' yes, Raf left me behind, refusin' to tell me where he was goin', whom he's seein', why he was leavin' me or when, exactly, he'd be back. I reserve me right to cry a little."

Kököle leaned forward, prompting, "Might there be anything else upsetting you, Miss MacKenna?"

Lord, yes! "No ..."

"Well, whether you want it or not, we're here for you."

"That's what I hear."

Kököle put a gentle hand to Maeve's arm. "You might as well accept it."

Maeve didn't reply.

"I know you're carrying Rafaele's child. Care for some lunch?"

If it were possible for a heart to drop and leap simultaneously, Maeve's would've done it then. "I am *not*—" Under Kököle's unimpressed stare, Maeve sighed in resignation. "How'd ye know?"

"Call it ... intuition."

Maeve wanted to call that a lie. Instead, she said, "'N' I can assume everyone else knows?"

Kököle's eyes flickered downward.

She groaned. *Of course they all know.* "Can we maybe not discuss it?"

With a smirk, Kököle bargained, "If you come eat. You needn't eat much."

Although Maeve wasn't hungry, she consented, catching a glimpse of her tear-marred face in the mirror. How nice it would be to not cry at the drop of a hat.

How wonderful to return to normal.

As she understood it, the side effects of being bagged were temporary. And she was fortunate, indeed, that hers thus far were not constant companions; the uncontrolled weepiness would give way to her normal mood just as the nausea flowed and ebbed.

Kököle escorted Maeve to the dining room.

"Miss MacKenna."

Maeve snapped the book shut, straightening in her seat and fluffing her hair. She turned to address Alexis but words escaped her.

"I apologize for interrupting—"

Maeve replied haltingly, "Ye weren't interruptin'."

"Oh please." Alexis cocked her head and grinned. "I see the stars in your eyes and the flush in your cheeks. Were you at least still clothed? In your head, I mean."

She put a hand to her collarbone; Rafaele's searing lips were but a dissipating reverie. "The daydreams help me not miss him quite so much."

"Loath as I am to suggest it, you'd benefit from getting out of the house."

Maeve was too tired for such excursions, and Kököle and Moencopi tailing them made the idea even less alluring.

After a hesitation, Alexis added, "I wouldn't mind some company since otherwise I'd be going to the Western Union office—" She hesitated and emphasized, "—all alone."

"Oh?" Maeve's eyebrows shot up. "Oh! Well—I—I wouldn't want ye bein' lonely."

Alexis snorted. "Of course you wouldn't. Thanks for your sacrifice."

She smiled and stood. "Think nothin' of it."

The walk to the telegrapher's station was filled with trite conversation as both skirted around the issues of Rafaele's absence and the presence of the other women in Alexis's household.

Ahmad Akbar greeted the ladies with a wide smile. "Miss Chesterfield! I've word from San Diego."

Maeve held her breath but Alexis clapped. "Splendid! Give her here."

"You should be warned." Akbar gave her a telegram slip. "It's ... colorful."

Alexis made a face while she read the missive. She cleared her throat, seeming to struggle suppressing a smile. "He's safe, in case you were concerned."

Maeve frowned. "Of course I'm concerned! Is tha' all?"

"Uh ... sure, why not?"

"Chesterfield," said Maeve sternly. "What else does it say?"

"Hang on." She hummed while she skimmed the telegram before summarizing: "Bad words, bad words, bad words ... cursing, anger. Ah, here's the part for you: 'Give my love to Maeve. On second thought, don't.'" She doubled over with laughter.

"What?" cried Maeve. "It does not say tha'!"

"See for yourself."

Maeve snatched the telegram from Alexis.

ALEX BITCH CHESTERFIELD

STILL IN SAN DIEGO. KNOW YOU DON'T FUCKING CARE.
HAVE BEEN TRYING TO REACH SHITTEN TUCSON TELEGRAPH OFFICE.
NOT A FUCKING WORD FROM YOU IN A WEEK.
WHAT WERE YOU THINKING MOVING MAYV FROM THE MACTAVISH HOME?
DELIBERATELY DEFYING MY GODDAMN ORDERS AND PUTTING MAYV IN DANGER.
HAVE MUCH WORK LEFT HERE. NOT HAVING LUCK.
FRUSTRATED. YOUR DISREGARD FOR ME NOT HELPING.
SPENT NIGHT HERE. HEADING OUT SHORTLY. WILL BE IN TOUCH AS NEEDED.
REPLY PROMPTLY.

GIVE MAYV MY LOVE.
ON SECOND THOUGHT, DON'T.

-RLF

"If you don't close your mouth, you'll have a terrible jaw ache later," Akbar told Maeve gently.

She glared at Alexis. "Why are ye laughin' at tha'?"

"It's funny!" Her laughter punctuated in what might've been darling squeaks any other time.

"Rafaele sayin' he doesn't love me is funny to ye?"

"Oh." Alexis sobered. "That's not what he meant, dear."

Maeve's face darkened. "How do ye figure?"

With a sigh, Alexis cast Akbar a long look before addressing Maeve. "Raf asked me to relay his message of love to you, but then realized he chose words that were … open to interpretation. Especially when the one receiving the instructions is a woman who would appreciate loving other women the way he loves you."

Maeve blinked. "Oh." Her face went hot. "*Oh.*"

"See?" Alexis smirked. "Funny!"

"If you have to explain the joke—" started Akbar.

"Then be thankful Wolf's not here to be offended by your insinuation," Alexis replied with a grin.

Maeve cleared her throat. "I didn't realize he aired his lungs."

"Of course he does." Alexis's voice was soft. "He's a man. In the West. It'd be suspect if he didn't use bad language at least when occasion warrants it. If not more often. In this case he's, um … he's furious with me. He gets testy when we don't listen to him, as I'm sure you've discovered."

"Well … yes. But he didn't use any of these words around me …"

Akbar and Alexis exchanged glances before saying in unison, "Classic courting behavior."

Maeve didn't appreciate what they implied, nor how it sounded her future would be once a wedding band was on her finger. Her face hot, she turned her attention to the telegram once more. "He calls ye Alex?"

"Yea. I prefer it."

"Do … Do ye want me to?"

"You do as you please. Address me however you're comfortable. Just please, not Lexie. Honestly, I'd prefer to be called a bitch."

She asked of the sign-off: "RLF?"

"No idea what his middle name is. Sorry." She shrugged. "You might try asking him."

Maeve frowned, unable to put out of her mind his language. "When I asked for ye to take me away from the MacTavishes, I didn't think what it might do to him."

"Truth be told, when I let you wheedle me into bringing you back here, I didn't give much thought to why he wanted you to stay there. I mean on the surface, the obvious thing was how easy it'd be to get you on the train when you were already mere feet from the station."

"So why all the awful words?"

"Well … Charming as he is, he's got enemies in the area. You now have 'em, too. No matter how allegedly handled things were in Tombstone, and how sweet you otherwise are, the law won't protect you from the people who were wronged by my well-aimed shot and your subsequent failure to hang." Alexis inhaled deeply. "All week when I didn't reply, he might've thought you were dead. Or *we* were dead, although I suppose my death wouldn't bother him as much as yours."

"Oh," Maeve exhaled. "Listen … I didn't want ye gettin' in trouble with Raf on me account."

Alexis waved it off. "Oh waren't nothin', li'l filly."

Maeve leaned back with a frown.

"Don't worry. It'll blow over easy enough. You give a little of this action —" She rolled her shoulders in, tilted forward, and pressed her glorious breasts together. "—maybe throw in a pout and some eyelash-batting with a well-placed 'I'm sorry Wolfie' and I expect you'll be golden."

"Golden?"

"The moment he sees you? Forget it. All of this will be a distant memory."

It had been several days of an emotional jumble for Maeve; great times with Alexis followed by worries about the pregnancy, and agitation with Moencopi's and Kököle's constant presence.

Luckily Maeve conjured a plan to get some alone-time and visited what remained of the Tiff and Tawny in the late afternoon.

She had an hour or two before she returned—by sunset, as she'd promised Alexis—and figured if she didn't return as night fell, the women would come for her.

So there Maeve stood, alone, bathed in the lurid burgundy of sunset, an intermittent cool breeze carrying on it smoke from nearby wood-burning cookstoves.

Voices petered out, replaced by the occasional echo of a closing door or window snapping shut; shadows stretched across the desert floor like a lazy black leopard dotted by small flames appearing in windows.

The electric *peent* of a Nighthawk cut through some distant chatter of flycatchers and drew Maeve's attention skyward, where she caught the lone bird in flight, his wings an arched boomerang as he looped through the air before diving into distant brush and silence.

There were no yipping coyotes and Maeve realized she hadn't heard a single wolf howl since Rafaele left.

She wanted to be by herself and even the desert accommodated her desires.

Except she wasn't alone. Something was there with her.

It was the feeling she often had in her bedroom in Letterkenny at night, when the candlelight couldn't cut through the darkness, instead merely impeding her night vision. The suffocating atmospheric change in the presence of a reaper come to visit.

The hairs on the back of her neck stood on end and the far reaches of her brain filled with a primal fear of monsters far scarier than she.

Unseen claws raked faintly along her forearms, drawing those hairs, too, upright.

Her breathing came faster, pulse thundering through her veins. It took every shred of self-control not to run.

Maeve knew the biggest monsters were human and that she could defend herself from them.

She cleared her throat, composing herself before she spoke, in general, to the only entity who should've been there.

"Listen, Tiffany. Ye leave me alone now. I amn't talkin' with things like ye anymore."

At least not for a while. She wasn't sure what opportunities that ability could open, but also figured dealing so closely with the dead was nothing but an invitation for trouble. At least not until she had a better idea what she was doing.

The presence came closer, bearing down on her as if her words had been a dare.

For how much it felt like something physical was exhaling on Maeve's neck, there was nothing as far as she could see.

It wasn't the entity she'd always assumed was Tiffany.

No.

This was different: nothing visual. Just a silent presence. An echo of emotions.

It wasn't happy.

Unhappy wasn't right either.

Scared? No. Angry? No.

Lost, Maeve realized sullenly. *It's lost.*

She'd never encountered anything like it before. "How can I help ye?" Maeve whispered. "What do ye need?"

When there was no answer, she glanced around. There was no living person within eyeshot. *Good.* She didn't need unwelcome ears listening in on the intimate ceremony.

"I can say a blessin' for ye." She paused, listening for an answer—any answer—before she began. Once again, she was met with silence. Maeve kneeled. "I give ye me blessin'. I release ye from this place. Be free, go on to be with—"

Her voice caught when a chilly breeze slammed into her, a shadow closing in. She lifted her head to see what blocked the fading sunlight.

"Liam," she cried in disbelief.

Liam O'Doherty stared at Maeve, his eyes wide and lips parted.

"Maeve? MacKenna? How can it be—?"

For several moments, they regarded each other before talking at the same time; he in Irish for her, she in English for him.

"Let me help you; where are my manners?" Liam offered his hand.

Though Maeve was hesitant to accept it, she gave him her right hand and he hoisted her to her feet.

"What're ye doin' here?" gasped Maeve.

"You speak English!"

"Ye're so shocked," replied Maeve. "I had to learn it. It's not as if they're gonna learn *Gaeilge* for me. Certainly, I wouldn't expect them to."

Liam shook his head as if he hadn't heard a thing she said. "Look at you." He swept the upper half of her body with an appraising gaze. "You're beautiful. The United States has been kind to you."

Maeve begged to differ, but she said, "So I'm told."

"Could I—?" Liam opened his arms to Maeve. "Old friend?"

At the mere invitation for a hug, she became keenly aware of carrying a baby not yet the size of her pinky fingernail, and of the ring gracing her left hand. Maeve permitted the embrace—stiff, uncomfortable, and still attempting to maintain her distance. She watched over his shoulder as the last sliver of sun disappeared over the horizon and left a painful red glow in its wake.

Maeve pulled back quickly. "Ye didn't tell me ... Why are ye here, of all places?" He couldn't have come searching for her; at least, she hoped he hadn't.

"Oh ... Marshal Cummings sent a request for help in the investigation of a building explosion." Liam smiled. "They sent the best they had." He clarified: "They sent me."

"Ye're a—"

"Detective. Yea. Surprised? Nobody guesses by looking at me." Liam was much taller than Maeve remembered; her memory must've been playing tricks on her. She couldn't decide if he was taller than Rafaele. If not, he was close. He was still a lanky fellow, a crop of curly red hair atop his head, impeccably groomed red handlebar mustache above his upper lip, and thin, wire-framed spectacles perched upon his perfectly straight nose.

He wasn't at all an unattractive young man and she wouldn't have been surprised if half the women in Letterkenny had been vying for his affections before he left.

To Maeve, however, he was an old friend. And she resented him for taking what she wished she'd given to Rafaele.

Having nothing else she could say, Maeve answered, "Wow."

"It's remarkable, wouldn't you say, that we found each other with all the odds against us? You wouldn't write something so incredible, no one would believe it."

She gave him a crooked smile. "I suppose not."

"It's kismet."

"Excuse me?"

"Kismet." He flashed her what she guessed was supposed to be a charming smile. "Fate. Destiny. It was meant to be." Liam hesitated. "And now there's a young unchaperoned woman who needs a safe escort home. In case you haven't noticed, the sun's set."

What were the odds of reuniting after over a year apart, neither of them purposefully seeking out the other, in Redington, of all places?

After Maeve struggled to find a response, she opened her mouth. "I—"

"Miss MacKenna," said Kököle as she, her sister, and Alexis approached. "Have you found anything of value?"

Liam smiled at Maeve, his gaze answering differently from his words. "Good evening, ma'am. Detective O'Doherty." He shifted his gaze to address the women, a flicker of sourness marring his otherwise gentlemanly demeanor. "Who might you three be?"

Maeve assumed the acrid expression was for the two Natives and the woman wearing men's clothing. She was used to it—at least used to Alexis— but imagined the three, especially walking as a group, were off-putting to a newcomer.

Liam glowered. "And what are you doing here so late? This is neither the place nor the time for women to be out unescorted."

"We're Miss MacKenna's friends. We're helping her salvage her belongings," scowled Alexis, her eyes narrowing on the badge gracing his chest. "There's no law against that, is there?"

Brows furrowed, Liam regarded Maeve. "… Your belongings? Why would you have belongings here?"

"I—" She hesitated. "I lived here. I worked here."

"Why are you interrogating Miss MacKenna?" Alexis demanded. "She was convalescing in Tucson at the time of the explosion."

Liam ran his fingertips over his mustache, puckering his lips. "Clearly, Maeve, you and I need to catch up."

"Catch up?" Moencopi gawked. "Are you somehow acquainted with this man?"

Maeve nodded, an overwhelming feeling of numb blanketing her body. She couldn't deny the feeling like they were pawns being moved by the hand of a greater power. "Yes. We were neighbors in Letterkenny."

"I must attend to some business with the marshal," Liam said, clearing his throat. He smiled at Maeve. "I hope you might come to his office to speak with me soon."

"I—I can do tha'."

He leaned in for another hug, but under the disapproving glares of Alexis and the twins, Maeve stumbled back. Kököle caught her.

"'Evening," Liam said, tipping his head toward the women before he departed.

As he walked off, the chill of a spirit swept through Maeve after him; the entity, whatever it was, departed with him.

She exhaled.

Going to bed sounded glorious; Maeve was fatigued and emotionally drained, hoping she could get under some covers, block out the world and never have to deal with any of this mess ever again.

"*So.* Tell me about this copper friend of yours."

Maeve didn't say anything for a while after requesting some coffee, expecting her bed would want for an occupant that evening. The twins excused themselves from dinner without finishing their meals, leaving her with Alexis over dishes of cold food.

Alexis ventured into the kitchen, returning with two mugs dangling by their handles from her pinky and ring finger, and a tall pot of coffee in her other hand. She planted them on the table and sat back in her chair.

And here they were, Alexis still eyeballing Maeve, awaiting answers Maeve didn't want to provide.

As she poured the coffee into both mugs, Alexis commented, "Miss MacKenna, I do hope you aren't hiding something."

Something? No. Many things? Absolutely. She cleared her throat. "Liam O'Doherty was me family's neighbor-boy."

There was a long silence as Alexis slid the mug toward Maeve.

Maeve hoped that statement was enough for her.

"So he came here searching for you."

Of course not. "He claimed otherwise." Maeve studied the holes in the crocheted lace of the tablecloth, taking note of several snags.

"You mean to tell me he just happened to appear here, of all places, to investigate the suspicious destruction of your former home?"

Maeve shrugged. "I guess the world is small."

"Getting smaller every day, it seems," Alexis groused.

"We grew up together, Liam 'n' me."

"... Oh?" Alexis cocked her head.

"Me parents secluded me to keep me safe because of me magic. They said people wouldn't understand it, tha' it'd be frightenin'. So ..." Maeve sighed. "They kept me in me family's small cottage away from everyone. But then the neighbor-boy moved in. I watched his family from me bedroom window 'n' took a shine to him. I started sneakin' out to see him."

Alexis raised her eyebrows. "Scandalous," she teased.

Maeve frowned.

"What's that look for?"

"We swam in the nearby pond together, he in his drawers, 'n' me in me nightgown. I had less sense of propriety then; I was seven, maybe eight years old. I don't recall, exactly."

"Oh." Alexis exhaled. "You were a child. No harm done. Probably didn't even notice any differences between you two!"

"No," muttered Maeve. "It was innocent. *Tha'* was innocent." She savored a sip of her drink. "We stargazed together at night, 'n' read clouds by day. We climbed trees, skinned knees, chased butterflies 'round in the fields ... He was me best-friend." She closed her eyes; it still hurt. "He was me only friend."

"You must've been lonesome, you poor thing."

Maeve's head bobbed once. It was silent for a while before she spoke again. "He attended public school, 'n' spoke English like everyone else. He was normal 'n' had other friends. I was so, so jealous. I didn't want to be just his friend. I wanted to be his best-friend, the way he was mine. I wanted to be the best friend ever. So ... I started conjurin'."

"... Fire?" assumed Alexis.

Maeve made eye-contact long enough to correct, "Fae-folk."

"Fae—oh, fairies."

"I did everythin' in me powers to make him like me. 'N' since I had the kind of powers to make fairy-tale creatures real ... I used 'em. I hid gnomes 'round trees 'n' rocks in our yards. He ... even found a tiny pot o' gold. I gave up me smallest cauldron to do it, but oh! The way his face lit up made it worthwhile." Maybe now she regretted it a little. By now, it would've been long gone, anyway.

"You've done that stuff for Raf, too. Right?"

No. When was there time to? Guilt tugged at Maeve's heart. *It'll only feel worse to admit it.* "For a while, his parents even convinced him it was nothin' more than his imagination ... 'n' tha' I was touched because I believed me fantasies were real."

"Oh, Maeve. How cruel."

Maeve sniffled. "We were thirteen when tha' happened. I was positively heartbroken."

"I've no doubt."

"I couldn't hide it 'n' after one particular awful night, me ma pulled the truth from me: I'd been sneakin' out, seein' Liam, conjurin'. Then the accusations about me bein' crazy started. Me ma was furious for it all, but mostly for me screwin' up our Smithfield Bargain. She demanded I go back 'n' do whatever I needed to ... to prove I wasn't a lunatic."

Alexis's face went red, her jaw visibly clenched. "And how, pray-tell, did you accomplish that?"

"I ..." Maeve shrugged; a little spastic twitch of her shoulders and head. "I had no idea so I asked him what he thought."

Alexis's voice dropped. "What did he say?"

"He said if he could kiss me cheek, it might help convince him. So ... I let him."

"That's ..." Alexis exhaled, her face etched with disgust. "... not OK."

"Afterward, he decided he still wasn't convinced." Maeve swallowed. "He asked for me lips."

"Despicable."

"'N' suddenly tha' wasn't enough, either." Maeve sighed. "I let him peek beneath me skirts. I ..." Her voice shook; divulging this to Alexis, of *all* people, seemed immeasurably stupid. "I was desperate to get him to believe me. I was afeard what me ma would do if I came back 'n' hadn't fixed things. So ... I gave him what was rightfully due me husband."

Alexis drew in a long breath through flared nostrils. "You mean he stole it!"

Maeve couldn't tell the difference; she hadn't stopped him when he pursued it. She'd thought she might enjoy it; after all, she'd enjoyed watching someone else enjoy it once, so she didn't argue.

Alexis's mouth fell open in a loud gasp over Maeve's silence. "You were thirteen!"

"I know how old I was," snapped Maeve. "What else was I supposed to do? Risk goin' home to me parents without havin' set things straight? I —it's—"

"Your mother had you so terrified that you were willing to be screwed by someone who wasn't your husband when you were still a child?"

"Ye didn't know her."

"Well it's a damn good thing she's not here. Maybe you forgive her but I wouldn't!"

"She was still me ma. I only ever wanted to be a good daughter for her."

"Was she aware of the lengths you went to for her?"

Of course not! Maeve cleared her throat and shook her head. "All tha' mattered was tha' they stopped callin' me daft."

"Gotta tell you: I'm feeling even less fond of Mr. O'Doherty now."

"Why? What'd he do?"

"You!" Alexis flailed at her. "Oh my God! Don't you see it? He took advantage of you—and I don't mean in the obvious way. He saw how desperate you were to make things right by your mother."

"He was just a boy," Maeve replied quietly. "He didn't know any better."

"'Just a boy?'" Alexis seethed. "'Just a boy,' my lily-white arse! He was thirteen and plenty old enough to know what that ... *worm* ... in his pants does!" She pushed her chair back and stood. "Maybe I can't kill your parents but I can sure as hell kill him—"

Maeve jumped to her feet. "Ye wouldn't dare!"

A tense silence was exchanged before Alexis lowered herself into her seat, a wary gaze locked on the woman across the table from her. "I'm just saying my finger may slip while it's on the trigger. Accidents happen." She grinned.

Maeve hesitated, certain Alexis was joking. Against her better judgment, she said: "Anyway, I amn't the best-friend I'd tried to be for Liam. Not only tha' but I'm the worst woman in the world." She put her cheek to the table, wrapping her arms over her head. "I let Rafaele think I was ... pure."

She'd rationalized it was only that one time and hoped she could somehow regain her virginity after so long. Upon leaving Ireland, Maeve didn't expect to encounter anyone who'd traipse into her womanly area again and figured it wouldn't be anything to worry about.

She hadn't bled the night she consummated her relationship with Rafaele and though he didn't say anything, she had no doubt he'd noticed it. Men always did—or so she'd been told.

Alexis found her voice though it was nothing more than a whisper. "Do you mean to tell me Raf doesn't know any of this?"

Maeve shook her head. "Please do not ye tell him!"

"I meant what I said that he's so in love with you that you could easily destroy him." Alexis exhaled. "I've no doubt this news would be overwhelming to him. Distressing. Good Lord, why would I want to tell him something that'd break his heart?"

"Oh," breathed Maeve, "thank ye! Thank ye so much!"

There was a long silence before Alexis stood abruptly. "You can't see O'Doherty again."

"I beg yer pardon?" Maeve frowned. "Why not?"

Agape, Alexis replied, "Because it's not wise?"

"He's just an old friend."

"With all due respect, we need to revisit the definition of 'friend' if this is what you think a friend is."

Maeve glared at her. "What's the harm in it?"

Alexis returned the expression in spades. "Do you mean in addition to everything you confided in me? Imagine Mr. O'Doherty thinks he has some claim to you because of that marriage contract with your parents. Imagine he sees the beautiful woman he's already had a taste of and believes it wouldn't take much to complete the transaction. I'm not telling anyone what you two did together, but would he? Might he blackmail you with your history?"

"No," cried Maeve. "He's a good man."

"Really? Does a good man deflower his best friend at thirteen?"

Maeve frowned. "What difference is it thirteen or eighteen? Does tha' fact make Rafaele any less of a good man?"

"Ohh," Alexis growled, "I hope what you did with Rafaele at eighteen was consensual. If you hadn't been trying to convince Mr. O'Doherty of anything, would you still have done it?"

Maeve wasn't sure. If she hadn't been the least bit curious, she would've said no—or so she'd convinced herself.

Alexis threw her hands into the air. "For Christ's sake, Maeve! I'm just trying to protect you!"

"Protect me? From what?" Maeve stood as well, though she didn't gain much vertical ground on a woman a half foot taller than she. "Havin' another friend here? Reunitin' with the last tie I have to Ireland, 'n' me family?"

"Maybe the O'Dohertys were on to something about you being touched in the head. Please! I'm afraid you just might *reunite* with him. Sexually. In case my euphemism wasn't obvious."

Maeve's face flooded red. "Listen to me, Chesterfield. I love Rafaele with all me heart." She clasped both hands against her breasts for emphasis, wincing at their tenderness. "Nobody is gonna change tha'. Yer fears are unfounded, 'n' frankly, insultin'. I amn't gonna go off with another man. Any other man."

Her voice low and chilly, Alexis replied, "You didn't notice how he stared at you. I've seen it before. It's the same hunger and mental undressing in Wolf's eyes when he looks at you. You think a man who sets his mind to claiming a woman is going to back off just because she tells him to? You believe he'll back off because you're wearing a ring from a man who isn't even around to defend his prize from the competition?"

"I'm no prize 'n' he's not the competition. He's me friend!" Maeve yelled, her face flushing. "Besides. What do ye know of what men want?"

"I'm willing to bet I understand them better than you do; as you so astutely put it when we first met, since I *am* a man, myself?"

"Regardless, ye have no right tellin' me who I can 'n' cannot associate with. I'm sick to death of others tellin' me what to do."

"You naïve little pisser!" Alexis slammed her fist against the table and their mugs hopped.

Maeve bristled. "Maybe ye're right 'n' I *do* need to reevaluate what the word 'friend' means."

Alexis planted her hands on the table and stared hard. "You can listen to me and do the smart thing by steering clear of him … or ignore me, same as everyone else does. But the second things go south, I will *not* be held responsible for what I might do to him."

"For the last time: Nothin' is gonna happen!"

"How can you be so confident about that?" Alexis steepled her hands over the tabletop, leaning forward. Her fingertips went white. "You tend to miss some painfully obvious stuff."

"Oh?" Maeve said. "Give one instance!"

Alexis dropped a pair of imaginary goggles over her eyes from their equally imaginary perch atop her head. "I'm Shadow Wolf." She motioned as if raising them from her face. "Now I'm Raf!" She pretended to put them back over her eyes. "No, wait a minute, no I'm not. I'm Shadow Wolf!"

It *had* been obvious. Had she seriously not seen it, or had she been in denial? Her opinions on the topic shifted wildly and even she didn't know anymore.

"Don't deny you couldn't tell."

"Fine. Give me two more instances," Maeve demanded.

"One stupid example is too many! With all due respect, this world is unforgiving of stupidity—"

"I amn't stupid!"

"What's all this yelling?" Kököle yawned as she wandered into the parlor, wearing her cotton night gown and rubbing sleep from her eyes.

Neither Maeve nor Alexis volunteered an answer.

"Lex, you know better than to get Miss MacKenna riled. Apologize to each other and get to sleep already. What is it, after midnight now?"

Alexis glared at Kököle, who looked mortally wounded for it. Her glare softened to a scowl. "Were you aware Miss MacKenna was engaged before she met Wolf?"

Maeve blanched. "Do not ye dare tell her—"

"And were you aware the engagement was to a man named Mr. O'Doherty? She's convinced herself that despite the arrangement, it's wise to rekindle her relationship with him!"

"Mr. O'Doherty," Kököle echoed, as if she didn't make the connection at first. "Miss MacKenna … Is this true?"

"Well—yes—" Maeve was flustered. "But it's not like tha'—"

"This is fantastic." Kököle clapped.

"What?" Alexis and Maeve cried in unison; the former in disgust, the latter in surprise.

"Marshal Cummings is convinced Moencopi and I were the ones who destroyed the saloon. Miss MacKenna, maybe he would believe the detective if you told him we didn't do it."

"Oh, no," interrupted Alexis, her voice strained. "No, no! She cannot see him again!"

"I beg to differ," Maeve shot back. To Kököle, she said, "Miss Chesterfield thinks I'm somehow puttin' meself in danger by bein' near him. He's a detective now! He's a good guy!" To them both: "All tha' aside, I can take care of meself."

"I know you can," replied Alexis. "But will you?"

"I did with Esquivar—"

"And it only cost you half a leg! What will O'Doherty's price be?"

"Ye have to trust me. Please!"

Kököle sighed. "Alexis ... We need Miss MacKenna to knock some sense into this man however she can do it. The marshal's prepared to arrest us."

"This wouldn't be the first time she had to do whatever it takes to convince that man of something," replied Alexis. To Maeve, she said, "And I'm afraid of the same outcome. You regret what you did last time. How would you feel now if the same events came to pass?"

"I want to help," Maeve said resolutely. "'N' trust me, Miss Chesterfield. I've learnt some tricks in the last six years."

"Yea," Alexis murmured. "At Rafaele's hands."

Kököle caught Maeve as she charged for Alexis, restraining her; as strong as Maeve was, Kököle was stronger. Maeve wrenched herself from the woman's grip and steadied herself. She pointed at Alexis. "Ye rotten—"

"Miss MacKenna." Kököle swept her out of the dining room before anything was uttered, curse or otherwise. "Why don't you and I take a little trip to the marshal's office tomorrow?"

Maeve replied, her hot head cooling, "Certainly, Miss Redbird. I'd like tha.'"

CHAPTER 6

 aeve held her breath, stepping unaccompanied into the marshal's office.

"Ducky!" he greeted her with a wide smile. "How good to see you. Have you news from Forino?"

"Not much. He's … doin' well." *Fury aside.* She cleared her throat, scuffing the wood floor of his office with the toe of her boot. "I was actually callin' for Mr. O'Doherty." How strange to address him formally, their history considered. "Is he available?"

Marshal Cummings narrowed his eyes. "I'll fetch him for you."

He ducked into the back of the office and Maeve glanced out the front windows to where she'd left Kököle waiting; there was no sign of her. *Good.*

If Kököle was a suspect, Maeve hadn't thought it prudent she enter the station, too. *They might not allow her to leave.*

Someone cleared his throat from just behind her and she turned with a start. It unnerved Maeve how a man so tall made such little sound on his feet.

"Miss MacKenna," Liam greeted her. "What a pleasant surprise."

She wondered if he was part cat. His voice was certainly akin to a jaguar's—if it could speak.

Maeve was slow to reply. "Mr. O'Doherty, hello."

"I'd be happy to get reacquainted but your timing is less than opportune; I'm just familiarizing myself with Marshal Cummings's notes—"

"Actually, I wanted to talk to ye about the Red—"

Liam waved her off with a quick flip of his gargantuan hand. "I wouldn't want to bore you with all the fiddle-faddle. And, besides, I'm sure the tedious details of recreating a crime scene would be over your pretty little head." Though he mentioned her head, his gaze was incapable of staying above her shoulders—or even anywhere near them. "You've no reason to worry yourself over it, anyway."

"Mr. O'Doherty, is somethin' the matter?" Of course something was the matter. She had no doubt he was distracted by her nearly glowing-white prosthetic limb. How could he miss the dreadful thing?

"I'm sorry—" Liam cleared his throat. "I don't mean to offend but—" He bowed his head and peered over the upper edge of his glasses. "Your shins are showing, and ... didn't you wear that gown when last I saw you?"

"Oh!" Maeve was dumbfounded into several moments of silence. "Oh, well, I lost all me possessions in the saloon fire—"

"And me: being the reason you have to reminisce such awful reminiscings. My apologies, Miss MacKenna, but I've scarcely given thought how difficult this must have been for you, how much you've lost. I'm so grateful you have charitable friends who give you a place at which to stay. It all must be so wretched."

Maeve shrugged. "I couldn't call it a walk in the park but there are certainly worse things out in the world." She put on what she hoped was a convincing smile such that he wouldn't be compelled to inquire about those 'worse things.'

"Listen, Miss MacKenna: I'm unsure how best to approach so delicate a proposition ..."

Her right eyebrow darted up. With an uncomfortable chuckle and her voice unusually high, she replied, "What's in yer head, Mr. O'Doherty?"

He chewed his lip. "Would you accompany me for dinner on Thursday?"

Maeve's mouth dropped open. "Are ye sure that's entirely appropriate?"

"I'm asking as an old friend. Nothing more, I promise."

"Well … as long as ye promise, I suppose there's no harm in me acceptin'." *Hopefully Alexis will feel tha' way, too.*
Who'm I kiddin'? She won't.

Rafaele slid the empty tankard across the bar top. "Another."

The bartender wordlessly prompted him for some sort of gratitude.

"Please," Rafaele sighed.

"Mmmhmm," replied the bartender.

In San Diego, stiff pleasantries begat stiff pleasantries, but Rafaele was in no mood to care. He watched as the tankard wandered beyond his reach in the capable hands of the cold bartender miles upon miles away from the miserable warmth of his old home, and the sensual heat of his little Maeve.

His last missive regarding her hadn't been the kind of telegram he'd enjoyed sending, especially not under the aghast stare of the dandy who had the misfortune of being charged with the task of transmitting it.

Akbar never batted an eyelash when in similar circumstances.

But then again, that dandy was hardly his old friend who sat behind the desk at Redington's telegraphy station.

And Redington was hardly San Diego.

San Diego was not the city Rafaele expected; from architecture to attire, foliage to fauna, and weather to technology, it presented him a thorough culture shock.

He himself didn't come close to blending in with the San Diegans in his decidedly more rustic clothing and unshaven face, so the first order of business upon his arrival was to buy fresh toggery. He purchased trousers a size larger than what he'd left Redington wearing—after struggling the last couple days to button his old ones—along with a nice new brown jacket and a smart matching derby hat.

He followed that with a visit to the nearest barber for some grooming proper for local society, afterward settling at the nearest watering hole with the unpleasant bartender, whiling away the rest of the evening dousing himself in alcohol and pining for the woman he chose to leave behind.

Daily, he went through the same motions. By now, a week later, he should've at least known the bartender's name.

Rafaele reminded himself this was temporary, but currently, temporary might as well have been permanent. This trip wasn't going as planned; unoccupied existing residences available for purchase were scarce, and the city's exploding population caused tenements to fill quickly, leaving few viable options for his plans for a family.

New Town was ripe with jobs, but to Rafaele's dismay, finding any suitable for his unmarketable skill set continued to lead him down a frustrated, unemployed path.

The only thing left for him was a lonely seat at a bar one block from the Stingaree.

The bartender dropped off his refilled drink.

Rafaele occupied himself by keeping his prosthetic hand wrapped around a tankard filled with alcohol, the other dipped in a bowl of peanuts. So absorbed in his brandy-soaked misery, he didn't acknowledge the grating wood-on-wood scraping of the seat beside his being pulled away from the table and then groaning with the weight of a full-grown man settling on it.

"Hey. You call that peach fuzz a mustache?"

Rafaele dragged his gaze from the empty mug in his fist to the gentleman now seated beside him. "You call the dead rodent on your head a hat?" His somber expression erupted into Rafaele, joyful as he ever was. He put the tankard down and pounded the man in the shoulder with his first. "Cosimo Benito, old prick-eared coffin-head! How've you been?"

"No hard feelings, huh? Good!" He winced, his eyes widening at the sight of Rafaele's metal fist. "I go by Bennett now, thanks. Duke Bennett," he corrected, rubbing his shoulder brusquely. "Interesting appendage growth you've had since last I saw you, Southpaw."

"Now there's a name I haven't heard in an age." He laughed. "They say 'cold hand, cold heart.' Suits me."

Duke grinned. "Sense of humor's intact. That's good." His stare lingered on the prosthesis and he nodded in appreciation before he openly assessed Rafaele's frame. "Boy you're ... robust ... these days."

Rafaele's laughter died. "What's that supposed to mean?"

"Nothing, nothing, just ... last I saw you, you were damn near skin and bones. You couldn't exactly feed yourself, I suppose. You've filled out nicely, since." Duke nodded toward Rafaele's torso. "Yea."

Rafaele pulled his hand from the bowl of peanuts. If it was noticeable beyond the size pant he wore, Maeve would notice it. He didn't want to return to her in that state. "What're you doing here?"

"That's a convoluted story involving a wretched she-beast I don't particularly care to revisit. 'Least, not 'til I'm far more topheavy than I am right now. What are you doing here? Tired of the cattle drives and reeking of buffalo?"

"You could say so. I've got a little lady who deserves an upstanding, fine-smelling husband."

"She must be an incredible woman to have convinced you to marry her."

"Trust me: there was no convincing."

Duke's eyes narrowed, his head cocking. "She voluptuous? Quiet and obedient?"

"Cosi—" Rafaele grunted; he was certain Cosimo had legitimate reasons for assuming a new moniker but wouldn't have been surprised if it was done for the sole purpose of irritating him. *He probably made it up now just to spite me.* "She's gorgeous, Duke. And no ... she's not boring. Far from it." *A little too far from it sometimes. Often.* He sighed. *All the damn time.*

Duke drummed his fingertips on the bar top. "So ... if your past is behind you, what are you doing for a living?"

"I dunno yet. Came to San Diego searching for a house."

"Much luck to you. These days, homes here are spoken for before they've even been built."

"Yea." Rafaele turned his attention to his tankard; he saw straight to the bottom. "I've noticed."

"The best way to sidestep that is to buy the land and build your own place."

Rafaele hadn't time for such things but the universal allure of the town at the foot of Presidio Hill left him little choice; he couldn't return to Maeve and expect her to live in nothing. He had to be responsible. "Not until I've secured a job." In retrospect, he hadn't planned any of this well at all, but in his defense, it was a necessary knee-jerk reaction.

"Maybe I can help you," offered Duke. "I've got some connections here. What are you looking for?"

"Whatever I'm qualified for. My experience is buffalo skinning." *Among other things.*

"Mine as well. Took me years to get over it." Duke made a face. "Hey ...

It's a long shot, but I know of a well-to-do widow who needs security at her home."

"How well-to-do are we talking here?" It would do him no good to be employed by someone who couldn't afford to pay him well, and Duke's idea of affluence may not have been as well-heeled as his.

Duke leaned in and lowered his voice. "Let's just say," he drawled, "Alonzo Horton asks what he can do for *her*."

"Who the hell's Horton?"

"Horton's the real estate baron who owns New Town."

"Ah." Rafaele swallowed a scowl; Horton was the reason he'd been having a hell of a time finding a home for his blushing bride. He bristled. "So. Why does this widow need security at her home?"

"Things have been disappearing. I'm unsure what qualifications she's looking for in a guard but you're a ..." Duke's appraising gaze swept Rafaele's frame, his lips lifting briefly into a flirtatious smile. "... a big guy. That should be good enough for her intents and purposes."

"Oh?" Rafaele raised an eyebrow. "What kinds of things are disappearing?"

"Items of illicit nature, I'd wager. She's rather secretive."

"Well do you suppose you could put in a good word for me?"

Duke smirked. "For my old friend Forino?"

"No. No, no, no. For your morally upstanding, law-abiding friend, Rafaele."

"Oh, for him?" Duke's smirk grew into a wide smile. "I'll put in *all* the good words for him." His wide smile was eclipsed by his drink and when he came up for air, he was somber. "Be careful around her."

"Why?"

"She makes a valuable ally, but she'll destroy you if you get on her bad side. Power is deadly, old friend, and she's the most powerful person I know."

"I don't trust him."

"What's yer problem with Mr. O'Doherty?" Maeve snapped. "He's been nothin' but nice to ye."

Alexis did a double-take. "How drunk were you the other night? Do you mean besides the skeleton in your joint closet?" She over-enunciated: "He's a copper."

Maeve would've been stunned if Alexis mustered any more disdain. "'N' I'm a barmaid. What's it to ye? Ye're too focused on labels."

With a roll of her eyes, Alexis said, "In my line of work—in *our* line of work, I hesitate to remind you—you don't want to have anything to do with peelers. No matter how charming they act, because that's all the charm is: an act. To get information, or … other things."

"Mmm-hmm." Maeve turned her attention to the mirror to continue her preening.

"I recognize when someone's being a dismissive little bitch—" Alexis grabbed her by the arm and turned her around. "I want you to stop and think, just for a second, about your last encounter with an officer. How'd that work out for you?"

Maeve slid her arm from Alexis's grasp, turning her attention to the mattress. *Liam isn't a copper or a peeler. He's just Liam, 'n' he'd not ever put me in danger. She won't understand.*

Alexis exhaled. "Think about it." After a hesitation, she asked, "Why are you going on an outing, anyway? It's not exactly as if you're not spoken for."

Maeve had to consider the statement with its conglomeration of negatives and positive before she could answer. "It's not an outin', just dinner between old friends to discuss his investigation."

"Something that should've been done at the marshal's office."

"Maybe …" Maeve faltered. "Maybe he didn't want to discuss it where others could overhear."

Alexis scoffed and flailed. "So instead he's taking you to a busy restaurant? This is no dinner between friends." She exhaled. "He's got designs on you."

Though she didn't follow the logic of Alexis's last statement, Maeve replied, "Oh, please."

"I must say I can't blame him for how he must feel—"

"Why?" Maeve snapped. "Because ye feel tha' way about me, too?"

"No," Alexis growled, "because you've been leading him on."

"Miss Chesterfield!" Maeve bristled, preferring her assumption to Alexis's accusation. "I've seen him all of twice since he arrived. I couldn't have had more than a half hour to talk to him!"

"Have you bothered mentioning to him that you have a fiancé?"

"No, it didn't come up in conversation, but I will. Of course I will. Tonight!" Maeve hesitated. "It sort of slipped me mind. Ye'll have to beg me pardon but, I remind ye, I haven't been affianced to Rafaele all tha' long."

"Excuses. You were emotionally affianced to Rafaele from the moment you first laid eyes on him."

"That's entirely beside the point!"

"And you've been affianced long enough to learn the word in English. How often does it come up in conversation in a languishing desert town?"

Maeve griped, "More often for a single lady than ye'd think."

"Listen: you'd better tell Red about Rafaele or I swear to God I'll do it and you do *not* want that."

Maeve frowned.

"I'll mention the embarrassing things. I was there. Me, every cactus, desert shrew, rock, and every damn thing for five miles around heard every sordid detail of the racket you two made." Alexis's eyes narrowed. "I'll call you by one of your in-the-throes-of-passion nicknames."

Maeve's heart pounded. "Ye didn't hear any of tha'. Ye're—oh—what's the word?"

"Bluffing?" Alexis grinned wickedly. "I'm not." She cast a purposeful glance at Maeve's crotch. *"Buttercup."*

A knock at the front door drew their attention.

Alexis answered the caller with Maeve acting as her copper-haired tail.

"I do apologize for interrupting your evening festivities," said the shop-keeper's son.

"What are you doing here, William?" Alexis shifted against the doorjamb, blocking Maeve's view of him.

"I have a delivery."

"I don't recall having ordered anything," said Alexis. "And I'm not paying—"

"I'm told Miss MacKenna is staying with you."

Alexis straightened and scowled. "By who?"

"Everyone in town knows it. This parcel is for Miss MacKenna, if you please. Let me deliver it. Pap will beat me good if I botch another."

Maeve's heart fluttered; who else would buy her gifts if not Rafaele? She put a hand on Alexis's shoulder to move her aside.

"Evenin'," Maeve greeted him. "Ye've brought me somethin'?"

"Oh—" he faltered, his gaze flickering to her right leg. "Uh, yes. Yes, here." He grabbed a large, flat box from his handcart. Passing it to Maeve, he said, "Take it easy. So sorry about—" He nodded toward the Parkesine limb. "—oh, everything."

Maeve stumbled, attempting to tuck the Parkesine limb behind her real one. "Thank ye kindly. Good evenin' to ye."

"And—and to you." William doffed his hat and grabbed the handcart, rushing from the house.

Alexis shut the door and turned to Maeve. "Oh, where are my manners? Let me take that; it looks heavy." She snatched the box from Maeve's hands.

"Excuse me!" Maeve replied. "What're ye doin'?"

"Just being a good host is all." Alexis bustled into the parlor with Maeve in close pursuit.

"Ye're bein' nosy is all!" Maeve shoved her aside before Alexis stole the honor of opening the box, and to her chagrin Kököle and Moencopi joined them in the room.

Inside the box was a deep blue visiting dress with teal accent embroidery, and a small note written with impeccable penmanship—unfortunately in cursive, which Maeve had yet to learn. She doubted, then, that this gift was from Rafaele unless he dictated the note from afar.

The writing didn't match Ahmad's, either, so it wasn't a telegraphic dictation.

Maeve sighed. "Can someone please read this to me?"

Alexis snatched it. "'It's not much,'" she read, "'but I wanted to help you recover from your hardships. Wear it in good health.'" She paused. "Oh, yech. 'L.O.'"

Kököle and Moencopi exchanged glances, questioning in unison: "L.O.?"

"Liam," whispered Maeve, extracting the bodice of the new gown from the box. "How kind of him."

"How romantic," Kököle said, pulling out more fabric.

Moencopi chimed in: "How generous."

Alexis, however, folded her arms across her chest with a glower. "How despicable."

Maeve was in the middle of closing her corset when Kököle walked by her bedroom. At the sound of her footfalls on the hallway carpet, Maeve turned. "Miss Redbird."

Kököle stopped. "Yes, Miss MacKenna?" She hesitated. "Do you need help with your corset?"

Maeve hesitated. "Please, if ye would."

Kököle removed the laces from where Maeve had looped them around the knob on the bedroom door. "You'll tell me if I do this too tightly, won't you? The last thing I want to do is hurt you—or the little one."

Maeve braced herself using the bed post while Kököle tightened the laces. "Trust me, ye're not goin' to hurt anybody."

"This outfit will be quite becoming on you. Although ..."

"*Although?*"

"Although you should have something far finer."

"Me? Oh, no." Maeve pulled on the bodice. "I'm just a barmaid 'n' have no use for fineries." She grunted, struggling to manipulate the little pearl buttons through their matching holes. The fabric strained so much it left unsightly gaps with flashes of the pale pink corset beneath.

She unbuttoned the bodice and slipped it off. "Tighten the corset more if ye please."

Kököle hesitated. "Are you sure?"

"Yes. I'm certain."

"But this is tight already—"

"Corsets don't bother me. I've worn 'em practically me whole life, to be sure."

"I wear them from time to time," Kököle replied, "but not as often as you. And never to social events." She grunted as she pulled the laces tighter; Maeve bit her lip to keep from groaning and put out of her head that before long, she'd need new clothing she couldn't afford.

"Have you got the knack of those buttons?"

"Yes."

Kököle said, "Here. Let me help with your hair."

"Oh, ye don't need to—"

Kököle smiled. "It's my pleasure; you have such lovely hair. It's so soft. I'd love to braid it sometime."

Maeve cast a sideways glance at her. "Ye say tha' like there's somethin' wrong with *yer* hair."

"Mine is coarse," Kököle explained. "I bust brushes regularly. But *yours*. Yours is soft and beautiful."

Maeve's cheeks swiftly matched her hair color. "Well … Thank ye, but it's nothin' special."

"Let's look at you." Kököle spun Maeve around in her spot. "You're lovely."

"Really?"

"Definitely," Kököle replied. "Have a nice dinner with Mr. O'Doherty, clear the air for us, and don't worry about what Alexis said. She's paranoid. After all, you know him better than we do."

"I'll try. Thanks again."

"Don't mention it."

Alexis sat in her room and wrung a handkerchief between her shaking hands, the only light a sliver of moonbeam cutting across the carpet. She swiped her cheeks with the abused cloth before pulling and twisting it more. Outside her window, she watched a lone shadow depart her house; an additional slight to the whole evening was O'Doherty failing to escort Maeve away. *Some gentleman.*

On the whole, as rude as his behavior was, it remained a blessing, as Alexis didn't want him coming to her door. *God help him should he ever.*

The sound of footfalls in the hall shifted Alexis's attention from her woes and she turned to the door as Kököle walked by, pausing long enough for their stares to meet through the night. No words were exchanged before Kököle continued on.

Alexis exhaled, turning to face the window. There was no sign of Maeve outside.

How angry would Rafaele be that Maeve was going on outings with another man? He disliked her friendship with Milton—and even with Edison, who posed no threat whatsoever to their relationship.

And Alexis let her go. She'd promised Rafaele she'd keep Maeve safe. Alexis scrunched her face against the heat rising behind her eyes. "Dammit," she hissed.

When she opened her eyes, she saw the unmistakable brightening in her room that an unwelcome candle brought with it. "I didn't say you could come in, Kökö. Don't start with me; I'm not in the mood—"

Despite her warning, the candle's glow grew closer. Alexis turned to lash out at Kököle but was stunned into silence when Moencopi flowed into her room.

Moencopi smiled wryly. "Kököle knows better than to bother you when you are in such a state."

"But clearly you don't."

"Are you upset with me?"

"I'm not upset at anybody," lied Alexis.

"You are upset because you do not understand the way Miss MacKenna is acting. Correct me if I am wrong but you are hurt because you lost a friend."

"Oh of course not. Don't be ridiculous. We were never friends." Alexis turned her back to Moencopi and drew her legs up, resting her heels on the edge of her bed and clasped her knees to her chest. "Rafaele made me swear I'd take care of the girl and if not for that, I don't care what she was does with her stupid life or who she does it with. Don't mistake my promise to Raf for caring about Maeve." In the ensuing silence, Alexis watched as the shadows across her bedroom furniture shifted with Moencopi's pacing.

Of course she wouldn't leave. She had a rebuttal—one that would certainly aggravate Alexis. So she attempted to preempt any possible argument: "Maeve's behaving so strangely since Liam appeared." She sighed, knowing the words were doing the opposite of what she wanted; and yet they wouldn't cease. "We'd finally gotten back to normal, things were even good between us. And now this." *I liked the Maeve I was discovering ... Honest, vulnerable. Even kinda scary.* She was beginning to resent how she could see what attracted Rafaele.

"Nothing you say is out of the ordinary for fire." As Moencopi drifted around the room in her graceful pacing, Alexis watched the flame on the candle she held. It undulated around the wick, a single yellow-white light contrasting against black; flirting with her, flirting with the night. Illuminating what little it reached yet perpetually on the edge of darkness.

"Fire. Tithu once called her that." She'd shrugged it off as having to do with Maeve's hair color but found it increasingly hard to dismiss as a metaphorical description.

"Fire is … unpredictable. Unstable. How are you certain the way she is behaving now is abnormal? Perhaps the way she acted before was not the …" Moencopi sighed and the flame flickered wildly, threatening to bow out. "… the real her?"

"I do. I just do, OK?" A lengthy silence followed, and Alexis caught Moencopi's pressing stare over the candlelight. "Because of the way she behaved around Rafaele."

"How can you be certain *that* was not the act? A phase … a moment in time, but not the true Maeve? Courting behavior to capture the interest of a suitor?"

Alexis clutched the handkerchief, beating her fists into the mattress on either side of herself. "Because! The real Maeve is the girl who fell in love with Raf! Nobody can wear a mask in the circumstances under which they met. She didn't have a chance to preen, to do whatever her version of courting behavior must be, while bound and gagged before a group of strangers. She didn't have the chance to act like someone she isn't while clinging for her life to the back of an out-of-control horseless stagecoach.

"People show their true colors in those situations more than at any other time." After a brief pause, Alexis added, "Except maybe in the throes of passion." She shook her head to clear it.

Alexis continued, "These moments are enlightening. They're the moments that define people, the moments we find out we're stronger or wiser or more compassionate than we believed. Terrible times bring out the best in people, so they say, and strips them of any mask they might be hiding behind. In those moments, they're more themselves than at any other time. And that's when those two met. They were real Maeve and real Raf." And dammit all, if they weren't perfect for each other.

Alexis glanced at Moencopi; to her surprise, she was smiling.

"Perhaps you are learning more about yourself under stressful conditions, too. You care more than you let on about both—one maybe more than the other and now I am unsure whom it is. Whatever the case, you need to be there for them. For her." There was a fat pause with a long, quiet breath. "When fire loses control, that is when it most needs someone tending it."

"That's Raf's job," Alexis snapped. "I didn't sign up for this."

"And yet ... here you are." Moencopi turned and approached the bedroom door in her ethereally elegant way, the light from her candle throwing her shadow across the floor. She paused, shooing at Kököle who must've been eavesdropping. Moencopi lowered her voice, turning to Alexis once more. "Watch your behavior concerning Maeve around my sister. It would be imprudent to incite her jealousy."

Alexis swallowed, a crushing fear pressing on her chest. She sank into the mattress, now unable to put Maeve from her mind.

CHAPTER 7

iss MacKenna, how lovely you do look tonight." Liam held out his arm for her to take. "It's my honor to have your companionship."

Maeve stared at his arm before warily looping hers with it. "Thank ye kindly, Mr. O'Doherty. It was nice of ye to ask me out."

He escorted her inside through double doors set deep within the side of the hotel building. From the little wooden sidewalk tucked between the restaurant and the hotel, Maeve watched fashionably attired diners enjoying their meals, candlelight from their tables glittering through the beveled glass windows along that wall. It was an elegant respite from the rest of the town and a far cry from the Tiff and Tawny—both before and after the arson.

"Good evening, Miss MacKenna," the host at the Cosmopolitan greeted her. He regarded Liam. "And I can't say I'm familiar with the newcomer on your arm."

"Detective O'Doherty," Liam introduced himself.

"Detective? Oh? You must be here for the dreadful business—well, I'm sure you know why you're here better than I." The host cleared his throat. "Miss MacKenna? The usual—uh—private booth in the back?"

"A special booth won't be necessary," Liam assured him.

"If you insist." With a twitch of his snobbish, pencil-thin mustache, he escorted Liam and Maeve to a table in the middle of the dining area.

Her stomach tumbled. It was a nice change of pace to not be treated as a whore, yet she couldn't ignore the feeling as if she were somehow cheating, sneaking in to be seated where polite society got to enjoy its meals.

She was a fraud, and although she'd played one recently in Tucson, parading herself around as Rafaele's wife, it was different here. In Redington, she wasn't fooling anyone; they knew she had no right eating out on shameless display among them.

Much to her amazement, she wasn't on the receiving end of any disparaging looks. On the contrary, the men nodded her direction with upward quirks of their lips; all men she knew well as they frequented the Tiff and Tawny to enjoy her drinks.

Here, they dressed in Sunday best, sitting alongside their wives, many with small broods. All frauds, like Maeve; she guessed they did what they did today to maintain appearances.

Things would be so much better in this world if everyone stopped makin' themselves out to be what they're not 'n' could behave as they truly are.

That applied doubly to Maeve. The problem being she still hadn't a clue as to who—or what—she really was.

She was vaguely aware of Liam pulling out her seat before she settled in it; Maeve was preoccupied with watching the strangers accompanying such familiar men.

Hugh Kaylock's wife was present, with her long, severely angled nose and wrinkled neck; the way her dark, beady eyes pierced anything she set her gaze on, she really did resemble the turkey to which he oft compared her on his drunken rants.

And another, watching wistfully as his wife socialized with a different family across the dining room—she doted like an unwed harlot on the man at the table—while he remained at his own with two ill-mannered children flinging bits of food at each other. Maeve had little doubt he missed Caitlyn.

"You seem preoccupied, Miss MacKenna. I hope everything was in proper order with my little gift, there." Liam motioned to her gown. "You look—I mean *it* looks—lovely." He snatched his glass of water and took a painful-sounding swallow.

"Oh—uh—yes. It was." Maeve pried her attention from people-watching and turned it to him. "Seems I'm havin' the most dreadful time concentratin' these days. Terrible sorry about tha'."

"Poor dear, you've been through so much recently. I couldn't hold that against you."

The waiter dropped off a pair of menus, lingering long enough to give Maeve a double-take.

Once he departed, she addressed Liam: "Thank ye for yer patience with me, 'n' I've so much gratitude for yer generous gift. I haven't had a gown this nice since—"

Liam leaned in, his eyes twinkling from behind his spectacles. "—Since …?"

"Since me fiancé gifted me one." Maeve sighed; there it was: the first really painful pang of missing Rafaele. How unwelcome it was.

"You have a fiancé?" Sadness flashed across Liam's face before he gave what appeared to be an understanding nod and an honest smile. "Of course, you have a fiancé. Look at you: how could you not? If you didn't, there would have to be something wrong with the men around you. What joyous news. Blessings upon your future union."

"I have to admit, yer reaction's a relief—I expected ye might be in some way upset by the news."

He arched a brow. "Why?"

"I don't know … Never ye mind tha'; I'm just babblin' now."

"So." Liam dipped his head. "Tell me about your fiancé."

"Well, his name's Rafaele."

"He's Spanish? Italian?"

Maeve frowned and answered, "Italian, yes. He's tall. Yer height, I'd s'pose, within an inch or two. Big frontiersman type. Poor man, though, he can't build a fire to save his life."

"That sounds like it'd be a pretty considerable inconvenience in the middle of nowhere." He smirked.

She was barely able to stop herself from correcting him; it was only an inconvenience when she wasn't around to help him with it.

"Smart, is he?"

"Oh, yes, very," Maeve replied without hesitation, "though his use of language might lead ye to believe otherwise."

"Foulmouthed?"

"I didn't think so, 'least not 'til recently."

"I wouldn't have taken you for someone to pursue a man with such lack of propriety in front of a lady."

"Yes, well." Maeve lowered her head, trying to hide her smile. "He's sweaty, always smells of horse, 'n' not ever clean shaved."

Liam replied with a sound that was a blend of disbelief and disgust.

"It must sound ... unconceivable to ye." She shrugged. "To be honest, I don't understand it meself. But ..." *He wouldn't be me Raf without those things.*

"But?" prompted Liam.

"Miss MacKenna," a couple voices sang from the front of the dining room.

Maeve waved at Jia Li and Bristol as they were escorted hastily to the back area.

"Introduce us to your handsome friend," said Bristol, insisting to the *maître d'hôtel* that they socialize before being tucked away from polite society.

Maeve hesitated. "Liam," she muttered. "O'Doherty."

"Liam—" Jia Li gasped. "*This?* This is the legendary neighbor-boy?" She clapped and bounced. "My goodness, oh, Miss MacKenna, all this time we took you for a fibber! I'm so sorry we didn't believe you!"

Following her outburst, silence lingered throughout the restaurant and Maeve was so filled with embarrassment that she figured even her teeny, tiny, secret baby was humiliated, too.

The host cleared his throat. "Come along, now, to the back with both of you."

Bristol blew Liam a kiss. "If you're sticking around long enough, do pay me a visit at the reopened brothel."

Maeve swallowed a scoff at Bristol's loaded invitation.

"Can't decide if I should be flattered or offended," muttered Liam. He cleared his throat, his expression stony. "So. I'm the neighbor of legend. What, exactly, have you been telling people about me, Miss MacKenna?"

Her face red as ever, she replied, "Well—I mean—tha' is to say—a-after closin' at the Tiff, I used to—um—entertain the girls with stories from home, 'n' ye remember tha' me experience in Éire was ... limited." Maeve focused on the table. "Ye may have come up in conversation once." In the ensuing silence, she glanced at him.

Liam looked unconvinced.

"Or twice."

His cold, calculating expression erupted into a Cheshire-cat grin.

Maeve exhaled, placing a hand to her breast. "Ye had me for a minute there!"

His grin went into a charming smile. "Did I? I thought that Rafaele fellow did."

"Oh—no—I meant—It seemed ye were angry tha' I'd been speakin' about ye behind yer back ..."

Liam winked at her. "I know what you meant. Just teasing. Between old friends?"

"Yea ..." Maeve echoed, "old friends." She dropped her gaze, wishing the flush in her cheeks would cool; blushing was the only time heat bothered her.

And like that, she got her wish, a tingling icy sensation going through her toward Liam.

A spirit literally injected itself into her conversation, though Maeve saw nothing of it. Nonetheless, she was familiar with the presence; it was the same one she'd noticed at the Tiff and Tawny. *What's it doin' here?*

A single, hard, head-to-toe shiver racked her small frame.

"Miss MacKenna? Are you cold?"

"Yea—" Maeve's voice cracked. "Yea," she said with conviction.

She cleared her throat, placing both palms on the table between them. "Listen. Mr. O'Doherty: ye said ye were sent here to investigate the Tiff 'n' Tawny explosion."

Liam nodded, leaning against the edge of the table to get a little closer to her as she had done for him. "Go on."

"I don't understand why *ye*. I mean no offense by it, but I find it a little too coincidental they sent *ye* to where I'm now livin'." Maeve smiled impishly. "Ye're absolutely certain ye weren't huntin' for an excuse to find me?"

"Word got around the precinct that I have ... experience ... with things outside the norm," he said, sliding his fingertip along the outside of his ear. "Fairies, gnomes, spirits, whatnot."

What makes them think anythin' outside the norm happened here? Maeve's impish smile dissolved into a frown as she couldn't decide if he was making a joke at her expense.

He continued, "They thought my abilities suited this investigation. That's the honest-to-God truth why I came here."

"Oh." Why was she disappointed?

"It's not as though I didn't think often of finding you, Miss MacKenna, but I had no idea where even to start searching."

"—says the great detective."

He squinted at her, jaw clenched through his reply, "Missing persons is not my area of expertise."

"I was just teasin'. I'm sorry."

"Funny," he replied disingenuously. "Very funny."

Maeve forced a smile, grateful she'd agreed to a single outing.

"I always wondered what happened to my closest friend. One day, we were skipping stones across a lake together. You made a daisy chain crown for your brow. We spoke of the veil you'd soon be wearing, and you tried on my last name for size. The next day, you were gone. Nobody knew to where you and your parents disappeared and my parents stopped speaking altogether of your family. When I asked, they yelled ... I remember the volume of their voices but neither the 'what' or 'why.' I really *did* start thinking maybe you were an imaginary friend." He laughed nervously. "I was starting to doubt my sanity."

"We ..." Maeve sighed. She couldn't tell Liam about the sick little girl Dallahan had stolen from a small family. Nor could she tell him of the mother and her baby who died despite her help on the ship from the Bridge of Tears; he wouldn't understand.

And of course, she couldn't speak of the potato famine as she had with Rafaele. Liam was there; he knew she hadn't even been born yet by the time it ended.

"We had to leave. Me parents longed for the land of opportunity. I didn't tell ye we were leavin' because they didn't tell me until the day of." Which was sort of true. *I need to stop lyin' to everyone.* "We were goin' to live in Manhattan, but me mother wasn't comfortable there." Another partial truth. "As the train pulled into the Tucson station, me parents were brutally murdered. 'N' here I am in Redington. Smith gave me a job as a waitress for the saloon—the Tiff 'n' Tawny … that's pretty much it."

Liam sat in silence.

Staring.

Maeve dropped her gaze. "Do tell … How's yer investigation goin'? Surely ye understand why I'm worried. The Tiff was me home. The employees are me friends."

"I wish I could tell you it's going better," Liam replied. "I'm incredibly suspicious of those two savages. They appeared in town, as I understand it, the same day the Tiff and Tawny exploded."

She sighed, relieved he broached the topic of the Hopi women. "Maybe ye should turn yer investigation on someone else. They'd not ever do somethin' so heinous." And yet she still didn't believe it, herself.

Liam frowned, and she feared he noticed the misgiving in her words.

"I must admit," he said, "I'm not sure why someone like you is associating with those two … why you'd defend them. The marshal tells me you weren't even here at the time of the explosion, so you can't provide their alibi. You seem to have a lot invested in those two that you couldn't possibly confirm."

"They're me friends," Maeve blurted, surprising no one more than herself.

Kököle was growing on her. *Maybe.*

A little.

Liam's gaze darted around the room and Maeve followed them; people were, indeed, staring.

His voice low and head bowed, he replied stiffly, "Your choice in friends is concerning me, Miss MacKenna: the Indians, the woman wearing mannish habiliments … The doves working the upstairs of your saloon? This is hardly the way to elevate your social standing."

Maeve grit her teeth, tucking her shaking hands beneath the table and clasping them tightly. "It isn't yer place to express concern, Mr. O'Doherty. It'd be wise of ye to stop. Now."

Liam's eyes went wide, silence spanning their table, drawing it into a chasm of hostility. He cleared his throat and dropped her gaze. "I apologize. You're right. It's not my place. Old habits die hard, I suppose, and I will always worry about you."

Loath as she was to admit it, the sentiment was sweet. She refused to accept his apology in as many words, though she asked, "Are there any other suspects?"

"I keep seeing articles that would suggest a ruffian named Esquivar."

She rolled her eyes. "It's not Esquivar."

"How can you say that with such certainty?"

Maeve bit her lip. "Esquivar ..." She wished she hadn't said anything about it. "There was an explosion in a granary in Tucson, 'n' Esquivar didn't survive it."

"I didn't realize buildings in the west were so combustible."

She couldn't decide if he was joking; she didn't reply.

"When I asked, Marshal Cummings said there was no report of him dying, nor a body turned up. There isn't a reliable alibi showing he was ever in Tucson."

Of course not. Anyone who would've been an alibi died tha' night. "Mr. MacTavish provided a statement to the area newspapers—"

"And Mr. MacTavish's story changed. Repeatedly. You can understand, I'm sure, how a history of lies would make it difficult to believe anything else he might say."

"But ye believe me, do ye not? I've given ye no reason to distrust me."

His jaw clenched and the vein running down his neck strained; she suspected the lies his parents told him about her clouded his judgment even to this day.

"N—y—I—" Liam grunted. "How could you know about Esquivar and the explosion in Tucson?"

Against her better judgment, Maeve nodded toward her right leg, discretely sliding it forward and raising her skirts just enough to reveal her prosthesis. There was something sickening to her about again allowing this man a glimpse beneath her skirts. *This time,* she assured herself, *it stops here.*

Liam frowned, cocking his head to peek beneath the table.

"I was there, Mr. O'Doherty. I saw the beam fall on him with me own eyes," she fibbed. "Nobody could survive somethin' like tha'."

"Why haven't they found a body? They've been working tirelessly—"

"Give it time," she lied. *Again.* "It was a miracle I got out with me life. Only ... with one fewer leg."

He straightened, the color draining from his already pale face. "It's—" his normally dulcet deep voice rose an octave. Liam swallowed, his Adam's apple shifting considerably with the act. "I thought—I'm so sorry, Maeve. I saw that the other day and dismissed it as a mismatched stocking."

Her gaze lingered on him. He'd called her Maeve. Such indiscretions required scolding but instead she focused on the topic. "It's disgustin'. It's awful. I hate it. But ... Esquivar was a murderer. Please trust me when I say it's no big loss he's dead."

"That's callous."

"It's truth. Do ye let a killer free? Do ye give a killer the chance to murder again? We're all far safer now without him." Under her breath, Maeve added, "Some of us more than others."

"Am I to understand you ... dealt with him?"

"Yes. Unfortunately. He was a regular patron at the Tiff 'n' Tawny. He was a miserable little man who was responsible for the death of at least one workin' woman at the saloon ... 'n' the murder of me parents, too."

Open shock washed fleetingly over Liam's face before it vanished and he smoothed his mustache with thumb and index finger in a single motion. "I would guess you had some interaction with many of Redington's residents while working in the saloon."

The realization was sullen: *He doesn't care. He's interrogatin' me.* "Most of them," she admitted, "at some point or other. But not everyone." She hadn't seen Alexis there her whole year as a beer-jugger.

"No. I suppose mostly the unsavories." He paused, glancing around the dining room before turning his attention back to her with a hesitated question: "Members of Shadow Wolf Pack?"

Maeve broke out in gooseflesh beneath her gown, thankful Liam couldn't see it.

"You've heard of them," guessed Liam.

"Oh ... Well who here hasn't?" Maeve chuckled weakly. "They're as much a staple in Redington as the Tiff 'n' Tawny was. As much a landmark as the San Pedro River."

Liam studied her with all the intensity of a predator on the prowl. "I fear you speak of the hoodlums fondly."

She couldn't speak any more fondly of the man she loved. "The group may have a wicked reputation, but they're not all bad people."

His eyes narrowed. "You're toying with my trust."

"I saved the lives of two children I didn't know from dyin' at Esquivar's hands, 'n' ... I'm a member of the Pack."

After a couple moments of silence, Liam burst out laughing. Heads all around the restaurant turned, and Maeve ducked hers in embarrassment.

"You. *You*, Miss MacKenna? Part and parcel of a nefarious group?" Liam kept laughing. "Why don't I recall you being so funny?"

"Surely, I amn't jokin'." Humiliation seared her cheeks from within. "It must've been all over the papers. I was convicted, there was a big jail break —I almost hanged for me association with Shadow Wolf."

He promptly sobered. "I beg your pardon? You mean to tell me you've dealt with Shadow Wolf directly?"

Maeve turned her head away, relieved that of everything she'd told him, that was the only part to have stuck. She focused on the floor to the left of her seat. *Ye could say tha'. Ye might even say I had as direct interaction with Shadow Wolf as a person could have.*

"What're you smiling for?" Liam asked.

"Oh—I—it's—" She couldn't conjure an even remotely reasonable response.

Slowly, Liam smiled, "Ah. You *are* teasing me. Guileful little creature."

Maeve gritted her teeth, hoping it was a convincing smile. If it wasn't, he didn't acknowledge it.

"So tell me, Miss MacKenna." Liam rested his elbow on the table, putting his chin in his palm, fingers curled toward a clean-shaven cheek. He smiled sweetly. "Who do you think did it?"

Maeve shrugged and shook her head. "I assure ye, Mr. O'Doherty, if I knew, I'd have been the first to—" She had to stop herself. Probably it wouldn't be wise to admit a desire for killing the culprit, even if she meant it figuratively. *Maybe.* Lately, she wasn't so sure. "I'd have been the first to—oh, what's the word?" she asked. "Interrogate?"

Liam chuckled. "How darling."

"I just wish I knew why he did it."

"Don't worry, we'll figure it out."

Maeve's eyebrows shot up. "We?"

"Marshal Cummings and I."

"Oh. Yes." She blushed. "Yes, of course that's what ye meant."

"We'll get to the bottom of it. Whoever did this will be held accountable for his—" Liam paused. "Or her actions."

Maeve swallowed hard.

"Miss MacKenna, I must tell you: this evening has been enlightening."

CHAPTER 8

 aving exhausted himself reviewing all of Cummings's paperwork on the investigation—nothing new of note since last he was in the marshal's office—Liam visited the rubble formerly known as the Tiff and Tawny to do some sniffing around.

Certainly, he figured, *something must've been disregarded in the initial investigation. A perpetually soused man, after all, can't have too keen an eye for detail, nor a mind with clarity enough to spot when something's amiss. If he possessed a keen enough eye or sharp enough intellect for such things in the first place.*

Doubtful.

The marshal noted a strong kerosene scent and wadding of hay, newspaper, napkins, tablecloths, and bedsheets around what remained of the service door; evidence of a simple arson. At face value, those things weren't indicative of the need to outsource to more capable investigators.

Liam paced the perimeter based on his knowledge of the floorplan to find where the door in question once stood.

Assuming evidence hadn't been removed—deliberately by the arsonist or innocently by a group of women thinking they were lending a combined hand in the task of cleaning away debris—there had to be something in this mess to solve the crime.

He shifted aside a blackened board with the side of his shoe.

A fire at that hour would've been observed, as people were awake and doing their daily business.

There would have been catastrophic damage, all the same, due to Redington's drought; there were but a handful of small wells near residences and a few select businesses, in addition to the San Pedro which scarcely deserved its river moniker.

God, I hate it here.

This wasn't done to damage property, he concluded. If it had been, there still would've been time for the residents and patrons to escape before the fire overtook them. There shouldn't have been as many, if any deaths.

No.

It wasn't a simple arson as Marshal Cummings asserted. It had an explosive element to it; victims hadn't the chance to flee.

This was murder.

He scanned the property, drinking in its damage, altered already from its post-explosive state.

The perpetrators prepared the building and doused it with kerosene.

Liam slid a metal bowl roughly the size of his hand to the side, discovering a small stick protruding from the dirt. It wasn't a twig or other plant debris. One of its ends was charred. He plucked it from its spot.

A strike match. White phosphorus.

He doused it with kerosene to start the fire.

If he's going to blow up the building, why not just set off the explosives to begin with? Yet another question with no obvious answer.

It would nag him incessantly.

Liam raised the match to sniff it.

The arsonist was clearly not a miner who would have been able to do the trick with tools he'd have readily at his disposal—safely using an electric detonator from yards away.

This fiend had to improvise.

He stood, following bits and pieces of remaining junk into what was likely the saloon's storage room.

The building was set on fire using kindling of dry paper and greasy rags as a rudimentary wick for the flame to travel along while the arsonist escaped.

In the store room were the remnants of bottles, barrels, table legs—and no further line of rags, paper, or batting. A dead-end. There, right where he expected them: two damaged barrel rings buried beneath it all.

Propellant. The barrel was made to store his material, so it should've been made in such a way as to protect it from any accidents during transport. The wood needed to be pretreated. But if the fire was channeled inside the barrel deliberately ...

He looked around the store room, collecting a series of blackened, curved wood pieces and lining them up on the floor, wiping the soot from them as he went. Like a puzzle, he arranged them, squinting to read a faint mark left behind. When that failed, Liam lifted his glasses and leaned in closer.

Bocere Herb Remedies.

He turned his attention back to the match and set his jaw.

William Bailey came by again, this time dropping off a long, skinny box. Maeve was there to accept it without anyone to peer over her shoulder and hurried back to her bedroom with it.

The note read in simple print: *A little something to brighten your day. – L.O.*

With a smile, she opened the box to find flowers within.

She dropped them into a decorative vase before glancing around at the small myriad of gifts she'd received from Liam. Dresses, shoes, hats, gloves; every essential a woman could want other than unmentionables, since apparently his generosity was limited by his sense of propriety.

Maeve emerged from the room to head toward the kitchen for a cup of coffee.

"So," Alexis popped out of the neighboring bedroom.

Maeve clutched her chest, gasping for air. "Miss Chesterfield! Ye surprised me!"

"What is this, now ... the sixth, seventh delivery for you from O'Doherty in the last couple days?"

"Oh, it's half tha' many." Truthfully it was more than twice Alexis's estimate. "I told Liam about Raf 'n' everything's fine, like I told ye it'd be. He's been nothin' but friendly 'n' carin'."

"Yep," Alexis scowled, "and you're playing the Little Darling of the West with him, aren't you? You're eating it up that he's giving you a new wardrobe, traipsing around town as if you're one of them high-society ladies."

"Oh, come on! Even ye can understand it's nice to be doted on."

"It's an act! Seriously you—or others in this town—are gonna reveal the real you ... not this façade you're putting on."

"What's tha' supposed to mean?"

"Look at who you really are, what your life was like here. Where you worked, what you did, who your friends at the Tiff were."

"He knows tha' stuff ..." Maeve faltered. *'N' thought less of me for it.*

"And what's he gonna do when he finds out what you've done with the Pack ..." Alexis smirked, continuing, "... and with the Pack's leader?"

"He knows all tha' too!" *'N' didn't believe me.*

"Does he?" Alexis crossed her arms over her chest, leaning against the china cabinet. "You told him every sordid detail about what you did with Raf."

"Well no, but tha' wasn't necessary. It's nobody's business but Rafaele's 'n' mine. 'N' it's especially not yers!"

"Believe me: I wish it wasn't, but you both managed to make it my business. How much exactly did you reveal to him?"

"Only what was needed."

"So ... you withheld information?"

Maeve turned away.

"Naw, that's not suspicious at all ... to a man whose job it is to be suspicious of everyone!"

Until then, Maeve had been patient with Alexis venting her frustrations. Now she feared Alexis had a good point in how much she'd divulged to Liam. Had she made a terrible mistake? Or a series of them?

"Tell me what happens when he remembers those little treats you used to conjure for him. You think those folks in Tombstone were on a witch hunt, but your copper friend won't do the same?"

Maeve stomped her foot, not realizing until after the loud smack of

Parkesine on tile that she'd done so with her right leg. "For the last time, Miss Chesterfield! He's not like them!"

Alexis laughed, pulling herself away from the china cabinet and turning a circle in her spot, smacking her hands on her thighs. "And I'm Her Royal Highness, Queen of Mars." With a flourish or gesture of exasperation—Maeve couldn't tell the difference—the Martian monarch excused herself from the room.

Liam returned to the marshal's office at sunset, expecting to be greeted by his old friends: solitude and silence. He cringed upon hearing, instead, laughter emanating from the back where Redington's two holding cells were located.

He soundlessly shut the door behind himself.

"You think you'd know better than to get caught cutting down a cactus, Byrd," Cummings said through his laughter.

"It's a stupid law," slurred Jethro. He burst out laughing. "You gunna help me with summa these spines in my hand'r not?"

"Ha, no, pal. Removing saguaro quills is beyond my expertise."

"Miss MacKenna'do it fer me."

"Maybe," Cummings snorted, "but nothing else you've ever asked her to do."

"Hey c'mon now, no foolin', I'm standin' right here," Jethro whined.

Liam inhaled and stalked in, reminding himself Maeve's honor was now another man's to defend. He approached the small stove in the corner across from the cells to pour himself a cup of freshly brewed coffee.

He poured a second cup and offered it to Marshal Cummings.

"Haven't seen you in a while," remarked the marshal, accepting the drink with a grateful smile. He sipped and his smile faltered. "Not as good as Maeve's—you should take some tips from her."

Liam didn't dignify that with a response.

Cummings continued, "Figured you went home. What've you been doing?"

Scratching the side of his nose, Liam shifted his spectacles to where they belonged were it not for his sweaty skin.

He'd followed the little discovery at the scene of the crime with a trip from business door to business door, asking for matchbooks.

Not the general store. Not the restaurant where he'd taken Maeve last night, nor the hotel he'd thought of taking her after.

On the bright side, he amassed an impressive collection of matches. Regrettably, none matched *his*.

Liam replied, "I discovered a match while double-checking the ruins."

Cummings sniffed. "A match?" His obnoxious robust laughter followed. "Obviously a match was involved. It was a fire! That's nuttin' to write home about!"

Taking a steady drink, Liam sneered at the portly marshal; the man needed to lay off his doughnuts.

I wonder what Maeve's fiancé looks like?

He choked on the coffee. *What a cruel thought!* Coughing through his words, Liam croaked, "There are other ways to start a fire."

Even the drunkard in the cell sobered at the remark.

"Yes, well, we agree that'd be the easiest and most obvious way to do it," said Cummings.

Which was more reason it couldn't have been the case.

"What'syern-name again?" Jethro asked through a long belch, his gaunt face pressed against the wrought-iron bars of his cell, withered branch-like arms sticking out like half-naked porcupines stuck with what Liam assumed were saguaro needles.

"O'Doherty."

Jethro shifted, peering at him with sunken eyes filled with years of heartache. "Y'er 'at boy who took out Miss MacKenna in public, 'uh?"

"What's it to you?" snapped Liam.

"Nothin' much I s'pose," Jethro drawled, turning his attention to plucking a cactus barb from his left hand with a quivering pincer grip. He flicked the liberated quill to the floor. "Just 'at I wouldn't think a feller who took out a lady affianced ta another feller would have any spine ta look down his nose on anyone."

Liam was sorely tempted to punch some respect for authority into the parasite. Instead he pulled a cigar from an inside jacket pocket, running it lengthwise beneath his nostrils with an exaggerated inhalation. "It's been a long day. Either of you have a light?"

"I gotta fistful of shit stickers," offered Jethro, waving a shaking old hand.

Cummings muttered, "Good-for-nothing dipso," as he produced a match from the matchbook he stored in his trousers pocket. He struck it on the edge of the desk and held its flame to the tip of Liam's cigar.

Liam snatched the marshal's wrist, inspecting the match before comparing it side-by-side with the one he recovered from the Tiff and Tawny. He demanded, "Where did you get this?" The cigar bounced in his mouth as he spoke.

"What, the match? It's from the Tiff and Tawny." Cummings groaned. "Don't tell me you're going on again about—"

"You frequented the saloon, Marshal?"

"Well—yea ... What man in this town didn't? Hell, Jethro practically lived there. It was the best saloon in Redington. 'Course, it was the only one we had—"

"Yes, yes, I'm aware of that." Liam waved off Cummings's prattling. "Felled by its own match." He cleared his throat. "Can you tell me about Bocere Herb Remedies?

Marshal Cummings straightened. "Can't say it rings a bell. Sorry."

"Yea," muttered Liam. "I'm sure you are."

"Oh son of a bitch! O'Doherty's calling folks in for another set of interviews." Alexis pounded a clenched fist against her parlor doorjamb.

"Huuuh-he's not going to g-get anything new; everyone's already t-t-told the marshal all they knew about the explosion," replied Milton.

"Apparently, O'Doherty uncovered something new. But if he pries, Cummings may not play along the way he always has and won't be able to continue to ignore that we've been moonlighting."

"He seems like a guh-good enough man, b-but his investigation's making me uhhh-anxious. Sure, he's covering the basics, going through the marshal's information, but it's a pretty safe bet he's going to talk to people. To us," Milton said. "There's only so much we'd be able to sidestep his questions. He's nnn-not stupid."

"You're absolutely right. And if one of us slips ..." Alexis folded her arms across her chest. "Or if the marshal does, or if any of our associates in this town decides there's money in it, the Pack's no longer gonna be disregarded. Rather than let them get the jump on us, we make sure they don't have the chance to by being real good and scarce." She paused, waiting for complaints, objections, or even comments.

"Does this mean the Pack's disbanded?" Cookey said, his voice and expression hopeful.

"Nobody but Shadow Wolf can make that decision," Alexis said, fully aware the thought had already been in Rafaele's head. It had to be breaking his heart. "No. But this means the Pack survives. Even if it does mean tucking our tails and running. Just for now."

Silence.

Alexis turned. "The Redbirds, Miss MacKenna, and I can't skip town at this point for—" she glanced at the twins. "—reasons. But the rest of you should." She looked between Cookey, Tithu, Edison, and Milton.

Cookey nodded in understanding. "I have friends in San Bernardino. I can stay with them."

"I can't go far," Edison replied, rubbing his temples on either side of a forehead etched with concern. "I'm old and incapable of venturing reasonable distances without assistance."

Alexis scoffed though she was smiling; it was a blatant excuse to stay nearby.

Edison added, "And Milton gets into trouble outside his element. You know that better than anyone, Chesterfield."

"Oh," she groaned, "fine. If you want to stick around town to keep your eyes on Maeve, so be it. It's unnecessary; we women-folk have things under control. But if you're gonna be stubborn and stay here, gather whatever provisions you'd need to survive a long-haul. Then go home and stay there. Close your curtains, lock your doors, and don't open them for anyone. No lamps, fires, noise. When the sun goes down, you suck it up and sit in the dark. Sleep. Whatever. I'll keep you informed of any changes, but I can't be making social calls each day. Don't answer letters. You act like you're not at home." She paused. "Better yet, pretend you're dead. I mean it: don't open the door for anyone. Not for anyone else in the Pack. Not even me. It may be a trick; we may have a gun to our heads … do not trust anyone. The only person who can give you the all clear— and that goes to all of you—is Wolf. In person." Alexis turned to Tithu.

"Young Redbird? I'm afraid you'll be safest going back to your reservation."

Tithu nodded. "I'll depart at sunrise."

"I hate admitting it but I'm worried about you," said Alexis.

He flashed an uncharacteristically cocky grin. "I have a way of being untraceable. I can take care of myself."

"You, young man—" Alexis wagged her finger at him. "—have been under Wolf's influence a little too long, I fear."

Soft chuckles spread through the group.

"Stay safe, dear brother," Kököle told Tithu, embracing him fiercely.

Moencopi followed suit with a gentler hug and similar sentiment.

The sound of the front door opening turned heads throughout the group.

Maeve entered—thankfully unescorted—a dazzling smile on her face that faded once she saw the gathering of people in Alexis's parlor.

"What's goin' on? Is everythin' OK? Is it Raf?" Maeve's voice pitched higher with each question; if she inquired on anything else, soon only the coyotes would hear her.

Kököle hustled to Maeve, taking the bag from her hands and guiding her to a seat. "Wolf's fine, dear, I'm sure of it."

Alexis cleared her throat, casting purposeful glances at the men in the room.

"Actually, I'm peckish," Edison announced, rising from the chair amid the crackling and snapping of his joints.

Milton echoed, "Well now that you muh-mention it, I'm starved."

"I could certainly have a bite," Tithu said quietly.

"I'll be happy to put something together for us," said Cookey, rising to his feet. He led the men from Alexis's house, casting a lingering glance at Alexis.

Maeve smiled at each in passing; Cookey returned the smile, Edison patted her on the shoulder, Milton held her hands briefly, and Tithu nodded a silent acknowledgment.

Milton's words to Cookey were the last from the group: "Puh-please none of your beans."

The front door closed and Alexis hurried to lock it. When she turned to Maeve, she was greeted with eye-daggers. "What?" yelped Alexis.

"Back to treatin' me like I amn't a Pack member, are ye?" Maeve scowled. "Holdin' a meetin' without me?"

"It was hardly a meeting—urgent matters which don't concern you," replied Alexis, "and I didn't want to interrupt your outing. Speaking of which: do tell."

"There isn't much to tell. We strolled 'n' spoke of old times."

Alexis wondered if they spoke of any one 'old time' in particular. With Moencopi and Kököle present, she didn't dare betray Maeve's trust to ask.

"Where did you go?" Alexis's stare didn't stray from the bag Kököle had retrieved from Maeve.

"No place remarkable. We paid a visit to the general mercantile 'n' he insisted on buyin' me a small bottle of fragrance. I told him not to but ..."

"Oh that's lovely." Alexis smiled fleetingly. "Now was this before or after you told him to stop calling on you, stop sending you flowers, and to—oh, you know—generally leave you right the hell alone?"

Maeve's cheeks warmed. "Well, I ... I didn't get 'round to tha'. Alexis, please try 'n' understand, it's so nice to see him again. He's familiar, 'n' comfortable. We're nothin' more than old friends, 'n' ... it was nice."

Glowering, Alexis replied, "How nice."

⟿⟣☙⟢⟾

Rafaele never imagined he would be so hard-pressed to find a Roman Catholic Church in a populated area. He exhaled, as relieved as he was anxious to go inside Saint Joseph Cathedral. *It'd be a lovely place to marry Maeve.* If they were allowed.

He stood before the quaint, unassuming building not much unlike Redington's church in its outward appearance, the chief difference being in the construction of what could someday grow into a grand cathedral. Did Roman Catholics ever do anything by halves?

There was a column several stories high at least, composed of bricks. It didn't seem prudent to build with brick considering the kinds of things California did.

Until now, Rafaele had seen these once great Catholic buildings reduced to ruin, or in various stages well before completion, but nothing in between.

Was he one of but a handful of Catholics in California? There were a few stragglers following Mass; maybe twenty present for the service, to Rafaele's best guess. Such a small number.

He needn't another way in which to be an outcast here.

Rafaele smoothed the wrinkles in his jacket and pulled the hat from his head. He didn't bother neatening his hair; his jet curls were a lost cause and something he could add to his extensive list of affronts to his savior.

All joking aside, Rafaele squeezed his eyes shut and prayed to the Holy Spirit for the light to see all his sins; he had so many that the light would have to be blinding. He chuckled before steeling his nerves.

This is serious business, he reminded himself. It'd been so long since his last confession that if he didn't deemphasize its significance, he'd be too overwhelmed to go through with it and be worse off in the long run. If he didn't cleanse his soul now, he—and it—would be beyond salvation. And God forbid he died before he had the opportunity to do this.

Rafaele crossed himself and ascended the few steps leading into the building, where he sat in the empty pews to pray for a while.

Once the giggles were out of his system, he helped himself to the confessional.

Rafaele knelt before the screen, clasping between metal and flesh the only thing he had on him to take the place of his beloved rosary left at home: a single match from the Tiff and Tawny.

"I confess to Almighty God and to you, Father, that I have sinned." *Boy have I ever.* "My last confession was—" Rafaele's shaking voice trailed off.

"Bless you, my son. How long has it been?" said a voice from the other side of the screen.

"Uh ... a while? When was the last time a Democrat was president?" Rafaele smiled despite himself.

"I'm listening."

"How much time have you got?"

There was a fat pause followed by a quiet sigh. "Let's start with today."

With a smirk, Rafaele repeated, "How much time have you got?" Actually, he'd been well-behaved thus far. More or less.

His joke was met with silence.

Unlike Padre Mut, this priest didn't appear to have a sense of humor.

"I'm sorry, I'm sorry, I couldn't resist. I'm off to a good start today but—"

he sighed contentedly, rolling the matchstick back and forth between his thumb and forefinger. "—the day's still young."

"You're wasting my time," said Liam through his teeth. "I'll tell you again: state your name."

"We've been over this."

"Do it anyway," he snapped.

"Alexis Chesterfield."

"And your occupation, Miss Chesterfield?"

Her jaw clenched as she turned her gaze to the tabletop between them. "I was a sharp-shooter with Whittemore & Thompson's New England Circus. As I previously told you."

Liam rested his elbow on the table, curled his left hand into a fist save his index finger, and pressed it into his cheek. Well, this was a marked improvement; at least she was being consistent with the fabricated story she'd told him before. It was convenient, too, as he'd been able to follow up on the assertions since last they spoke. "Work must be slow for you with no circus passing through Redington."

"Yea, well—"

"Ever."

"Yes. That's why I'm no longer a sharp-shooter with said circus. I've long since retired, as I also previously told you. It pays to be frugal." She scowled: "Rather than to spend frivolously on a woman who's not legally yours."

"You'd be an expert on the topic, wouldn't you, filthy sapphist?"

Alexis smiled. She was either a spectacular actress or was genuinely sublime in her reply: "Yes, well, that's just one of many laws that doesn't suit my best interests."

"Don't think you're going to somehow lure Miss MacKenna into some … disgusting … Boston Marriage."

Alexis laughed. "You figured me out. Good for you."

Liam vowed he wouldn't allow this woman to best his temper and currently, he struggled not to break said promise. "Why did you leave Massachusetts? Did that have anything to do with the owner of Whittemore & Thompson's being found dead and riddled with bullet holes?"

"Oh of course not." All too chipper, she folded her hands over her lap and answered, "I left because of men like you, sir."

It was taking his full breadth of self-control not to knock some respect into her; of everyone he'd interviewed, she was worst by far. "I'm going to list some names—"

"OK."

"Edison Stilwell. Milton Price." He choked through Maeve's name before continuing, "Tithu, Moencopi, and Kököle Redbird. Francisco Esquivar. Reginald de la Cloche. Ryan 'Cookey' Brown. Harry Kartchner, Joseph Schieffelin, Zeke Prescott."

A shadow darkened Alexis's eyes.

"Ah. The last one: That name mean something to you?"

Blinking furiously, she replied, "Yes. He did."

Liam smirked, leaning forward. "Tell me: what do all those names have in common?"

"They're all people," Alexis spat.

"In—"

"Redington?"

Liam slammed his open palms on the desktop and roared, "In Shadow Wolf Pack!"

Alexis flinched. "Who told you?" she whispered, her voice shaking.

He granted himself a steadying breath before replying, "It came up in previous questioning—"

"Who told you?" she yelled.

"—and your response doesn't seem to be a denial that it exists. Now." Relishing his reclaimed control of the situation, Liam reclined in his chair, tweaking his glasses to wipe something from the inner corner of his left eye. Paying more attention to the eye-goo he rolled between his thumb and forefinger than he did to Alexis, he continued, "Who's in charge of the 'Pack,' Miss Chesterfield?" He overenunciated her name so she knew he didn't believe it was really hers.

It was silent for a long time before she muttered, "I am."

"Preposterous!" Liam said through his laughter.

"Ask any of them. I'm Pack leader."

"Well I don't presume I could ask Esquivar, de la Cloche, Kartchner, Schieffelin, or ... Prescott. Could I?"

Alexis scowled, and she lowered her head. "Not unless you know someone who can talk to ghosts."

Liam groaned. "Who's missing from the group?"

"Nobody."

Liar. She was a good liar, granted, but a liar nonetheless; she wasn't head of the Pack and neither were any of the other people he'd listed. "Where were you on September tenth?"

After several moments, Alexis lifted her gaze and met his head-on. She cleared her throat. With a nearly imperceptive shake of her head, she answered, "I was at Church."

"I highly doubt you have ever been to church. Leastly on a Monday."

"I'm offended!" she countered. "I've been baptized and everything."

"Well you're hardly following the Bible's teachings, given what you've already provided in your testimony."

"I don't see how that's the least bit relevant to this investigation. Besides. A lot of folks are Sunday Christians ... as if going to pray one day makes up for all their sins and lack of prayer for the other six. I'm sure your type does the same. If you were godly all days, what's the need to go to confessional on your day of rest?"

"The semantics of religion is not my concern."

She smirked. "Then remember as much the next time you claim someone doesn't seem like a churchgoer."

"Miss! Chesterfield!"

"And if you insist on trying to pin this on me, why don't you stop by the church yourself and talk to the people there. Maybe actually investigate? I'm sure they'll confirm my whereabouts when the Tiff blew."

CHAPTER 9

 t was a lovely day for a walk though Maeve couldn't help but notice the sweat beading at Liam's brows and trickling along his sideburns. The sight of it made her stomach turn and so she put her attention to the boardwalk, focusing on her left boot when the toe popped out from beneath her skirts with each step.

"Care to stop for a meal?" Liam asked.

The thought of eating brought with it a fierce wave of nausea. "Oh, no, thank ye. I amn't hungry."

He stopped her with a hand to her upper arm and she glanced at him. The sensation of a second hand—made of ice—covered the same area.

Don't.

"You're a little green around the gills. We could pop into the druggist … maybe get you a Tummy Tonic?"

Maeve found the suggestion laughable and didn't hide her thoughts on the matter.

"What's so funny?" said Liam.

"Oh, it's just … The druggist stocks Booker's potions."

"One might serve you well if you're under the weather."

"Surely Mr. Angelino is a nice enough gentleman but anyone who's been in Redington more than a few weeks would tell ye how useless his concoctions are. I shouldn't want to waste yer money on it." She added hastily at his odd expression, "Or mine. Because I'd pay for such things. Of course."

He waved her off. "It was my suggestion and as such, would've been my responsibility. I know you've been struggling, given your ... misadventures." He smiled and continued strolling.

She followed, having difficulty keeping at pace with his long-legged strides. She took two—sometimes three—for each one of his.

"Taking all things into consideration, I must give you credit."

"Me goodness, for what?"

"I marvel at how well you've done for yourself given everything ... and not just recent events."

Maeve gave him a crooked smile. "Oh?"

"Being stuck in a wild, lawless town, fending for yourself—maybe even successfully."

"Thanks?"

"No, Miss MacKenna, give yourself more credit. It must be difficult to be such a lady under these circumstances and yet to have found a place for yourself in a man's world. No doubt it's the glory of the church."

"No doubt," she echoed weakly.

"You do attend faithfully, don't you? It's essential for your immortal soul."

Maeve gritted her teeth, hoping it made a convincing smile. "Oh, yes, of course I go. Faithful, even."

"I haven't seen you there in recent weeks."

"I've been unwell 'n' didn't want to spread the illness." She hadn't proof, of course, but couldn't guarantee pregnancy wasn't contagious. Nor could she say the same of lying, though one fib led to another, ad nauseam.

"You're well enough to entertain a walk with me." He cocked his head and offered a small smile. "Perhaps you'll be in attendance this Sunday. Please?"

"With luck," Maeve chirped.

Liam stopped outside the druggist's storefront. "Say ... what was that name again?"

She swallowed hard. "What name?"

"Buster—Broker—"

"Oh, Booker? Angelino?"

As if it had somehow offended him, he turned a frown to the store.

"Oh, come on," Alexis cried. "Why in God's name are we having to go to church, now?"

Maeve flinched. "I ... may have told Liam I go, 'n' now he expects me there. I'll be happy to go by meself—"

"Like hell you will!"

"I have to go. If I don't, he'll know I lied."

Alexis crossed her arms over her chest. "Why, exactly, are you lying to him?"

"Do not ye judge me! Who here hasn't lied to him?" Maeve shot back. "Ye've been honest? If so, why didn't he recognize Angelino's name? Ye talked to him about the Pack, did ye not?"

Alexis's eyes bored a hole through Maeve's face.

Maeve shrunk away. "We were just talkin'; it wasn't about the investigation. I couldn't very well tell him anythin' incriminatin' when I have no information on it."

"I suppose ..." Alexis replied through her teeth. "Tell me: you ever been to church?"

Maeve dropped her gaze and shook her head.

"I've never known to enjoy the institution myself but under these circumstances—between you, Moencopi, and Kököle? Maybe it'll even be interesting."

Maeve wanted to ask what those circumstances were but after all the problems she'd already caused, she kept her mouth shut instead and was thankful Alexis wasn't more upset about what she'd been dragged into.

Rafaele woke drenched in sweat; these recurring dreams were so vivid he feared he'd wake one of these mornings to find an actual bird tearing at his guts.

It proved difficult to shake visions of his nightmare: the swallows gathered around him, his blood drenching their white breasts, and anointing their little heads crimson.

That was not an ideal start to the day of a big job interview. He prayed it wasn't an omen, missing Maeve more than usual. It wasn't difficult to think of a few things she could've done for him to soothe his raw nerves.

Rafaele drank some sludge that barely passed for potable coffee before touching up the shave established by the San Diegan barber. He prided himself in looking dapper; Maeve would undoubtedly be smitten by his new style.

With a steadying breath, Rafaele departed.

He had no way of knowing Aria's home was walking-distance from the hotel in which he was staying, otherwise he wouldn't have wasted the money taking a Hansom cab.

Perhaps it was the optimism talking, but he made mental note to procure and learn to ride a bicycle. Certainly it would be no more complicated than riding a horse, and bicycles didn't require stops for rest or watering.

The cab slowed to a stop and swayed a few times as the driver dismounted and opened the doors. Rafaele thanked him and dropped to the ground before the driver opened the folded step.

"Sir, I could have—"

"Eheh." Rafaele waved it off. Pressing fare into the driver's palm, he said, "Don't wait for me. I'll walk back." He certainly needed the exercise.

The cab departed and Rafaele turned, breath whisking from his lungs as he set his gaze upon Aria's home.

Before him stood a seemingly endless and stately three-story mansion on sprawling, lushly manicured grounds: a vast lawn with a backdrop of Kyanite-blue ocean and a cloudless sky that paled in comparison to the water beneath it.

The meandering gravel path leading to the mansion was lined with trees; their spindly, leaf-filled branches skyward reaching and their thick trunks sporting dry, wan bark peeling away to reveal even lighter bark beneath. They smelled glorious.

Somehow distinctly San Diegan.

Maeve was going to love it there.

Along the foundation of the mansion was an impeccably trimmed hedge punctuated with two tall fan palm trees on either side of the dual staircases.

The staircases led to wood pillars supporting gold scroll-worked archways on the front patio. There was nothing about this American palace that didn't exude sophistication.

Beyond the archways and inset below the central conical, wood shingle roof: a single, dark wood-paneled door.

Rafaele hesitated. From Duke's description, he expected some display of wealth, something akin to MacTavish's abode—which was an outhouse when compared to Aria's home.

What sprawled before him was magnificently rich, bordering on gaudy. The errant thought crossed his mind that he didn't deserve to breathe the air there.

What was he doing?

He wasn't qualified for this job, wasn't qualified for the caste and had done nothing to deserve the opportunity to work there. Rafaele turned to leave, annoyed he'd sent the cab away.

"Excuse me," a meek voice chirped.

Emerging from the brush was a svelte teenager half a foot shorter than he. She had full lips up-turned in a charmingly crooked smile with equally crooked front teeth, a constellation of freckles across her cheeks and nose, and mousy brown strands of hair escaping a white, wide-brimmed straw hat. She dressed in what Rafaele figured was the household uniform: a plain gown of percale over which she wore a large off-white apron caked in dirt.

He questioned how so pristine an outfit could get so soiled until she brushed her filthy hands on it, leaving behind russet-colored smudges.

She was unassuming, so why did she—like the house—make him want to tuck tail and run?

"Hallo? I can help you." The words were laced with the hint of an unfamiliar accent.

Rafaele cleared his throat and yet his voice came out an embarrassing squeak: "Perhaps?" He swallowed before recovering his normal baritone. "I have an appointment with Mrs. Blanc."

The maid craned her neck to meet his gaze. She had stunning eyes: one green-hazel, the other brown, and both with grass-green limbal rings encircling their irises.

His dislike of her was intense.

Primal.

She smiled as if she had no earthly clue what was going through his head and said, "Please follow me."

The sooner I go in, the sooner I get this over with. Perhaps he'd even have good news to telegraph to Redington. *Unlikely at this rate.* He swallowed a sigh and walked a respectable distance behind her, watching as the enormous bow of her apron bobbed above her modest bustle. The bow was mostly off-white with dust marks on either side, probably where she adjusted it as necessary.

The maid glanced over her shoulder as she ascended the steps two at a time to the front door of the mansion. Where his feet echoed off the staircase, hers were noiseless.

"Who shall I say is calling?" she said in the same sickeningly chipper voice.

She moved with such grace, even the slightest movements like choreographed dance. Between that, her friendly demeanor, and her beautiful little face, his detestation of her mounted.

He was now hopeful the widow forgot their meeting altogether and he could depart without further reason to hate this young woman.

"Sir?"

Too late: she'd caught him with his guard down. He cleared his throat. "Mr. Rafaele Forino."

She nodded. "Very good." She reached for the gold doorknob attached to a plate in which there was a bas relief carving of what looked like a fairy, her arms folded over her chest, head tilted to the roof and eyes closed.

A strange thing for a fairy to have feathered wings.

No; it was an angel. But where was its halo?

Then he saw it: the doorknob within the maid's grasp.

Despite himself, he smiled. *How clever.*

The maid pulled her hand from it when it didn't rotate. "They've gone and locked me out again." She patted herself fervently in several places. "Oh, I'm embarrassed …" Her cheeks went an obnoxiously adorable shade of rose as she met his gaze. "I've misplaced the housekey. It must've fallen somewhere in the garden during my chores." She raised a hand to use the ornate twist doorbell in the middle of the door but recoiled. "I mustn't. I can't."

Rafaele frowned. "Excuse me?"

"This makes my fifth lost key this month. I've been reprimanded for this before and if Ma'am finds out—I can't—I can't lose this job. It's all I've got. I'll have no place to live!"

Despite his revulsion to her, there was something gut-wrenching about her distress he couldn't ignore. "Is there some way I can help?"

"*Ja*." She turned her piercing gaze to him. "Let me slip off to the side. Ring the doorbell and someone will be along to answer it shortly. I'll follow you in."

He slowly reached the doorbell and gave the small knob at center a twist, hearing it ring within the building.

"Thank you," the maid said, bowing as she scooted away from him. "I'll repay this favor. Somehow. Someday. I swear it." She hurried down the stairs three at a time without a sound.

Sure you will. Damn near impossible to repay someone you'll never see again.

A stout blonde woman answered the door, her amber eyes narrowing at the sight of him. "Yes." She pressed a sturdy fist to her thick hip and nodded impatiently at him to answer.

"Forino—Mr. Rafaele Forino to see Mrs. Blanc," he said, stumbling over his words. "I have an appointment?"

"Are you asking me or telling me?" she huffed.

"I have an appointment," he replied decisively, barely withholding a well-deserved scowl.

She glowered at him before bellowing, "Adi!"

Rafaele flinched at her abrasiveness.

There was a long silence before the woman leaned outside, peering around. She mumbled, "Where is that girl?"

Rafaele noticed she was wearing an outfit the same cut and style as the maid's but in far nicer fabric—velvet, he figured. It was freshly washed and pressed.

The blonde raised her voice again: "Adi! Quit playing with the rodents! You have a guest to tend!"

Moments later, the maid who walked Rafaele to the door came rushing up the steps, replacing her straw gardening hat with a proper white cap similar to the one worn by the woman at the door. "I wasn't playing with the rodents, Missus Lucht. I was weeding and tending the oleander."

"No. This gentleman needs you. He shall wait in the parlor until Mrs. Blanc is ready to receive him. And don't you take your eyes off him, not even for a moment." Missus Lucht wagged a long finger tipped with a sharp nail before retreating down the hall, muttering, "Too many things go missing as it is. Don't need some strange man adding to the fray."

"Jenet comes across as curt but she isn't really," Adi reassured Rafaele. She smiled at him with such affection his stomach turned. "This way, please."

Adi led Rafaele down the hall.

The parlor was filled with an impressive variety of small statues—some of which Rafaele recognized as likenesses of saints, a few angels. A lot of idols carved in diverse styles, many appearing to be centuries old at least. The sculpture on a pedestal in the southern corner of the room immediately drew his attention; it had to be the oldest among them.

Rafaele approached, reaching out to touch it, restraining himself at the last second.

"It's my favorite, too," Adi remarked. "That's goddess Proserpina. Mr. Blanc, rest his soul, recovered it himself during an excavation in Pompeii ... Must've been ... almost a decade ago now? The Blancs—" She lowered her voice. "—They refused to surrender it to the Italian government and smuggled it to England."

Lovely Proserpina, wreathed in flowers. The comely bronze sculpture donning floor-length robes held a small round object in her hands over the apex of her thighs. There wasn't enough detail to differentiate it from other objects but he had no doubt it was a pomegranate.

And he swore he saw color in the statue's floor-length metal robes: Cherry red.

He squeezed his eyes shut; the stress from his trip and this interview was certainly causing hallucinations.

Rafaele opened them on the sculpture; never had he been more compelled to steal something. *After all*, he rationalized, *it belongs to me more than it belongs to them. If I could hold it, just for a moment—*

"Adi." Jenet strode by the parlor door without stopping, making a quick gesture as she went.

"*Jaja*, Missus Lucht." Adi cleared her throat, purposefully tapping the crown of her head as she regarded Rafaele.

Rafaele frowned. "Beg pardon?"

"Your hat. Mrs. Blanc is particular about such things. I wouldn't want you embarrassing yourself."

"Oh." A slight warmth flowing into his cheeks, Rafaele pulled off his hat and made a sorry attempt at neatening his hair, checking it in the mirror behind the items in an elaborate dark wood curio cabinet. "Thank you, Miss—"

"Adi."

"Miss Adi?"

She bobbed her head. "Miss Adi Kätzchendorf."

Rafaele had no hope of pronouncing her name properly and despite his inherent detestation of her, she'd done nothing to deserve such disrespect. He nodded stiffly in acknowledgment.

"Follow me, please, Mr. Forino."

Without further conversation, Adi led Rafaele down another long hall, up the wide staircase and into a room filled with packed bookshelves and more artifacts.

"Ma'am," said Adi. "Mr. Forino." She soundlessly excused herself, leaving Rafaele standing dumbly in the doorway.

Aria Blanc was not what he expected from how Duke spoke of her. He'd envisioned a waiflike woman with spindly white hair in a big, lonely estate.

What he got instead was a sturdy, curvaceous woman whose beautiful skin was darker even than his. She wasn't as old as he'd expected, being within his age, he wagered, by a few years.

And her beauty dropped his jaw.

Although she kept her head downturned, Aria's greeting floated to him carried on a faded British accent: "Mr. Forino." It was apparent she couldn't care less he was there.

"Good afternoon, Mrs. Blanc."

She was seated in a plush chair with elaborately carved arm rests, powder blue gown spread out all around her. Her black hair was immaculately styled. In her lap was a well-worn copy of *Viaggio di un Naturalista Intorno al Mondo*. She closed it, glancing at him with a quiet, "Oh," followed by a longer look. "Oh me, oh my." With a wide smile, she gracefully rose from her seat. "Pardon me." Aria turned her back to him, adjusting her ample breasts with a couple jerks of her gown's neckline.

She patted her perfect hair, smoothing imaginary flyaways. "The horror. I'm such a mess."

Rafaele frowned, taken aback not only by her throaty voice but by her flawless appearance and insincerity on her last statement; she must've known damn good and well she looked flawless.

Aria faced him again, taking unabashed inventory of his physique and making him exceedingly self-conscious about his additional weight.

Her gaze locked on Rafaele's. "Mr. Bennett failed to tell me how handsome you are." With a cock of her head, she scolded Duke, "Shame on him. You, fine sir, are an impeccable specimen." Extending her hand, Aria said, "I do believe it's my pleasure."

Rafaele crossed the study to take her hand, and after a heartbeat of deliberation, decided against kissing it in salutation; instead, he held on for a couple breaths before withdrawing. "I appreciate your willingness to meet with me."

"Hmm." She gestured for him to sit. "Please, won't you take a seat?"

Rafaele glanced around; there was one chair in the study other than the one in which Aria had been sitting. He settled in the previously vacant seat. "Thank you," he said. "Duke gave me little information about what you need. I was hoping to get some clarification."

Aria crossed her study in several quiet strides, closing its French doors. She inspected the room casually before taking her seat again. "Mr. Forino," Aria said, her voice low. "My beloved husband—*god rest his soul*—had a great deal of wealth. I bore him no children, so upon his untimely passing, he left everything to me. Land. Servants. Investments. His brainchild, as well: the *Whitefeather Dirigibles Company*, whose profits, alone, keep this household running.

"Between him and me, we accumulated many valuable artifacts. He had a dreadful interest in taxidermy and I sold his collection of skulls and other dead-animal related paraphernalia shortly following his death—much to Miss Adi's elation. Myself? I ... have an interest in items of a ... Oh, how to put this?" Aria paused, searching the room for her words. "My interests are of a religious nature."

Nodding, Rafaele said, "I see," though he didn't understand the difficulty in Aria's choice of words. What was wrong with religious artifacts?

"Every now and again, I notice something of great value, occasionally priceless and irreplaceable, goes missing. I suspect it may be one of my many servants. I need a guard who can put the fear of Christ into them. And, perhaps, to even recover what's gone missing."

She shifted in her seat. "You are, indeed, a big gentleman, Mr. Forino. But I'm concerned you'll woo my servants with those dashing good looks of yours rather than intimidate them. I would hate to have had you come here for naught." There was a hesitation. "I suppose I'd hate it more to not see you every day. You might imagine the quandary in which I've found myself.

"I'm a lonely woman who has yearned far too long for a good man's touch." With a sultry smile, she leaned toward him, moistened her mouth as if anticipating a rich dessert, and bit her bottom lip. "Let me make this simple: it won't take much to convince me to hire you, Mr. Forino."

Her intense stare could've straightened his curls; otherwise, he would've been certain this was a joke. Where was this woman when he couldn't get anybody but a whore to entertain him in bed?

Unable to deny her brazen behavior was pleasing, he smiled. "Mrs. Blanc, I'm flattered by your proposition, but I'm happily spoken for."

"And how much does this other woman speak for you? Can she speak for you in as many languages as I?"

At least two he was aware of. Certainly, she'd learn a third as they spent more time together.

"Is she as skilled with her tongue as I?"

Rafaele swallowed his groan; there went the only viable employment option he'd found. "I don't imagine my wife wants me to have this job that badly." When she wordlessly accepted his challenge, he leaned forward and added pointedly, "Nor do I."

Aria flared her nostrils and pursed her lips. She opened her mouth to reply, the skin beneath her right eye twitching now and her pupils contracting to pin-pricks.

Yea. This was a spectacular waste of time. He put his hands on the armrests of his chair to hoist himself off it. If he valued his safety, he figured a speedy exit would serve him well.

Aria burst out laughing and applauded his response jovially. "I can't say I'm the least bit surprised you're married, by the looks of you! Disappointed? Oh, absolutely. But not surprised. I still require some credentials before I offer you this job."

He blinked furiously.

A long silence stretched between them as Rafaele gave her request some consideration. Probably being Maeve's personal watch-dog wouldn't qualify. Discussing his exploits as Shadow Wolf wouldn't impress her, either.

I've stolen plenty in my lifetime and I was genuinely considering pocketing the statue that doesn't belong to you. Dammit all, he still wanted it. Out of sight wasn't out of mind.

What skill could he exploit to set himself apart from anyone else offering to help Aria Blanc? He wasn't so foolish to believe he was the sole applicant.

Without thinking, he removed his left glove and rolled up that sleeve, figuring—if nothing else—his skeletal hand and arm would be turnoff enough to douse Aria's unwelcome sexual advances with a large bucket of ice water. And maybe it would be enough to sell her on the idea of offering him employment for the position in question.

"Goodness," she breathed, her eyes going wide as she pressed fingertips to her mouth delicately. "It's certainly—"

"Unattractive? Ghastly, even?" replied Rafaele. "I'm aware of it. That was the intention." Before Aria commented further, he cycled through the tools Edison built into it.

First, a fat, wide blade; then a second blade just as long but half as thick. And the third: a curved sickle blade longer than the others by several inches.

Then he pulled out the thick bonecutter blade from above his hand.

He said nothing of their purpose, his stare locked on Aria's.

Lastly, he triggered the gun and it popped up from the forearm, its barrel larger than any of the knives.

"Oh! *My.*" Aria said with a throaty chuckle as she regarded Rafaele through her lashes. "Would you look at the size of that thing. It doesn't leave much to the imagination."

Rafaele set his jaw. "Historically this weapon has done an excellent job of 'putting the fear of Christ' into people."

Her voice deeper yet, Aria replied, "I haven't doubt."

"And the ones who didn't fear it didn't live long enough to learn why they should have. It's no ordinary gun."

She cleared her throat. "May I inquire as to …" Aria made circles in the air with her right hand. "… how …?"

Rafaele didn't skip a beat. "Coyotes."

"Coyotes!"

"That's all you need to know." It was all the lie he was going to share, anyway.

"Tell me: From what part of *Italia* is your family?"

"Napoli."

Aria smiled. "Ah, Naples! *Checazz'*! Such a lovely city, lovely people. My beloved Calvin took me to Verdi's *Aida* at Teatro di San Carlo. Have you been?"

Rafaele wondered if she meant the theater or the opera but asking for clarification wouldn't change his answer. "Unfortunately, no." His family scarcely afforded the clothing and food they'd needed, and there were countless times his father went without. "I have promised myself time and again I'll go should my fortunes turn."

"Quite the admirable aspiration. I wish you well in your pursuits." Aria stood, straightening her gown. "Well, Mr. Forino?"

With a deep breath, Rafaele followed her lead. "I appreciate your taking the time to meet with me." He took a few long, heavy strides toward the French doors, opening them but pausing in the doorway. Over his shoulder, he commented, "It's not my place to say but I'd be remiss if I didn't tell you: you *do* need better security here, regardless of your in-house thief."

"How so?" Aria's eyes flashed as she lowered her head in challenge, her whole frame stiffening.

He turned enough to brandish his prosthetic arm's gun. "I was a foot away from you with a cache of weapons. Nobody even attempted to check me when I entered your home. If I weren't applying for the job and had it in my mind to do so, you and your whole staff of nothing but the fairer sex would be dead, and everything you own would now be mine." *Including my Proserpina.*

Aria's mouth fell open soundlessly.

"I'll see myself out, ma'am." Rafaele settled his hat back atop his curls with a firm push.

She squared her shoulders and raised her head. With the regality of a queen, Aria replied, "You shall do nothing of the sort."

He froze, the distinct sensation of a frigid wind blasting him in the face, pushing him back into the room by several steps. There were no open windows nearby and she couldn't have had one of Edison's cooling machines installed.

She was like Maeve.

Oh, hell. Not another witch.

He refused to turn around, forcing a daring reply in the face of his terror: "Excuse me?"

"You've made your case. I don't imagine I'll find anybody better suited for this job. You're hired."

Liam's excitement was palpable, his skin prickling as he plopped a stack of papers onto the marshal's desk.

Cummings raised his head from his bottle of beer, pulling his feet from the desk top. "You're as excited as a virgin with a fistful of tokens at a brothel."

"Thanks for that visual." Liam's grin inverted to a sneer. "I've spoken with some of the residents around town who were so kind as to verify Bocere Herb Remedies as being operated by Booker Angelino." He, too, was being kind; the residents who divulged the information had to be coerced into doing so. It hadn't been difficult to—just obnoxious.

"Don't be absurd."

"Not if you spare it fleeting consideration. Bocere is the Old English version of the name Booker. He named his business after himself but chose a derivation of his name so he could distance himself from it when there came the inevitable problems with his shoddy products. Now: this all would be obvious had anyone previously mentioned someone in this town went by the name 'Booker.'" Liam arched his eyebrow.

"Ah—uh—yea—yes," Marshal Cummings replied, his eyebrows a mile off his forehead but gaze still locked on the floor. "Oh, Angelino? Right. His products and solutions are dreadful. Their results speak for themselves." He patted his rotund stomach which was more the result of overeating than it was the failing of Booker's concoctions. "Bought some of Angelino's so-called diet water and I swear it's made me larger. 'Course he used the company name 'Dr. Angelino's Fine Vigors' then, but his 'yote-drool tonics remain the same and no clever business title change is fooling anyone, eh?"

He exhaled. "Seems he changes names every time he's run out of Redington. He's always coming back with something stupider than the last."

"Here I thought snake oil salesmen were the fabrication of dime store novels." Liam's smirk fell. "And yet, with such a sordid record, Angelino doesn't appear even once in your paperwork. Imagine that."

Cummings at long last dragged his gaze to meet Liam's. "You don't think it was Angelino—"

"No."

The marshal cocked his head.

"And I take it you think he did?" pressed Liam.

Cummings's eyes went wide with fear.

If he believed it was Booker's doing, he would've—and should've—said as much. Why didn't he suggest it, then? Inquiring after it would result in lies or excuses, so he chose to save them both time and said, "I hear Angelino was part of the cowboy faction in the territory—Shadow Wolf Pack."

Marshal Cummings blinked a blatant acknowledgment that none of this was news to him.

Curious.

"I've also followed a tip and had two gentlemen confirm Angelino was the pyrotechnics expert in said group. I did a little digging and found information regarding a jailbreak in Tombstone a couple months ago involving Shadow Wolf, his gang, and an impressive explosive display."

"And you somehow don't think it was Booker?"

"No. I've been in contact with Sheriff Ward as well as several eyewitnesses, and they verified the event at the jailyard was a professional job involving intricate timepieces connected to explosives. Obviously it was highly technical; Angelino may be a snake oil salesman but his real talent is in fireworks. I'm told what happened in Tombstone made the explosion at the Tiff and Tawny look like amateur hour." Liam shook his head. "No. At best, Angelino supplied our arsonist—" *you?* "—with the barrel of Bocere kerosene. Were this a civilized town, and were Angelino an upstanding citizen, I'd locate him and request his record of sales."

The marshal chuckled. "Booker sells out of the back of his wagon and he's far from an honest man. Fat chance he's left any paper trail."

"Yes," said Liam with a hefty roll of his eyes. "That's where I was going.

Besides, the odds are high, I'm willing to wager, that our criminal wasn't the primary buyer anyway and the kerosene switched hands any number of times between Angelino and the arsonist."

"That'd complicate issues."

"Do you think?" Liam wanted to thank Marshal Cummings for stating the obvious. He plucked a newspaper from the desk, skimming its columns. Nothing of significance stood out. "I'm retiring for the weekend," *you unbelievable dullard.* "If you would, please keep in contact with the neighboring communities and attempt to track Angelino's movements. I need to talk to him."

"Oh come now! Even you must realize that's gonna be as futile as chasing shadows at midnight."

"If there's a dead-end with Angelino, so be it." He snapped the newspaper against the edge of the desk before tossing it into the middle of the mess. "But at least there will be no question we're missing leads." Liam adjusted his glasses. "Good evening to you, Marshal."

CHAPTER 10

 he trip to church was going to be an uncomfortable imposition from beginning to end.

Maeve dressed in the clothing she owned that most closely resembled any normal churchgoer's Sunday best, opting for her new boot on the off chance it might be seen as she walked. She tried putting on her engagement ring but decided against wearing it as it was uncomfortably snug at her knuckle.

Having neither gold eagle in her new boot nor gold ring on her finger, she hunted instead for her hair pin.

Alexis rapped on the open bedroom door. "Frantic searching and hand-wringing are sure signs of a woman ready to leave," she said with a jovial smile.

"I need me hairpin," replied Maeve. She pulled back the sheet on her bed; nothing. Nothing under her pillow, either.

"Why? Your hair's fine without it. This … wouldn't happen to be something you need to impress someone you shouldn't need to impress, would it? Some red-haired copper, maybe?"

"No." Maeve leaned over, smoothing the bedsheet as if perhaps she'd feel what she couldn't see. "It's gold."

"… and?"

Maeve turned to Alexis in a huff. "It's important!"

"What? Is it some sort of magical, life-saving pin?"

She resumed searching around the dresser, muttering, "Now isn't the best time for me to get reaped."

"Is there ever an opportune time for that?" Alexis said through her laughter.

Kököle peeked into her room. "Ladies? We should be on our way."

"We're just going to church, Maeve." Alexis said, her voice soft. "What's the worst that could happen?"

Still glowering at Alexis, Maeve replied, "I could burst into flames?" She resumed her search, opening each dresser drawer and rifling through its contents. Nothing, nothing, nothing. More nothing.

"Are you serious?"

"Of course she's not. Don't be ridiculous," replied Kököle. She tilted her head, resting it against the doorjamb, her gaze settling toward the floor. "I see something gold against the baseboard behind the bed."

Maeve rushed to investigate. "There it is!" She jerked the headboard to pull it away from the wall but Alexis stopped her with a gentle hand pressed to her shoulder.

"You don't need to exert yourself. The ladies and I will retrieve it when we get back from the service. I promise."

"If I get reaped at church, I'm blamin' *ye*."

Alexis smiled. "Death will have to get by me, first. I'd like to see him try."

Maeve gaped at her, pale cheeks abnormally ashen. Though he was an ocean away, she snapped, "Do not ye challenge Dallahan."

"Come, come, ladies," Moencopi called from the hall. "We must not leave the pastor waiting."

Maeve had always wondered about the seemingly vacant building at the far east end of town beyond the first little cluster of homes. It was relatively new and small, comprised of a single room that couldn't comfortably hold more than two dozen people.

Townsfolk Maeve only saw in passing were waiting to go inside shortly before the Sunday service began.

They chattered about the new preacher, and the air cooling system of Edison's that was still the center of everyone's excitement even though it wasn't so hot during the day anymore.

"It works like a charm," somebody remarked. "It's practically magic! I was in there helping to clean and wow! No more sweating in church ... unless you've good reason to."

Though they couldn't possibly know the plethora of reasons Maeve had for being nervous in church, she assumed the comment was directed at her.

While they waited outside, Maeve studied the crowd. Brandon had Tawny on his arm, Jia Li escorted Monroe, the shopkeeper was with his family, and even Jethro Byrd was in attendance, with the faintest glimmer of sobriety in his eyes. Maybe the new preacher had gotten through to him. Or maybe it was the lack of town saloon.

And of course, separated from everyone else was Liam chatting quietly with Marshal Cummings.

Maeve bemoaned that Edison and Milton were nowhere to be found; in fact, she didn't recall seeing them since the Pack meeting Alexis claimed wasn't a Pack meeting.

Much to Maeve's surprise, she recognized the town's newest resident and preacher: Brother Thurman. She didn't expect to see him again after the Tombstone jailbreak, and, further, couldn't have anticipated how overjoyed she would be by it since she assumed she was to him nothing more than a soul in need of salvation.

He was heading for the church doors while trailed by an entourage and talking to a tall, slender gentleman with a limp and a dashing bowler hat.

Maeve had no hope of getting Thurman's attention, let alone chatting with him; perhaps he'd be a little less busy after the service.

She was left with her current housemates.

Maeve tried investing in the conversation with Kököle and Moencopi, vaguely aware they weren't speaking English.

Alexis was pacing, her arms crossed tightly over her chest, an unpleasant expression on her downturned face. She'd be no good for companionship. *Not surprisin'.*

So Maeve milled around, wondering what to do with herself. She felt unwelcome. Like a ghost.

"Miss MacKenna?"

Mr. Davidson approached, dapper as ever in an aubergine suit with burgundy-colored accents, his subtly uneven gait slowing him as he pulled the black bowler hat from his head and balanced it atop a small round tin he carried.

He was who'd had Brother Thurman's ear. Her face lit up at his affectionate smile. "Mr. Davidson, how good it is to see ye!"

"Likewise, little dear. You're positively radiant, absolutely full of life." He reached for her hand and after a hesitation, took it and left a warm kiss on it.

Maeve gave a tight-lipped smile though her thoughts lingered on his remark about her complexion. *I'm radiant because it takes a surprisin' amount of effort to refrain from pukin'.* "It seems a lifetime since I've seen ye."

"I'm sure I could say the same, Miss MacKenna." He faltered. "It ... is ... still 'Miss MacKenna?'"

"Oh, yes, it is." *Hopefully not for long. Best before anyone notices the bastard baby.* "Word spreads like wildfire, yea?"

His charming smile became a roguish smirk. "I've heard you had yourself some misadventures recently. Are you well?"

Maeve's stomach turned somersaults and she delicately splayed her fingers across the lower half of her bodice. "I must admit I've been better."

"Are you hungry? Care for a few cookies?" He jostled the hat and tin, removing its lid before offering it to her.

"Thank ye, no—me stomach's feelin' a bit off today."

"You're sure? The Widow Marsden made them for me. They're ginger-snaps—I hear ginger is wonderful for settling an uneasy stomach."

Maeve plucked one from the tin. Thoughts of eating still nauseated her, and she paused with the thin, hard, biscuit-like cookie against her lips.

He smiled in encouragement.

She took a tentative bite and her senses were flooded with flavor: among those she recognized were ginger, followed by something that tasted like peppermint. With the immediate settling of her stomach, Maeve finished the cookie and helped herself to a few more.

"Tasty little things, aren't they?"

Maeve nodded.

"I don't care what everyone else thinks; Widow Marsden is such a love. A real dear old lady."

"I'll … I'll have to take yer word for it." The dear old lady had, after all, seen fit to stay as far as possible from the Tiff and Tawny, so Maeve never had any personal interactions with her.

While Maeve helped herself to a few more cookies, Brother Thurman's voice carried over the din of the crowd.

"Church doors are open; please come inside where it's temperate."

Mr. Davidson cleared his throat and cast a smile upon Maeve. "Let's not be strangers, now."

"Are ye not joinin' us for the service?"

"Oh," he drawled with a lazy shrug. "I don't have any interest in participating in this type of idolatry. I was only here to discuss some business arrangements with the pastor."

"Excuse me," Alexis interrupted loudly, cutting between the two. "Dalliers get the pews farthest from the cooling machines." She looped her arm with Maeve's, knocking the remaining cookie to the dirt. "Oopsie."

Maeve waved at Mr. Davidson as Alexis jerked her into the tiny church. As she stepped over the threshold, Maeve winced at the blast of chilly air striking her face, and she shivered violently.

She snapped at Alexis, "Tha' was rude!"

"What the hell are you doing?" hissed Alexis.

"Tremblin'?" said Maeve through chattering teeth.

"Don't play dumb. That's not what I meant!"

"Oh. I was just havin' some pleasantries with Mr. Davidson." Maeve twisted in her spot. He stared after her with a peculiar look on his face. She glared at Alexis. "Or are pleasantries no longer allowed?"

"Not with men they aren't. It's bad enough you're pleasant with Mr. O'Doherty!"

Maeve couldn't help but roll her eyes. "Ye're bein' absurd." She yanked her arm from Alexis's grasp. "They mean me no harm."

"No." Alexis prodded Maeve's collarbone with a single finger. "*You're* being absurd. Men are only ever after one thing and so long as you're in Mr. Forino's keeping and my responsibility in his absence, I can't have you having pleasantries with other men. Your beauty is a terrible liability."

"But havin' pleasantries with other women would be acceptable?"

Alexis's jaw dropped.

"What?"

Alexis sputtered: "Do you even know what we're talking about here?"

Maeve wasn't entirely sure but figured such topics were fantastically inappropriate—especially on hallowed grounds. It was a relief when Brother Thurman changed the subject for her.

"Welcome, welcome," he spoke to the congregation. "It gives me such joy to have so many smiling faces in the Lord's house this morning." His already wide smile broadened when he caught sight of Maeve in the pews. "Good morning, all!"

A chorus of voices rose around Maeve: "Good morning!"

"Lovely weather we're having inside the building, isn't it?"

"Beats the hell out of being outside," someone from the back of the church laughed.

Uncomfortable chuckles rippled through the pews. Brother Thurman shook his head and replied, "I'll pretend I didn't hear that."

Less uncomfortable laughter followed.

"Please find a seat, greet your neighbors, and enjoy the blessings bestowed upon us by the wondrous talents of Mr. Stilwell."

While the church filled with the unintelligible murmur of many conversations at once, Maeve became keenly aware a heated stare was boring a hole into the side of her head.

She turned. "What?"

Alexis blanched and leaned away.

"Why are ye starin' at me?"

"I'm sorry, I was just waiting for you to burst into flames. You promised."

"I don't actually do tha' … I merely implied it was a possibility."

"Oh?" Alexis giggled. "Try telling Esquivar that."

Maeve chewed her cheek, neither wanting to laugh or lash out. So instead she opted for the diplomatic: "I may be new to this church business, but I'm pretty sure ye're not supposed to giggle in here."

The din petered out and Brother Thurman continued, "As I watched the sun set last night, I reflected on recent tragedies, from the volcanic eruption of Krakatoa—you might imagine it was the sunset which inspired me—to the storms in Rochester, Minnesota … Even in our remote little desert oasis, tragedy befalls us with the unexplained explosion of the Tiff and Tawny."

Maeve shrunk in her seat as much as her clothing allowed. Even though she knew he wasn't blaming any of those things on her, she still felt guilty.

She was lucky she'd been in Tucson at the time of the saloon explosion, not just because she escaped death or injury, but also because in so doing, she escaped blame.

She had no doubt there were people like Gaylene who attributed the granary explosion in Tucson to her—and they would've been right to.

Her gaze flickered to her hands clasped in her lap. She resented they were swollen so she couldn't wear her engagement ring.

There was no good reason they would be bloated, so she assumed it was due to the pregnancy.

Time was running out on her little secret staying so little and secret. She would soon outgrow her clothing due to bloat. And then fat, and eventually, the baby.

"—But in these trying times, it's important to not lose sight of even the Lord's smallest blessings. As an example, God recently sent me a divine message that somebody in our flock is in the family way but is none too happy about it. I want to remind this woman: God has a plan for you, and for your baby, too. For every person and for all things. And you need to trust in His plan."

Excited chatter filled the building, heads turning every which way, wide-eyed gazes searching for the mother-to-be. Maeve's heart flew into her throat and she lowered her head in hopes of dodging the stares, wracking her brain to figure out who told Brother Thurman because it sure as hell couldn't have been divine words from on high.

Which housemate betrayed her fragile trust?

Maeve clenched her jaw against her lip's quiver and squeezed her stinging eyes shut.

This whole pregnancy thing was absolute hell: the mood swings were keeping her perpetually on the verge of losing her sanity, she'd rather be dead than nauseated, and she was tired of the constant fatigue.

All these things fanned the flames of her anxiety over social repercussions, Rafaele's response to her news, and, of course, a labor and delivery that could kill her in a plethora of terrible ways.

And then? She could worry for years about the baby dying.

I wish this hadn't happened. If only I could go back in time 'n' prevent it.

Dear God...dess? Whoever's up there?

I know this is a part of yer grand design, but I amn't strong enough for this. I amn't built for it.

I'm tryin' so hard to trust ye 'n' in yer decisions tha' everythin' will work out but ... I wish I wasn't with child.

It was an accident.

A mistake.

A moment of weakness, 'n' I'm sorry. Forgive me weakness, I'm tryin' so hard to be perfect but I—

The crowd laughed, jarring Maeve from her thoughts. She turned watery eyes on Brother Thurman.

"Now, when the unexpected happens, it's important to always remember to trust. Trust in God, and in His plans for us. Trust in each other. We need to live our lives with trust in God during all times, but especially during times of uncertainty. Let's read Psalm Thirty-One."

Bibles opened all around Maeve. She felt like such a fraud and wondered why she hadn't burst into flames upon entering the building. And as his sermon continued, Maeve supposed she may as well have, given the burning questions she held for the young pastor.

After what seemed an eternity, Brother Thurman concluded his service and dismissed the congregation, most of who were happy to leave and attend their Sunday plans. A few lingered near the cooling machines.

Before Alexis or the twins interfered, Maeve rushed to the pulpit.

"Miss MacKenna," Brother Thurman greeted Maeve with great affection, cupping her left hand in both of his. "I can't tell you how glad I am to see you!"

Her smile at him was, at least, half sincere. "Hello, Brother Thurman. What a surprise to see ye in Redington."

"I kinda had to leave Tombstone, as siding with a condemned woman sullied my name there. A little." He smiled despite her frown. "I wouldn't have it any other way. They were wrong, and I wasn't willing to stand with them when they were murdering an innocent woman. By-the-way, that was quite the little get-away you had."

Maeve blushed. "Ye heard about tha', did ye?"

"I was there," Brother Thurman chuckled. "God certainly answered my prayers in an ... unexpected and entertaining way."

"I suppose then ye know it's me fiancé who deserves the credit for it."

"Fian—" The preacher gasped, his face lighting up. He clasped his hands together with a single loud clap. "Forino proposed!"

"Yes," Maeve bobbed her head shyly. "He did."

"You two have a bright future together. Can I expect he'll be here with you some Sunday?"

"I—" She swallowed. "He's away. On business. 'N' I amn't sure when he's due to return." *Due.* Maeve closed her eyes. "I ... I had a terrible accident." *Had one ... Am goin' to have it.* Was there much difference? "Oh, I hate to impose, but ... I'd appreciate if ye prayed for me. Again. I guess."

"Of course I'll pray for you. It's no imposition." He took her hand and squeezed. "What kind of accident? Do you need help?"

Maeve didn't want to dismiss his question, nor his kind offer. She also didn't want him knowing she was pregnant. So although it wasn't the accident to which she referred, she said, "*Ssh,*" and hiked her skirts barely enough to reveal the fake leg.

Brother Thurman's jaw dropped. "Miss MacKenna—" he gasped.

Maeve adjusted her skirts on the off-chance someone might look their way at the preacher's gasp. "There was a granary explosion in Tucson."

"Oh, yes, I heard. Such dreadful business!"

"I was ... a little too close to it."

"Oh," he sighed. "Trouble *does* find you, doesn't it?"

"Ye could say tha', I suppose."

"How can one little lady be so unlucky, I wonder?"

Not lucky. Cursed. Despite herself, Maeve chuckled. "I've asked meself tha' very question, time 'n' again."

"A little luck of the Irish, huh? Well maybe things will settle once you marry Forino. Get his sweet little family started."

Maeve's face went crimson and she glanced away.

"Don't be ashamed. The Lord *did* command 'go forth and be fruitful.'" Brother Thurman furrowed his brow, rubbing the side of his index finger beneath his lip. "Then again, the Lord was angry when He said that. Oh, never you mind."

"The lord gets angry?" she squeaked. How many things had she done— and in recent months, alone—to earn God's ire?

Brother Thurman replied, "That's, um ... a conversation for some other time. Don't forget, God is forgiving, too."

"Is there a limit to what he'll forgive?"

The preacher frowned. "I owe your fiancé a staggering debt of gratitude."

She didn't appreciate his blatant change of subject. *God must have a finite amount of mercy in him.* "Ye do? Whatever for?"

"Well, I helped him out in Tombstone, and he insisted on returning the favor, so I asked him to bring me more parishioners, thinking—figuring—he wouldn't. Not through any fault of his, mind you; How does somebody drive people *into* a church?"

"Ye threaten them?" Maeve guessed with a crooked smile.

He chuckled. "You make the church the most comfortable building for miles around. The air coolant system? Forino's idea, Stilwell's execution."

Maeve smiled. Her tiny secret baby couldn't have asked for a better father. "He *is* a good man."

More than you know.

Thinking how great a father Rafaele would be, Maeve already wondered if she could pray away a previous prayer.

After a brief, uncomfortable silence, Maeve asked, "Brother Thurman? What do ye pray for?"

The preacher's eyebrows went up. "First I give thanks to the Lord for His many blessings."

"Like what?"

"This morning, I thanked Him for my good health. Each meal, I thank Him for the food I eat. Every Sunday, I thank Him for a church full of parishioners, and for their generosity when the collection plate goes around. And for all those parishioners, I have your fiancé to thank, so I thank God for Mr. Forino, as well."

Maeve nodded, her gaze focused on the ground. "Do ye ever ask God for ... things?"

"Things? Like guidance, patience, and strength? Yes. When my faith falters—and believe me, even the most faithful and pious have our moments of doubt—I ask God to renew my trust in Him."

"Do ye ask for ..." Maeve shrugged. "I dunno ... Specific things?"

"You have something in mind."

"Well, if ye were sick, would ye ask God to make ye well again?"

Brother Thurman nodded, a sweet smile tugging his lips where his eyebrows were still crimped in concern. "Wouldn't you?"

"Yes, I suppose. If he listened."

"Let's sit. You could use some rest." Brother Thurman took Maeve by the elbow and led her to a pew at the back of the church, observing, "Mr. O'Doherty certainly is a watchful gentleman, isn't he?"

Maeve waved off the comment. "He's an old friend with steadfast concern for me."

"Miss MacKenna …" Thurman raised his hand as if he wanted to settle it on her knee, then pulled it away. "Why would you think God doesn't listen?"

No man ever made a habit of listening to her: From her father to Rafaele; Judge Pinney in Tombstone to Liam, here, and now. Maeve opted for a tactful, more general assessment: "Nobody listens to me."

"I'm sure that's not true." The preacher cocked his head and smiled. "I listen. I did in Tombstone and I am now."

Maeve said in revelation, "Ye did. Ye are."

"And I've no reason to believe our Lord and savior wouldn't be listening to you, as well."

Shite! How do I undo a prayer?

To be sure, she followed with: "He even listens to heathens?"

Brother Thurman chuckled. "You're no heathen."

He didn't say yes; she was reassured. "I …" Maeve swallowed. "I want to ask god for help. How would I do tha'?"

"Well," said Brother Thurman, "we are instructed to pray in secret, and not to ramble or be repetitious. We give honor to God, we ask for His Kingdom to come, or for His will to be done—no matter how much we might not like what His will is. We request for a heavenly or godly presence here on Earth. We ask for daily provision. We ask He forgive us our sins and offer forgiveness for others who've wronged us. We are to pray that God keep us from temptation and deliver us from Satan's power. The Bible assures us when God is pleased with our prayers, He answers them."

Maeve exhaled, all stress rushing from her body. She hoped no loving god would be pleased with a prayer to end a life—especially an unborn life. *Except Thurman said god gets angry.*

Brother Thurman continued, "Pray with the heart of a child: with simplicity, and reverence. With trust. I've no doubt you can do that. You have all those things in spades."

"If I do, god will answer me prayers?"

"I'm sure of it." He hesitated.

"What?"

"Just be patient with His answers," Thurman said slowly. "Sometimes He says 'no.' And sometimes it's 'not yet.' But He always knows what's best for you, even if it may not feel like it."

They sat in silence for a few moments before Maeve asked, "How do ye do it?"

"I ... I don't understand."

"How do ye pray? People here bow their heads. Is tha' how I should do it at home?"

He stared, his jaw slack. "You really were raised outside the church, huh?"

Maeve's cheeks dimpled in a forced smile. "I wasn't jokin' when I told ye tha'."

"So I see! Well, at night, I kneel at bedside. I clasp my hands together—palm to palm—and bow my head and give thanks."

"'N' then ye ask god for help?"

"Miss MacKenna, are you in trouble? Perhaps it's something I could help with." He paused, smiling weakly. "You might get a more immediate response that way. Perhaps God placed me in your life to help you, just as He placed Mr. Forino in mine."

Maeve stood slowly. "Thank ye, Brother Thurman." She smoothed her skirts as casually as possible, well aware she had multiple people staring intently at her. "I appreciate yer offer, but ... this is somethin' for a higher authority."

"Please remember, Miss MacKenna: I'm here for you in the interim."

Maeve rested in bed, wearing nothing more than the nightgown in which she'd spent a fitful night following the day she attended church.

The cramps woke her and came at regular intervals from their pre-dawn onset. She said nothing of them, hoping she hid her discomfort well enough that the women wouldn't notice. She didn't want them fussing over her or being more of an imposition than she'd already been.

It was a relief when Alexis departed as the sun rose to check for missives and shop for groceries, leaving Maeve with some kind words and orders to take it easy until she improved. She heard Alexis charging Kököle and Moencopi with her care, but thus far they'd left her alone.

So Maeve slept off and on, waking with the cramps and dozing as they tapered, but she woke with a start following a loud, single knock at the front door—a familiar knock that sent an electric sizzle of terror through her body.

The knock itself wasn't remarkable and under other circumstances could've been mistaken for something carried on a hard wind bumping against the door.

What made it unique was the knock coupling with silence.

No noise from the street; no horses, no wagons driving through dirt and gravel, nor voices. Not even bird song from the nearby trees.

The absolute lack of life otherwise ever-present in Redington made the silent, lifeless thump of a knock so terrifying. It was the same lifeless thump she heard in County Donegal just prior to the death of the little girl who'd spent her waning hours in Maeve's care.

"No—" she breathed. "It can't be. Oh please no, not this—"

The twins chattered as they went down the hall toward the front door.

"No!" Maeve tumbled from her bed, misstepping on the prosthetic leg and landing hard on the carpet, a shock of pain shooting through both thighs; she yelled. "Don't answer it!"

An unmistakable, familiar voice carried down the hall: "Ladies," he greeted Moencopi and Kököle. "Hello, I'm the doctor. Poor Miss MacKenna needs my service. I hear she's been ailing."

"What business do you have with her?" Though Maeve couldn't differentiate between their identical voices, she assumed by the curt tone those words belonged to Moencopi.

"I'm here to check on her injury. Her leg surely gives her grief, doesn't it?" He drawled, "Reminds me of a blessing from back in the old country." He raised his voice, presumably so she could hear it in her room: "Now, how did it go, Maeve?"

The front door creaked, and she swore it was the keening of a banshee.

He quoted, "'May those who love us, love us. Those who do not love us, may god turn their hearts. And if he cannot turn their hearts, let him turn their ankles, that we may know them by their limping.'"

There were two thuds followed by lifeless, hollow-sounding, uneven footfalls.

"Miss MacKenna," he sang, his voice drawing near.

Maeve attempted to hoist herself back on the bed but her limbs wouldn't cooperate, weakened by fear; instead, she scooted away from the bedroom door, retreating on her rear to the farthest corner of her room.

The whole house creaked as if even it were trying to withdraw from his presence. The lamp flames extinguished, choked of their lives in the stagnant air now filling with the stench of a thousand rotting corpses.

Maeve finally understand the air of danger surrounding Mr. Davidson; why everyone gave him wide berth and animals avoided his presence.

He was the old foe she thought she'd escaped. How could she have been so blinded by the handsome face he wore?

Her bedroom door swung open. On the other side was Mr. Davidson, not quite himself anymore with hollowed-out cheeks and sunken, soulless eyes. "MacKenna. MacKenna … MacKenna." He repeated her last name as if tasting it—and he thought it bitter. "How on earth did you fall in with those two?"

"Whatever are ye talkin' about?" she whispered.

"I hear you've taken unwell." He cocked his head and grimaced something she didn't recognize as his typical charming smile with its imperfect teeth. "I do hope it wasn't the cookies I gave you. Though I admit I wasn't entirely forthcoming about their ingredients. Ginger, yes … Tansy, too. You really mustn't trust so readily. Naivety oft proves dangerous in this world. Sorry I was the one to have to teach you that."

His features changed before Maeve's eyes; gone was the devilishly handsome man she knew in Redington.

The flesh on his brow cracked and flaked, peeling back to reveal deteriorating muscle. His nose turned ashen, the pores on it widening and separating, creating a moldy appearance.

"The name 'tansy,'" he continued through the decay, "comes from the Latin and Greek roots—in Greek, it's *athansia*, and means 'immortality.' In the middle ages, it was given to women to help them conceive and to prevent premature birth. Ironically, it was also given to induce spontaneous abortion. The plant is immortal yet causes death." There was a pregnant pause followed by a pointed question she didn't have the answer to: "Sound at all familiar?"

Patches of flesh remained on his ghoulish skull, dangling from his cheek bones like the curtains of a deadhouse, swaying as he gave his best approximation of a grin. Yellow pitted teeth clicked together as he took a whistling inhalation through the cavity forming in place of his nose.

Maeve's gaze darted around the room in desperation for a piece of gold —any piece of gold. The hairpin was still on the floor behind the bed and a monster now stood between her and the bedside table where she last set her engagement ring.

Her old work boots were within her reach, and her left housed the gold eagle Rafaele gave her the first time she served him at the saloon.

She lunged for the boot and there was a flash of white; Maeve shrieked at the sight of his spine whip as it curled around her wrist, restraining her.

"Oh," he drawled, "there shall be none of that."

He released her with a jerk of his skeletal hand, the whip shredding her flesh as it retreated, its cervical vertebrae coming to a rest on the floor beside his right shoe.

Maeve recoiled, pressing the injury to her abdomen; the pain was so intense she tasted it.

She searched his hollow eyes with a hoarse plea: "Why do ye do this to me?"

He continued as if he hadn't heard her. "If *athansia* prevents miscarriage but also induces it, a pregnant woman ingesting some creates a ... a real flutter for the life of the unborn baby." His jaw clicked. "And yours lost that gamble."

"No, no!" Maeve implored from her spot on the rug beside her bed. She shook her head fervently. "Do not ye do this! Please!"

"She held on tight, this one. Positively dying to be Forino's daughter ... though for the life of me I can't imagine why." He made a motion toward Maeve's abdomen and curled what remained of his index finger in a beckoning gesture. "But it's too late now. She's mine; a debt you owed me, repaid."

"No!" Maeve cried, squeezing the fabric over her abdomen as a tiny wisp of a soul drifted from her lower stomach to him, curling around his wrist like a ghostly vine. She screamed so loudly her voice broke: "Give her back!"

"Oh, stop carrying on." He stroked the little soul with a single bony fingertip and cooed at it, "My sweetest little pet. You're so much better off with me."

"How can ye be so heartless?"

He looked at her with impressive deadpan.

"Ye're a monster!"

"A monster?" Dallahan made a gurgling little gasp. "You hurt me! I was doing you a favor—settling our debt and saving you from abject humiliation, both. I answered your prayer and now you're angry with me?" He loomed over where she cowered on the floor, the precious little soul sinking into his bones and vanishing forever to a place Maeve could never reach her.

"Aibheaeg," he said, "I relieved you of a terrible encumbrance the likes of which you couldn't begin to fathom. And her?" A light in his soulless eyes flickered to the fading spirit coiled around his wrist. "I did her a favor beyond measure. This world is no home for a woman like her: the purest of the pure, a true innocent soul … she would have been treated like garbage. A queen relegated to circus sideshow mockery." Never had words carried such venom. "Next time?" He extended a single white digit, leaning in and pressing it over Maeve's heart. "Next time I'll just let you suffer your burden."

Without another word, he stalked from the bedroom.

Moments later, the front door slammed shut.

Sounds of life returned down the hall as the twins stirred. Outside, an owl hooted, answered by the *peent* of a nighthawk, then several gray foxes barking as if nothing had ever been wrong.

"What happened?" one of the women asked.

"I am unsure. I have vague recollections of being told to sleep."

Maeve struggled to the mattress, taking heaving breaths as she attempted to stand. The wound on her wrist was healing; yellowish scabs in the middle of the abrasion, pink and puckered along the outside. It burned as if the whip were still twisted around her, permanently embedded in her skin.

She pulled herself to her feet, the bedsheets clenched in tight fists.

Was it all over?

Dallahan claimed the soul of her unborn child and left her with—

Maeve frowned.

She'd been taught during her midwifery apprenticeship how pregnancy could fail under conventional circumstances, but Dallahan spirited hers away. Was she still susceptible to the experiences other women had?

She supposed he or some demon underling reaped all little unborn souls; though maybe not with the ghoulish glee he had with hers.

As if to answer her question, Maeve's lower abdomen seized in a cramp and she turned her attention downward on impulse. A single spot of bright red appeared between her feet. Fear lodged at the base of her throat. Another spot appeared on the carpet beside the first, then a thin trickle of red flowed down the inside of her left thigh.

The trickle became a gush that brought Maeve to her knees; blood saturated her undergarments, a puddle of it forming beneath her, pooling on the carpet. No matter how she clenched, there was no stopping it; Dallahan had opened a spigot in her body.

A scream tore from her throat as she stared in helpless shock.

The twins ran into the room, both blanching at the sight of Maeve, kneeling on the floor and bleeding profusely.

Maeve glanced between them, unable to articulate a plea for help.

Moencopi told Kököle, "Grab the linens," before rushing to Maeve, and taking her by her nightgown's sleeve. "Come on. Up."

Kököle brought an armful of linens, tucking them against Maeve's privates as she sat on the bed.

"We need to clean the carpet before stains set in," muttered Kököle to her sister, who nodded before excusing herself from the room.

Kököle sat on the bed beside Maeve, kneading her thigh through the nightgown. "I'm so sorry."

Maeve glanced at her. "It's goin' to get worse before it gets better."

"I know. I've seen this sort of thing before." Kököle squeezed her eyes shut. "We'll help you through it. We're not scared."

"I am." Maeve gasped as a cramp worse than all previous overtook her. She rolled onto her side, drawing her legs toward her chest with a long groan. It wasn't just pain anymore. There was something accompanying the cramp—something overwhelming, horrific. Inescapable.

"Breathe," said Kököle, massaging the small of Maeve's back, alternating gentle strokes with moderate pressure. When Maeve scowled over her shoulder, Kököle explained, "It's supposed to help alleviate the pain."

Maeve wasn't sure what alleviate meant but Kököle's unwelcome touch made things worse; she was narrowly focused on it. Her breath came loud and heavy, faster and faster.

"Chamber pot—" she cried, the words strangled. "Now!" Maeve got to her knees, bracing herself against the mattress as Kököle slid the pot between her legs.

She resumed rubbing Maeve's back.

Maeve jerked away from Kököle's touch with a long groan as the urge to bear down consumed her. She fought it for as long as possible, willing her body to keep a soulless baby.

But there was no battle left to win. "I can't—oh, I can't," she sobbed, her fingertips sinking into the mattress and eyes clenching shut. She was keenly aware of something solid escaping her body with another gush of blood.

The cramp ebbed, and so with it went the wretched urge to push.

Kököle stood beside her, staring, with a quivering hand pressed to her lips until they turned white with pressure, tears glistening on her cheeks.

When she had the strength, Maeve pulled herself onto the bed, her body shaking with exertion and blood continuing to trickle along the inside of both thighs. She turned to see the chamber pot out of compulsion but Kököle had already whisked it away, rushing with it to the door.

"Stop!"

Kököle paused midstride but didn't turn.

Maeve panted, "I want to see it."

Kököle tilted her head downward and there was a lengthy silence. Her voice was tight as she replied, "I assure you that's entirely unnecessary. It's just blood."

Maeve swallowed hard, her eyes narrowing on Kököle's back. "Ye're lyin'. Me baby's in there. Show her to me!"

Kököle cast a hard look over her shoulder at Maeve. "You don't. Need. To see. This." Without another word, Kököle left the room, exploiting how Maeve was too weak to follow.

Moencopi came back to start the arduous task of cleaning Alexis's carpet, and Maeve settled back on the bed, arranging the already blood-soaked linens beneath herself with violently shaking hands.

"I'm goin' to bleed to death."

"No," said Moencopi sternly, hard at work on the floor, "you are not."

"I'm still havin' cramps," Maeve replied weakly. "Why do they still hurt so much?"

Moencopi held her gaze with a somber expression that spoke volumes: She had no answer.

Kököle returned with the chamber pot in time for Maeve to need to use it again.

She assumed the same position, wailing through another urge to bear down; not because it hurt—although it did, terribly so—but because try as she might to resist, there was no denying nature's course and each push, each expulsion, left her with less of Rafaele's child.

The steady cramps by nightfall ebbed, the flow of blood subsiding to what Maeve was accustomed during her monthlies.

Rafaele's baby was gone.

The plot of land in New Town San Diego commanded a view of the harbor and was dotted with a few small shrubs. They didn't matter, considering Rafaele's master plan.

In fact, the barren landscape suited him well—the construction crew had less work prior to building.

Currently, not even his master plan mattered when the sun kissed the horizon and a cool ocean breeze sprayed his face. Seventy-five degrees Fahrenheit, though above autumnal average for San Diego, was nothing so miserable as the average high of Redington in summertime.

Rafaele could easily imagine Maeve adoring it. The harbor view was second to none, and the breeze, enchanting. It wasn't difficult to envision her standing at the open kitchen window, small daughter who was his spit and image on her hip, a thick little foot tucked into the bunch of fabric of her bustle. He sighed in contentment.

This fantasy was coming true. *Good things happen to—well, people.* He was hardly a good one.

"Mr. Forino?" The architect cleared his throat.

"Yea?" His reverie, wonderful as it was, dissipated.

"If I'm to move forward, I'll need details. Ideas at the very least."

"The kitchen needs a window, and I want it facing the harbor. And a room with a window—or the front door, maybe?—across the way. Something to give us a good cross-breeze. Same with the rooms on the upper story." Rafaele would be damned if he'd spend another night sweltering in his bed. "Otherwise ..." He shrugged, smacking both his hand and gloved prosthesis against his thighs. "I'm open to suggestions. I'm not in the business of building houses, as it were. That's why you're here."

"OK." He tore his attention from his notes and scanned the plot of land. "Kitchen, dining room, parlor downstairs?"

"Yes, yes, yes." All places he'd love bending Maeve over a surface to work on building their family.

"Den? Library?"

He nodded his approval, supposing Maeve would enjoy both those things; he'd need the décor and books with which to fill them.

"Two bedrooms and a master suite?"

"Yea—wait, no."

The architect kept his head bowed over his notes but peered at Rafaele expectantly.

"We'll need lots of bedrooms." *Would ten be considered obscene?*

"You have children?"

"No." Rafaele smiled. "Just planning on a fruitful future with the missus."

Chuckling, the architect stated, "Aren't *you* optimistic?"

"No. Catholic."

The men shared a laugh as the sun disappeared beyond the horizon.

"Let's go back to my office," said the architect, "and work out the particulars."

Rafaele agreed, though he was reluctant to leave his perfect little plot of land; this endeavor was certainly going to be a good test of his patience.

If nothing else, now that he'd seen where his home would stand, daydreams of his future with Maeve could be more accurate.

CHAPTER 11

ököle stayed the night in a nearby chair, keeping silent watch over Maeve while she slept.

Come morning, Moencopi brought Maeve breakfast in bed which she refused to eat, although she took the tea in cautious sips.

Moencopi undertook the dismal tasks of refreshing bedsheets and linens without complaint.

Maeve presently had a peculiar acceptance of her loss; feeling nothing but cold numbness. She put out of her head the things Dallahan told her and found respite in the lack of thoughts in their place.

She rested in bed, gazing unfocused at the wall as she absently fondled Caitlyn's gold necklace, opening and snapping shut the locket with a couple fingers. *Snap, click.* If only she'd worn it yesterday. It didn't save Caitlyn, but it could've saved her daughter. *Snap.*

"Maeve?" Alexis asked, tapping on the open bedroom door. "May I come in?"

Click. With a sigh, Maeve nodded.

Alexis entered, moved the chair to beside the headboard, and straddled its cushion. She put her arms on the back of the chair, resting her cheek against her arm. "The girls told me what happened. I ... There are no words." She shook her head where it rested against her arm, and the chair wobbled. "I'm so sorry."

Maeve exhaled, still playing with the locket. *Snap, click; snap, click.*

"How are you feeling?"

Snap, click. "I'm OK," replied Maeve, her voice tiny and muffled by the pillow.

"Listen ... if you wanna talk, I'm here. I maybe can't offer advice, and I surely haven't had this experience ... but I can listen."

She assumed it was a pleasantry, and that Alexis was silently praying Maeve wouldn't take her up on the offer.

For both their sakes, Maeve said, "There isn't much to discuss." It wasn't untrue. *Snap, click.* Her gaze flickered to Alexis in time to catch her sinking into a soundless sigh of what must've been relief.

"Take what time you need to recover. If you want us checking the Tiff for anything, or ..." She trailed off.

Maeve forced an entirely insincere smile.

"I've nothing I can offer right now but whatever you want, please tell me. I'll see to it."

Snap, click, snap, click, snap, click. "Ye ... didn't send a telegram to Raf about this, did ye?"

"No. I didn't. And I won't. Not unless you tell me otherwise."

She clutched the locket in her fist. "Please don't."

Alexis frowned, straightening on the chair. "You're gonna tell him, though, right? He deserves to know."

What could tha' accomplish? Worry 'n' scare him? So she fibbed: "I'll tell him when we're together again. They're the kind of words tha' need to be spoken in person."

They fell silent for a while before Alexis ventured a comment: "It'll happen for you someday."

Maeve glanced at her without moving her head from the pillow. "What will?"

"A family. I can't imagine a couple who'd have more beautiful babies than you two."

They were hollow words and Maeve stopped listening. "I amn't cut out to be anyone's ma."

Maybe Dallahan really saved her from me. She swallowed hard; the musing was an icepick to her heart. She clutched the locket to her tender breast, her hand shaking.

Alexis stood abruptly, a peculiar expression on her face. "Well. Good luck keeping a bun out of your oven with a man as amorous as Raf."

That was certainly an area of concern requiring address. Maeve wondered if, perhaps, Doctor Luff might have suggestions. Unfortunately, she'd then have to broach the sensitive topic let alone while unmarried. What business would an unmarried woman have asking for preventives?

Perhaps she could ask Kököle. She might've known ways to avoid bearing children and the thought of approaching the topic with her was far less embarrassing given what they'd just experienced together—courtesy one encounter with Rafaele, and one with Dallahan.

While Rafaele was away, she was afforded time to recover—and to figure out how best to proceed with him once they reunited.

Alexis returned early from the Tiff and Tawny after Maeve asked her the next day to search for clothing—though they both knew it was futile—and she greeted Kököle with a brief kiss on the lips.

"So?" said Alexis. "How is she?"

Kököle shook her head. "She's bled so much. It's still too early to tell."

"She'll get better," Alexis insisted. "Women get over stuff like this."

"She'll recover physically with a little divine providence. However, you can't imagine the agony of losing a child until it happens to you."

"You don't speak from experience." Alexis chewed her lip. "And she doesn't seem like she's in agony."

Kököle frowned. "She's in shock! The agony will come once that wears off and she realizes there's a hole in her heart where her baby should've been. And who knows what will accompany it? Confusion, possibly. Guilt?"

"Why guilt?"

"It's unfathomable. I pray she's not angry when the shock wears off. We wouldn't survive Maeve's wrath."

Alexis turned away. "Love's such a filthy business."

There was a loud gasp. "I'm not going to pretend that didn't strike true."

Kököle's voice wavered and Alexis turned to see her take a giant step back. She whispered, "You sound just like my sister."

"Hey! I didn't mean it—"

"Excuse me. It's my time to tend Miss MacKenna."

"Kökö, please!"

Without another word, Kököle retreated to Maeve's bedroom.

"God," Alexis sighed. "Dammit." She took a step in pursuit of reconciliation when there was a knock at the front door. "Sure," she sighed, smacking her palms against her thighs. "Why not?"

Her already sour disposition soured more when she opened the door to find Liam standing outside. "What now?" she snapped.

He greeted her, "I'm calling after Miss MacKenna—"

"Of course you are."

"I haven't seen her in town these last few days; I worry. Is she well?"

Alexis casually pushed the door open with the toes of her boot as Moencopi approached, her arms full of bloodied linens to be washed.

"It is a monthly difficulty," Moencopi explained curtly, edging by Liam in the doorway. "I beg your pardon."

The color drained from Liam's cheeks at the sight of the soiled linens and he turned away, gagging against the back of his hand. He waved at the women with the other, coughing on his words. "Say no more." Hustling down the front walk, he said, "I'll come back at week's end to check on Miss MacKenna."

"I'm sure you will." Alexis snarled. She didn't dare to hope Maeve might be in better shape by then so she, herself, might tell Liam to stop calling—not as though she seemed especially inclined to.

Alexis guessed Maeve enjoyed his attention in Rafaele's absence and worried she was enjoying it a little too much.

It was a week and a half before Maeve left bed for longer than the time required to freshen its linens.

She remained in her stained nightgown, checking herself in a mirror to find no hint of Death in her eyes though her complexion was pale as the bedsheets before she'd ruined them. The scar where Dallahan's whip encircled her wrist was faded to a shade of white scarcely differing from her natural skin tone. The injury wasn't going to fully heal.

It was especially upsetting; she'd never scarred before.

Maeve needed a break from the same ceiling, the same walls, the same mattress, the same carpet with the same blood stain beside the bed; she reluctantly emerged from the room, bracing herself against the wall as she toddled down the hallway. Being off the false leg so long made her uncertain on it again.

Sounds of China clinking against China and silverware scraping plates indicated the women were having tea and breakfast without conversation.

Maeve stood in the archway of the dining room, watching as they glanced at her, faces an array of emotions, and all three too stunned to stand upon her arrival.

"Miss Chesterfield," said Maeve, "I'm terrible sorry for ruinin' yer sheets 'n' carpet. When I have money, I'll replace them."

"Maeve—" Alexis gasped.

"Miss Redbird—both of ye—I can't thank ye enough for takin' care of me, 'n' I'm …" Maeve's voice shook, and she swallowed hard. "I'm sorry for what ye had to bear witness to."

"Miss MacKenna—" the twins cried in unison.

The women at the table chattered over one another, dismissing her apologies and gratitude as if she owed them none of it.

Alexis jumped from her seat. "Ladies mustn't lurk," she said, helping Maeve to a chair at the table.

She imagined Alexis feared for the upholstery's longevity; after all, it was no secret Maeve was still bleeding—albeit lightly.

"Please tell me you're hungry for breakfast," said Kököle, grabbing a clean plate and selecting bits and pieces of food from the communal platters at the center of the table: A helping of spinach pudding, some cream sauce, and several hardboiled eggs on the side. She set the full plate in front of Maeve and sat back down, watching her expectantly.

"I amn't, not especially."

It was a peculiar thing to be hungry and nauseated all at once; similar to what she experienced during pregnancy.

But she was no longer expecting and assumed the symptoms would vanish along with the baby. Still she was plagued by nausea, fatigue, and tender breasts.

Tears splattered her plate and she pushed it away, slumping forward and resting her cheek against the table. There, she wept.

Moments later, Kököle was at Maeve's side. She pulled her into a hug and just held her when Maeve didn't reciprocate.

Moencopi joined her at the opposite side, kneeling and resting a hand on Maeve's nightgown over her right thigh.

Alexis joined the silent condolences as best she could, caressing Maeve's head and back.

Maeve's constant companion of the last couple months was gone, and though she was small, she'd made a huge impact. Never had Maeve felt more alone.

Words she hadn't been able to articulate surfaced, pouring from her with brutal tears. "Two weeks ago, I had the world, 'n' now there's nothin'. No idea what she looked like. I didn't get to hold her, name her, love her. I've got nothin' to commemorate tha' sweet little life. Just memories of illness, loss, heartache 'n' nothin' more. It was to the outside world as if her heart didn't ever beat. She was rumors at a sermon for strangers to gossip about but she was me every-thin'." With a ragged breath, she bawled, "It's all me fault she's gone now!"

"Miss MacKenna," said Moencopi and Kököle.

Moencopi continued on her own, "Please do not blame yourself."

"Oh my God," Alexis said. "How could it be your fault? Nothing you said or did could cause something like this. Right, ladies?"

The twins were too quick to agree.

Maeve's head snapped up from the table. "Do not ye get it?" she cried. "I saw her as a burden 'n' an embarrassment 'n' I was terrified—" *of childbirth, of what the townsfolk would think of me ... Terrified of what Raf would do—* "'n' while we were at church, I ... I prayed to ... to not have her anymore. I didn't expect me prayers would be answered—"

And answer them, Dallahan did; the sleeveen had said as much.

Alexis frowned. "You can't honestly believe your thoughts resulted in—"

"Then ye explain to me what happened!" *Explain away Dallahan!*

She dropped her head with a sharp exhalation. "But I can't."

"Why not?"

"Because I ... I don't have the answers. I don't have any answers. I'm sorry."

"Yea," said Maeve with a shuddering sob. "Me, too."

After she choked down a little bit of the breakfast Kököle served her, Maeve retreated to her room, accompanied by Kököle and Moencopi. She asked them to leave. Twice. They were steadfast, expressing concern about what she might do if left alone.

It was for that reason Maeve challenged them: "Ye know it's true."

"What's true?" said Kököle warily.

"The reason I lost me baby. Tha' it was all me fault for askin' to be ... unencumbered."

The sisters exchanged glances. It was Moencopi to say, "I am certain we do not follow."

"'N' I'm certain ye're lyin'!" Maeve snapped. "Ye opened the door to Davidson." She corrected herself bitterly: "Dallahan."

At the blank stares, she went a step further. "Death. The collector of souls. The reaper?" When they still returned blank stares, she groaned; that groan became a growl. "The skeleton man, the skeleton man!"

The women sighed their recognition.

Maeve panted, slowly calming. "So ye *do* know who tha' is."

"Yes. We do," replied Moencopi, "but we call him Másauwu."

"He was at the church tha' mornin' I made tha' awful prayer. I spoke with him out front. He knew I was sick 'n' he gave me those tansy cookies, tha' poison, 'n' I ate them—"

Kököle pulled Maeve into her arms. "I'm sure had you known, you never would've done so."

Maeve wished she could be so certain, herself. It was the same with her parents' deaths.

"Shh—" Kököle cooed, rubbing Maeve's back.

Maeve's thoughts turned to being embraced; Kököle's sturdy frame enveloping hers, her skin warm, soft, and smooth. She smelled of lemon and apple.

Kököle was comfort embodied, and Maeve understood then what Alexis saw in her beyond her obvious physical beauty.

Alexis.

Maeve pulled back. "Ye mustn't ever tell Alexis. She won't understand."

Moencopi nodded. "Oh, we are in agreement about that."

"Alexis is … uneasy around the paranormal," Kököle commented. "To know Másauwu was in her house, I imagine, might lead her to do something rash."

"She chooses her company poorly given her aversions," said Moencopi.

Kököle chuckled knowingly. "I warned her about keeping company with Wolf but she must really love him since she didn't listen. I've seen no soul so narrow-mindedly loyal."

Maeve looked at Kököle sharply. "What do ye mean ye warned her about Rafaele?" She, too, had been warned about him, though by Edison. She, too, had failed to listen. And she, too, suffered the consequences.

Kököle and Moencopi exchanged glances before the former answered, "Our dear Wolf has a remarkable way of attracting unearthly creatures." She nodded, eyebrows raised, at Maeve.

A silence stretched between the three women and it seemed to Maeve that Moencopi and Kököle were engaging in wordless conversation.

Moencopi held out her hand to Maeve with a nod toward the dining room. "I am thirsty, and you could certainly benefit from a drink as well."

"Honest, I'm fine—" and yet Maeve's hand was encircled by Moencopi's, accompanied by pin-prickling pain as if she'd stuck her hand in cold water. She was pulled to her feet and led from the bedroom as she threw a pleading glance at Kököle, who smiled impishly and waved but made no motion to follow.

Moencopi pushed her into a seat and Maeve felt a small release of fluid from her quim with the motion; sitting, standing, anything other than lying prone did that. How she hated it, each sensation a reminder of what was no longer there. In addition, the constant wet made for constant welts on very sensitive skin. At least the misery would've been over by now with her regular monthly cycle.

"You enjoy this weather, do you not?" Moencopi asked while pouring some cooled tea from that morning's brew.

Maeve shrugged absently, turning her attention to her hand; she noticed tiny blisters where Moencopi's skin had touched hers. *What the—*

"This is my favorite time of the year. I assumed it would be too cold for you."

She pressed a blister with her fingertip, flinching; it hurt. They were moisture blisters.

"Yea, uh huh," she replied as absently as earlier. Maeve glanced up when the motion of Moencopi taking a seat caught her eye.

Moencopi cupped her glass between her hands and caught Maeve's gaze. A small smile toyed at the corners of her mouth, a twinkle of mischief in her gaze. She winked.

Maeve promptly turned her stare to the glass between Moencopi's hands. The tea inside was moving, congealing into the recognizable form of a female body, dancing and twirling gracefully.

She gasped, her gaze snapping to meet Moencopi's. "Ye're like me?"

"I am," Moencopi replied with strange brevity, "yes."

"Ye're like me!"

"We are sisters." Moencopi gave her a strange smile and held up the hand she'd taken Maeve's with, revealing a palm and fingertips blistered with a heat burn.

Maeve was awash with emotions: amazement, wonder, rapture, feelings of finally belonging. Someone else could possibly understand her.

There too was guilt. She hurt someone—accidentally or otherwise—who walked a path on Earth like hers. "I am ... so sorry. Moencopi. I—I did tha' to ye." She swallowed and motioned to Moencopi's wounded hand with her own.

"We should be careful with each other." There was a pause. "You have questions. I imagine you must."

Maeve opened her mouth but there were no words. She had questions—more than she could articulate. Instead of anything intelligent or at least carefully thought out, Maeve blurted, "How on earth are ye doin' tha'?"

"Not Earth," Moencopi chuckled, wagging a finger at her. "Water. I am of water, and it of me."

Maeve frowned, trying to make sense of what she'd just said—there must've been some loss in translation. "Ye're ... a ... *Moruadh?*"

"Merrow?" she repeated with a furrowed brow. "I have heard that term in my past." Moencopi's eyes tracked imaginary motion on the ceiling as if searching there for answers. "It is not incorrect. Let me say it this way: I am to water as you are to fire. And do not be so impressed by what I do. You have these capabilities as well, Miss MacKenna. Such skills are acquired through years of practice. Discipline. Control. But your soul is of fire, which is why you will struggle more to use your talents so … lackadaisically."

"Lackadaisically?" Maeve frowned. "I can use it—"

"When it has been necessary."

"Whenever I've wanted to!"

Moencopi's furrowed brow opened, her right arching. "You have not exercised restraint over what you have done. If it was a desire to revoke Francisco Esquivar of his right to live, why also cause the volcano Krakatoa to erupt? You lack self-control."

Maeve whispered, "What?"

Solemn as ever, Moencopi said, "You heard me."

"I—the volcano—tha' was me fault?" Her voice shook. To have her fear confirmed by someone who wasn't there was humbling. "How do ye know about the volcano, 'n' what happened to Esquivar?"

"When something of such significance happens, the mortals may miss it, but we—the greater ones—we do not." Moencopi reached across the table, hesitating with her hand over Maeve's before opting to rest it on her sleeve. "Though you were at fault, fault is hardly intention. You did what you needed to survive."

"Just like a monster."

"A monster no more than I … Or my darling sister. Or the couple others like us. But you *do* have so much to learn."

Maeve withdrew her arm from Moencopi's grasp and said nothing as she smoothed her sleeve.

"Fire is notoriously difficult to control. Consider this: Men have learned to control water, to bend it to their will. They stop it in its tracks by building dams. Even beavers have the strength and skill to do the latter. For centuries, men have forced water to go where they wished it; take the aqueducts in Rome for example. But fire, ah, fire: Fire rages. Fire consumes and must be fought. The desire of man to steal it that he would traipse where gods dwell … to risk the wrath of those gods; to risk injury, eternal torture, even death to possess fleetingly the beguiling tempest!" Moencopi caught her breath and tipped her head toward Maeve with a dazzling smile that revealed a beauty on par with Kököle's. "This is you, am I correct?"

"I … I amn't all tha'," whispered Maeve, scratching at the nape of her neck, and blinking furiously.

Moencopi coaxed the little tea sprite from her glass.

"Water is nothing more than a liquid. It is … uncomplicated."

The tea sprite danced over to Maeve where it evaporated near her hands.

"Fire, as I understand it, is neither liquid, solid, nor gas, but a chemical reaction. Surely you can tell where I am going with this?"

Maeve inhaled deeply, nodding in silence. If she were to learn to control her element, she'd have to find some way to simplify it first.

Maeve sat on the bed with a deep exhalation. The house was at rest and in its silence, she had renewed clarity. *I amn't gonna be a monster*, she decided. *I'm gonna at least try to do this right.*

Perhaps rather than conjuring fire, she could work to control existing flame. Maeve took the pillar candle from its nightstand and lit it with a strike match. She gazed at the single flame, watching it grow and shrink with her breath.

Fire *was* easy to manipulate; Moencopi was wrong. A single breath eliminated flame, but she could blow and blow, and no amount of huffing or puffing could have made floodwaters ebb.

She blew a single, sharp puff of air and the flame winked from existence, leaving behind a single curl of smoke and a pool of wax at the base of its wick.

Maeve tilted the candle slightly, watching the wax move like water in a glass. Her eyebrows jumped.

She held out her left palm, holding her breath as she tipped the candle until the wax poured out.

It met her skin and the world bloomed in sensation, a warmth spreading from her lower abdomen out through the rest of her body. Breath quickened, rushing in her throat with her thundering heartbeat.

It dawned on her like a flash-lamp going off: that was how she felt whenever Rafaele turned an amorous smile on her. The reaction at her point of no return, when she surrendered to his embrace and failed to emerge from it until after he was finished with her—and she with him.

Putting her finger on her reaction merely compounded her bewilderment. Why would the sensation arouse her?

The wax wasn't solidifying. She used her right-hand index-finger to manipulate it, creating first something vaguely wolf-shaped, and then a heart.

She willed her skin to cool enough for the wax to harden but when she touched the heart, it cracked into two pieces split vertically down its center.

There came a gentle knock on the bedroom door. "Miss MacKenna? May I come in?"

"It's Maeve. Call me Maeve." She squeezed her hand around the broken heart and pressed her fist to her still-tender breast, drawing a steadying breath. "Come in."

Kököle opened the door and stepped inside. "I hear you had a … little discovery about my sister?"

"I admit it's comfortin' tha' I amn't the only one who's like me." Maeve lifted her gaze from her fist. "'N' ye?"

"Me?"

"Ye're also like us."

Kököle regarded Maeve with expression unchanged.

Maeve swallowed. "… Aren't ye?"

She bobbed her head. "I am."

"Ye must be earth."

Kököle's lips raised into a tiny smile and she shook her head slightly.

"Air?"

"Spirit. The center of all things." After a pause, she augmented, "Love."

"I have … ye to thank for Rafaele lovin' me?" Her face went hot.

Kököle laughed. "Strictly speaking, you have yourself to thank, and I, the two of you for me."

"Huh?"

"My existence is a bit more complicated and a discussion for another time."

Maeve opened her hand, her gaze flickering to it.

"Oh, honey." Kököle pouted, covering the broken heart in Maeve's palm with her own.

"I had this comin', ye know. I've … I've taken lives, 'n' I deserved to be punished for me misdeeds."

"Oh—no!" she gasped. "No! Why would you think something so dreadful?"

"Because of the Rede. Ye Moqui believe in the Rede, don't ye?"

Kököle shook her head. "The Rede?"

"First do no harm. Whatever ye give the universe is returned to ye threefold."

"Mmm." She stood and walked to the window, bracing herself against the sill. "What a narrow view of our world."

"Excuse me?"

"Maybe the universe isn't as ... unbending as it is the way you view it. Sure, we of course strive to use our gifts benevolently. The Hopituh Shi-nu-mu wiiki of balance and harmony are more understanding and less ... strict. In time, this balance and harmony is to become our source of power. Listen: Sometimes it's necessary to do something undesirable to accomplish a greater good. Even our benign gods behave impishly ... Make mistakes." She turned to Maeve with her hand pressed between her breasts and a sour face. "Or make terrible errors in judgment."

"What happened to ye tha' ye feel tha' way?"

Kököle whispered, "Even love can suffer a broken heart."

Maeve pouted. "I appreciate tha' ye're tryin' to lift me spirits. How I wish it were the way ye describe it. But that's not me belief 'n' I must still abide the Rede, strict as it may sound to ye. Tha' means reapin' the punishment I sow."

"I hope you will grant yourself permission to heal. You deserve closure."

She closed her eyes against the threat of tears. "Please go," Maeve whispered, her voice raspy.

Kököle exhaled. "I'll respect your wishes. Should you desire to talk, you know where to find me."

CHAPTER 12

 iam had always prided himself on his emotional constitution. But this town, its people, the desert, and his hotel room were all conspiring to test his resolve. That he couldn't tell a living shrub from a dead one, find a single honest resident, and the walls of his rental room were encroaching on him inch by steady inch, Liam was developing a solid hatred of the place and this regrettable situation.

The only thing to keep this from escalating to full-blown detestation was the single friendly face for miles around; the woman who was, he was sure, being deliberately hidden from him. Initially, he'd given it little consideration; he knew how bad womanly problems could be from observing how poorly his dear Elizabeth weathered her monthlies.

But it had been longer than a week now.

Weeks, as it were, of the same old stacks of paperwork at Marshal Cummings's office. Weeks of the same old files hauled back to weeks of the same old barren hotel room walls as they further intruded on his space. Weeks of daily being turned away at Alexis's door.

He'd finally—begrudgingly—allowed others to make the deliveries for him.

Thank the good Lord it was Sunday.

Today he would reap the results of his hard-fought patience and courtesy, with the bonus of getting out of that God-forsaken room.

Liam adjusted his lapels and straightened his tie, taking lengthy inventory of his appearance in the mirror atop the bureau before departing.

Redington's weather had become far kinder in recent weeks. It must've been in the mid-sixties when he stepped out.

It would've been a marvelous day for a walk with a friend; if, as it were, those wretched shrews allowed him to call. They were hiding something.

There was no time to dwell as the church came into view, its parishioners being led inside by Brother Thurman.

Seeing as the outside weather wasn't so hellish, Liam noticed the separation of the pious from the devout; that is, the unsurprising disappearance from church those who were going less for spiritual enlightenment and more for relief from the unforgiving desert elements.

Notably absent from the group: the women residing with Alexis Chesterfield. Liam didn't presume Alexis or the Native Americans would be in attendance but he prayed Maeve would be. He hated thinking of her as a liar but so far, she'd been to church once since he pressured her to go.

He hoped it was because she was still unwell; he refused to believe otherwise.

Liam sat by himself in the last row of pews, several rows empty between him and anyone else. Nobody acknowledged his presence and that was just as well; he wasn't there to be seen, or to socialize.

He was a silent observer throughout the service, taking copious mental notes of who closed her eyes or who bowed his head in prayer, which folks looked like they could benefit from a confessional—if, of course, they followed the true faith.

The theme of this sermon revolved around weathering life's difficulties, and ways to handle the inevitabilities of disappointments, temptation, and betrayal.

Naturally, none of these things applied to Liam so he took the opportunity to pray.

A half hour later—short by Liam's standards—Brother Thurman dismissed the congregation and they quietly filed out of the building.

Liam lingered, taking in the solemn but peaceful atmosphere.

"Mr. O'Doherty," Brother Thurman greeted him from the pulpit. "I couldn't miss you all alone in the back during my sermon. God does miracles when His followers work together."

Liam didn't recall ever hearing such bollocks.

"How goes it?"

He wandered to the nearest cooling unit to feign interest in inspecting it. "Days are long," Liam replied, "and my work unforgiving. I was ... hoping Miss MacKenna and her entourage would be in attendance today." He hated missing the young woman so much.

"You and me both." The preacher closed his bible. "I take it you miss your friends."

Friends? thought Liam. *I don't have friends.* He asked, "Is it uncommon for those ladies to miss church?"

Brother Thurman sighed. "I'm afraid not."

"Do you ever ... work during the week?"

He chuckled. "I'm a student of God. Students seldom take time off."

Liam cringed inwardly. "Oh, I meant ... are you in church during the week?"

The preacher nodded.

"The reason I ask is ... Well, I've been told Miss Chesterfield was here on a Monday ... September tenth, I believe."

"September tenth?" Brother Thurman nodded once more, this time smiling. "I remember it well. That was the day the cooling machines were installed."

Liam's heart plummeted. "Was Miss Chesterfield here then?"

"Oh yes. It was her whole little team working together to fulfill a promise."

Dammit! "Excuse me? What do you mean 'her whole little team?'"

"Miss Chesterfield, Price, Stilwell, and Brown—though mostly Brown stood watch while the others toiled. Struck me as a nervous fellow."

"I see." Liam bobbed his head somberly. "These machines are some remarkable business."

"They were an answer to my prayers," replied Brother Thurman. "A testament to God's wonder and promises."

Trying not to scowl, Liam replied, "Indeed."

Mr. Bailey folded the set of ivory dressing table brushes in some plain brown packing paper. "I believe you're going to single-handedly fund my new home in California."

Liam made no comment, which the shopkeeper acknowledged with a frown.

"I can assume this is going to Miss MacKenna as usual?"

The brush, comb, and mirror would soon be in good company, following the clothing, shoes, satin slippers, perfume, down-filled pillows, earrings, a necklace, several dainty hats, handbags, and a couple pairs of gloves.

He sent them with the intent of helping her recoup her losses and rebuild her life, and assumed she appreciated it.

It was all in the name of love.

Friendship, he swiftly corrected himself. *Friendship*! Maeve was the closest thing he had to a friend.

After Liam wrote the requisite note that shrunk in length with each gift, he hastened to his hotel room, as the pile of papers he received yesterday wouldn't research itself. *Such a shame it won't.*

Lately, the same old stacks enjoyed rearranging themselves when his back was turned; a pastime he didn't appreciate. It brought back memories of things he once believed and remembered more clearly than he cared for. It reminded him of all those cases that he bent over backward to disprove were not entirely disproved. The cases he'd lied about just to be able to call them "closed."

Liam shook his head. *No.* Such things were fairytale foolishness, games played by a young girl he once knew who had a fantastic sleight of hand and a vivid imagination.

Amid the new stack of paper were numerous newspaper articles recounting a stagecoach heist, its resulting deaths and the search for the culprits, then the apprehension of their chief suspect; a complete transcript of the subsequent court hearing; images taken and sketches drawn from the day of the execution.

While her name was butchered several different ways throughout the articles and court transcript, and the sketches left much to be desired, the images were unmistakably of Maeve standing on the gallows.

Liam recounted what happened to the poor woman from the point she arrived in Arizona Territory: she'd traveled hundreds of miles just to deal with the murder of both parents and was forced to survive on her own—first in the unforgiving desert and then in the lawless wild west town. It hardly seemed fair that hanging would be her fate.

But she escaped the execution against jury's decision and judge's order. And numerous newspaper articles indicated there were others in Tombstone who wished lynching upon her. There had been a call for vigilante justice.

Out of the blue, her verdict was changed to not guilty; Francisco Esquivar, deceased, was blamed instead—and had already served his death sentence in a spectacular explosion in a Tucson granary.

Somehow Liam doubted those events absolved Maeve of her guilt in the eyes of those who lost loved ones or property that fateful day. And those in attendance of the trial knew where her home was in Redington after she was forced to provide her address to the court.

He reached for a smaller stack of paperwork to verify some of her testimony against what had been written in multiple newspaper articles; the stack wasn't where he left it.

Liam was certain he'd set it right on the corner of his desk. Nonplussed, he resumed his musing, flipping through what was where he actually put it.

Anybody in attendance at Maeve's trial could've been the one who destroyed the Tiff and Tawny.

It stood to reason they had more motive to destroy her home—presumably with her inside it—than anyone in Redington.

More than anyone in Shadow Wolf Pack.

Liam groaned, retreating from the paperwork to fetch himself coffee and roll around in his head information about the town and its residents. Much to his dismay his mug was nowhere to be found. Without his drink, he went to his bed to review another file he'd left on the bedside table.

Brother Thurman's history revealed a few points that at least gave Liam reason to chuckle even if they were entirely irrelevant to the investigation.

Thurman—whose Christian name was Brother—was raised from infancy at an orphanage with a twin named Sister by the matron of the institution. Brother became a preacher, and Sister, a nun. The circumstances were a bit of topsy-turvy whimsy befitting a Gilbert and Sullivan comic opera. Reminiscing about it made Liam smile as few things did anymore.

From there, he reviewed his notes on the testimony given by the restaurant and hotel staff and owners. As the restaurant had—albeit limited—bar service, if he 'followed the money' as he'd been taught, he could conceive the Tiff and Tawny was considered its chief competition.

To his surprise—and disappointment—the restaurant and the saloon had a history of mutually beneficial transactions. The Tiff and Tawny sold some snacks and appetizers purchased from the hotel's restaurant while the restaurant, in turn, had exclusive access to a handful of alcoholic blends Maeve concocted that proved delicious and popular.

Liam sniffed around for anyone else who may have wanted the saloon closed but there wasn't much in terms of representation from the Temperance and purity movements in Redington; nobody in town claimed to be familiar with either group and he hadn't known those people to ever downplay association with them, so it was likely they were being honest.

For once.

Going door-to-door yielded little in the way of significant progress toward pinpointing the culprit, only revealing petty intrigue: Widow Marsden promptly blamed her neighbor Mrs. Kaylock, describing in detail the turkey-resembling Kaylock entering and setting fire to a downtown building.

Liam smiled wryly in recollection. The building didn't match the appearance of the Tiff and Tawny, and remained standing to that day.

Naturally, he followed up with Mrs. Kaylock next door, who denied the accusations as expected, and explained to him that Marsden was bent out of shape—not much unlike her own prominent aquiline nose—following Kaylock's Newfoundland urinating in Marsden's flowerbed, subsequently killing her garden.

He verified with ease Mrs. Kaylock's alibi, which left him nobody who might've been seeking revenge against a Tiff and Tawny resident.

As far as Liam deduced, Maeve was the primary target—and there were people out there who wanted her dead no matter how he wished otherwise. Though he didn't want to admit it to himself, the investigation of this seemingly straight-forward arson had taken another turn.

No wonder they'd called for his expertise.

The bad news was that he needed to go investigate the families and friends of Joe Stanifor and Pat Lynch.

On the bright side, it meant leaving Redington; unfortunately, heading to Tombstone merely meant trading one god-forsaken hellhole for another.

The bloody terror finally stopped, taking with it Alexis's fear Maeve would succumb to the miscarriage.

Maeve's tears were ebbing as well, though she was slipping bit by bit into what Alexis recognized as melancholy. She'd last seen the likes of it in Rafaele, and it scared her as much now—if not more. She didn't want to lose Maeve to it and couldn't imagine what Rafaele would do under such circumstances.

Maeve failed to take her up on her offer to talk. This was as much a relief as it was a disappointment.

The moments when Maeve was herself, Alexis enjoyed her company. Not in the same way she enjoyed Kököle's, and she kept telling herself as much to ensure she wouldn't forget it.

Alexis reminisced to when she and the twins brought Maeve to Redington. She'd had to convince herself that when she was certain Maeve could've been coerced into being receptive to her affectionate overtures, it was all in her imagination.

And the points Maeve might've instigated affectionate overtures were doubly her imagination.

Maybe what Francisco once told her was less absurd than she wanted to believe; she was jealous of Maeve and Rafaele. Jealous he could have Maeve when she couldn't. Jealous another woman commanded his attention so thoroughly. Jealous—even fearful—of the idea Maeve would replace her as Rafaele's trusted right-hand. Someday when they said their "I do's," Alexis would find herself alone. Again.

Alexis turned yet another page of Jules Verne's *The Green Ray* without having read a single word of it. Because that's what she was doing: reading.

Any case, Alexis had numerous reasons to be thankful Moencopi and Kököle chose to stay in Redington. Having to deal with Maeve and the loss of her baby was even more terrifying than being alone with her and awash with whatever tension she was sure they had between them.

The paper gave a juicy rip as she turned another page in the book. With a growl, she smacked the book on her bedside table and squeezed her eyes shut.

After a few moments, Alexis swung her legs off the side of her bed and ran both hands down her face. It made her ill to think that under other circumstances, Maeve could've been her spoon.

I need Kököle.

Or maybe a kiss from Maeve ... to leave no doubt.

Maeve wouldn't be the first lover Alexis couldn't have due to—among other things—irreconcilable differences in sexual preferences.

It didn't matter.

Alexis jumped to her feet.

Maeve had Rafaele, she had Kököle, and everybody was perfectly happy with both arrangements.

Except for Liam and Moencopi, respectively.

Being in such close quarters with the three women was driving Alexis crazy. She wondered if the straitjacket Marshal Cummings kept at his desk would fit a woman of her proportions.

Taking a steadying breath, Alexis left the relative sanctuary of her bedroom to pursue breakfast.

Maeve came from the dining room and bustled by her, making fleeting eye-contact as she passed.

"Morning?" Alexis offered, getting nothing in reply.

When her friendship with Maeve was tenuous at best, introducing a romantic element into it would certainly be their ruin; Alexis was better off maintaining her distance and keeping with Kököle, though neither had ever considered their relationship a long-term solution.

Or she needed someone with whom she could happily spend the rest of her life, not as though she could marry. Did she need that formality to feel permanently and wholly loved?

It still would've been a nice option to have available, she supposed.

Alexis stood in the archway, watching Moencopi corral water into a glass from a puddle on the table.

"Studies going well?" said Alexis, leaning against the doorjamb.

"Miss MacKenna is not at her best so early in the day … and she frustrates easily." Moencopi glanced at Alexis. "I apologize for the mess."

"Don't be so hard on her; she's only a teener."

Moencopi gave Alexis a peculiar look she didn't much care for so she changed the subject. "I … never got the chance to say thanks."

"For?"

"Staying!" Despite herself, Alexis laughed. "God only knows what I'd have done with Maeve had you two not been here a month ago." *Panic, certainly.* "And … for everything you and Kökö have done for—with—her, since."

Moencopi shrugged. "It is in the best interests of everybody that Maeve learn to better handle her gifts."

"You mean her temper," said Alexis, "and that's not what I'm talking about."

"Oh?" Moencopi arched her eyebrows.

"You forget I've worked in the circus."

Her eyebrows falling along with the corners of her mouth, Moencopi said, "Tread here carefully."

Yet Alexis smiled. "Hear me out, let me finish. I've seen my fair share of rigged games and card tricks executed deftly by magicians to recognize sleight of hand when I see it."

Moencopi looked no less unamused.

Alexis dropped her voice. "The lessons with Maeve? Don't tell me you elected to start coaching her right now and *didn't* intend it as a distraction from her loss. So … thanks."

"We are family." The twinkle returned to Moencopi's eyes. "It is what we do."

CHAPTER 13

t had been quiet; a blessing and curse in equal measure. In the silence of his office, Liam heard the voices bicker in his head but none said anything helpful. He sorted through the paperwork strewn across his desk, organizing it into stacks according to its uselessness.

Useless.

More useless.

Most useless.

The paperwork in its infinite uselessness was like most of the bodies wasting space in Redington. He was going to die there a failure. A nobody. And that, he feared above all else.

The front door of the marshal's office popped open, followed by the man himself, lowering from his mouth a bottle of mother's ruin.

Cummings did an unabashed double-take. "What in the blazes of all hell are you doing? It's a holiday. Lay off for God's sake and let everyone enjoy himself for once. Nobody's gonna come by anyway. You're working yourself dumb."

Liam working himself literally dumb was in all likelihood the marshal's thinly-veiled wishful thinking.

"Just because President Arthur decided willy-nilly to call this 'a day of thanks,'" Liam mocked, "is no reason for me to stop my investigation." He turned his attention to some receipts brought in from the town grocer. They didn't reek of alcohol the way certain marshals did. "Until those who perished find justice, this town hasn't seen God's grace." He muttered to himself, "A woman pregnant out of wedlock mentioned during a church sermon a month ago. What *is* this world coming to? Disgrace."

He spelled it out in the likely event Cummings didn't catch his drift, enunciating each word: "There is nothing to celebrate."

Marshal Cummings cleared his throat.

Liam glanced up in time to see him shrug.

"Everyone's in church. So good luck to you."

"You're not there," Liam pointed out as Cummings turned to leave.

"Got to drinking early, showed up late, forgot there was even a service today." Seemingly to himself, he added, "Thursday's a strange day for being in church."

"May that serve as a lesson to you."

Cummings let himself out of the office muttering, "What a joy *you* are to have around."

Liam exhaled. Loose-Morals-Marshal wasn't worth a rebuttal.

He resumed a review of his notes on the case once the desk was more organized.

He spent the last month of his life re-interviewing every soul in town following Cummings's so-called initial investigation. There were holes in testimony as wide as the Canyon Diablo crater, and differing answers from one person to the next. Hell, even one person's story changed from day to day.

The more perceivably honest people talked about Shadow Wolf Pack, likely because Liam was the impartial outsider they were waiting for to rescue them from an uncontrolled criminal element in their sad little lawless town. But even following the earful about everything the Pack was, everything it did, everyone who was rumored to have any connection to it in even the most minute capacity, there were still holes.

Redington's dirty laundry was out on the clothesline, so to speak, but Liam was still no closer to finding a suspect.

Cummings couldn't even be ruled out. After all, his investigation scarcely deserved to bear the name—as if he were hiding his own trail of evidence.

The marshal was a smoker who used the same brand of matches as those recovered at the crime scene and he'd reacted peculiarly to the discovery of the barrels of accelerant.

The reason Liam had been reluctant to pin the crime on the badge was because he was desperate to implicate Shadow Wolf instead.

He imagined he'd receive accolade upon accolade for putting that character behind bars.

How sublime the celebration, how sweet the justice; he could taste it.

The door swung open again. "O'Doherty."

Liam suppressed a groan at Marshal Cummings's voice. "What."

"You've got some work today after all. Got someone here you haven't interviewed yet."

Without glancing from the record in his hands, Liam muttered, "Send him in."

Footfalls came near, the door clicking shut and a chair grating across the floor, then creaking with the weight of a body settling on it.

No rustling skirts, nor tell-tale *chink* of rowels. A large dandy with what was likely an old war injury to his leg, reluctant to be there—all judging by his shuffling, uneven gait.

This was going to be a rollicking waste of time same as every interrogation prior, with the added nuisance of it not being accompanied by a mellifluous voice and a fair chest. Liam's sigh came out a little louder than he intended.

"Am I in trouble, Mr. Detective?" said a meek voice.

"No," droned Liam, "it's just questioning. Name?"

A loud swallow. "Nioclás."

"First or last."

"First. It's, uh, Nioclás Davidson."

Liam pressed his index finger into his cheek and glanced up. Davidson was a proper skinny fellow with heavy five o'clock shadow and weary brown eyes beneath a substantial flip of dark brown hair. He was a dandy alright, donning his Sunday best in tones of deep blues and purples that in contrast made his skin appear sallow. Maybe he was ill or even dying; Liam couldn't decide. Further, he didn't care.

"Your profession?"

Davidson leaned back, wringing his hand in the air and seeming to search for a response from the ceiling. "Oh ... I don't know ... Undertaker?"

Liam frowned. Redington had no resident undertaker of which he had been informed. He supposed it had to have one, whether it was a man dedicated to the chore or somebody who moonlighted when work at his day job grew scant. "Why are you being disingenuous?"

Meek matchstick man Davidson shot forward, slapping his palms on the desk, his face screwed into a maniacal expression of equal parts teeth and animosity. "Because," he overenunciated, "I'm lying."

Liam drew in a deep breath as his recently organized paperwork scattered, much of it fluttering to the floor. He met Davidson's stare over the rim of his glasses with a twitch in his lower eyelid.

"Having some trouble with your ... little investigation, are you?" Davidson taunted. "Can't find the culprit in a small town of but a handful of players? The needle in a haystack where the hay's already been cleared away for you? It's almost as if you're choosing to fail in such a woefully simple task. Going to go back to your wife with your tail tucked between your legs?"

"How do you—"

"—know about your wife when your dreams stray to Miss MacKenna? Isn't it obvious? Everyone sees you doting on her, spending scads of money that would better serve Elizabeth and your unborn son ... Stephen Vincent, is it?"

Nobody knew of the names he and his wife had tossed around while in the comfort of their marriage bed.

Between his words, his demeanor, and his—something strange, Liam couldn't put a finger on—Davidson was driving him to frenzy. Davidson was driving him to—

"Go ahead." He smirked. "Draw your gun."

Liam followed through, aiming the muzzle at Davidson's face. Davidson wasn't concerned, licking his upper lip in a swift, tic-like gesture. He spoke to something off to his side: "This one has a temper, doesn't he, Love?"

As he reclined in his seat, Davidson's gaze casually slid back to Liam and he kicked his feet onto the desk, folding his hands together over his lap. "Pull the trigger. See what happens."

With a wordless yell, Liam charged forward, jamming the muzzle of his gun to the center of Davidson's forehead. Beads of sweat appeared across Liam's brow, his hand shaking, jaw clenched, neck and face aflame.

"Pathetic," clucked Davidson, raising his cool gaze to meet Liam's wild eyes. "Did you just sweat on my trousers?" He tilted his head down. "You did. You got sweat on my leg, you impertinent child. And look at you: still unable to shoot me."

Liam groaned, staggering back several feet awash with throbbing behind his eyes; the gun thumped unceremoniously to the wood floor.

Davidson smiled. "Coward."

Never in his life had Liam wanted to do something more than he wanted to kill Davidson, and yet while he had the power, he lacked strength enough to squeeze the trigger. He felt drunk; it was positively dreadful.

"Really can't handle the heat here, can you?"

Doused in sweat and shaking violently, Liam's gaze turned to the desk between them. The paperwork scattered the way it was before he'd organized it. *Exactly* the way it had been upon his arrival that morning; he remembered it. His voice trembling, Liam answered, "Information is being withheld from me." His voice cracked, "People in this town are lying."

"I know the truth," offered Davidson with a devious smile. "And you can trust me. I know everything."

Gripping the table around its edge, Liam raised his gaze to meet Davidson's. "Given your behavior toward me, I highly doubt I can trust you. Everyone else in this hell-hole has stood in my way during my investigation. Why should you, of all people, be different?"

"Me, 'of all people,' Mr. O'Doherty? Why … I'm offended, my fun little plaything."

"Then answer my question!" roared Liam.

Davidson replied apathetically, "I don't hold Shadow Wolf in high esteem."

"And may I ask why?" Liam adjusted his fogged-over spectacles with a shaking hand.

"He's a common criminal. A thief. In fact, Shadow Wolf stole something of great value from me—priceless, really—and I'm desperate to possess it again before he ruins it. Barring that item's return, I'd take the Wolf's head on a platter. Or in a noose. His body riddled with lead. Picked apart by vultures. Whichever."

"So what information do you think you can provide me?"

Davidson stood from his chair, stretching out across the desk like a cat waking from a nap, manipulating some of the remaining pieces of paper around. He read them upside-down, emphasizing two words: "Shadow Wolf. Shadow Wolf. Shadow Wolf, Shadow Wolf, Shadow Wolf!" He caught Liam's glare and pouted. "Oh, I'm sorry. Did I make a mess of your little desk?"

"How is this helping?"

Davidson sighed. "I do hate it when the pawns are resistant to play. There's an awful lot of testimony vis-à-vis *Shadow Wolf* and his so-called Pack. But no given name provided by anyone. An accidental oversight among the townsfolk, mebbeh? Oh," he drawled, his voice deepening considerably, "I doubt that. The rest of Shadow Wolf's gang of ruffians at least have the courtesy to use their real names." He glanced briefly toward the marshal's door. "I never could trust anyone who uses an alias."

Liam's face grew increasingly hot, his fingers curling into tighter fists. Where was his damned gun when he needed it?

"Oh," Davidson chuckled, kicking back in his chair once more, "you did realize Shadow Wolf is Rafaele Forino. Maeve MacKenna's beau. Ahem—fiancé." He added in a tone oozing mockery, "The love of her life."

Blood rushed in Liam's ears while he watched Davidson pout insincerely. Was it for his benefit or was he that poor an actor? Somehow Liam doubted it was the latter.

"Wh—what you say is intrigue but irrelevant to this investigation. Forino was out of town when the explosion occurred." Yet Maeve's voice echoed in his head: *Poor man, though, he can't build a fire to save his life.*

It's an alibi.

"And Miss MacKenna was out of town too, at the time. Is there anything more convenient?" Davidson cocked his head and smirked. "Do you suppose Forino would do his own dirty work? It's more his style to assign the job to a lackey. Seriously. Have you never investigated before? The truth couldn't be more obvious."

Liam wanted so desperately to assign the crime to Forino, knowing of Shadow Wolf what he did. Yet he couldn't ignore facts: "There's no motivation for such an act. Everyone here tells me the saloo—brothel—was a base of operations for Shadow Wolf Pack where they mixed business—" He sneered. "—with pleasure. Why destroy it? Why would Shadow Wolf —Forino—destroy Miss MacKenna's home? Especially if he loves her. Lacking motive, this is nothing but conjecture." Liam added in his defense, "And conclusions I could've come to on my own if I favored sloppy investigation."

Davidson scoffed, casting a disparaging look at the papers strewn across the desk and floor. "And clearly you don't favor sloppiness."

"Help, Davidson," said Liam haltingly through his clenched teeth, "or leave me be. I have work that needs doing. Not all of us can be as flippant regarding our jobs as you are."

"I assure you, O'Doherty, I take my job deadly serious." Davidson showed himself to the door but paused with his hand on the knob. "I do apologize if I in any way impeded your—" He chuckled through the last word: "Investigation. Oh—uh … I don't suppose it would be of any consequence that among the deceased: Caitlyn Burke, harlot, lightskirt, soiled dove, lady of questionable morals, rental cunt … and Rafaele Forino's common-law wife." He shrugged. "Before he left her for Miss MacKenna. O'Doherty, tell me this, would you: how does a pious Catholic man divorce his wife?"

If he were in the market to do the same with Elizabeth in the event she shared a town with Maeve? Liam opened his mouth to reply.

"Bring me MacKenna's engagement ring, would you? She mustn't have it." Davidson tipped his head and stepped outside. "Good day to you."

With a roar, Liam leapt from his chair and swept the remaining papers off his desk.

A few days later, Liam took his trip to Tombstone, still feeling under the weather as he had ever since Davidson's visit to the marshal's office. It wasn't quite illness, nor quite bottle-aching, but something left him feeling decidedly not himself.

Liam thanked Duncan for the ride as he hopped from the carriage, closing the door behind himself. "I expect it should be a while before I'll be ready to return to Redington. Make yourself at home at a nearby public house, restaurant, boarding house—" He mumbled, "Outhouse."

Duncan straightened in his seat, his eyebrows high. "Excuse me?"

"I'll call for you when I'm ready."

"I *can* presume I will be compensated properly for my—"

"Yes, yes," Liam said, waving off Duncan as well as his concerns. "Of course."

With narrowed eyes, Duncan repositioned himself on his seat and set the carriage in motion.

Liam discovered the coachman was no idiot during previous interrogation and that made him even more suspicious. He had a lingering hunch Duncan was in some way tied to Shadow Wolf Pack. This warranted some additional questioning on the return to Redington.

Liam rapped on the front door at the corner of Second and Tough Nut in Tombstone, and listened. There were children inside whose voices hushed at his knocks, then footsteps. Heavy ones; Liam wagered a man's.

Good.

The door opened to a sour-faced cowboy with an abundance of wrinkles etching his face and nothing but a thin ring of brown hair circumnavigating his head by way of the nape of his neck.

His voice as sour as his face, the man greeted Liam: "What do you want?"

"I'm calling for Bernard Stanifor."

"Yea that's me. Who's asking?" Bernard snapped.

"Liam O'Doherty. Private investigator."

"We don't take kindly to your ... kind."

The door came rushing at Liam's face; he stopped it with a sturdy palm before it shut, a brief shock shooting through his wrist at the contact.

"You might take kindly to my kind if I were permitted to impose on you a moment of your time."

The door creaked open, Bernard passing glances between the two children watching their exchange from a sparsely decorated parlor, and Liam still standing outside.

"Henry. Junior. Play outside a bit, will you?"

The boys nodded and rushed out, ducking their heads as they hustled by Liam.

"C'min." Bernard motioned what Liam assumed was supposed to be a welcoming gesture; that would be the best he'd hoped to get from any of these folks. "Ain't got no coffee or tea. Brandy do ya?"

Liam sighed and accepted after a lengthy hesitation.

Bernard sat at the tiny table in the kitchen and Liam sat across from him, dirty little glass of golden-brown alcohol in hand.

"There's hardly room for a meal at this table for the four of you," noted Liam, being deliberately obtuse.

"The four of us?" Bernard frowned; it seemed his typical state.

"You, those boys, and their mother?"

For once, something other than a frown came from Bernard: a bitter laugh. "I'm a bachelor, sure to be confirmed thanks to my lot. Henry and Junior—Joseph—are my nephews."

Again, though he knew why, Liam asked, "How did they come into your keeping?"

Bernard exhaled. "O'Doherty, have I done something to deserve this interrogation?"

Likely. Everyone has. These people in Tombstone could've destroyed the Tiff and Tawny hoping Maeve was still inside, aiming to take her life with it.

But Liam was there with an ulterior motive; remove Shadow Wolf Pack, Forino, the whole bunch of them. One way or another, he'd remove a major obstacle—and would still apprehend the criminal responsible for this whole mess.

"This is no interrogation," he lied.

"Their father was killed at his job. Burdened by the death of her husband, the boys' mother sought relief from her heartache with what turned out to be a lethal dose of heroin. 'N' now it's just me, Joseph, and Henry."

Liam feigned sincerity. "My condolences."

"Yea." Bernard dropped his head.

Once more, though he knew the answer through prior research, Liam asked, "May I inquire as to what felled your brother?"

Bernard sought the answer from his drink.

Liam hadn't the heart to inform him there was nothing but misery at the bottom of an empty bottle; his father, bless his soul, never stopped searching for answers there. He'd always found trouble instead. Liam had a few well-hidden scars as souvenirs from those nights.

"The bandits were faster to their weird guns than he was to his Colt."

"Were those bandits brought to justice?"

"You come to help? Well you're too damn late." Bernard smacked his mug on the table with such force Liam was stunned neither drinking vessel nor furniture were rewarded with cracks. "The little witch was sentenced to hang."

Liam swallowed hard, barely keeping his temper in check. "And …?"

"Members of her gang rescued her at last minute. Was sure they got there too late. She dropped through the trap door on the gallows and everything, but they grabbed her and as they got away on horseback, I heard her screaming. Must've been in agony the way she carried on." He huffed. "*Good.*"

"So you don't believe justice was served," Liam assumed.

"'Course not. Would you?"

Liam frowned. *If it weren't Maeve—* He cleared his throat. "Has there been talk of a vendetta ride? I understand your brother wasn't the only one to lose his life that day."

"They had the ropes, we have the trees."

"… But?"

"Look around you, Detective." Bernard motioned to his home. "… *Detect.*"

To call Bernard poor would've been a generous description. And if the vendetta ride was proposed after his sister-in-law committed suicide, it stood to reason there would've been nobody else to watch Bernard's nephews. "You couldn't join them."

"I couldn't and it's not for lack of wanting. Just makes me hate her more."

Liam bristled. "Well, Mr. Stanifor? There may be justice for your family, yet."

CHAPTER 14

 his," said Kököle, "is *toosi*. It's ground-up baked sweet corn."

"Is this it?" Maeve peered into the bowl Kököle held out to her in demonstration. "Is it done?"

"Not yet. Next, we add water, stir and knead it until it's the desired consistency."

"'N' then what?"

"Then it'll be called *qömi* and it's eaten cold."

"Ah." Maeve watched Kököle add water to the bowl and stir it. "It's like *min arbhair.*"

"I have it on authority," said Kököle, her disposition and tone carefree, "a certain Italian rogue was partial to the flavor of sweet corn cake. You might make *qömi* for him sometime soon."

"Yea. I might." Maeve wondered what Rafaele would do if she made him food without his having to pay her for it. *He'll probably expect it of his wife,* she realized. *'N' when I give tha' to him he'll come to take it for granted.*

"Are you OK?" Kököle frowned.

Maeve was as 'OK' as she ever was those days. Lonely. Barren of babe but filled with regrets. Nodding absently as Kököle kneaded her concoction, Maeve replied, "Just … Thinkin', is all."

"Well whatever it is," said Kököle between grunts of effort, "stop it. It's making you unhappy."

"Yes—well—"

A series of knocks at the front door interrupted Maeve. She stood. "I'll get tha'—"

"Oh no, I will—" Kököle waved her hands, sending bits of *qömi* dough this way and that.

"'N' leave a trail of sweet corn cake? Have I not soiled Miss Chesterfield's house enough on me own?"

"Maeve—"

"I'll have none of tha'. Excuse me."

As Maeve left the room, Kököle sighed, "Fine."

Upon her approach to the front of the house, Maeve was greeted by a painful, cold rush through her body and was all too aware of the pounding of her heart. It was too quiet.

She was dragged backward by an icy current and struggled to fight both it and the whisper in her ear: *What if it's Dallahan?*

She swallowed hard. *It could be Rafaele.* She took the door handle firmly in her hand. *'N' if it's Dallahan, he's gonna rue the day he came back here.*

"Liam," gasped Maeve after she opened the door. "What a pleasant surprise." Not as good as Rafaele by a long-shot but not as bad as Dallahan; a fair middle-ground.

Liam's face lit up. "I could say the same, Miss MacKenna. I wasn't expecting I'd ever see you again. I assume you're feeling better? You're out of bed."

She attempted to rub the flush from her cheeks while staring at the ground. "I do hope the—the ladies—" Maeve faltered when she lacked a better descriptor for her housemates, "didn't burden ye too terrible with me ailments."

Liam hesitated. "Oh no, no, not at all."

Maeve met his gaze with a crooked smile.

He sighed. "Look at you."

"What? Why?"

"You're lovely—" He caught himself. "You cut a fine figure in proper garments; the very image of grace and beauty." Liam prattled on under her stare: "I was starting to suspect you didn't care for the gifts I sent ... that perhaps the west had trained the lady out of you."

"Oh—yes, I've enjoyed them. Very much! I just ... Haven't been well enough to properly thank ye." Guilt compelled her to open her arms for a hug.

Liam enveloped Maeve in a tight embrace and his nose pressed into the elaborate braid circling the top of her head.

He inhaled deeply.

Maeve pulled away at his inhalation, glimpsing several men behind Liam, all standing with weapons at the ready.

She recoiled with a gasp, clutching the door as if it would protect her from them. "Liam—"

"What's the matter?"

Her voice strangled, she replied, "I know a posse when I see one!"

He tilted his head in question before answering, "Oh—yes. Yes, Maeve! I have leads. The investigation is moving along at last."

"That's fantastic!" At least something was going well for someone there.

"Yea ... Unfortunately, my leads will mean I'll be out of town for ... well, quite some time, I'm sure."

Maeve nodded, forcing a smile. "Congratulations. 'N' ... Go get yer man."

Liam tipped his hat with a wink. "I'll be back ... We'll celebrate."

"I'm lookin' forward to it."

"Congratulations on the new job," said Duke as he stepped carefully through the half-dead shrubs on his approach to Rafaele.

Rafaele tore his attention from his inspection of the building, well into its construction. It was amazing how willingly people worked for him when generosity of pay was involved. He did a mental calculation of how long it'd been since he last saw Duke; almost two months. His former cohort continued to be exceptionally good at his vanishing acts, as always. "What have you heard?"

"What haven't I?" muttered Duke.

Rafaele cocked an eyebrow at him.

He augmented, "You've … made an impression."

It must be good, Rafaele surmised, *since she hasn't withdrawn her job offer.* "I'll take that as a compliment." He held his breath before continuing, "She didn't seem especially happy I couldn't get to work same-day. I … I needed to take care of some pressing matters, first." With a purposeful glance around the frame of the building, he added, "I wanted to bring Maeve and our belongings before starting my job. Not so sure how well that's going to work out." He kicked himself for botching this trip.

"So." Duke folded his arms across his chest, nudging some dirt with the toe of his boot. "This your big to-do?"

"My new home?" Rafaele inhaled deeply, marveling at the smell of the ocean. There were but few things that gave him such satisfaction. The smell of Maeve after sex, perhaps? He cleared his throat. "It will be, in a matter of time." It depended upon how picky he was going to be with the work quality his carpenters were producing; thus far he had few complaints. It wasn't their fault time was dragging, nor could they do anything to speed it along.

Duke snorted. "I'm not sure that's big enough for you and the missus. It's … what: seven bedrooms?"

"Ten. Can't be too conservative there."

"You old dog."

Rafaele smirked, glancing at Duke. "I can't keep my hand off her."

"Mmm." Duke looked both unhappy and disgusted.

It was serendipitous that Duke should appear out of nowhere for a visit, as Rafaele had questions nagging at the back of his head for weeks now. He placed his attention on mentally pacing out the space between two-by-four studs. Several were, he'd deemed, too close together, and he noted which to bring to the foreman's attention. "I've been meaning to ask … how, exactly, did you find Mrs. Blanc? You hardly run in the same circles."

"All it takes is one magic encounter to change that. Hell: you could say the same of her."

"Why send me to her?"

Duke shrugged, turning his attention to a nearby two-by-four. He tapped it gently and it paid him no mind.

"Running into you when and where I did was certainly advantageous. I recognize cosmic signs—" Duke turned his back to Rafaele.

"You would," Rafaele muttered, provoking him deliberately.

"Beg pardon?" Duke cut him a glare over his shoulder.

"I know when someone's screwing with me."

"Do you?" Duke slowly turned and cocked his head with a wicked little grin. "Then why go on the interview?"

"My desperation for work trumped my better judgment ... and—" the word hung there as if dangling over an ocean bluff. "I'm grateful." He blurted, "What exactly is Mrs. Blanc capable of?"

With a laugh, Duke said, "I didn't mean she's literally dangerous. You take things so seriously, Raf. Thought you'd learned better by now!" He paused. "Remember the journey to Zavala County when we ran into a *lechuza?*"

Rafaele shuddered violently. "Don't remind me." He still had vivid nightmares of the beast.

"Saved your sorry ass." Duke leaned over, pointedly evaluating Rafaele's posterior. "Yea, still sorry."

"You don't understand," replied Rafaele. "I've experienced a great deal since then. I'm not a naïve young man anymore. Native spirits, witches, never-seens, the Wolf Girl ..." he stopped himself shy of mentioning Maeve. That experience was too personal.

There were other things he recalled, but he didn't want to open old emotional wounds he had no doubt Duke hadn't forgotten, either.

They were silent for a while and Rafaele busied himself with making some minor adjustments around the construction site, Duke keeping nearby.

"What attracted you to her?" said Rafaele.

Duke leaned back, his eyes wide. After a hesitation, he sighed. "I'm in love with her."

"Really." Rafaele sneered. "She hardly seems your type."

"What can I say? The heart wants what it wants." Under Rafaele's disbelieving stare, he augmented, "OK, fine, ya got me: one of my little toys registered a hell of an energy pattern when I arrived in San Diego. It was an electro-magnetic anomaly ... even though as best I could tell, whatever it detected wasn't magnetic or electric. It was more akin to those spiritual sites you find all over the world. Thing is? It wasn't concentrated around an area. It was around a single person."

"Mrs. Blanc. Huh. Still messing around with that stuff, are you?"

"I—"

"She's just an experiment to you!"

"Well, sure at first—hey now! She's not just an experiment. She's ... remarkable. Through everything we ever encountered, I'd always managed to maintain my skepticism. But Aria changed things. She threw all my beliefs right out the window and made me never want to go back to the way I was. And I haven't."

Rafaele swallowed; Duke had always been the more devout of the duo. Now he feared he was in danger of the same experience with Maeve.

Duke sighed, gazing wistfully off into the distance. "Aria's a real goddess."

"Dammit, Duke! You set me up!"

"Like old times?" Duke's gaze flickered to Rafaele. "Well, if you're so angry about it, why are you smiling?"

A group of seven men on horseback traversed the parched land of Three Mesas, puffs of dust rising from their mounts' hooves as they veered toward First Mesa.

The man leading the group held out his hand as they came upon the villages. The men who accompanied him stopped at his direction before he dropped to the ground, making the remainder of his approach on foot.

The mesas provided the Hopi a defendable spot for their homes, as intruders would have to ride up the pathways around the mesa, itself—or climb, if they decided to veer from the trail—giving the residents the advantage to rain upon on them death and destruction should necessity call for it.

The location had kept their settlements secure for thousands of years.

Watching the outsiders approach, Tithu couldn't decide if what he witnessed was bravery or stupidity.

The head of Redbird clan naturally had another opinion: "They are armed. They have not come with peaceful intentions."

"No, Father," corrected Tithu, "they've come for me. The one approaching is a lawman."

Cheveyo frowned. "Has this unwelcome visitor anything to do with your relationship or antics with Shadow Wolf?"

Tithu bobbed his head. "I'm afraid this wouldn't be the first my loyalty to the Pack has been tested." He addressed his father as many other eyes watched the single man upon his approach. "Though he may wear a badge of peace, he's not doing what's right, nor even following his own people's laws. He's on a vendetta against Wolf for perceived wrongdoing."

"I see. So I am to lose my only son for loyalty to … to acquaintances?"

"Father … the Pack is to me as Forino is to you."

Cheveyo grunted, as if unwilling to see it the same way.

Tithu continued, "They aren't mere acquaintances, just as Forino isn't just your old friend. It's so much more. They're my found family. I wasn't given them by grace as I was you and my sisters; I earned my place in their lives, and they in mine. They've cared for me, and I them. Please trust you won't lose me. I've kept my nose clean despite associations and I'm sure once this gentleman sees as much, I'll be free to go."

"I hope he has half the sense you do. You make me proud."

Tithu stepped toward the man when Cheveyo stopped him with a firm hand on his shoulder. "Remember: what is here is yours should you want it. You are needed here more than in any other place."

"I never forget. It's a responsibility I've no intention of shirking."

Cheveyo nodded though he was far from smiling. "We worry."

There was no sense in Tithu telling his father agonizing was unnecessary, so he wordlessly put his hand atop his father's before departing.

So confident in his eventual return to Hopi, Tithu didn't bother looking back.

He approached the red-haired man, whose lips beneath a thick mustache raised in a smirk. The man flashed him a glinting silver badge. "Redbird?"

The lawman could've been asking for Cheveyo but he figured it would be easier to take responsibility for whatever this confrontation was about; if it avoided any possible skirmish between the Hopi and these white men, he was in favor of it.

So Tithu went along willingly.

"I'm wuh-worried about Ducky." Milton set a plate of pork griskins before Edison. Though he was a guest in Edison's home, Milton felt responsible for serving the older man; he *was* the decidedly more able-bodied of the two.

"So am I," said Edison. He plucked a thin slice of meat from the plate and nodded toward the bowl of burnt cream. "Thanks."

"Do you think we ought pay her a vuh-visit?" Milton sat across from Edison, helping himself to some black coffee—the hardest drink he typically had.

"As it is, you're disobeying Alexis's orders by being here. And I disobeyed by letting you in." Edison said with a lengthy sigh and doleful expression. "Dare we risk it? Can you imagine the look on her face if we appeared at her door?"

Milton chuckled, layering the meat with a couple slices of bread. "She may have suh-saved my life years ago—" He paused to stuff his mouth with the crude sandwich. "—but my loyalty to you ruh-ruuuns deeper and I c-couldn't have you lonesome."

"My thoughts keep me occupied," said Edison. He dropped his gaze and muttered, "When I can catch them."

"Is it getting worse?"

"It's hard to say. Half the time I can't remember. I'm uncertain if I'm well or if I've forgotten my mind's failing me."

Milton didn't want to think about it; Edison had been this way as long as they'd known each other, and his mental health was never far from Milton's mind.

Milton exhaled and cleared his throat but it was Edison to continue the conversation.

"How did your interviews with Detective O'Doherty go?"

They'd discussed this previously, but Milton humored his old friend as if they hadn't. "I m-met with him in total of three times of increasing aaaanimosity. He's duh-distrustful, which I suppose comes with the profession."

"What did you tell him?"

"The same things you did, I sup-sup …" He snapped, agitated at himself, "Suppose. All three times."

Edison gave him a stern stare, silently pressing for further detail.

"He keh-kept trying to get detail about the Pack members," Milton said, retrieving another slice of meat from the shared plate. "Obviously I'm not the outlaw t-t-type … and didn't have direct interaction with the Pack—"

Winking, he reminded Edison, "I'm an artist, after all. I did provide him the d-details of a few hideouts to check."

Edison gasped. "You didn't!"

"Provide him any places we currently use? N-no, only ones which would pruh-prove vacant if searched. My intent was to have him tracking from Utah Territory to Mexico."

"Well. May that be the last we hear from him."

Someone knocked insistently on the front door.

"Of course," Milton added, "it was a f-f-finite list, and eventually he'll run out of places to search. Hopefully not for a while."

Likely his impulse at the sound, Edison rose from his seat.

"No," snapped Milton, waving at him to sit. "Alexis suh-said to not answer the d-door."

Edison may well have forgotten himself; he wasn't the type to answer his door on the average day even when friends called on him. As it were, Edison answering the door for *him* alarmed Milton. What would he do if someone knocked when Milton wasn't around to protect him—his ability to protect being what it was?

Edison lowered himself into his seat.

The caller knocked again.

"Sssh," Milton whispered. "If you don't suh-seem to be home, they'll g-give up and leave."

"What if it's Wolf?"

"He'll let himself in j-j-just as always." It was silent for a while before Milton sighed his relief. "Tell me," he said, his voice low. "What did *you* t-tell the detective duuuring your interrogations?"

"I was honest but provided him little of what he wanted: I explained how Wolf's arm functions. That's the upshot, I suppose, of having a more hands-off role in the Pack. Everything else, he seemed to dismiss as the ramblings of a useless codger. I'm the decrepit, forgetful fogey to your artist."

If Milton weren't mistaken, it sounded as though Edison felt left out of the Pack's adventures. He must've felt like a knight in shining armor for rescuing Maeve from the middle of the desert after they botched the stagecoach heist.

"If we n-never steal anything fruh-from anybody again," Milton decided, "it'll be too soon."

"Agreed." Edison bobbed his head. "I've always disapproved—"

Both men jumped in their seats with more pounding on the door.

"Open up! We know you're in there!"

It was decidedly not Rafaele.

"What do we do?" Edison gasped.

"C-c-continue to pretend we're not here," whispered Milton. "It's not as if they'll—"

With a thunderous crash, the front door was kicked in.

"S-ss-sstay calm."

Liam stomped into the dining room flanked by several men who looked vaguely familiar.

"Can't you see we're having tea and innocent conversation?" Edison addressed Liam.

Milton groaned inwardly.

"Milton Price? Edison Stilwell? You're both under arrest."

"F-for what?" Milton cried. "We've done nothing wrong!"

"You can cooperate, or we can drag you out," said Liam.

"T-t-tell us the ch-charges, first."

Liam ticked off the charges on his fingers as he recounted them: "Aiding and abetting a criminal organization, numerous criminal acts with Shadow Wolf Pack; too many to count, really." He glanced at his two extended fingers and lowered his hand with a shrug.

"Y-you have no proof—"

"Don't I? There was ample evidence at those abandoned meeting places you sent me to linking you with the bandit gang. Plans, blueprints, illustrations, letters, telegrams. Any of these ring a bell?" He addressed Edison pointedly: "Sparky?" And Milton: "Dandy?" He added with a smirk, "I didn't need to leave this territory to figure it out."

Following a nod from their leader, the posse split; two grabbed Edison with far more force than was necessary, and the other three yanked Milton from his chair.

Through jolts of pain, and thrashing against their grips, Milton yelled, "Don't hurt him!"

"A little brotherly romance is there?" Liam sneered at Milton. To the posse, he ordered, "Incapacitate them."

The last thing Milton heard was scoffed commentary: "Imagine that: there *is* honor among thieves. How positively dreadful."

❦

Liam latched the cell door shut, making a grand flourish of closing the lock.

The whooping and hollering of his posse faded into the distance as they dispersed from the marshal's office to celebrate.

"That's the last of them," said Cummings with a sour expression across his features, watching the culmination of an entire month's work: Edison and Milton joining the already overpopulated cell. "The dawning of a new age in Redington, I guess. I can't believe you caught them all."

From his spot standing beside Tithu in the lockup, Milton exchanged wordless glances with Edison and the marshal.

"No." Liam shook his head. "Forino's still at large. As are Angelino and Brown. And the ladies Redbird, Miss Chesterfield ... Miss MacKenna—" His voice dipped into sadness on Maeve's name. "They're all part of this as well, loath as I am to admit it, but I couldn't very well bring them in with a single cell to go around."

There was also the matter of the non-Pack associates Liam couldn't help but believe should be arrested as well; people like the telegrapher, the owners of the Tiff and Tawny, possibly even Brother Thurman, and the rotund marshal, himself.

And Davidson—well, he was a problem all his own.

While he wouldn't entertain the idea of jailing the women with the men, he had no qualms packing the space with every last man in Redington if necessity dictated.

"What's your plan?" said Cummings warily.

"For the women?" Liam set his jaw. "Constant surveillance."

"You cuh-can't do that," Milton cried, slamming his fist into the strap iron bars of the cell.

"Can't I?" Liam turned a disinterested glance at him. "Watch me. Oh wait —you won't be able to from in there."

"Close arrest?" cried Alexis. "On what grounds?"

"Your involvement with Shadow Wolf Pack." Liam stepped into Alexis's home, his stature and proximity driving her backward to get away from him.

"You have no proof of any wrongdoing—"

"Stilwell and Price both vouched for your playing second fiddle to Forino."

She gasped. "What? They wouldn't—"

"I strongly advise against disobeying my orders," said Liam, closing the front door and locking it.

"And if I refuse?"

He snatched her upper arm, dragging her into the parlor. His voice a cold whisper, he said, "Your insubordination will cost MacKenna her life."

Alexis's gaze darted around the room in search of anything that could pass as a weapon, but her gun belt—with its holstered firearm—was on the counter where she'd left it.

In the kitchen.

It may as well have been on another continent for how useful it was to her there.

Liam drew his gun as if sensing that she longed for her own, pressing it to the hollow of her throat. "And by-the-by, I am never unprepared." He twisted her arm behind her and try as she might, she couldn't fight the tears springing to her eyes.

It was partly the pain, but primarily the realization of her weakness. Her vulnerability.

Her sheer stupidity at letting her guard down, ever—even within the perceived safety of her home, which now would never again feel safe.

She could fight him, and he could break her with little effort. If she landed a punch, she wagered he wouldn't so much as bruise.

"Now be a good, subservient little woman and do as I say. Neither you nor any of the—" he scoffed, "*ladies* in this house are to entertain unauthorized visitors. Nor are any of you at any hour to leave the premises unescorted."

Alexis caught motion outside as the members of Liam's posse dismounted their horses and approached the building, fanning out, she presumed, to cover the sides and back of her residence. The group he amassed was cutting them off from the outside world.

With Moencopi and Kököle being of peaceable nature, and Maeve not being in her right mind due to any number of reasonable circumstances, they would be too much for Alexis to fight by herself.

The strength of the Pack could prevail.

But there was no Pack.

Alexis's skin crawled at how easily he'd subdued her.

If they weren't detained, they would still have been laying low on her orders and she couldn't anticipate any of them coming to her—or Maeve's, Moencopi's, and Kököle's—rescue.

Something about the nature of Liam's choice of lockdown told her the odds were that no Pack member remained in hiding, and Lord only knew when Shadow Wolf would return.

No. This was failure.

She closed her eyes and growled through clenched teeth, "I'll obey."

Liam released her arm, lowering his gun from her throat but keeping it trained on her. "Good girl. Don't test my patience. You wouldn't care to see I have none left."

He backed out of the parlor and beyond her view before she heard the front door open and close again.

Alexis dropped to her knees with a full-body shudder, and she pounded her fists into the carpeted floor with a strangled cry.

"Alex?" Kököle's soft voice broke the silence of the parlor. "What's the matter?"

"Nothing." She managed to swallow a sob but couldn't conceal the sniffle.

"That's horse's bollocks."

Alexis glanced up at her harsh tone and straightened. "We're under armed guard."

"What?" Kököle rushed to the nearest window and threw open the curtains. She snapped them closed, turning to Alexis and demanding, "Why?"

"It's a way of incarcerating us without using valuable cell space—which I suspect is at a premium if the rest of the Pack is in the hoosegow."

"There's more," said Kököle with an intense stare. "Isn't there?"

"I don't—" Alexis faltered. "I don't know what you're referring to."

"I can understand your being distressed over the news but you're fighting off tears. There must be something else upsetting you."

She swallowed. It was bad enough to feel these things but to have to articulate them was nauseating. "O'Doherty had me at a disadvantage. I was unprepared, unprotected." She spat, "Vulnerable. He made me feel helpless." She shook her head; the tears were flowing, damn them. "No. He made me feel like a frail little girl!"

"But ... you're none of those things."

Her eyes narrowing, Alexis said, "Never again." She stood, swiping the tears from her face as she stalked into the kitchen.

The gun belt was not where she'd left it on the counter, but in the middle of the floor instead. A silly, fleeting thought crossed Alexis's mind that she was learning to move items without touching them. Could any of the other women in the house do so? Maybe she was absorbing their powers simply by being near them.

She put on her gun belt, stooping and opening a drawer, where she retrieved one of Edison's weapons. Giving it to Kököle, she said, "You shoot on sight anyone trying to get in who isn't a Pack member."

"I—I couldn't," Kököle stuttered. "It goes against everything I believe in."

"But you need to protect the helpless, too. Protect Maeve."

"She's perfectly capable of defending herself—"

"But she won't if it means possibly hurting her attacker, and you know it. Protect her like you promised Wolf you would."

Kököle groaned, then sighed. "Yes, Alexis."

Alexis jammed her hat on. "Hold down the fort, beautiful. I'll be back as soon as I can."

"Be safe," Kököle whispered after her.

Outside the front door, Alexis was greeted as she anticipated: with scowls and drawn guns.

"Hey. Dudes!" She raised her hands, gun still holstered. How she detested playing submissive. "I've just gotta send a telegraph."

Reluctant glances were exchanged.

"What?" She mocked, "Does some big *man* need to hold my hand and escort me to Akbar? Afraid I might get lost in this big, mean world?"

Nobody budged, nor even cracked a smile. Ridiculing them may not have been the best approach. "Look, fellas: getting arrested wasn't on my agenda today but this is a critical missive I've gotta send. Either somebody's gonna have to walk it to town for me—best of luck if your boss catches you off duty—or one of you can walk me down there at gunpoint and, hey, still be doing your job!"

The shortest man of the set heaved a heavy sigh. "Fine. Come on." As they departed, he muttered, "'S a good thing you're so easy on the eyes ... Breasterfield, is it?"

She scowled but didn't answer. *It's a damn good thing for you I'm a woman on a mission.* And she couldn't risk said mission for an easy—but satisfying—kill. *Your time will come, pig. Soon.*

He smiled back at her and licked his lip lasciviously.

It took every shred of restraint not to kill him, or to at least punch the suggestive expression from his awful face. So instead she focused on how she was going to send her message.

It would need to be ciphered in such a way as to not arouse suspicions as being anything of significance.

Ahmad Akbar greeted Alexis with a wide smile and a chipper, "Hello," as if he hadn't just been on a half hour walk through the desert with the scum of the earth as his escort.

No, wait. That was me.

"I need you to send Gram a message," replied Alexis with a grim expression that came without struggle.

Ahmad cleared his throat and nodded. "And what will you be saying to your grandmother today?"

"If you would, please tell her I fed her fish, but I'll be unable to continue feeding them. I've ... run out of food."

His eyebrows flickered upward in a fleeting display of concern. "Oh, that's ... unfortunate. And what of her old dog? How fairs she?"

Oh, thank God he's following! She barely withheld her sigh of relief. "The old bitch is woefully ill." It was cathartic to refer to Maeve as a bitch—even if in code. "We're hoping to find someone to check her before it's too late."

"Well I'm sorry to hear it."

She swallowed thickly. "Yea. Me too."

CHAPTER 15

 afaele reviewed the telegram for the nth time. Something rubbed him the wrong way—and it wasn't just the obvious code indicating Alexis had somehow lost control of the situation in Redington.

He dipped into the nightstand drawer to retrieve the last few missives from the territory. The second most recent came yesterday and all was as it should've been.

RAFAELE:

THINGS ARE FINE.
MAEVE IS WELL.
SHE DESPERATELY MISSES YOU AND COUNTS DAYS UNTIL YOUR RETURN
BEST NOT MISS YOUR TRAIN BACK.

—ALEXIS

He re-read the new one.

GRAM:

CANNOT CONTINUE TO FEED YOUR FISH. HAVE RUN OUT OF FOOD.
OLD BITCH IS DYING. NEED VET IMMEDIATELY.

—ALEX

The distress call was bad enough, but Rafaele couldn't figure out why Alexis's sign-off changed. Was that code as well?

He could've panicked but it was due to the incongruities that he didn't act rashly. All but one telegram indicated everything was fine.

He studied the odd man out. The sign-off wasn't something Alexis was likely to forget; as far as Rafaele remembered, she never had.

But what if there was another operator at the transmitter? Maybe Akbar was sick and was replaced. Or captured.

Rafaele swallowed. *Or dead?*

Two of those scenarios meant there was a legitimate issue. And considering Redington was the kind of place where things went to hell overnight, there was ample cause for concern. Doubly so with that group of women—things could've gone horribly wrong in an instant. And that was what he knew of them as individuals. As a group, their mischief-making capabilities could've been ten-fold.

With a deep breath, Rafaele pulled out a sheet of paper and a pencil to draft what would eventually become his telegraphed reply; it would require careful wording and an abundance of patience. Even the coded distress message could've been faked or coerced, so he needed confirmation. Preferably from Alexis or Akbar as both were familiar with Shadow Wolf Pack telegram protocols.

If he received the correct reply to a telegram that wasn't even sent using his name—or his usual alias—he'd be on the next train out. A lack of reply meant everything was OK or that the telegraph office had been in some way compromised, and he would stick to the existing plan. *Just one more month is all I need to finish here.*

Now he worried he'd be taking Maeve to a new home of little more than lumber.

Until he knew more, he had yet another reason to count the seconds for his return trip.

And—by all evidence thus far—Rafaele anticipated a bumpy ride.

Liam jerked Akbar into the marshal's office, grunting with exertion as he pitched the telegrapher into a chair.

His gaze flickered to the packed jail cell. If Akbar thought Liam wouldn't attempt to squeeze another body in there, he was sorely mistaken.

"Don't take me for a fool, Akbar," yelled Liam. "I know enough of Morse's code to know you weren't transmitting the message I told you to. What else did you send?"

Akbar studied numerous points in the room before he replied, "I assure you, I was sending the message provided. It's standard protocol to send an opening and ending statement so the receiving end knows when the message concludes."

"That's a cock-and-bull story if ever I heard one." Liam yanked him from the chair and slammed him against the bars of the cell, the men inside it taking a collective step away—as much as they could. "The truth, Akbar! What did you send?"

"What's all the ruckus?" Cummings stepped into his office, brushing off his sleeves. When he saw the packed cell, the expressions of their detainees, and Liam throttling Akbar, the marshal drew his gun. "You've lost your mind, Detective. I'm relieving you of your responsibilities. Take the first train back east."

"You don't have any such authority," Liam replied, releasing Akbar roughly. "I'm in charge of this investigation and it's far from over."

"Well I can no longer stand idly by while you have these decent gentlemen jailed for no good reason."

"No good reason?" Liam gawked. "They're active members in the gang linked to countless crimes and murders in this area alone."

"Not Smith, not Byrd, and certainly not Price, Stilwell, or the boy—" countered the marshal, shaking his head. "You were brought here to assist in the investigation of the arson, and you have no jurisdiction over any other matters. You've jailed innocent men, trapped blameless ladies in their home, and—and—to deputize your little posse was inexcusable! They may call themselves deputies but none of them are and what that group of yours has done under the guise of investigation is unlawful. You—you should be jailed, yourself!"

"Are you quite finished flapping your mandible?" snapped Liam. He inhaled through flared nostrils. "You, I do believe, thought these folks a legitimate posse when Sheriff Ward arrived from Tombstone with them to arrest Miss MacKenna last summer. They were affective enough you accepted their warrant, did you not?"

Marshal Cummings cleared his throat. "Well, that … was … entirely different."

"I had a need for experienced men and the Lynches, Stanifor, and their acquaintances fit the bill, as it were. Now, then, if you are quite done, I have evidence tying Forino to the saloon explosion—"

"I don't care about your so-called evidence," Cummings yelled, his face flooding red. "Booker had the explosives, not to mention the expertise to use them effectively. Forino and MacKenna were both out of town—"

"That's an alibi and I remain unconvinced it's a good one. Even if Forino didn't set the fire, he's responsible if he mandated it. And he is, to date, the only man I can find with motive." Which was, of course, deliberately dismissing the motives of the members of his own posse.

"You think Forino had a motive?" Cummings punctuated his question with a stiff laugh. "What, pray-tell, would be the use of destroying his intended's home? No doubt she was already making plans to move in with him upon their nuptials."

"He needed to murder his common-law wife before he could marry MacKenna."

Silence lingered over the marshal's office as if validating his assertion.

It was Edison behind cell bars to respond: "Ask anybody: Forino never called Miss Burke his wife, common-law or otherwise. Nor was there a child born of their union."

"That you know of," Liam was quick to point out.

"Their reh-relationship was not a m-marriage. Only Caitlyn ever said it was," Milton added. "And she never had a child—Forino's or otherwise."

"Wouldn't her assertions be reason enough to make a man with designs on a woman desperate enough to kill another?" Liam ran his fingers through his thick red curls with a calming breath. "Forino is the head of Shadow Wolf Pack and he must answer for the crimes of his gang. Cut the head off the octopus and its tentacles do nothing but writhe aimlessly. Like you lot." Under several blank stares, he augmented, "It's not a perfect metaphor."

"Regardless," Marshal Cummings said, "you can't detain people indefinitely over a hunch or because you don't approve of who they once associated with. There's no actual evidence, no charges filed against them. You need to release them. Now!"

"They're at risk for decamping and as such, they will remain behind bars."

"You're planning on personally handling this even if it doesn't go to court. This isn't an investigation, it's a vendetta. It's jealousy. You want what you can't have: Forino's woman!" He puffed out his chest, adding, "I know when I've been screwed over, O'Doherty, and that's just what your precinct did. You weren't the best they could send us; they sent you here to clear their garden of its weeds!"

Liam's eyes widened before narrowing as he imagined throwing daggers at Cummings.

It was one thing to concede he was on a vendetta, quite another to see other people recognized it; it took every shred of self-restraint not to pummel the man.

"Just be aware," added Cummings, "that your sad excuse for a posse isn't going to defend you against Forino. They're not stupid and know him better than you think you know his reputation. You don't have a warrant, you don't have evidence, you don't have loyal companions. You don't stand a snowball's chance in hell against Forino. Face facts, O'Doherty: you've got nothing. And once I release everybody you've rounded up—"

"Not until I have my man!" Liam roared, his face beet-red and veins bulging in his neck. He steadied himself against the desk and inhaled a cleansing breath. His voice low and deadly calm, he continued, "If anybody from this cell is caught outside the room prior to Forino's death, I will personally delight in the task of hunting each of you down—man or woman —and killing you. Including you, Cummings." He met the marshal's gaze directly. "Oh, *especially* you."

Nobody uttered a word as Liam departed.

Liam could tell it was Booker Angelino; even from afar and with his back turned, he looked slimy as a slug drenched in grease: a snake oil salesman through and through. While tempted to rush in and apprehend the man, Liam figured patience would serve him well. It often did.

He gestured for his posse to stay back as he approached, keeping his steps light and mentally reviewing this final part of his plan.

Narrowly avoiding the globular and unfriendly barrel cactus to his right and the equally hostile cluster of cacti to his left, Liam crouched in the nearby brush. He spared the plants but a single passing thought: *What a miserable place to grow such abominations of nature.*

Booker was right at home among them, paying the barbed plants no mind as he built a small fire with a single strike match and a few branches he'd removed deftly from a nearby mesquite tree.

He scrounged his mount's saddlebags for food and came up literally empty-handed. "No food," Booker groaned. "No money." With a roar, he kicked at the sand by the horse's feet.

Liam smiled, watching as Booker had to calm his horse or risk her stranding him in the middle of the desert. The human ball of slime would've deserved it.

Having successfully calmed the mare, Booker pressed his forehead to her neck. "I shouldn't go back to Redington old girl, but I've got no choice."

She nickered.

The lunatic chatted with his animal, "I'll try to barter with Paul in the morning I guess. He's always been receptive to my suggestions."

Liam wasn't too sure anyone did business by trade anymore and supposed Booker and Redington's chief shopkeeper had some sort of special relationship.

He watched as Booker elected to forego even attempting to forage himself a meal from the desert—what there was in Arizona Territory that was edible, Liam didn't know—and erected a pathetic excuse for an encampment. He dropped his gun belt beside the fire and stepped a few feet away, opening his slacks before watering a jumping cholla.

Liam sneered. Everything about Booker, this situation: all of it, dreadful. Notwithstanding, here was his chance. He stood from his spot, drawing his weapon and approaching, keenly aware of the soft crunching of his own boots in the sandy dirt. Positioning himself between Booker and his gun belt, Liam leveled the gun at his head, cocking it.

"If you're gonna shoot me," Booker sighed without turning, "couldja at least wait 'til I'm done pissing here?"

"Hurry it up, Angelino," snapped Liam with a wave of his gun. "I haven't got all night."

Booker urinated as if his life depended on it, grunting and groaning as the stream turned to a trickle, the trickle to drops. Even the tips of his ears went burgundy as he forced a couple brief sprays.

But the desire to prolong things couldn't change the simple fact he'd drained his well dry.

With the last few drops, he cursed he hadn't had more to drink, and closed the buttons of his trousers.

Stiffly he turned to face Liam's gun.

"You're Booker Angelino."

"Yea," replied Booker. "What do you want?"

Liam took a chance on the accusation: "You blew up the saloon in Redington."

Booker's eyes narrowed. He was at an obvious disadvantage with his guns so far away, but his mouth ran away without him regardless. "Who the hell *are* you?"

"I'll take that as a yes."

"What's it to you? You gonna shoot me or not?"

He lowered the gun, extending his hand in greeting. "Liam O'Doherty."

Booker accepted Liam's hand with marked wariness.

"It was my plan to kill you," replied Liam.

Booker yanked his hand away.

"But plans change. Tell me, Angelino: What do you know about Rafaele Forino?"

"That all depends."

Liam sighed. Of course he was going to be this way. "... On what?"

"How much you willin' to pay me."

Liam felt foolish for thinking maybe they could've been friends. His arm whipped upward, aiming the muzzle of the gun between Booker's eyes. "I'll pay you with your life. It's probably worth more to you than me."

Sighing in defeat, Booker said, "Whaddaya want from me?"

"Everything you can tell me."

Booker grunted and rolled his eyes.

"First, confirm my suspicion if you would: Why'd you blow up the saloon?" Liam paused. Attempting to lead him to a confession, he asked, "Were you trying to kill Forino?"

"No—you got it all wrong. Betraying a Pack member is grounds for death."

Liam looked to the side in exasperation. "If not—"

"He had me do it."

"Why?" Liam demanded, surging forward until the gun pressed to Booker's brows where they met in a sad attempt at a unified caterpillar over his nose.

"I dunno."

"Why?" He pressed harder.

"I told you, I dunno!" Booker cried. "He never gave me a reason, just told me what he wanted and when he wanted it. I was just following his orders, like always."

"And you didn't bother asking?"

"Of course not." Sweat beaded on Booker's forehead. "We know better than to question the Pack leader. How stupid are you? Christ!"

"Hmm." Liam lowered the gun. "I hear you're a pyrotechnics expert and the explosion was nothing close to your style or quality."

Booker turned his stare to the dirt.

"You're lying to protect Forino."

"No—yes—oh, what do you want me to say?"

Liam wanted to be overjoyed he had someone pinning this entirely on Forino. Or someone who would with little coercion, anyway, and Booker seemed like the man for the job. "I want you to tell me why you did it."

"He wanted me to destroy the Tiff and Tawny with Burke inside to get out of his common-law marriage."

It seemed too easy, however, and much too convenient. He feared Booker was taking him for a fool.

He eyeballed the man, realizing with a knot in his stomach that his initial impression may not have been accurate.

Booker may have been cleverer than he let on. Yes, he claimed Forino planned the explosion. He may even have been telling the truth. He may also have been operating alone, smart enough to avoid using his signature method of operations to throw others off his trail, and merely suggested Forino as a suspect based on Liam's line of questioning; he'd made it no secret he held Forino responsible.

With Booker's testimony and admission so unreliable, Liam was no closer to attributing the explosion to Forino—or anybody, to his chagrin.

This interlude was flying in the face of what he desperately wanted to believe; it was a good thing he wasn't seeking facts anymore.

After a moment, Liam smiled wryly. Booker *did* provide him something of great significance: unmistakable evidence he had no sense of camaraderie with his leader.

Perhaps there was another way to conclude this investigation and make Forino answer for the crimes he'd committed.

With two finger-widths separating sun from horizon, Rafaele boarded the train burdened with foreboding, and carrying a full suitcase, his stomach knotted upon itself. But there was little doubt he needed to get back to Maeve as quickly as possible, and get back to her, he would.

He sat in the combines, his luggage in the empty seat beside his. Several other passengers boarded after him and before long—though any amount of time was too long when he was rushing back to Maeve—the train pulled from its station.

Rafaele sorted through the facts again, wagering at some point along the line, the train would be searched; specifically, someone would be looking for him.

His mind wandered haplessly back to the telegram he received when rushing from the hotel room. It was, he thought, in reply to his carefully coded message but included the usual weird incorrect details, similar to many others he'd received recently—starting with being addressed to him rather than the name he'd last used: Jim MacKenna. He'd addressed it to his daughter, Mayv, and expected the reply to be addressed appropriately.

This was the first he'd received from Maeve and there was a desperation in it; not only from her—or whoever dictated it—but from the telegraph operator. Rafaele didn't even want to assume Akbar had been at the transmission key.

Whoever it was had included something mismatched from the rest of the message; something that likely cost a great friend and ally his life.

Maybe Rafaele misread something in his haste to catch the train, and with a shaking hand he opened his war bag and pulled out the telegram to review it, hoping he might find something he missed the first time. Maybe something that would soothe his nerves.

DEAREST RAFAEL

WISH FOR YOUR RETURN
MISS YOUR TOUCH
NEED YOUR BODY
HURRY HOME

WITH BURNING DESIRE
MAEVE

Rafaele swallowed, his gaze settling on the last line:

IT'S A TRAP – A. AK

He hadn't even finished signing off.

This wasn't the answer Rafaele had been waiting for, which amplified his fears. This Alexis and this Maeve were not who they appeared to be and while Akbar may have been at the wire, he mustn't have had time to send the proper response.

Someone wanted Rafaele on this train; something was coming for him down the tracks. If it were a Pack operation, that would've been how he'd handled it.

Given how careful whoever this was had been to ensure Rafaele was on that train and in that seat, it wasn't prudent to play this trip by chance.

As the train departed Painted Rock around three thirty in the morning, he had his hunch confirmed in the form of a twerp of a man, standing at the head of the combines and sorting through a handful of familiar daguerrotypes by lamplight, glancing from them and peering through the darkness to review the faces of the passengers aboard.

Never would he feel so good for his weight gain, nor as confident in the style of his clothing and facial hair; he didn't resemble even his most recent images.

But then the little weasel snagged the sleeve of the conductor and after a brief whispered conversation, the conductor pointed a level hand toward Rafaele's seat.

That served as sad validation who his adversary might've been; he'd purchased the train ticket under a false name and the only people who were familiar with it were Pack members.

Either someone he knew had targeted him, or someone he loved provided the information under duress. Though neither possibility was good, the latter made his stomach sink as if he'd swallowed an anvil.

With positive identification made, the weasel nodded and hastily retreated. He'd likely detrain at the next stop, Rafaele supposed, if the architect of this imminent ambush was as predictable as he seemed.

Unless the banality was by design.

Though he may have been privy to Pack information, Twerp was certainly expendable; Rafaele would ride to his doom waiting for him to detrain if Twerp wasn't expected to walk away either.

Perhaps Twerp's departure and indiscreet behavior was intended to force Rafaele off the train early and right into whatever they'd planned.

It would've been all too easy to panic and act rashly, but instead he took steadying breaths.

I need to make a decision and nothing more. I could make myself ill trying to stay ahead of him. And so, he planned his actions irrespective of what Twerp did.

Rafaele wouldn't stay on board to watch things unfold.

The question remained: were they—whoever 'they' were—targeting him alone, or was there going to be collateral damage? He wanted to assume the former but be prepared for the latter.

Rafaele casually scanned his surroundings. Nobody of even passably Italian descent sat in the combines with him—in which case, he doubted there were any other Italians on the train.

The closest there were to Italians sat in the last group of seats in the cabin—a small family Rafaele guessed were former cotton plantation workers. Judging by their emaciated appearance beside a beautifully plump baby, this couple appeared to be forgoing all they had to provide a good future— or at least a full belly—for their child.

Nobody should go without. It was, perhaps, rationalization for his actions.

Rafaele removed his belt buckle, tapping his metal fingers against it. *Tink, tink, tink.* It had been a gift from Eliseo when Rafaele had given him the gift of eternal freedom from his ills. Having to give it to someone else felt as though an icy hand crushed his heart.

With a deep breath, he approached the small family at the back of the train. "I couldn't help but notice the two of you back here with your beautiful baby."

The woman clutched her baby closer to her breast, wide-eyed gaze focused on his left hand.

The wretched claw.

"I wanna help you," Rafaele explained, putting the horrified stare out of his head. "I've been in hard times myself and know how it is to go without. Here." His voice cracked as he pressed the buckle into the man's callused hands. "This is sterling silver all the way through. When sold, it should garner enough to buy your family food for quite some time."

The man regarded Rafaele, hesitation in his gaze. Yet he curled his fingers tightly around the buckle. "Why do you do this?"

Rafaele hesitated in replying. He hoped by moving himself away from the train, it would ensure these innocent folks would no longer be within his adversary's crosshairs. In which case, this was a charitable act if ever he'd seen one. And if not—

"I'm paying what fortune I have forward." It was a half-truth—maybe a quarter-truth—and Rafaele hated himself for it.

They were slowing into the Gila Bend station. He glanced out the windows. "This is my stop. Take care of your little one." *God save him.*

"Thank you—" the man stuttered, dropping his head to more closely inspect the buckle. "Thank you so much."

Rafaele mustered a smile before returning to his seat and rifled through his war bag to check his supplies—spare parts for prosthesis repairs, extra ammunition, a couple telegrams—and tucked it back safely beneath his duster.

The rest of his few possessions would have to stay in his luggage aboard the train; maybe, with luck on his side, he'd get to reunite with it at the Tucson station.

He didn't, however, genuinely believe he deserved it.

Rafaele made his way to the front of the car where he watched the platform during the brief whistle-stop. Sure as horse shit, there went Twerp.

The train's whistle blew again followed by the familiar shake of the cabin as it continued on its way. Praying there wasn't another person keeping a more discreet eye on him, Rafaele walked several cars toward the front of the locomotive, finding an unattended side door. As they gained speed and the station shrunk into the distance, he pushed the door open and leaped into the world outside.

⤙☽✲☾⤚

It was a spectacular, ear-ringing explosion reminiscent of what preluded Maeve's jailyard break. This one, however, had the addition of a brilliant display of fireworks against the pre-dawn sky.

While Rafaele was eager to return to Redington, he needed to spend time at the site of the not-so-accidental accident.

He sheltered beneath a rocky overhang concealed by brush and protected by a pair of viciously-spined cacti. It was there he waited for the fire from the steam engine to burn itself out.

With the rumbling of an imminent storm, Rafaele anticipated the rain would help cool any lingering hot spots, after which he'd investigate.

He rested with his war bag beneath his head as a pathetic pillow and slept, enjoying a respite from the worst of the winds and rain.

With the early light of morning, Rafaele awakened, emerging to find the ground still muddy.

He cursed the weight he'd gained and adjusted his suspenders a little, thankful for having them since he'd been unable to button the trousers of his tracking attire.

Rafaele made his way toward the wreckage and crouched behind the line of trees separating fertile soil from the loose sand near the gulley. He watched through a pair of Edison's enhanced binoculars.

It came as no surprise several men were sifting through the remnants of the explosion and subsequent fire. It *was* surprising, however, when none of them were removing valuables from the victims.

No; theirs was a more specialized search: they were hunting for him. His hunch was verified when one of them located the wolf-engraved belt buckle with a whoop and a holler, another finding his trunk which they carefully dissected, removing what could be valuable to brokers of pawn.

Their cheers lured in another man from the outskirts of the debris. Rafaele lowered his binoculars and silently made his way to get a better view of the newcomer who was shouting orders at the group.

The buckle was handed from man to man, heads nodding, arms swinging out to what Rafaele left behind.

They were, indeed, pleased with their get.

Once he repositioned himself, Rafaele again looked through the binoculars and was dismayed though unsurprised to see a so-called friendly face.

Booker.

The Devil's pubic hair, himself.

Of course it was Booker; between not being fooled by Rafaele's usual alias and the orchestrated explosion that destroyed the trestle being nothing short of a professional display, he shouldn't have been surprised.

The explosion wasn't just effective, it had a sense of show he guessed made everyone on the train know their fate before meeting it.

Such was Booker's style.

As Booker listened to his men, he turned the buckle over in his hands and looked unconvinced of their claims, as Rafaele feared.

He hoped the traces of his presence would be convincing enough since he couldn't leave behind his body. How convenient it would've been.

Rafaele remained in hiding while Booker and his men finished their search, mounted their horses and rode east.

He sighed, vowing a second time he would get Shadow Wolf's buckle back. Undoubtedly, he would encounter those men again upon his return to Redington—if not sooner. He had no plan for that eventuality.

Yet.

But with a little time and a lot of patience, he was confident he'd think of something brilliant—such was *his* style.

After they'd been gone for a couple hours, Rafaele made his careful descent into the wash, the dried and cracked mud crunching beneath his moccasins.

It took another hour or so to reach the wreckage, after which he spent the rest of the evening carefully sifting through the mess, collecting a hefty bounty of money and valuables from the luggage and bodies while he reflected on the situation.

Though he prepared for the eventuality, he wasn't keen on having to return to Redington via any other means of transport. Worst was realizing this could add a week to his travels if he didn't encounter any complications.

Given the circumstances, Rafaele expected plenty.

CHAPTER 16

aeve answered the pounding at the front door, stunned to find Liam there, haggard and breathless.

"Ye look dreadful," she gasped. "What's the matter?"

"Terrible news from the rails."

Maeve leaned back, her eyebrows kinking together so hard they ached. Where the statement should've been exclaimed to match his physical appearance, it was delivered with utter indifference, as if he were an automaton, his lines previously dictated to him by another person.

When Maeve didn't move, Liam slapped her in the chest with the newspaper. "Read."

Her gaze skimmed the text, and with it, her heart dropped to her feet; for a moment, she feared the world would drop away from her, as well. "It—can't be—" *Oh, lord. That's Raf's train.*

"I'm sorry, but it is. And as such, I believe you're in grave danger and must vacate Miss Chesterfield's home at once."

"Yes—Let me—just—get everyone—" Sounds were fading away, Maeve's entire body succumbing to numbness. Liam may have been prattling on, but she was focused on the article and its implications.

She wanted so badly for this to be some awful story fabricated by Liam, but with Dallahan torturing her all this time, deliciating in making her life hell, it was hard to dismiss the news as fiction.

"I could've played this nicely, but you're expecting those insufferable women to come along, and I simply can't have that. This is an invitation for you, alone." With his gun aimed at her chest, he wiped the corner of his eye. "Let's not belabor this, shall we? As if you have a choice in the matter."

Liam didn't appear any more like the man she knew or the boy she remembered—his eyes wide, sunken, soulless. For a split second, he resembled Dallahan come for more torment.

He over-enunciated, "If you're not at my room with your worldly possessions by 1:45, I will find and kill the ladies of this household on my way to you."

Maeve was so taken aback by his orders, his behavior, and the news, she couldn't find any words with which to respond before he turned to depart.

Liam paused long enough to repeat, "1:45, Miss MacKenna. Don't be late."

She turned and looked at the grandfather clock in Alexis's front hall. 1:45 was less than two hours away. An eternity in the blinking of an eye.

Maeve moved as if within a bad dream, treading water merely to prolong her inevitable drowning. Even rushing to her room felt like dragging herself through molasses.

It was Kököle who first appeared at her door. "Maeve?"

She couldn't answer through her tears and the ever-mounting effort to not vomit.

"Please talk to me."

Maeve dropped the newspaper on her pillow and frantically pawed through her belongings, too harried to be able to determine what was worth keeping. Without Rafaele, none of it was. She gagged on her words: "This can't be happenin'."

"What's going on?" Kököle asked, her voice rising.

"I have to go."

"You have to go?" Moencopi joined her sister in Maeve's bedroom. "Where?"

"Oh, hell no," said Alexis, pushing by the twins on her way into the room. "You're not going anywhere."

Maeve glanced at Alexis with a glower. "I'm too tired to fight. 'N' ..." *without Raf or his baby* ... "What's even the point anymore?"

"So ..." Alexis cleared her throat and blurted, "You lose a baby and you're completely giving up on fighting for anything?" She gasped, slapping her hands against her mouth. "I—I didn't mean that."

But Maeve knew she *did* mean it; such unforgivable sentiment wasn't the sort of thing to get thrown around flippantly. For how long had the cruel thought been festering in Alexis's head?

There was a long silence while the twins backed away from them.

Maeve slammed the half-empty trunk shut. "All me life I've been runnin' from Death 'n' it seems he finds me wherever I go. He followed me thousands upon thousands of miles to take away the single thing I'd have at this point tha' actually meant somethin' to me. He hunts down those I love. Wants me life to be nothin' but misery. I need to accept tha' constant presence as me fate." *Maybe I should just go with him already.*

Her breathing heavy, Alexis replied, "I've been biting my tongue all this time but now you've reached a point where I've gotta say it: you should be grateful Raf's not here. If he saw this, I'm sure he'd be having second thoughts about marrying you."

"How dare ye say tha'," Maeve seethed. "I killed Esquivar for sayin' less hurtful things!"

"Maeve, please—" Kököle interjected.

Though Maeve couldn't bear to be around Alexis anymore, she attempted to verbalize the more pressing issue: "Liam ... after he told me ..." But the words wouldn't come. If she said them, they'd become real. "... He said I needed to leave, else he'd kill ye all."

"Screw that," replied Alexis. "Let's fight him!"

"If I fight, I'll kill him. If I flee, he'll kill ye all before findin' me. He'll endanger anyone who attempts to help me. I can't risk tha'!"

"No. No, no. You've gotta get over this—this 'Rede' business you're hiding behind and stand up for yourself. Fight back, for God's sake! With your help, we could stand our ground. Surely between the four of us we can! Especially if you did to Liam what you did to Frank."

Maeve whipped around, her eyes flashing. "Ye've done nothin' but insult me, break me heart worse than it already was, 'n' belittle everythin' I believe in. 'N' there's no point in arguin' with ye because ye'll not ever understand. Ye can't understand. We're too different. Too different from everyone else 'n' too different from each other. I don't want to do to Liam what I did to Esquivar! Get tha' through yer thick skull, ye eejit!"

Alexis put her hands out in defense, her breath catching in her throat. "My God—your … your hands!" She swallowed hard. "They're glowing red! Calm down—please—before you do something we all regret!"

"I'll do no such thing!"

"Listen to me: I do understand how it is to be different." Alexis gripped her by the upper arms. "Don't you remember?"

Maeve yanked her arms from Alexis's grasp. "How can ye possibly compare our situations? We—'n' they—are nothin' alike. Havin' to go around makin' yerself out to toleratin' wearin' a skirt for a few hours a day is not the same as … as … not even bein' human!"

Alexis's eyes shimmered. "You miserable harpy," she whispered. "How dare you trivialize my plight?"

Maeve gaped at her before blurting, "Yer plight? Ye don't have a plight; ye have what ye perceive as problems. 'N' tha' is why ye cannot possibly understand me difficulties. Now for the last time: I cannot—I *will* not—kill him! 'N' I will not let him kill ye. I refuse to be responsible for anyone havin' to kill anyone. There *has* to be another way; death can't always be the answer!" *That's what Dallahan wants.*

"You don't get it," Alexis snapped. "Sometimes there's no other answer." She over-enunciated, "He will kill you."

"Then I'll die. As a human. As a woman. But not as a monster. Ye promise me ye won't do anythin' to endanger yerself."

"Whatever. Sure. Fine, go. Don't let me stop you." Alexis grunted, storming from the room.

Maeve stared after her. In one way, she was relieved. In another: stunned.

In the ensuing silence, Kököle sat on the bed. "You don't have to do this because O'Doherty says to."

"Yes. I do. So either help me … or get out of me way." She opened the trunk and dropped a couple more garments into it before drilling her knuckles into her eyelids with a long groan.

After several moments, Kököle ventured: "Maeve?"

Around the fire in her throat, Maeve replied, "Me ma used to call me tha: 'harpy.' Wretched harpy, awful harpy. Wicked harpy. I amn't." She yelled, slamming the trunk shut again. "I amn't!"

"We are quite certain you are not those things," Moencopi said softly.

"I'm goin' to prove it. Someday." She hoped sooner rather than later as she curled her fingers around the handle of her athame. Thinking better of packing it, Maeve deliberately left it out of the trunk. Taking it would breed temptation to use it in ways for which it wasn't meant.

"Please don't die just to prove a point."

Maeve finished packing without acknowledging Kököle's request and changed into a travelling gown before making certain her luggage was retrieved from Alexis's front door on schedule.

Unsurprisingly, Alexis refused to bid Maeve farewell. Moencopi and Kököle stood wordlessly at the door as she departed.

The guards all followed Maeve away from Alexis's home, their weapons trained on her. She realized sullenly that they were only there to watch for her, to keep her in compliance.

As she walked through Redington, she committed each building, every desert plant to memory, expecting this would be the last she would see of this place. There was a disquieting acceptance of her fate; perhaps Alexis was right about those hurtful things she'd said.

She raised her collar against the mist falling from grey skies to protect herself from the elements and to give herself as much time as possible outside.

Drizzle gave way to deluge like a great goddess wept from the clouds.

Redington's streets and their lack of drainage turned dirt to mud in the batting of an eye, Maeve's boot heels sinking into it and adding to her grief as she struggled now to walk.

The welts on her skin appeared, but as with her tears earlier, she was so numb that the accompanying pain didn't even register. It was of greater concern to maintain her footing where traction failed.

She rushed into the Redington hotel and approached the clerk at the front desk to ask breathlessly for directions to Liam's room.

The clerk—a spindly man she'd never spoken to but who she'd seen emerging on numerous occasions from Jia Li's room at the Tiff and Tawny

—startled when he addressed her, stumbling backward and bumping into the cubbies and key rack behind him.

"Miss MacKenna," he said with a yelp. He cleared his throat, regaining his composure. "Mr. O'Doherty's expecting you. He's in 203." He leaned over the desk to gesture. "Up those stairs, second door on the left."

Maeve nodded. "Thank ye."

She ascended the staircase, her uneven gait echoing on hollow steps. As she walked by the mirror at the second story landing, Maeve caught her reflection, flinching at her angry red, puffy face. She assumed her appearance was what caught the clerk off-guard.

The door of room 203 remained ajar, a shaft of flickering lamplight thrown across the hotel hallway's ornate runner.

She rapped on the door with her knuckles. No answer.

With her fingers splayed against it, Maeve eased open the door. Amid its creaking, she whispered, "Hello?"

Still nothing.

Holding her breath, she stepped inside.

A small cloth slapped over her nose and mouth, and in a single gasp of surprise, everything went black.

Alexis reviewed the newspaper article again: there were no survivors among the wreckage of the Southern Pacific. Her first thought had been the unfortunate timing of the disaster and how it'd delay Rafaele's return. He could catch a stage or several between San Diego and Redington although he was much more likely to go on horseback. Taking horses had always been his preferred mode.

But when she couldn't ignore the nagging fear at the back of her head—the same fears Maeve so readily gave in to—Alexis pulled out the telegram she'd most recently received.

Addressed to Mayv MacKenna from her father, Jim, the message detailed his pending visit to Redington, including the train he'd planned on taking: the very same locomotive that met its end at the bottom of an Arizonan wash.

Alexis felt as if she'd been doused by a bucket of ice. "Oh, my God." She crunched the newspaper in her fist.

And while Maeve had quietly kept the news to herself, Alexis had behaved like the very she-beast she'd accused Maeve of being. "Oh, my God!" she yelled.

Feeling sick to her stomach, she hoisted herself from her bed and padded through her house, listening.

Moencopi was taking Maeve's leaving harder than Alexis thought she should, her weeping audible over the pouring rain outside. Between sobs and the crashing of thunder, she chastised herself for being so weak. She apologized repeatedly; for what, Alexis could only speculate.

Kököle emerged from Moencopi's room, shutting the door quietly behind herself. Turning to Alexis with eyes rimmed red, she commented with an irrepressible smile, "The plants here won't want for rain for months."

Oh, how Alexis disliked thinking these women had such powers. She drew in a deep breath. "The monsoons surely do such things." She retreated to the parlor, where she'd watched with wretched tears streaming down her cheeks as Maeve walked to certain death, followed by Liam's posted guards.

Kököle settled on the edge of her mattress as Alexis flopped into her chair.

"Why're you so happy?"

"You have to ask?" gawked Kököle. "Maeve's training with Moen to control her magic succeeded! Maeve said so herself: she laid waste to Esquivar for less than the unforgivable things you hurled at her."

"Hey! I couldn't have been the only one thinking them."

"Oh, I assure you, you could've. And if Maeve learned nothing from all those lessons, you and I certainly wouldn't be having this conversation."

"Yay," Alexis said flatly.

"Alexis?"

She turned away to hide her face from Kököle. "Maeve must believe she has nothing left to live for with the news of—" Alexis choked on her phlegm. "The train—"

"What news?"

Alexis offered the crumpled newspaper over her shoulder. "Front page, top center."

Kököle took her time with the article—all its three short paragraphs. She'd never been a strong reader and Alexis was grateful she hadn't been asked to speak those words aloud.

There was a sharp sniffle, the sounds of the newspaper being further crumpled. "You know as well as I Rafaele's still alive."

Alexis mumbled, "Glad to hear I'm not alone in my denial." It was what kept her from crying harder than Moencopi. *They* thought they'd lost someone significant to them? Rafaele meant the most to her of any of them —Maeve, included.

"Rafaele is alive," Kököle snapped. "And Maeve will be fine."

Alexis turned in her chair to look at Kököle, too afraid to reply as she was inclined: *If you insist.*

"Your plan? Don't make me come up with one. I'm not so good with those as you may recall."

Despite herself, Alexis smiled. She spoke, her mouth thick with saliva. "I —I remember." Glancing at the Ansonia mantle clock atop her curio cabinet, she thought aloud, "It's been an hour. Plenty of time for her to get where she's going, don't you think?"

Kököle's face lit up. "We're going after her?"

"I let her go. She's gone. But … I *did* promise Raf I'd keep her safe. So that's what we're gonna do." Alexis squared her shoulders. "Get Moen and we'll head out."

Kököle's gaze flickered in the direction of Moencopi's bedroom, then to the window bathed in sheets of rain. "We'd probably be better off leaving her here."

"You sure?"

A long rumble of thunder seemed to answer affirmative.

"It's a damn good thing I'm waterproof," muttered Alexis. To Kököle she said, "Let's go get our girl back."

Alexis's determination washed away once she and Kököle stepped outside amid the storm. "Oh shit." She rushed into the street, splashing ankle-high flood waters around her. In desperation, she dropped to her knees and tried bailing the flooding from itself, searching for clear water amid toffee-colored mud. "No, no, no, no, *no!*"

"What's wrong?"

"Any tracks there were are completely washed out now. Everything's washed out. We've got nothing to follow!" She inhaled through clenched teeth, glowering at the clouds.

"You're not going to get anywhere taking it out on the sky."

"No, I'm going to take it out on your sister." Alexis shouted, "God dammit, she needs to keep her emotions under control. She's gonna drown us all!" She jumped to her feet, kicking at the water and bellowing.

Kököle squeezed her eyes shut and said quietly, "There's gotta be something we can still do."

"Of course there's something we can do." She clenched the grip of her gun in its holster and shuddered. "We go door to door as quickly as possible and threaten people until we find her."

"That's not a good way to make friends."

"I'm not in this business to make friends." Alexis sneered at her. "I'm in it to keep what few I have."

Several hours later, Alexis concluded her Redington search in its hotel.

"O'Doherty was here," she told the clerk. "And he's taken Miss MacKenna. That would make you the last person to see her alive."

"My sincerest apologies," said the clerk, "but I cannot divulge any information about my customers. Surely you understand—"

Alexis brandished her firearm. "As the last person to see her alive, you're now the main suspect. I can take this exchange to Marshal Cummings, or I can forget I ever talked to you. Surely *you* understand you're in no position to withhold this information from us."

His stare locked on her pistol, the clerk cried, "Alright, alright, listen, I don't got no information on O'Doherty and the barwhore, OK? She came by hours ago, yea, but they ain't here no more! There was a scuffle 'n' by the time I got to room 203 it was empty. Check for yourself if'n you don't trust me."

"This game you play being what you're obviously not is reason enough to distrust you." She nodded at Kököle to follow and sprinted up the staircase two steps at a time.

To her crippling disappointment, room 203 was, indeed, vacant. Alexis kicked the bureau. "God dammit!"

"Now what?" said Kököle.

Alexis ran her hands over her face. "I have no idea."

Rain plinked against the barred window. The weather created a lovely respite from a cramped cell heated with too many big male bodies, although Milton objected to the accompanying damp.

Someone, somehow smelled of wet dog—and Rafaele was nowhere in sight.

In the month they'd all been incarcerated, there had been better days filled with lighthearted conversation and surprisingly good humor, or so Milton believed. There had also been plenty of bad ones where he was amazed they hadn't all tried to find some way to kill each other or somehow render one another permanently mute. Likely they wanted him dumbstruck most of all.

That Friday afternoon—it somehow felt like a Friday, anyway—was almost certainly one of the better ones.

Jethro proved a witty man when he was sober enough to think straight, and nobody bothered sneaking him alcohol in a month; half the time Tithu spoke, which was on the whole infrequently, Jethro remarked how much Rafaele had rubbed off on him.

Edison regaled his cellmates with the story of Rafaele's rescuing him from an asylum as if none of them knew it; he told his story with such panache that Milton's jealousy of his masterful oratory skills choked him— even if they'd all grown tired of hearing the same old story for the forty-second time.

Give or take.

Embittered by his envy, Milton criticized Edison's clothing, pointing out under the guise of lighthearted teasing: "Are you m-mending your shirt with metal? D-do you have no spare thread?"

"It's silver filament," Edison replied, toying with a patch where its thread gleamed in the light. "It was left over from a new mechanism I've been perfecting over the last year or so, and I've been using it to mend my clothing. It's unfortunate the mend will outlive the garment though. Maybe someday I'll use the thread to weave some silver fabric—"

The front door to the Redington jail squeaked open and shut quietly.

"It's gonna be hell if you're ever c-caught wearing that in wuh-winter," Milton remarked. "Fah-fabric made of silver thread? I like you, S-stilwell, I truly do, buuut we better get outta here soon. I couldn't take you as a cell mate much longer."

"Well, Dandy," said Marshal Cummings upon his approach, "I'm afraid 'soon' has come." He withdrew a key from his pocket and slipped it into the lock on the cell door.

"Given circumstances I was just informed of, I'm sorry to say ..." He sighed, opening the cell door as wide as he could. "I'm sorry to say you're all free to go."

None of the incarcerated men moved from his spot as stunned glances were exchanged; there was no joy in newfound freedom if it meant Rafaele had died.

Patches of a waxing gibbous moon appeared amid thick clouds as the God-forsaken storm at long last ebbed.

Rafaele was soaked to his bones, cold, thoroughly done with being out-of-doors, starved half-to-death, exhausted, in a great deal of pain, and covered in mud from his moccasins to his curls. And it was becoming harder to dismiss that the black-tailed prairie dogs were reading his mind.

On the bright side, as the desert was a giant mud-puddle and the moon soon to set, he was adequately camouflaged against its backdrop.

The flash flood at Rio Santa Cruz and a risky maneuver had ensured the posse tailing him lost all trace of him—at least for the time being.

Would it be too much to hope Booker and his lackeys assumed he drowned in the flood alongside his poor sweet mount, and that they all were crowbait now?

Better yet, would it have been too much to ask that *they* had drowned in place of the innocent animal?

He permitted himself a small campfire for a warm meal —not as if Rafaele could make anything larger, especially not when natural kindling was soaked.

"*Sto morendo di fame*," he muttered, suturing by touch alone a wide though shallow gash he'd sustained on his left thigh while battling a wild boar over its delicious little life.

Although it would've been easy to sleep, he was more famished than he was exhausted. Unfortunately, he'd have to put in a lot of work to satiate his hunger.

It was only afterward did he realize he'd lapsed into Italian and chastised himself for what he considered a weakness; when distracted, wounded, exhausted, or all three at once as he was now, it was all too easy to forget he'd ever learned any English at all. For all his linguistic struggles, he didn't want to forget it.

He severed the string from its spool and knotted the fresh sutures, fearing the pain would never subside. He glared at the hog now bleeding out beside the fire. Historically, Rafaele would say a prayer for the creature as he had for the horse he'd lost to the flood waters.

"Ma questo bastardo—" He growled, finishing the sentiment in English: "—kind of deserved to die for what he did to me."

He wished it wouldn't spend its last breaths squealing so.

But there was no rest for the weary—or the wounded. Rafaele limped a few yards to the nearest opuntia, carefully removing a couple of its lightest green paddles. He used his knife to scrape them clean of their spines and prickles—perhaps going overboard to compensate for his exhaustion and the darkness. On the other hand, he didn't need his tongue pierced by its barbs for want of care in preparation.

Some rustling in the nearby brush wrenched his attention from his meal plans. He turned his gun to his pathetic excuse for a campsite as several pigs rushed in to investigate the slaughter of their brother-in-hams.

He thought fleetingly of having a feast at their expense and his stomach snarled in agreement. Much to his disgust, Rafaele watched as the living pigs lapped the blood pooling in the dirt.

Of everything he'd witnessed and experienced lately, it was that behavior to cause him to gag on his bile.

What sort of foul beasts revel in drinking the blood of their brother?

He watched from a safe distance, helpless, fearing the pigs might steal away his dinner once they were done drinking the blood. He didn't want to shoot any more than he already had as he didn't have an infinite supply of bullets and he didn't want to draw any attention to himself on the off-chance those pursuing him were within earshot. He also didn't want to kill any more animals and firing near the pigs would likely have the opposite effect than intended.

He exercised patience. After all, the boar he'd killed wasn't terribly large and would run out of blood sometime soon. With luck, the others would leave afterward.

Vampires, Rafaele realized. *Vampires drink the blood of their brothers. Sisters. Fathers, mothers. Anyone.*

He held his breath as several pigs nipped repeatedly at the hooves of his dinner.

And probably zombies would have no qualms eating their neighbor zombies if they got in each other's way. Zombie brains can't be especially nutritious for another zombie, can they?

Having exhausted his hog's supply of blood, the vile beasts trotted off in different directions, grunting, snorting, and oinking into the distance.

Rafaele limped back to the dead boar to begin the grueling chore of preparing it for eventual consumption.

He castrated it and removed its scent gland, hoping to have avoided taint, though he was sure the time for that passed while he tended his wound.

With its belly facing the sky, he pulled its skin back, using the boning knife of his prosthetic arm to work his way down, reducing an hour-long chore to fifteen minutes in his carelessness to preserve its fat. This would be no gourmet meal.

He exhaled, switching to a smaller knife to make the cuts necessary to remove its entrails.

Rafaele would've been inclined to rest or to give up preparing the animal altogether but its death—and his injury—would've been in vain. So he continued, making a cut from the sternum to the groin to finish removing its entrails.

He manipulated the animal so gravity assisted in removing its internal organs, though he still needed to do much of the work with his bare hand; its connective tissues proved especially stubborn. Following that, he separated the ribs, cleared out the remaining organs and severed its head with the skinning knife on his prosthesis, each of many slashes accompanied by a staccato Italian expletive.

After taking several minutes to catch his breath, he hacked through the pig's backbones and pelvic bone, separating it into two sad little halves. He removed the hams near the fleshy part of its thighs with his boning knife and tended to removing the meat from its shoulders; he planned on letting that cook longest and eating it last.

Grateful the worst of it over, he spread out the meat on rocks placed around the fire.

He appreciated also that the demise of a small wild boar was a far less gory ordeal than a buffalo. On one hand, a smaller body produced less blood; on the other hand, it would result in less food.

This little piggy—under ten pounds in all—was going to be the slowest cooked pork in the history of all white meats.

He found a moderately-sized puddle in which to wash his hands; of course it wasn't optimal but muddy hands were better than bloody ones, he supposed.

To stave off his hunger while the beast roasted for the better part of the night, Rafaele set to warming the opuntia paddles over the fire.

Francisco favored them to Cookey's meals on nights the Pack was away from civilization. He called them *napoles* and ate them raw, adept at ignoring the stares of disgust he received all the while.

The cur was long gone and still Rafaele scolded himself for not dispatching Francisco any number of times he'd had the opportunity.

Rafaele attempted to wipe the opuntia's secretions from his fingertips; it reminded him of aloe vera sap.

His eyebrow quirked.

Kököle once told him of aloe's healing properties during their many exchanges about the medicinal potential of the land surrounding them. Perhaps opuntia could do similar things.

Praying it wouldn't make matters worse or be the death of him, Rafaele squeezed the juice from a paddle onto the stitched-up gash on his thigh.

To his relief, it *was* a relief; not as good as if the boar hadn't caught him with its hoof, but it was soothed enough he believed he might be able to sleep tonight—once he ate enough to silence his stomach's growling.

Rafaele closed his eyes and bit into the opuntia pad. The experience was surreal; it had the crunch of raw bell pepper with an essence of lemon. Perhaps he was so ravenous, he didn't find it as objectionable as anticipated.

He devoured both paddles and considered having at least a couple more while the pig cooked. Instead, he curled up on his side as close as he could safely get to the fire, clinging to the thoughts of Maeve that would carry him through the night.

In the crackling of the fire, Maeve's voice whispered his name, broiling seduction cloaking him in much-needed warmth.

Visions tormented Maeve in her sleep of Rafaele alive but alone and injured; Rafaele being torn from her embrace; earthquakes rending apart the ground beneath her feet, towering evergreen trees all around her one-by-one ravaged by flame. Falling, falling into blackness without end. And ice water. Drowning, being pulled from the brink of death by Dallahan, himself—the most excruciating experience of them all.

She woke, her skin still prickling from the water in what she hoped was nothing more than a brutal dream.

When she discovered she was unable to move—not her body, neither her head—she closed her eyes and attempted to stay calm. Maeve couldn't tell if she were tethered to something or if the paralysis was an upshot of being injured or drugged. Who knew what happened after she was knocked out?

So there she lay, mentally scrambling to recover the fading tendrils of her dreams—or premonitions—before they were lost forever. And maybe, considering how awful they were, that wasn't a bad thing.

Some time later, in the darkness, Maeve tilted her head slightly, then shook it side-to-side. She exhaled in relief.

Use of her fingers was returning, too. Though her arms felt like leaden weights, her fingers rubbed against what she was resting on.

A bed.

I'm in a ... comfortable 'n' ... oddly familiar bed. Not MacTavish's.

'N' it's not Alexis's, to be sure.

She inhaled, surrounded by scents she recognized: a mild and sweet wood, lamp and machine oils, a touch of sweat that made her wild inside.

Her eyes popped open, her pulse quickening. Though the room was dark, Maeve's night vision was excellent. All around her was familiar décor and furniture.

Rafaele's home! But tha' would have to mean— Her heart thudded. *I'm still dreamin'. I have to be.*

Maybe this one wouldn't go bad and she could live in it for the rest of her life.

The floor creaked outside the bedroom accompanied by the light foot-falls of a small animal, or maybe a child.

Undoubtedly it was Rafaele, returned home from his adventure. In a heartbeat, he'd be there with her. Because in this dream world, that outcome was still possible.

So why did her chest ache and her tear ducts burn? If this were a dream, she had no reason to cry.

The bedroom door whined as it eased open, a tall silhouette backlit by oil lamps.

Maeve squinted against the cruel light. "O'Doherty—?" she choked on her breath. "No!" Rather than being trapped in a wonderful dream, she was trapped in hell.

"No?" he replied. "You're breaking my heart."

"Liar!" Maeve spat, still too weak to lunge at him the way she wanted. "Ye'd have to have a heart for it to break."

"I don't deserve that," warned Liam, wagging his finger at her. "Apologize to me."

She scowled, "Make me."

Liam charged for her and wrapped his giant hand around her neck, pressing her into the mattress until she could scarcely breathe. "Apologize!"

Her impulse was to ask why she should but his crushing the life from her was the apparent answer.

"I'm—sorry—" Maeve rasped.

He pulled his hand away but didn't retreat, glowering at her. "Good little girl."

She struggled to put her fingertips to her neck, still without strength enough to rub away her pain.

"I expect your full compliance from here on out. And I demand your respect."

Again, Maeve fought the desire to ask why she should but lost the battle: "Why?" she croaked.

"'Why' what?" Liam snapped.

She'd faced off with Dallahan and lived—twice, now—and had the power to make people cease to exist. Yet Maeve's fear of Liam didn't seem irrational to her.

"Why—are ye doin' this? What have I done to deserve yer hatred?" she whispered, her voice shaking.

"Oh, my dear," cooed Liam, stroking her cheek with the back of his hand. "How simple you must be to confuse love with hatred. What did that louse Forino poison you with that you don't recognize pure adoration?"

Maeve had memories of love, but also memories of antagonism pure as it got. *Have I mistaken lust for love? Did Raf want me only the same as he used Caitlyn? Dear god, was Esquivar tellin' me the truth 'n' I was too stupid 'n' stubborn to believe him?*

But surely love didn't threaten or belittle as Liam did here and now.

It didn't strangle—of that, she was certain.

What difference did any of it make? Rafaele was gone and with him, whatever it was they had together—love, lust, infatuation, or otherwise.

She wracked her brain for memories of her parents to serve as example. Had Ashling and Colin been in love with each other? Did she even know what love was? A chill washed over her; she doubted she'd ever seen it from Ashling—either toward Colin or herself.

Maeve may not have been able to recognize love in retrospect. That her skin crawled at Liam's touch, however, was anything but.

He cleared his throat. "Rest, little church mouse. We won't be staying here more than a few days. It's a mere stop-over on a much longer trip."

"What are we waitin' for?" Perhaps if she interfered with whatever it was, she could put off this 'much longer trip.' She feared he planned to take her back to County Donegal; Maeve would sooner die in Redington and spare them both the misery.

"Angelino is expecting to be paid for his job."

"For his job?" Maeve's mouth fell open with a gasp as it all struck her at once. "Ye put Booker up to destroyin' tha' train. Ye did tha' to kill Raf!"

"My dear little Maeve, how crude." Liam clucked. "Forino died on the train due to some old vendetta Booker had. I will admit it's all gravy to my solving the saloon mystery and eradicating Redington of its criminal element. I'm this place's St. Patrick and everyone here will thank me for it. And then you'll accompany me to better places."

CHAPTER 17

 afaele had lost all track of time and barely recognized where he was after so many attempts at changing his course to lose the posse trailing him. He was maybe outside Benson, somewhere roughly southeast of his destination. Though unsuccessful at losing them so far, Rafaele was keeping a day ahead—barely. They must've been resting whereas he went without.

To that point, Rafaele couldn't be sure anymore what was real and what was hallucination; Maeve, standing on the hillside and beckoning to him while the prairie dogs watched him struggle to reach her—continuing to chitter amongst themselves about his thoughts.

Criticizing his religious convictions.

They were saying Catholicism was wrong.

Well what the hell do they know? They're dumb, Godless rodents.

He shook his head, trying to snap himself from his daze as he trudged uphill through the desert, too tired and pained to lift his feet from the sand as he walked.

His enemies hadn't been shy with their gunfire; fortunately for Rafaele, nobody in that group had Billy Dixon's—or Alexis's—aim.

He wondered if they were deliberately missing him, making a twisted game of this hunt. No man deserved such torture. With a grimace, he realized he'd given his wild boar more respect, which spoke volumes considering he'd castrated and beheaded the poor thing. *The poor, delicious thing. I could go for another poor, delicious thing like that right now.*

Alas, he hadn't such luxuries; neither time nor distance were on his side and he hadn't seen a wild pig in days. Plenty of quail, though, but one hardly passed as an appetizer. And to prepare it for eating meant touching it.

Rafaele's stomach protested and he instead set his mind to analyzing the behavior of this gang chasing him. There was a significant chance they were trying to guide him to a specific place, likely into an ambush. Lord only knew how many men were after him. He'd never seen more than two at any given time, but he wasn't sure if they were the same duo. If so, good. If not, he was going against nine—at least.

Those odds were not in his favor.

Rafaele reached an overlook and hissed, *"Merda,"* as he dropped to the ground.

In the ravine below, a makeshift camp had been erected. He counted eight horses grazing on damp brush and six tents situated around a little fire. A small army's worth of munitions was scattered throughout the encampment, the men's supplies unpacked from their mounts. This was an established site and they were waiting.

As they had yet to shoot at him, Rafaele assumed the men below hadn't seen him. He skulked along the ground, availing himself of his muddied camouflage.

Despite the layout of the camp and its arsenal of weaponry, the four men below didn't appear to be on sentry duty, huddled in a group facing each other. Probably talking.

It was nice for once to have an advantage.

The dirt a few feet from him kicked up in a spray; there went his perceived advantage. There was another spray of dirt a few feet to his other side. Rafaele paused long enough to watch the men in the ravine scrambling for their guns.

Several more shots landed close enough in the dirt that they sprayed it against his trousers; unlike the previous, these shots came from behind.

He scrambled for safety before freezing, flattening himself to the mud, his heart racing. The edge of the ravine was inches away, a cliff that would lead him into an assortment of cacti waiting to impale him, and crevices certainly home to diamondbacks and bark scorpions waiting to strike at him on his descent.

From his spot, however, through a couple scraggly desert shrubs, Rafaele watched the men frantically scouring the area.

He suspected those shots were made not to scare or harm him but to alert the others of his proximity.

Well, he reasoned, *if they already know I'm here, I may as well hurry along the inevitable.*

Rafaele fiddled with the weapon on his arm, stopping before he activated Edison's light gun.

No.

Instead, he went for the pistol he'd tucked into his belt at the small of his back, favoring it to Edison's fanciful invention. *They'll hear the noise but not see the flash of light from its barrel,* he thought, giving himself confidence to see his idea to fruition. *Yes.*

He fired at the rocks across the way and held his breath as the sound echoed off the eroded chasm walls, the bullet ricocheting before it hit the dirt near their encampment. Falling rocks and dust drew the gang's attention to the wall opposite his position.

Perfetto.

Rafaele sneaked down the hill while the two men who were trailing him gave up their pursuit and joined their group at the camp. They didn't receive the warmest reception. The lead cowboy flailed toward the crumbling cliffside while yelling something about Forino getting pushed too close to the edge.

He may not have recognized the clothing, but the voice was Booker's.

A wicked smile spread across Rafaele's lips as Booker sent his men the wrong way to locate him.

Now he had time to safely put some distance between them, which afforded him the best chance to make it back to Redington, maybe even within a day or two if he didn't stop long to eat or rest.

And he departed with a headcount: six. If he weren't exhausted, those odds would almost be in his favor.

Liam had scoured the kitchen numerous times—from the countertop to the pantry, from every drawer to each cabinet—ensuring he hadn't missed removing a single blade from the premises. Certainly it would make food preparation a tedious affair but when Mr. Davidson revisited him and gave a convincing argument suggesting Maeve's temperament wasn't beyond turning a butter knife into a weapon, the upshot of his well-being was worth her inconvenience. While Liam assumed the warning was for his safety, the alleged undertaker continued with little restraint and a wicked grin: *You wouldn't be much loss if she turned on you, but I don't want her escaping. It'd be such a chore*, he'd asserted, *to track her down again.*

Out of spite for the man, Liam would make him work to find her—with the additional benefit of keeping her for himself.

He patted the only weapon in the cabin—where it belonged, holstered to his hip—and scowled in recollection; this detour wasn't part of the bargain. He meant to remove Forino from Maeve's life but otherwise refused to follow Davidson's instructions to the letter despite his overwhelming compulsion.

Mr. Davidson had a real way about him that made Liam abhor him.

On the bright side, Liam had made a small fortune pawning those items —along with many others he curated from Rafaele's residence. Among them, the item which reaped the highest return from an unlikely gentleman who happened to be at Rosenzweig's at the right time: Maeve's engagement ring.

Once he again verified the lack of knives in the cabin, Liam peered into the bedroom.

Maeve appeared especially vulnerable in a state of undress as she struggled into her clothing with her back to the door.

She wore nothing but her boot, stocking, combinations, and corset— inadvertently presenting him an absolutely titillating silhouette. On the bed was her most conservative outfit in shades of deep blues and black. Had she laid out an outfit he'd given her as an attempt to curry his favor or to play the modest woman she obviously wasn't?

Liam's breath caught in his throat as she bent at the waist to adjust the laces of her boot, exposing herself enough that he saw she kept herself bare. Just as he remembered her.

Blood rushed to his cheeks.

Maeve straightened and raised her bustle, carefully stepping into it.

Blood drained from his cheeks.

It was when she put on the underskirt that Liam let his hand wander to his trousers.

Maeve scowled as she scrubbed a stubborn crusty stain in the crotch of Liam's pants. When he shoved the garment in her face, he'd insisted he spilled his drink on his lap and demanded she fulfill her womanly duty by washing it.

She'd asked how a grown man made such a mess and he'd had the audacity to blame her; Maeve shuddered at the implications.

She was desperate to believe it was anything but what she knew in her heart it had to be.

Despicable, she scoured, *disgustin' man*!

If Liam did all this deliberately to break her spirits, she feared he was well on his way to succeeding.

There was no way her hands would ever feel clean again despite the boiling water she used to wash his pants. Her eyes settled on her left hand beneath the surface of the water, and its lack of engagement ring.

It was the most recent thing to have gone missing while she was interned at Rafaele's cottage. She hadn't witnessed Liam take anything but it was hard to dismiss the likelihood he was to blame.

Maeve had managed to hide a few things of Rafaele's to ensure they survived—perhaps, eventually, a Pack member might find them, and there could be some legacy or reminder Rafaele ever existed.

She swallowed hard, her anger rising.

After grinding the fabric along a washboard with more force than necessary, Maeve rinsed it and wrung it out with little care, even going so far as to hope she ruined the repulsive garment.

Rafaele had left no clothesline—understandable given he'd all but abandoned this place.

With a steaming, wet lump of fabric in her hands, Maeve stood and gazed at the small cabin.

It wasn't glamorous, it certainly wasn't big, what with its modestly-sized master bedroom and the second bedroom so small it only fit a cot and a small end table. Maeve wondered who'd inhabited that shoebox-sized bedroom prior to Liam.

The cabin could've been a castle with Rafaele there. Instead it appeared to be the kind of place where families were chopped into bite-sized pieces and a blood-doused axe was left embedded in a tree stump beyond the backdoor.

There was an appallingly graphic story printed in the newspaper about recent Apache raids that was much too similar to what Maeve's imagination conjured; perhaps she dredged it up subconsciously.

He's goin' to kill me, Maeve realized. *Or maybe I'm just hopin' he will.*

Of course it was wishful thinking; she hadn't earned release from this world. No—it would continue to test her resolve and loyalty to her adherence to the Rede.

First harm none.

Harm.

None.

So lost in thought, Maeve caught her right foot on a soft, raised patch of desert floor, stumbling for several steps before straightening. *Even the earth hates me.*

Maeve steadied herself and stalked into her little personal hell, greeted by Liam who'd waited for her at the door all the while.

"What a graceful little dance," he remarked with a smirk.

With a guttural yell, Maeve pitched the damp trousers into Liam's chest.

"Ow! That's hot!"

"I'm goin' to bed," she snarled, "'n' do not ye dare follow!"

So naturally, following Maeve to the bedroom despite her demand was just what Liam did. She slammed the door in his face, awash with a chill.

He's still out there.

"Of course he's still out there," she hissed to the voice in her head.

She held her breath. The floorboards creaked on the other side of the door.

So what are you gonna do about it?

"What *can* I do?"

I think you know—

Maeve shook her head fervently. "I amn't cracked enough in the head to continue arguin' with meself." *More.*

Seemingly in response, the small pedestal end table across the room jerked and slid several feet toward her.

She may not have been cracked enough to argue with the voice in her head, but she wondered if Liam's treatment was leading her to hallucinate.

Rafaele didn't want to admit to being lost but if he'd been on track, he'd have reached the San Pedro River already.

He was certain he'd seen that twisted pair of saguaros and the cholla covered in bird excrement in the saguaros' shadow several times already.

Hardly seeing straight and barely able to walk anymore, Rafaele's posture turned him into a human version of those saguaros, and as he clutched the waistband of his trousers to keep them from dropping to his ankles, he regretted having sacrificed his suspenders to use as a poor man's tourniquet on his thigh wound.

Against his judgment, he had to stop.

He had to rest. He had to hope they wouldn't find him yet.

I'll maybe stop here—

And regardless of his intent, Rafaele's knees buckled and he hit the sand beside a lush desert willow.

He heard Maeve's voice loud and clear as if he rested in her loving shadow: *Sleep well, me beloved. Ye've earned it. It is, after all Sunday, 'n' even God rested today. I can wait for ye to return to me ... but ye can return to me only if ye survive.*

Then, sure as if she kneeled beside him, Rafaele felt her hand brush his cheek. Gentle, warm, and soothing.

He exhaled, a smile gracing his lips as sleep stole him from this world.

Liam watched Maeve emerge from the bedroom looking a fright, her ghostly pale skin a striking pallor against what must've been the darkest gown she owned—a blue so deep that in Forino's cavernous excuse for a home it appeared black.

Jet drops dangled from her earlobes, swaying enough he glimpsed them among the matted strands of her filthy hair. This lack of self-care was excusable given current circumstances but there would be harsh correction should the behavior continue once they were on their way. He couldn't be seen in public with a woman so disheveled.

Maeve sat at the dining room table and he experienced an unwelcome twinge of pity for the thing. Nonetheless he couldn't resist making a saccharine observation: "I've given you a full wardrobe, and yet you choose to wear mourning colors again? Who the hell died?"

She kept her head down, unkempt hair concealing her face. "Ye know full well who died."

There was no anger in her voice. There was barely anything, anymore.

It was unsurprising she had little strength when she refused to eat, and at night fell victim to fits of faintness and hallucinations that included either talking to herself as if chatting with someone else or talking to Rafaele as if he were still alive and beside her.

Such behavior, too, would be remedied once they left Redington.

Where's Booker? Liam's patience—and time—was running out. Not that he intended on paying the bastard as promised, but he was a liability; the only person who could connect the train explosion to Liam. The sooner he showed up, the sooner he could be taken care of.

He cleared his throat. "Must you mope? The train incident is old news. Besides," Liam lied, "you're so much more attractive in lighter colors. The dark positively overwhelms you."

A spark of energy lit her face as her head snapped up, her abnormally dark gaze meeting his. "I will wear dark colors as long as I'm grievin' 'n' tha' is very likely to be for the rest of me life!"

Liam straightened in his seat; he had his work cut out for him if after so much, she was still prone to ill-tempered outbursts.

He would start by disposing of any garments she considered grieving attire. *What a waste of money.* He bristled.

"Why do ye insist on torturin' me, Mr. O'Doherty?"

"Liam," he sighed. "I've told you to call me Liam."

"Ye haven't earned as much. Mister. O'Doherty."

"Liam. Liam, Liam, Liam!" he yelled, slamming his fist on the table. "O'Doherty is the best ye'll ever get from me."

Maeve came to, a dreadful throbbing in her forehead spreading throughout her face. Her whole body hurt; he must've broken numerous bones in addition to knocking her unconscious. There wasn't much point in moving as it would do nothing but exacerbate her injuries and agony and delay her healing time. *Me country for some laudanum.*

What had caused the beating this time? Shooting off her mouth? Refusing to behave as he demanded or just being on the receiving end of a physical thrashing for no other reason than to torment her? She couldn't recall what set him off.

She was so miserable that forcing her mind to wander met with little success; even thoughts of Rafaele couldn't distract her from the deep radiating pains throughout her arm and torso. *I wish I could leave me body behind to heal.*

Her eyes popped open. She knew of astral projection—both from her old Book of Shadows and from providing a special powder to help magicless insomniacs find rest—but she'd never tried it herself for fear of being lost in the spirit plane forever. She'd had a lot to live for back then, things which Liam and Dallahan both recently stripped her of.

If she couldn't find her way back to her body, would it be such a loss? Perhaps she could even seek out Rafaele and their baby on that plane. Maeve saw no downside.

There would be no 'letting go' and relaxing her way into this state; she was in too much agony for any kind of tranquility. She'd have to try a different method, though she hadn't much confidence that would work, either.

Tears slipped from her eyes and settled in her ears as she focused on a particularly large knot in the wood ceiling overhead. It could've been mere minutes, but it felt like hours before Maeve noticed the shift happening: the aches, the pain, the electric shock of her injuries falling away from her, replaced by strange though welcome sensations.

Tingles of intense energy overtook her small frame, a hiss buzzed in her ears like billions of voices whispering. Was it warning?

No. Encouragement.

Keep going! You're almost there!

It would've been easy to give in to the fear tethering her to her wounded body, but she wouldn't be deterred. Maeve remained still, relaxing deeper into herself, deeper and deeper until her view of the immediate surroundings altered. She slipped from her body and fell through the mattress beneath it before she forced her spirit to stop on the floor.

Rafaele's bed was comprised, as Maeve learned from falling through it, of three individual mattresses—the top a pad of feathers, the middle filled with a blend of animal hair and wool, and the bottom entirely straw. How was any of that comfortable?

Not taking especial pleasure from where she'd ended up, her consciousness crawled out from amidst the mattress and stood, taking in the not-quite-right visions of the world around it.

She felt light, free, and wonderfully without aches as she turned a circle in her spot. Was she clothed as an astral form on this other plane? Did she have both her legs here—or no legs at all? *Or still only one and a half?* Maeve waved her hand in front of her face and saw nothing. She turned her gaze toward the ground; again, nothing. She wasn't sure if this was the result of being a spirit or being inexperienced, but whatever the case, it disappointed her.

She wandered into the neighboring room through the closed door, noticing a faint campfire scent along the way. When she glanced behind her, she caught gentle tendrils of smoke coming from the door itself and curling after her.

The mirror across the room afforded her no better insight into her appearance on this plane; just the faintest orb easily missed by the uninitiated. Maeve, however, was anything but inexpert.

A decidedly-not-Maeve motion caught her incorporeal eye; she followed it as it circled her. It was all black and blue shadow, human-shaped, featureless, but recognizable as a feminine figure.

Despite a lifetime of experience with spirit-entities, Maeve was intimidated by whatever this was: an absence of light, a black shape with piercing white dots where its eyes might have been. It approached her, standing within reaching distance.

Maeve went awash with ice, as if her blood ran cold; an unpleasant sensation on a typical day, but especially disconcerting when she considered she lacked the physical body to feel it.

From somewhere behind her, Maeve heard several knocks but remained rooted to her spot, afraid to address them as the ghostly figure drew closer to her again.

She convinced herself the entity spoke to her: foreign sounds, including one that may have been her name.

She was vaguely aware of the sound of a door opening behind her.

The shadow vanished through the wall into the bedroom where her body, unguarded, remained.

She was keenly aware of being alone.

It dawned on her: the knocking on the bedroom door and its being opened meant Liam was in there with her and she was unable to defend herself.

She rushed in through the open door to find Liam half-dressed, standing at the foot of the bed as the shadow thrashed at him, enveloped him, and whipped around him—all to no avail. He didn't acknowledge any of it, so transfixed on watching her motionless body on the bed.

There was the fleeting motion of his hair, some papers on the dresser lifting so slightly Maeve thought she'd imagined it.

She moved beside him, following his gaze to her body: battered, bruised, its ashen complexion and open, unfocused eyes appearing all but lifeless.

Did he believe her to be dead? *I couldn't be so lucky.*

Despite what must've been the wraith's frantic attempts at intervention, Liam put his knee on the bed, then the other, crawling toward her.

Whatever he had in mind, Maeve knew she couldn't abide it. With his physical body blocking her ethereal path to return to hers, she was helpless in protecting herself.

Stop! yelled Maeve, which he ignored—either deliberately or because he couldn't hear her. *Get off me!* She attempted to will her body to fight him off but no strength of thought accomplished the impossible.

As Liam's face neared hers, she heard the wraith's words—difficult to understand, fragments of statements but it was inarguable they were directed at her.

L—ep—y—

T—me—h—p—you—

Maeve glanced toward the shadow, noticing what appeared to be hands wrapped around the base of the bedside lamp, motioning to pick it up and throw it.

I can't, Maeve cried. It wasn't because of the Rede, and it wasn't for lack of wanting to; she hadn't the strength to physically impact the world around her. And if not for that, Liam's head would've been bashed in.

Y—spir—t—act—n—

I can't do anythin', she replied to it.

The wraith's voice finally came loud, clear, and belittling: *You're a spirit, act like one and pass through him!*

Maeve hesitated.

Now! it shrieked.

She took what would have been a deep breath before diving for her body.

The moment her spirit merged with Liam she experienced an overwhelming rush of antagonism: rage, fear, confusion, an irrepressible need to dominate, and something else just beyond her reach. Something he, himself, scarcely resisted but was so deeply buried that it was like a starless night sky. An abyss.

Like searching Dallahan for his soul.

It was but a heartbeat they shared space and Maeve couldn't have been out the other side of him quickly enough, falling toward her body as Liam yelled in agony, pressing a hand to his chest where she passed through him.

He collapsed atop her.

The sensation of a fully-grown man's body hitting hers where broken bones were still healing was brutal and with her vocal chords within her reach, she screeched herself awake, her voice cracking and breaking around the edges, the ground beneath them shaking with its force when she momentarily lost control.

Maeve fought against him, throwing his body off and scurrying away through palatable agony until she tottered over the edge of the mattress. In desperation not to fall on the floor, she tried to grab onto the footboard of

the bed with her foot. Her right caught the ornamental metal frame and held fleetingly before she lost her grip and fell, collapsing beside the bed, the back of her head knocking against the wall. She stood despite the stars dancing in her vision.

When she put weight on her right foot, however, her leg shot out from under her as if the floor had iced over.

It took until after her third attempt to run before she noticed why she couldn't: her right leg tapered to a point near its ankle. Where her foot was supposed to be was nothing but damaged metal and pipe. Her stomach pitched to the floor at the sight of it.

Sound returned to her then: Liam's unwelcome footfalls as he rounded the bed toward her. She scooted back on her bustle to escape him and ended up cornered, instead. He kicked at something between them, and she flinched at the sound of metal scraping across the floor. On his second kick, she watched as her foot clattered into view.

It *had* been her right leg she'd tried gripping the bedframe with. She hadn't lost her grip, no: the ankle joint had come completely off her leg and sent her tumbling from the mattress.

Liam regarded Maeve with what may have been remorse—once upon a time, anyway—before his gaze travelled to her leg.

His lip curled in disgust as he snapped, "Fix it! I expect you back on your feet by dinner!"

Without another word or second glance, he stormed out.

Maeve exhaled a shaky breath before crawling to where he'd kicked her foot, picking it up and cradling it as she would the baby she lost.

She studied the exposed parts before checking her leg where it terminated at her ankle. Why hadn't she paid attention to Milton and Edison when they taught her to maintain and repair it? Where were they now? She feared Liam had killed them as he had, Rafaele. Likely soon she would be joining them.

The thought shouldn't have brought such profound relief, so she focused on her ankle.

Amid the ankle joint's mechanism, there was a single, inch-wide slot.

Her gaze traveled her shin and she ran her fingers over a long gash where the bedframe scraped the Parkesine, revealing gold-colored metal beneath it. She cursed.

Maeve studied the pipe protruding from the bottom of her leg—what replaced her shin bone, she supposed. It'd be a relatively easy fix if she applied a little ingenuity and a lot of elbow-grease.

She lined up the pipe with the hole in her prosthetic foot, pulling it on as if it were a shoe. While it fit and slid on a bit, there was still a good inch of the pipe exposed. She was pretty sure it wasn't on properly.

Slowly, Maeve stood, and gave the prosthesis a solid stomp, hoping to force the pipe into position.

Rather than sliding in the rest of the way, the pipe bent forty-five degrees.

"Shite!"

Not very ladylike there.

Now she could neither pull the pipe out nor force it the remaining length in and would have to walk on the edge of a sole without the heel touching ground, her right leg so much longer than the left that it made a significant difference to her gait. Walking became a horrible ordeal—almost as bad, she imagined, as if she didn't have a leg below her knee at all.

Maeve collapsed to the floor, tears streaming down her face.

Alexis slid her empty tankard across the table. All trails literal and figurative leading to Maeve had long-since dried out and now she was doing nothing but chasing cruel rumors.

She found the only place left in town still standing and serving drinks so she could drown her sorrows somewhere outside her dining room, which now was a cesspool of unwelcome memories.

"I'd search the whole Territory for her if I could," she sighed.

"There juh-just isn't enough of us left," replied Milton. "Believe me, I'd be r-r-right beside you."

Alexis gave him a pitying look. "You have been, old friend."

"Old." He scoffed, "I'm younger than you."

"I'm in no mood to discuss the particulars of your birthday."

"S-s-suh-sorry."

"Please don't be this hard on yourself." Kököle sat at the table beside Alexis.

"Why shouldn't I be? I failed Wolf. I failed Maeve. What the hell was I thinking waiting a full hour to go after her? A half hour would've been well more than enough! I should've left the second the guards did—"

"Enough, Alex," said Moencopi sternly.

"No. No, it's not enough. Raf would never have failed so spectacularly. He'd set us right."

"He'd also never stop trying," added Edison. "And neither should you. You were his right-hand and, in his absence, you *are* Shadow Wolf."

"Maeve's still out there," Kököle said. "And if she is, Raf is too. He wouldn't give her up without a fight. He'd cheat death to get back to her."

"I've never heard anything truer in all my life," Mr. Davidson scowled from the front door of the Cosmopolitan. "I couldn't help but overhear you're hunting for Miss MacKenna."

Kököle and Moencopi jumped from their seats and took defensive positions at the sight of him.

"Maintain your distance," Moencopi warned, her voice abnormally deep and sinister. "I will not be held accountable for what I do should you step closer."

He heaved a heavy sigh, turning a much-aggrieved look on Alexis. "Frail, emotional women. I have no time for them." To Moencopi: "It has been a time, hasn't it? How fairs your lovely daughter?"

Moencopi growled. "You would know!"

"The world is cruel," he responded blithely.

Alexis grit her teeth. "Your timing is impeccable, Davidson."

Mr. Davidson smirked. "You might say timing is my business."

"I *might* say 'tell me what the hell you know about Maeve before I shoot you in the face.'"

"Crude." He sniffed. "Mr. O'Doherty was meant to return one of my belongings but he's stealing it, instead. It was a business arrangement he failed to follow through on."

He still wasn't providing a place, and that was all Alexis wanted. She pulled her gun from its holster. "Oh, I'm sorry, did I ask for your life story?"

Mr. Davidson rolled his eyes. "You searched everywhere, did you? Including your beloved Pack leader's former homes? I can't imagine you were thorough if you haven't yet found her." He excused himself from the restaurant, his last statement a taunting invitation: "May be interesting to see what's taken residence where Forino lives."

The stiff smile melted from Alexis's lips once he disappeared outside. She turned to the twins, addressing neither in particular, "What the hell got into you?"

"Davidson is not who he appears," replied Moencopi.

That it was Moencopi to reply made Alexis wary.

She explained, "He is the human façade of Másauwu—whom Maeve calls Dallahan." Moencopi inhaled. "Death."

"Oh, come on," scoffed Alexis. "I'm not some naïve child. You're talking about a … a ghost story. Something parents tell the little ones to keep them in bed at night."

Moencopi's expression remained unchanged and when Alexis glanced at Kököle for backup, Kököle dropped her gaze, her face every bit as somber.

Alexis whispered on a shaky breath, "… Right?"

"Why can you not believe it? We are … what is the word?" Moencopi regarded her sister for help.

"Witches?" Kököle supplied her.

Moencopi shook her head, yet said, "Yes. All three women who shared your home can bend reality to their wills with nothing but desire. And you cannot believe Death is a flesh-and-blood entity who walks the earth?"

Kököle augmented her sister's comment: "Flesh and blood, relatively speaking."

"Please," Alexis snorted, physically turning away from the twins. She snatched her tankard from where she'd slid it and put it to her lips, recalling with agitation she already emptied it. At the bottom of the empty tankard was a faint reflection of a pasty face. The tankard chattered against her teeth. "You let me sass Death?" Alexis smacked the tankard on the table and leaned back in her chair as the words sank in. "You let me sass Death!"

"Well there was no stopping you—" Kököle started.

"Oh my Christ! Maeve talked about him before, but I didn't realize they were personally acquainted! I thought it was just a … a turn of phrase. When I say, 'Thank God,' I'm not literally thanking Him personally. I don't know Him like He lives down the street from me, pops in to borrow a cup of sugar every now and then, had a beer with Him once, caught Him once with His pants dow—"

"Jesus, Alexis!" Milton yelped. "That's b-blasphemous!"

"Does He?" Alexis shot an accusatory glance at Kököle. "Does God live down the street? Is it Byrd?"

"Alexis!" Kököle's gaze darted to a neighboring table at which sat the town's preacher.

"Oh, God." Alexis forced a laugh at her own expense. "No offense there, Thurman?"

His complexion ashen, staring roughly where Mr. Davidson had been standing, Brother Thurman responded, "None taken?"

She turned back to the twins. "Why did none of you tell me? It's huge!"

"It was a need-to-know sort of thing," Kököle said, her voice soft. "Honestly, my darling, what would you have done had you known?"

"I—I—dunno but you should've let me decide—"

"Besides," Moencopi added, "none of us—not even Maeve—knew he is Dallahan until he revealed himself before stealing away her unborn child."

"What?" Thurman's forehead etched with concern and his lips turned down. "That was Miss MacKenna in the family way?"

Nobody verbally confirmed it for him but they all nodded.

"If Davidso—Dalla—whatever the hell he is—is right … how would O'Doherty even know about Rafaele's homes?" Alexis wondered.

Milton lowered his gaze, sliding his tankard away from himself with its beer untouched.

Eyebrows raised around the table.

"It was muh-my fault," said Milton, his voice tiny.

"What?" replied Alexis, covering her mouth with her hand.

"When O'Doherty was interrogating me trying to find the ruuuh-rest of the Pack, I told him places I knew were vacant, sending him on a wuh-wild goose chase: The livery. Raf's places since he's long gone from them. I never expected he'd—"

"Go in there and get his stink on everything?" Alexis patted his arm. "You couldn't have known." To the rest of the group, she announced, "Are we prepared to do battle?"

Edison looked uncertain. "What do you suppose Davihan meant by 'what's taken up residence' at Forino's home?"

"Davihan," Alexis chuckled wryly. "Funny. I'm hoping it was just a turn of phrase." She shot accusatory glances at Moencopi and Kököle. They both shrugged.

"Now what the hell are we dallying for?"

Alexis led the charge out of The Cosmopolitan, making a final remark: "I noticed neither of you said Jethro Byrd *isn't* God."

Rafaele crossed himself with a desperate prayer on his lips.

The bad news was he still had another day's travel to Redington. The good news was at least the location was familiar.

Sharp inclines riddled with desert trees and lush cacti populated the rocky locale. Off to his right, a robust waterfall descended into a canyon at the bottom of which was a cola-colored pool.

Rafaele's good fortune began—and ended—with being at Tanque Verde, near enough to home that he could taste it.

He hit the ground, his face narrowly missing a particularly jagged rock. There was no time to nurse his wounds; he groaned and pushed himself up, inspecting the steaming hole in his left sleeve. He thanked God they weren't trying to strike him, but they'd gotten close enough to nick a hose in his prosthetic bicep—air puffed from it when he moved the arm. Luckily it still functioned but it would soon fail if not tended.

He scrambled behind the largest boulder he could reach. With a bit of cover from the barrage of gunshots, he caught his breath and tore a strip of fabric from the hem of his pant leg to create a tourniquet for the hose.

Rafaele peered around the boulder as the men, most of them on horseback, came upon him—fanned out over the span of 180 degrees.

If Rafaele opened fire on them, he figured he'd strike two or maybe three, but it would make him vulnerable to their bullets—and he had little doubt the moment he retaliated, their collective aim would improve.

There had to be a better way.

He mulled over his options while trying to catch his breath.

There's no other choice. Dammit. Rafaele pulled his weapon from its holster and yelled, "Hey," tossing it over the rock behind which he hid.

It clattered to the ground.

There was silence, fleeting silence. Several men dismounted, their horses snorting and whinnying.

Rafaele inhaled, steeling his nerves before emerging from his shelter with both hands raised above his head, the whine from his fake arm's weapon muffled by his sleeve.

Genuinely surrendering had such an attractive ring to it, being done with it all. But for the young woman with the copper hair, piercing green eyes, and delicate bosom, Rafaele would've relinquished himself without hesitation. Instead, he stuck to his plan—which looked to the posse in all ways like he was doing what he longed to.

Rafaele moved along, his back scraping the rock as all six approached, trapping him.

Booker made his way over while the rest of his men dismounted and approached, their weapons trained on Rafaele.

"Well lookie what I have here," Booker said, his swagger as wide as his ego. "The great Shadow Wolf is surrendering." He turned with a flourish to his posse. "To me!"

Booker was behaving exactly as Rafaele expected.

They forced Rafaele to his knees, his body aching, sweat carving vertical trails in the mud caked on his skin. With his face inches from the ground and each speck of dust abrading his eyes and assaulting his nose, he was aware of the sickening fact he appeared a mere remnant of his former self.

Booker motioned to Twerp, after which Twerp retrieved Rafaele's weapon from where it landed.

Rafaele exhaled, dropping his head, shoulders slumping forward.

"Falling in love's made you stupid," said Booker.

"Falling in love's made me strong!"

"Oh, yuck. Is that why you're surrendering?" Book snapped his fingers. "S'pose it makes my job easier; O'Doherty left off 'or alive' on your wanted poster."

"O'Doherty, huh?" He committed the name to memory. Someday he'd get his revenge. "Figures you're following someone else's orders," Rafaele said, punctuating the statement with a well-placed snort. "You were never good at anything beyond setting fires."

"You think anything you say insults me, you sorry excuse for a man? At least I can set fires! You're no threat to me."

Rafaele raised his head enough to spy Booker slipping his gun back into its holster.

Fingers laced into the curls at his crown before Booker yanked Rafaele's head up; the end was nigh.

Booker continued talking, Twerp still watching Rafaele as his hand moved to the gun. The split second became eternity. Twerp's fingers clutched the firearm, and as he lifted it, for an instant, his attention dropped to their prize.

It was now or never. Rafaele shot Booker in the leg with Edison's weapon, and he dropped to his knees with a tormented yell. In a single sweeping motion, Rafaele was on his feet, dispatching the two men standing to his right as well as the one who'd snatched his gun with brilliant flashes of red light propelling the bullets.

Shots from the two remaining posse members narrowly missed as Rafaele scurried to the side.

He snatched his handgun from Twerp's lifeless fingers and whipped around, riddling the two men with bullets.

As their bodies fell, Booker managed to suppress his agony enough to retrieve his gun from its holster. With a violently shaking hand, he aimed at the man towering over him with two weapons pointed at his head and pulled the trigger.

Click.

Rafaele held his gaze, unflinching.

Click, click, clickclickclick! Booker managed a slimy smile though his breath was ragged. He chuckled weakly as he dropped his gun. "You're pathetic," he said, his voice pinched. "You really believe no Pack member should go against another Pack member? You're the only one left with any loyalty to Eliseo or his stupid ideals. You can't win."

"Really, Angelino? *Really?*" Rafaele scowled. "You're no Pack member. You've made that blatantly clear."

"You still won't shoot me. You wouldn't want your little Irish tart knowing you're nothing but a common fiend."

The throbbing whine emitted by the Edison's weapon seemed to grow to fever pitch as it awaited another round of use. Rafaele reminded him, "She already knows what I am."

CHAPTER 18

 aeve studied hard her reflection in the mirror above Rafaele's dresser, willing herself to see the Death omen in her eyes.

Another broken promise, another mornin' I amn't gonna die. Another mornin' I'm willin' to bet I won't see the omen in tha' man's eyes, either. Well of course not; tha' would be a grand mercy.

It was merciful, at least, the cabin was abnormally quiet.

Maeve needed a drink. She steeled her nerves for her next encounter with Liam but hoped the relative silence of the house meant he'd opted to sleep late.

But it wasn't silent for long; the voice she couldn't discern from her conscience chattered at her: *Kill the bastard.*

She squeezed her eyes shut against its words as well as the pain shooting from her stump into her right hip. *Will ye shut yer mouth 'n' hear me speakin'? Stop encouragin' me to kill him. Tha' isn't who I am.*

He's asleep in bed. His gun's on the end table. A single shot to his temple would do it. Stand right over him and you wouldn't miss. Hell, it'd even be humane!

No! Stop it, shut yer mouth!

Maeve reached and groped for the next thing to cling to that could bear her weight; she moved from one piece of furniture to the next not much unlike a baby learning to toddle.

The gun is your key to freedom. Ain't that something your father once told you, Chicky?

There it was: undeniable proof these words weren't hers. She exhaled her relief.

"Where are ye?" Maeve demanded, her arms shaking with exertion as she straightened and glanced around what would serve as a parlor in fancier homes. "Show yerself."

Ooooover heeeeeere, it sang, a voice like distant wind-chimes on a breeze.

Maeve pivoted in her spot, scanning the room and straining to find the apparition.

She spotted it in the corner, picking it out from where rays of light caught dust motes floating in the cabin: the fuzzy spot Maeve might have called a ghost if it were one.

Let's work together.

"Stop," Maeve whispered. "Dear lord, please stop!"

He's a bad man who deserves to meet the Dallahan. And you're the only person here who can introduce them.

"I amn't a monster. Nothin' is gonna change tha'."

The form slipped by her, fingers of ice teasing the delicate hairs on her arm to stand tall.

"What are ye?" Maeve demanded, keeping her voice low.

I'm dead. Don't you know? You've seen me. We spoke. I couldn't have imagined our conversation.

"Ye can't be a ghost. Ye've left this house. Ye're not confined here."

No. I follow the bastard.

"Of yer own free will?"

Would you? the voice snapped. *Would you follow around the wretch of your own free will? Oh. Wait. You're staying in your intended's home with him ... of what I assume is your own free will.*

"Ye take back those awful words," hissed Maeve.

I will do no such thing until you prove to me otherwise. I think you stay because you want to be with this brute. To keep with your kind. Or to break Forino's heart ... I'm not too terribly sure which it is.

"Ye take tha' back!" Maeve yelled.

Absolutely not. I'm stuck haunting this ghoul because of you! And we're both now stuck in this home—again!—because of you!

"I did not—"

Back at the Tiff. You gave me 'freedom,' ha! You told me to, and I quote, 'be free, go on to be with—'

"Liam," she breathed in recollection. "Oh, good lord. I—I was tryin' to help, 'n' I got distracted! I didn't mean it—"

Yea, well, then fix it! Fix it now! Release me!

"I don't know how!"

There was a clatter from the closet-sized bedroom.

Horse bollocks!

Maeve froze, her breath catching.

The voice taunted her: *Prove to me you're not this louse's possession. Prove to me you're not choosing to be with him. Prove to me your dedication to the man I lost to you!*

Maeve's hands flew to her ears as she dropped to her knees, imploring, "Stop!"

Prove it. Prove it, prove it, prove it—

The poltergeist's voice grew louder and closer until it shredded her ears with shrieking not far off a banshee's.

The noise stopped.

Maeve held her breath, pulling her hands from either side of her head, the only sound now was blood coursing in her ears.

The sensation of being impaled by an icepick ravaged Maeve's body and she cried out.

She was yanked to her feet and jerked around by her arm. Liam was practically atop her.

"What's all this yelling?" he snapped, his breath sour with last night's alcohol.

She suppressed a gag.

"Didn't I tell you not to wake me unless Angelino came by?" he yelled. "Disobedient bitch!"

"I'm sorry for the noise, I was just goin' to check on somethin'—"

"Liar!" Liam threw Maeve to the floor, agony of the impact wrenching a cry from her throat. "Let this be your lesson: I will not tolerate such insolence from any little woman. Least of all you."

He stood over her, his eyes Deathless yet bloodshot either from the drink or lacking sleep—possibly both. The expression on his features read of anticipating an apology.

Where Maeve had succeeded in wrangling her magic, she had yet to learn to keep her tongue in check: "Every mornin' I look at yer face, prayin'—I pray, for god's sake—tha' I'll find the Death-omen in yer eyes."

Though she refused to kill him, she couldn't stop wishing someone else would; when there was nobody else with them, such desires held no power.

"'N' when I don't see it there, I check the mirror 'n' hope to see it in mine instead. Every passin' day, Dallahan taunts me by leavin' me here trapped with ye in some never-endin' hell!"

"Well you can quit praying because I will never let that ghoul have you."

Maeve couldn't stop herself from blurting, "He's less of a ghoul than ye are!"

As disgusting as the sentiment was, it was worse that she genuinely believed it.

And the worst thing of all was the still Deathless look in Liam's eyes when he attacked her.

❧

Maeve studied the lingering marks from Liam's assault earlier that morning. They'd gone through the early stages of the bruising spectrum, swiftly as they always did, waning purple in places, blackish in others, and the less severe ones already green to yellow.

Though those, too, soon would fade, their lingering as they did reminded Maeve of the brutality of his physical anger.

Any other person would've died from such injuries. But Maeve got to endure the same fear and agony, fate leaving her to survive it happening again and again.

It took a solid quarter of an hour for Maeve to get from Rafaele's bedroom to his kitchen shortly after Liam left the house in the late morning. Her struggle was all for naught when she lost her balance while getting herself a glass for a drink; several plates and bowls fell from the cabinet and broke on the countertop beneath it, the glass popping upon impact with the floor, the dishware spraying her with pieces of glass and shards of porcelain.

She straightened to examine her right leg. The previously weakened metal in the damaged ankle joint had given up its ghost, bent beyond the prosthesis being useful anymore.

Maeve leaned over and rested her forehead against a debris-free spot on the floor, realizing how futile it was to hope for death. The one part of her body that wasn't flesh and bone was broken and could never magically restore itself.

Conversely, the soft, delicate flesh susceptible to mutilation would heal indefinitely, leaving her to suffer Liam's wrath forever.

Over, and over until he perished, she wouldn't have the release of death; his personal, human, everlasting punch bag would merely recover for his next round of abuse.

Too tired to fight anymore, she lay where she fell, resting her cheek against her arm and figuring one of Liam's guards would certainly come to check on things inside Rafaele's house with all the racket her fall made.

Hours went by and nobody bothered entering or even peeking in through the kitchen window. She knew they were out there and heard the clatter. They had to.

After so long, she lost her battle against her bladder and time, burying her head in her hands as though hiding from the world would make it all go away.

The room grew dim with encroaching nightfall and Maeve on the floor remained, still too tired to fight against the halo of glass shards surrounding her. Still alone. Still urine-soaked, welted, hopeless, and miserable.

The front door opened and closed, a few lamps in the parlor being lit. As her heart leapt into her throat at the thought of being rescued, Maeve grabbed the largest piece of broken plate and swept shards of glass with it into the largest piece of bowl she could reach.

She knew Liam was near by the requisite cold spot sweeping against her. Icy, ethereal hands wrapped around her wrists and pulled upward. She got to her hands and knees but kept her head down.

Maeve hoped if she failed to acknowledge Liam's presence he would leave her alone to wallow in her misery. She was also aware of the fallacy in her plan; a turned back meant vulnerability.

"Have a little accident, did you?"

She cringed at Liam's voice coming from the kitchen entry behind her. "A little accident?" replied Maeve through clenched teeth. "I can't stand, as ye might recall."

"You're still going on about that?" he said. "You can't stand and yet you decided to take a stroll to the kitchen."

"It was hardly a stroll."

"You needn't be angry; it wasn't your real leg you broke."

Ye broke it. She closed her eyes, praying for strength to control her temper and to keep the words off her tongue.

"You might be a little more grateful to me."

"Why?"

"I found a particularly elegant solution to your problem."

Maeve didn't know what to expect as she twisted in her spot to look at Liam, but a plain wood cane wasn't it.

He gave her the cane as if it were the biggest humanitarian gesture in human history.

"Ye think this is gonna make up for cripplin' me?" cried Maeve.

"I didn't cripple you, churlish invalid! You were broken goods when I got here. And I will thank you to remember your place, or I will make you remember it."

Seemingly in response, the kitchen cabinets burst open, an impossible amount of dishware pouring from them like porcelain floodwaters.

"Stop it!" Liam roared.

"I can't stop what I amn't doin'," Maeve cried, her heart in frantic beat; she was trapped in a house with a man from whom she couldn't protect herself, and an otherworldly entity she couldn't control.

"I don't believe you!"

Wallpaper peeled ceiling downward, panels of wood floor lifting and curling away from the foundation. Anything and everything the poltergeist could pick up and fling around, it was.

"I'll beat subservience into you if it's the last thing I do!" He snatched a fire iron from beside the stove.

The voice wouldn't stop chanting: *Do it, do it, do it!*

She was certain she was losing her mind, that it was her subconscious goading her to retaliate for how he'd treated her.

Hurt him, maim him, kill him! Slit his throat and scrawl your name in his blood on his forehead, on his chest, on his di—

"Stop!" Maeve cried.

Liam knocked her to her stomach, looming over her with the fire iron in his grip. "Maybe losing another limb will get you to end this nightmare!"

She kicked him with her prosthesis, knocking him backward, the fire iron clattering to the ground several feet away. As he clutched his shin, Maeve attempted to use the kitchen table to help herself stand but went right back to the floor with a painful thump.

Maeve's pulse bounded, a primal molten heat spreading from her abdomen to her appendages, every inch of skin aflame. Her muscles clenched in the rising tide, lips, toes and fingertips tingling with mounting energy; the earthquakes before the eruption.

Her breath came heaving, fingers raking the floor to maintain control before she became nothing but the animal embodiment of fire.

It was all she could do to fight the need to will Liam from existence the way she did Francisco.

The poltergeist goaded Maeve:

I've heard the things Liam's said to you. He hates women far more than Esquivar ever did. Liam judges people on their religion in ways Esquivar never said. He's more of a race-discriminating bastard, too. Liam killed far more people in the train wreck alone than Esquivar did in his whole life. He's said unforgivable things to you, beaten you half to death numerous times.

There was a long, merciful silence.

She continued, *He murdered Rafaele! What more must he do before you'll act? Chicky, if you don't do something, he's going to physically beat you and emotionally torture you for the rest of his God-given life.*

It bore no stating: Liam deserved far worse than Francisco received from a vengeful goddess-incarnate.

Ye have a weapon. He just gave it to ye. Ye can't kill him with it but ye can fend him off.

Maeve blinked, gasping when she realized that was her voice rather than the specter screaming at her. They were her thoughts, clear as day. Unmistakable.

And they'd made a brilliant suggestion.

She indeed had a weapon, but it was as useless as a life-jacket in the middle of the desert. If she were to touch it with her temper unchecked, she'd render it to ash.

Maeve closed her eyes and focused on calming herself, seeking her last memories of bliss.

Rafaele's voice echoed in her ear as if he kneeled beside her, assuring her he would soon be home, reminding her of the lifetime of love they had ahead of them. But to get there, she needed to survive the here and now.

Her fingers wrapped around the top of the cane.

It's not breaking your Rede if it's in self-defense.

She got back up to her hands and knees, dragging the cane as she crawled toward Liam.

At the sound of her movement, he turned around, grabbing a glass lamp from the table and pitching it at Maeve's head. Just as it left his hands, it flew off at an odd angle as if deflected by the unseen, and shattered against the wall behind her, kerosene splashing from its font.

Liam roared an unintelligible word and Maeve swung the cane at him; it connected with his right leg, the cracking of bone cutting through the cacophony around them when the cane broke in two.

He collapsed with a bellow, feebly clutching his leg.

Maeve's heart raced with victory, but it thudded when she looked toward the door; her breath whisked from her mouth with the realization it was mercilessly out of reach. It could've been in Letterkenny for as able-bodied as she was to get there.

Nonetheless, she scrambled on all fours toward it, getting a couple feet closer before her skirts got caught on something. In an instant, she was sliding on her belly back toward Liam, the bottom hem of her gown clutched in his hands.

He rolled her onto her back before grabbing the fire iron and using it to pin her skirts to the floor.

She clawed at whatever she could reach, splinters from the roughened wood assaulting her palms and embedding themselves beneath her fingernails; she kicked and flailed blindly, her feet meeting his chest.

He shouted, struggling to stand back up.

Porcelain shrapnel from the ever-flowing cabinets circled around them in close orbit. Liam got to his feet with the shard of her cane in his fist, turning toward her with blood seeping through his right pant leg, a crazed expression on his face. He limped toward her, raising the busted piece of cane as if preparing to stake a vampire.

"You deceitful witch," he spat. "The ... the fairies and the leprechauns, all those little things you did that I thought were childish dreams or sleights of hand, the things that caused our parents, all, to call you touched in the head ... I should've listened to your mother all along—you really are *Caorthannach* in beguiling skin!" Liam lunged for her.

"*No!*" the poltergeist shrieked, taking full ethereal form between Maeve and Liam, as if her non-corporeal body provided any kind of physical barrier.

When Liam passed right through her, she created a physical barrier: the items lapping them in the air started pelting him. Plates broke against his back, followed by lamps that doused him with kerosene. Despite the assault, he rampaged through it, his anger the fuel to propel him through his suffering.

A large lamp, fire and all, bounced off his arm and spiraled out of control, smashing against the kitchen wall; the oil spilled, igniting the wall and floor before flame wicked up the curtains.

For a second, Maeve considered squelching the fire; the last thing she wanted was for Rafaele's home to burn to the ground, no matter who was in it or what was happening.

She was grateful the urge passed quickly, realizing she couldn't miss a clear opportunity to get some distance while her captor was distracted.

Liam struggled against the poltergeist as it dragged him toward the flames ravaging the dry timbers of Rafaele's cabin.

The front door flew open as Maeve clawed at the floor in a second bid to escape, spotting a pair of familiar shoes entering the burning home amid the chaos. Though she was sure it couldn't be him, she called out anyway: "Raf! Save me!"

"Maeve! Oh, my God! What. The. Hell!"

Maeve's head whipped up. Alexis reeled in her moccasin boots, taking two giant strides backward, her eyes wide and mouth hanging open in soundless scream. She shook her head desperately against the horrific sight before her.

Liam dropped the cane in favor of pulling his gun on Maeve, the furniture around them sliding his direction to block his path. He stumbled and fell but pulled himself over the displaced settee, undaunted.

"Maeve!" Alexis yelled, charging into the room. She grabbed Maeve around her chest, ripping her skirt free of the fire iron before dragging her out, granting her an unobstructed view of the ghastly antics of the poltergeist.

The wraith grinned wickedly, winking toward Maeve before turning to Liam. *"All this time, I fought being chained to you. But in the end, all it means is you're chained to me, too ... forever. You're not going anywhere,"* she said, her voice growing in strength, clarity, and wrathfulness. *"You're my toy now, big boy!"*

One of Milton's paintings ripped off the wall and the frame struck Liam's arm, spilling his blood; books streamed endlessly from a shelf, assaulting his back and legs. He shouted incomprehensible words as the bookshelf, itself, toppled over on him.

Alexis pulled Maeve through the entry, the door slamming shut with a couple inches to spare from Maeve's soles.

Liam was trapped inside with a vindictive poltergeist.

Maeve heard the cacophony; the utter destruction of Rafaele's house at fever pitch, the tempest at its peak.

Alexis struggled to get Maeve farther away from the building. When it was obvious Maeve couldn't keep up burdened by her broken prosthetic leg, Alexis hoisted her from the ground and ran as best she could.

With the violent flickering of lamplight and flame through the windows, the painful cracking of wood, shattering glass and a low rumble that sounded like the house threatening to collapse on itself not so far behind them, Alexis juggled Maeve in her arms and slid on the gravel hillside. The dead bodies of Liam's posse went by in dark blurs as Alexis lost control of herself.

Maeve tumbled from her grip and hit the ground hard, the world flashing white. She and Alexis skidded to a rough stop in the dirt yards from where the rest of the Pack waited, everyone watching the activity in the house in abject horror.

"What the hell was that?" gasped Alexis.

Several moments went by before the fog in Maeve's head cleared enough for her to struggle semi-upright, the stars in her vision fading away until she could see normally again. "Tha' was Miss Burke."

"A—a ghost?" Alexis stared at her, wide-eyed and agape.

She nodded. "Yes, well, not a ghost … A poltergeist. I've not ever in me life seen anythin' like her."

Alexis cussed. Her voice shaking—in fear, anger, exhaustion, Maeve couldn't tell—she said, "You owe me so much right now." She prodded Maeve in the shoulder to punctuate each word: "I just faced everything I'm terrified of, everything I hate." Her shoulders sagged as she dropped her hands into the dirt. "'Cept for you. You: helpless, broken, right there in the middle of my waking nightmare. What I did for you? It was like if you swam through a sea of scorpions to save me from a giant scorpion made exclusively of scorpions."

"OK—"

"And the scorpion? It's spitting flying scorpions at you."

Maeve could've vomited at the mere suggestion. "OK, OK, I get it!"

"You're lucky I didn't just leave you there."

"I *am* lucky." Maeve offered a weak smile. "… 'n' thanks Lexie, for actually comin' to rescue me. Even when I didn't think I needed it. Even though I didn't want ye to."

Alexis gave her a sour face. "It's Al—" She sighed, then smiled. "Lexie. It's Lexie. But only to you. And just this once."

"Ye promised ye wouldn't come for me."

"Strictly speaking, I didn't promise anything. You left, and I didn't stop you. I said nothing about not coming to your rescue. Besides: *you* said you wouldn't hurt anyone, not even to defend yourself. What happened to harming none?"

"I didn't use me magic against him. I didn't destroy him. I did what a woman could." She smiled, tired but gratified. "In the end? *I* wasn't the monster."

Alexis gaped at her. "Aren't you finding a technicality to rationalize breaking the Rede?"

Maeve was quick to interject: "Didn't ye promise ye wouldn't do anythin' tha' would endanger yerself?"

With a smirk, Alexis glanced at the rest of the group, whistling and waving them over. "So I lied." As everyone approached, she instructed, "Let's all get the hell out of here before that nightmare inside spreads out here."

Edison and Milton brought over a horse which Alexis mounted easily. Kököle and Moencopi helped Maeve struggle onto him behind her.

Alexis watched the group disperse before she nudged the steed, directing him away from Rafaele's home.

"You finally learn something about being naïve ... especially regarding men?"

Maeve hoped she was teasing. "Time will tell."

There was so much she could've said in the following silence, but instead Maeve opted to keep her thoughts to herself. Her embrace tightened as she burrowed her face into Alexis's back.

Alexis inhaled sharply before her muscles relaxed. "You OK there, Miss MacKenna?"

"OK is a relative term. I'm alive—yes." Her voice faltering, she augmented, "No, I amn't." Maeve closed her eyes, resisting the urge to look back at Rafaele's home; it was certainly for the best she didn't indulge her compulsion. "But I will be." Of their friendship, she inquired, "Are ... we OK?"

They'd both said such hateful, unforgivable things when last they were together, and neither had apologized. Maybe Alexis forgot it, but Maeve hadn't.

Silence lingered between them before Alexis sighed, putting a hand over Maeve's where it rested on her stomach. Their fingers weaved together, followed by the faintest squeeze. "We have to be, yea? We're all we have left."

Without thinking, Maeve pressed her lips to Alexis's back.

Maeve looked around from the same bed in which she felt she'd spent now half her life recovering from some ailment or other. The blood stain was a mere ghost of itself, but still there all the same on the floor to her left. The chair Alexis once straddled to speak with her, neatly tucked away at the desk across from the foot of the bed.

Her injuries from Liam were nothing but memories and bad dreams she couldn't shake—including the one from which she'd recently awakened. What she wouldn't have given for dreamless sleep.

"Alex?" Maeve called. "Moencopi? Kököle?"

She held her breath, awaiting a reply. A knock on the door. Any acknowledgment.

But she was alone.

Her bed may have been a wicked temptress, but her will was stronger; and, besides, going back to sleep meant going back to horrid dreams. Taking a long inhalation, she pushed herself to sit upright.

With the women out of the house, Maeve could drag herself from bed without unnecessary celebrations or equally unnecessary interrogations.

Are you OK? How are you feeling? Do you wanna talk about it now? Is there anything I can do to help? Let me touch you—just a brief massage.

No; she wasn't going to drag herself from bed. She hoisted herself out of it and stretched to greet the day with a forced smile. If she did it enough, someday the smile would come naturally.

On the desk, Maeve found a note:

I LEFT THE TUB FULL OF CLEAN WATER FOR YOU. HAPPY BATHING!
WITH LOVE,
MOENCOPI

Cleaning herself had an appealing ring to it so she retreated to the bath with razor in hand. She heated the water to a comfortable roiling boil before stripping, removing her prosthetic leg, and lowering herself into the tub.

In her solitude while she groomed herself for the first time in maybe forever, Maeve allowed her mind to wander. Unfortunately, without close supervision, her mind strolled paths she wished it wouldn't.

"I haven't a job; Smith won't have a cripple barwhore."

She didn't suppose it was such a loss in retrospect; after all, what was so alluring about air so thick with smoke it gagged her, and being doused in alcohol and foods barely qualifying as edible so often the smell was permanently ingrained in her clothing? It wasn't as if she enjoyed waiting on others or having to swindle good people out of hard-earned money just because Brandon convinced her that was how business was done.

"It meant me freedom, that's what it meant." She swallowed thickly, her gaze falling on where she'd propped her prosthesis. "Esquivar right well managed to take me freedom away, anyhow."

"'N' now I have no home. Kind as they've been to me, I'm sure the women don't want me sharin' their home indefinitely. 'N' I wouldn't want tha', either."

"I wanted Rafaele." She exhaled.

"I want him. I always have, 'n' I always will."

'N' he's gone.

It was the first those words sunk in, and they stung as fiercely as the tears she fought off, even if she hadn't spoken them aloud.

Without a job or home, I need him.

Maeve cried out in agony, slamming her fist into the boiling water.

It wasn't the lack of his financial support and residence that hurt.

It's the lack of him.

There wasn't even a point in attempting to run through a list of eligible bachelors. She didn't want to settle. She wanted what she couldn't have.

"Oh, Rafaele."

Real love or otherwise, Maeve would never feel for another man the way she did for him.

Alexis was tired of arguing, and yet the disagreement seemed never-ending.

"We're going to need different weapons," said Kököle. "What we currently have doesn't stand a chance against that entity."

"I still don't understand why we need to fight it. Why do any of us need to go back there?" Alexis replied.

It was Edison to respond to Kököle with a dour expression. "How exactly do you fight what cannot be seen or felt? I welcome your ideas as to how such a weapon might function."

"Tuh-technically, we have a weapon against spirits: Miss MacKenna," added Milton.

"*Had* a weapon," Kököle corrected. "Maeve needs time to recover. She's tired. She's injured. She's lost and heartbroken. We'll be lucky if she ever recovers from this." She tapped the edge of her beer bottle against the wooden table with a sigh.

"Keep wuh-working with her," Milton said, giving Kököle a reassuring—though hesitant—pat atop her arm. "Sshh-she'll come around. She's stronger than we guh-give her credit for."

"I might have more faith if our deck was stacked. If she had some really good reason for getting out of bed in the morning." Alexis cast a sorrowful look at the saloon's canvas ceiling.

"Well ... How about muh-my birthday party?" Milton pouted. "It's not as though I get a proper one each year."

Kököle gave him a pitying smile. "I'll try. I'll even do my best, but I can't promise—" Her gaze flickered beside his head and her face brightened. "Wait—can it be?" She gasped, fingers flying to her lips. "No—yes! I think our deck was just stacked!" She jumped to her feet, *luluing*, drawing stares from patrons all around the birthday party.

Alexis leaped from her chair at the sound, her heart shooting into her throat. She charged for the door before she allowed herself to think this was impossible, pausing shy of throwing her arms around the man who towered above the rest, and was presently caked in layers upon layers of dirt. Instead, Alexis reeled back, slugging him in his right shoulder without restraint. "If you're alive, you answer your telegrams! God! Dammit! Raf, we thought you were dead!"

"I've gotta admit," Rafaele replied with a smirk and a weak chuckle, "there were times I thought I was dead, too."

"You've got enough dirt on you to fill a grave. Maybe even two."

"Who's to say that isn't where I picked it up?" He yanked her into a bear hug, clapping her on the back as he would any male member of the Pack. "It's good to see you again, Alex. Now that I'm back, I can assume you've gotten everything under control? Or has it actually been that way all this time? Those telegrams really scared me!"

Alexis shrugged from Rafaele's embrace, brushing his dirt from her chest and arms. "Your little lady is more trouble than she's worth. I aged ten years in your absence. Next time you tell me to take care of her for you? Here's an idea whose time has come: Don't!"

Rafaele laughed. "How I've missed your sarcasm."

"Sarcasm my ass," Alexis muttered.

"Now." He scanned the crowd, nodding greetings to members of the Pack as they approached. "Where's my intended?"

Alexis exchanged glances with Kököle and Moencopi. "Ducky's at my home. We'll bring her here. But ..." She sneered. "If you love her, you'll get washed first."

"Hey, uh ... Since she's not here, could I surprise her with my return?"

"What a lovely idea," said Kököle, hugging Rafaele from a respectable distance. "We won't tell her you've come back."

"Thanks. And ... please. Stop calling her Ducky." He regarded the Hopi women, Edison, and Milton in turn. "All of you."

"Your phobia has gone too fuh-far," replied Milton. "It's a cute nickname. There's n-nothing wrong with it."

"It's not a phobia," Rafaele shot back. "Phobias are irrational."

Alexis shook her head. "Bath's in the back, ya giant mud-pile." To Kököle she said with a nod toward the saloon door, "Let's go fetch the missus."

⁓⊱❀⊰⁓

Maeve cringed, hearing the front door open and close amid the excited chatter of Alexis and the twins. She held her breath and listened to them praise the efforts of Redington residents in erecting a makeshift saloon, followed by remarks of cause to celebrate. Nothing she knew of was worth celebrating on February twenty-ninth. Especially not this one.

"Maeve?" Kököle called. More quietly: "She's left her bedroom."

"I swear to Byrd, if she ran away—" Alexis started but was promptly hushed.

"Maeve?" Kököle's voice was much closer now. They found her.

She debated responding but thought it might be better not to—until the door opened and Kököle's face appeared.

"Oh!" The door closed, Kököle stuttering, "I'm so sorry, I didn't mean to barge in. I didn't see anything—wait! Was your bath water boiling?"

Despite everything, Maeve chuckled once. "It's how I can bathe comfortably. I thought ye knew."

"I'm sorry, I forgot." There was a soft thump against the door. "Um ...

Listen. There's this shindy going on in town tonight and we thought maybe it'd be nice if we all went."

Maeve scoffed, shaking her head. "Do not ye let me stop ye from enjoyin' yerselves."

"Please? The Tiff and Tawny won't be the same without you. You might just enjoy yourself if you came."

There were giggles and more hushing.

"The Tiff 'n' Tawny isn't the same regardless." It was of course a guess, as she hadn't seen it in a half year.

"OK," Alexis's voice chimed in from outside the bathroom. "I didn't want to have to stoop to this but here goes: today is Milton's birthday. Strictly speaking, he gets only one of these every four years. He specifically requested your presence at the party tonight. All you need to do is show up and it'll make his whole evening."

Maeve exhaled but said nothing. That would've been worth celebrating if she were in the right mood.

"It's the least you could do for him after all he's done for you," Alexis snapped.

So ... She's still mad at me. I suppose I can't blame her since I haven't exactly apologized. Though to be fair, Alexis never apologized for calling her a harpy and for saying such awful things about losing the baby. She should've been holding at least twice as much grudge.

Maeve's gaze fell on the fake limb; Milton and Edison repaired the damage it'd sustained but it worked as rigidly as it did before she got used to it when they first gave it to her. And the gash was still there. That couldn't be repaired, only replaced, and Maeve wouldn't stand for it when Milton had offered sculpting a new one.

She sighed, letting the back of her head bump the edge of the tub. "Fine. I'll go. Can I at least finish bathin' first?"

Someone chuckled through hushing.

Alexis replied, "Oh, I insist. Clean yourself really good. But don't dally."

Giggles faded down the hallway and Maeve concluded they already partook in celebratory drinks before retrieving her. Would joining them for a good drunkenness be so objectionable?

Well, I suppose the sooner I go, the sooner I can come home. 'Home' being what it was. *There are worse homes, Maeve.*

She soaped and rinsed, then balanced on the edge of the tub to dry off with a ratty linen, stained pale brown.

She'd ruined that towel, same as the carpet in the room where she slept. Why couldn't Alexis at least throw the damned linen away already?

Seeing her bare, flat little belly reminded her of the day she wished she'd forget. So she put the prosthesis back on hastily and retreated to her room to dress in the darkest, plainest clothing she had.

At least being groomed gave her satisfaction she hadn't had in the better part of a half year. How much she loved the silken draw of her stocking as she pulled it on over shaven skin. Even with the stocking on, she enjoyed feeling her skirts as they brushed her leg with each step.

I'll be OK. Yea. I was perfectly fine without a man before Rafaele. I'll be perfectly fine again. Someday. Eventually. Maybe.

"No, you can't wear that," said Kököle upon seeing Maeve in the hall after she dressed. She dragged Maeve right back into the bedroom and rooted through the wardrobe.

Maeve frowned at her attire. "What's wrong with it?"

"It's drab."

"I'm in mournin'."

"This is a birthday party, not a wake." Kököle flopped several garments onto the bed that Maeve guessed qualified as more appropriate for a birthday party. "Forgo the dismal dress tonight. Get back to it tomorrow if you must."

With a groan, Maeve looked over the opulent gold and cornflower blue fabric, pops of saffron-colored lace and ruffles catching the lamplight.

"Do not ye think it's a bit ... much?"

"Honey." Kököle smiled. "There's no such thing as 'a bit much.'"

There was no point in arguing; Maeve acquiesced.

CHAPTER 19

edington had erected a tent on the site of the old gaming building while the new saloon was being constructed where the previous Tiff and Tawny once stood.

Outside the tent it was dreary, the colors of daytime fading into a gloomy night; inside, it was bright and loud, a cheer swelling around her when she hobbled in, her gait uneven and stiff even with Kököle's assistance.

Maeve was passed from embrace to embrace with little time to even realize who was greeting her, up to and including the handsome older gentleman she didn't recognize until he spoke to her; with the Tiff and Tawny being non-existent for months, Jethro Byrd found sobriety and it looked good on him.

She was seated at the table beside the man of the hour.

"Ducky," Milton said. "I worried you wouldn't come."

"Well, the night's still young …" Kököle said with a smirk. She got elbowed on either side by Moencopi and Alexis. "Hey—ow—"

They'd definitely been drinking. Maeve ignored them and put on what she hoped was a convincing smile for Milton. "I wouldn't dream of missin' yer birthday celebration." Dodging Alexis's unimpressed stare from across the table, she added, "Happy Birthday, dear friend. I'm sorry I've no gift for ye."

"Your buh-being here is all the gift I need."

"Speaking of gifts," Edison interjected, "how's the ankle joint behaving?"

Maeve sighed, agitated he would raise the topic now. Agitated at everyone's attention being drawn to it—and her—on Milton's occasion. "It's ... great."

"Don't wuh-worry. It'll ease with use but it'll never be as good as it was—without fuh-fully replacing it."

She pouted at Milton.

Edison added to Milton's sentiment, "Count on repairs being fussy. Unfortunately, machinery can be ornery once damaged."

"'Kenna!" Brandon called, hurrying to drop off their drinks. "How glad I am to see you out and about." He set the drinks down, including a glass for her.

"Rotgut?"

"Of course."

"Tha' *ye* mixed?"

"Yea. Who else would do it in your stead?"

She sneered. "I amn't drinkin' this swill."

"It's made especially for you," he replied with a smile. "Only half the poison than what's in the usual house rotgut."

"You muh-mean half the alcohol," Milton laughed. "Miser."

"Drink your namby-pamby tea, Dandy," said Brandon before turning back to Maeve. He cleared his throat. "When will you be returning to work? I've got my hands full without you and the people need their drinks."

"Smith, I'm broken. Remember?"

He smiled sheepishly. "A broken beer-jugger is better than me serving customers or having them serve themselves. Nobody here can be trusted the way you can."

"We even reserved a room for you," said Tawny, joining Brandon's side with a smile brighter than the oil lamps scattered throughout the tent, marking the canvas above them with spots of soot. She took Brandon's hand and squeezed.

"I don't know—" She needed the work, though. And a home.

"At least see your room before you reject the job offer," Tawny replied.

Maeve glanced at Milton. "I can't. Not today."

"Go, Duck—Um—Maeve. See it. The dehh-décor's nice, if I do say so myssself."

She rose slowly, narrowed eyes on the birthday boy. There wasn't a thing about what he'd said that didn't raise red flags. "Fine." She followed Tawny to the last partitioned space in the back of the tent, Milton's party guests following behind closely.

"We'll give you a few minutes to get settled," said Tawny.

Brandon added, "You don't have to give us your decision right away. Maybe sleep on it."

Someone nudged Maeve through the curtain into the small room.

There was a single puny nightstand, a small bed, and a large man sitting on it with his back to her.

Tawny must've assumed Maeve would be desperate enough for work to take on employment with her rather than—or in addition to—Brandon.

Were it any other time under any other circumstance, Maeve might have dazzled this fellow with a humorous remark. Something on the wittier side of, 'ye can't afford me.'

She wasn't in the mood to even try.

"I'm terrible sorry," said Maeve with a sigh, "but I amn't for sale. Surely ye mean to be in the next bed over."

He shifted in his spot to regard her.

There he was: the most handsome man Maeve knew. She braced herself against the wood post beside her, awash with a waking swoon. "Raf—" she breathed, wildfire tears springing to her eyes. "I thought ye were dead!"

"No," replied Rafaele. "Never. Not while I've still got you to live for."

She stared at him, piecing together an image both familiar and strange. The obsidian, curly black hair she remembered was uncut and corralled into a tidy ponytail resting against the nape of his neck—not much unlike Milton's. His scruffy chin and jaw were shaved clean save for an impeccably groomed, thick, black handlebar mustache that overwhelmed his face. And there was the slightly crooked nose above his wolfish, painfully charming smile.

Rafaele's skin was darker than she remembered, his style of clothing less cowboy and more dandy.

And she was keenly aware of him gazing back at her, likely making similar comparisons about her appearance. Thankfully the bruises and cuts suffered at Liam's hands were healed.

"I brought you back a little gift." He offered her a single-strand pearl necklace.

"Oh! Goodness, it's beautiful! Where did ye get it?"

"It still pales in comparison to your beauty."

She noted the evasion to her question; he stole it.

Maeve glanced down at herself, suddenly feeling self-conscious as ever. She fluffed her hair frantically and straightened her already straight sleeves, gasping, "I'm a frightful mess!"

"No," he breathed, "not at all. You're a sight for sore eyes." He stood and approached her, putting the pearls on her before pulling her into a tight embrace.

Rafaele smelled unfamiliar. He was freshly bathed—which was no cause for complaint—but the clothes he wore must not have been his for long. There was no vague scent of outside or nighttime on his skin. She returned his hug as tightly as her trembling, slender arms allowed.

She craned her neck to meet his gaze without pulling away. "Ye are me Rafaele, aren't ye?"

"Of course I am." He smoothed her hair against the back of her head with his right hand. "Why do you ask?"

"Ye're not a ghost?" After encountering Mr. McLaury in the Tombstone jail, she couldn't be sure anymore. "I amn't dreamin'?"

"Not unless I am, too. And if that's so, I pray I never wake."

She swatted him on the arm and snapped, "Where have ye been?"

"Ow," Rafaele laughed before he sobered. "I've been in hell, my dear."

From outside the room, someone—likely Kököle—chirped: "Oh just kiss each other already!"

"Why don't you skedaddle," replied Rafaele. "Go get drunk."

A male voice—Maeve hoped it wasn't Jethro—slurred, "We're allrudy drenk!"

Rafaele smiled at Maeve, telling them, "Get drunker. This round's on me."

A cheer rose from the group and the chatter grew distant as they retreated from the makeshift hallway.

Maeve swallowed as he coaxed her into a kiss. For all intents and purposes, it was an innocent meeting of the lips, but flame shot through her veins as if it were more.

She impulsively put her hands on his face as if his mouth on hers wasn't proof enough they were together again. She crushed herself against him, desperate for his weight on her, for his warmth, for his scent, for everything Rafaele was to flood her senses, to penetrate her and to make her whole again. To take away the suffering of the past half year.

She gasped and pulled away, trying to sort her thoughts before they ran off without her. It was Milton's birthday after all, and they should've been celebrating with him. "We should go back out there—" Maeve stumbled over her words, straightening her sleeves, tending her skirts, and wishing the raging desire in her lower abdomen would take a brief respite before she ravaged her mate. "Is me *tournure* right?"

"It's a trifle crooked. Let me fix that." Rafaele sneaked his hand down the bustle's band around her back and tugged the fabric, moving to a spot over her hip where he tugged more.

He was so close to her again, his lips grazing her earlobe and neck.

Maeve inhaled, her pulse at a gallop as he slid his palm along the band of her skirt over her stomach before fiddling with the fabric there, too. The butterflies were wild, her tummy aching for more of his touch. For more of his skin against hers.

"There." He nodded decisively.

"Is it all better now?"

"Oh, wait. No, it's still screwed up." Rafaele put his hands on either side of her overskirt and tugged downward. Both skirts, her petticoat, and her bustle all dropped to the floor in a single heap. "*Now* it's better."

She gasped, her cheeks warming at the growing damp between her thighs. "Oh! How … Efficient." Coming to her senses, she met his gaze, her fingers undoing the buttons of her bodice seemingly of their own accord. "Not to mention new. Tell me: what else did ye learn while ye were away?"

"It's far from new," he replied, shucking his boots before opening the laces around the back of Maeve's corset. "Just an old trick I learned from … an old trick." Rafaele pulled her corset off and exhaled.

Maeve looked him over, her gaze settling on the trouser buttons she was struggling to undo as he strained against them. The physical manifestation of his attraction pleased her.

She helped him out of his trousers and shirt, and he removed her combinations.

Maeve took his manhood into her hand, marveling at its size and firmness. Rafaele's breath hitched at her touch and it dissolved into a low moan that stirred her inside.

There was much yet to discuss, so many questions, but thoughts escaped her when his hand slid to her backside. She couldn't even concentrate enough to fondle him as she was inclined so she squeezed his arousal, which he made no complaints about.

He stroked her bottom and cupped it before his fingers meandered between her thighs. "My dear Buttercup," he whispered, "how I longed for you."

Maeve gasped, falling against his chest with her eyes closed and head tilted back.

His lips warmed her neck as his fingers circled and explored her sensitive flesh. Between mouth and hand, Maeve's legs quivered and threatened to give out on her.

"Raf—" she sighed, "I'm afeard I might swoon—"

He chuckled, the laugh reverberating against her skin. "Don't. Not yet."

"Not yet?" Maeve whispered.

"Swoon after you're done." He squeezed her breast and toyed with her nipples one after the other. "Enjoy this first."

She shivered under his touch. "So now ye're tellin' me what to do?"

"Kind of." He smiled impishly. "Is that a problem?"

"Kind of," she deliberately echoed him with a lot less impishness. "Let's return to this later. Ye have me at a disadvantage here—"

His fingers dipped into her and she responded with a yelp of pleasure. He guided her over and pushed her backward onto the bed, kneeling to bury his face between her spread legs; his tongue teased her softly, the bristles of his mustache a stark contrast to her skin. As she arched her back, her necklace slid and settled into the hollow of her throat, the motion of the pearls seeming to amplify every sensation coursing through her body.

She tucked her fingers into what curls she could at his crown, biting her lip to swallow her moans. Her restraint was no match for his skill as he brought her to the precipice of resolution multiple times without the sweet release she longed for.

As he began building her up again, she twisted in her spot while she had the presence of mind to, grabbing a pillow from behind her and pitching it at him.

Rafaele raised his head, brows kinked and a frown on his delectable, glistening lips. "Why'd you do that?"

"Yer teasin' me," Maeve panted, "'n' I can't take anymore."

"Well then ..." He tousled with her, and they jockeyed for position again before Maeve pinned him to the mattress with a triumphant laugh.

"*Zio, zio del mio meglio!*" Rafaele laughed breathlessly.

If she weren't already undressed, that would've charmed the gown right off her. "What?"

"I surrender! Do to me as you will."

She leaned back. "Sit up."

He did as instructed. While straddling him, his erection bumped against the tender inside of her thigh and he adjusted himself.

Maeve lowered herself onto him bit by bit until he fully broached her. Rafaele pressed his forehead to hers, gazing at her with stars in his eyes. "Ah, I missed you so much, Gorgeous. You can't know."

"Can't I?" Maeve kissed him as he grabbed her hips. She granted him the privilege of guiding her motions; a lazy lap-dance where their chests touched, and their mouths didn't stray long from each other.

Rafaele's right hand wandered from her hip to the little space between her thighs, where it added glorious friction to Maeve's ride. Her pulse galloped, heat spreading through her body, every muscle in spasm. The euphoria of his undivided attention drove her to the most exquisite delirium; she panted, her skin atingle with the energy of their love, her fingers snaking into his hair as a cry of long-overdue ecstasy wrenched from her throat.

Another female voice joined her song of rapture somewhere in the distance, the candle flames around them flaring and stretching taller by several inches.

He arrested her movements abruptly, crushing her against himself, his heart pounding so fervently she felt it knocking back against hers. His heart wasn't the only thing she could feel throbbing.

After several minutes, Rafaele helped recline her beside himself, handling her as he would a porcelain doll. She snuggled in and he nuzzled the top of her head while lazily rotating the pearls against her neck.

Maeve closed her eyes and listened as his breathing slowed, vaguely aware parts of her face were burning. How wonderful it was to be back in his arms, to be secure, wanted, and loved. Not falsely loved, but really and unmistakably loved. How comforting it was to not doubt her feelings for him, nor his for her.

A world she feared would never be good was right again.

The world would be perfect, in fact, as long as the two of them were together.

Only the two of us.

Not the three of us.

Not Maeve 'n' Rafaele—'n' baby girl.

No, with just the two of them, a perfect world no longer existed. In a perfect world, she would've been halfway into her pregnancy, with a wonderful little round belly to show for it.

Why? Why did I have to think about tha' now? She choked on a sob. It was obvious: she needed to tell him.

"Maeve—?" Rafaele lifted her chin.

She met his gaze with a hard, shuddering breath.

His words were baffled: "You're crying." He brushed her tears away with the pad of his thumb. "Please don't mar your beautiful face."

"I can't help it—" But the words caught in her throat; she had no idea how to tell him what happened, to first admit to carrying his child and then to tell him she'd lost it. *Not 'it,'* she corrected herself. *Her.* Dallahan had confirmed what she knew in her heart of hearts: the baby she'd carried was a little girl. Maeve pressed her face into his chest with a groan before sniffling loudly.

The smell of soap on his skin had been replaced by the subtle, delectable scent of his sweat. She sighed through her tears. At least she still had him, which was more than she'd had a couple hours ago. Presently, it was everything. "Do not ye ever scare me like tha' again, Mr. Forino!"

"'Mr. Forino?' Why the formality?" Rafaele said, caressing her arm.

"Because. I'm mad at ye." She pulled her arm from his touch; she needed to be able to think straight. "Cannot ye tell?"

He sighed. "For what it's worth, I'm mad at me, too. I had terrible misgivings leaving you behind when I stepped aboard that westbound train, and I spent every moment of those following months ruing my decision. I hope the choices I made are a good exchange for the misery of our having been separated."

Maeve bolted upright. "The choices ye made? What choices?"

"You'll see in short order. We're here long enough for me to recover my strength from the past few weeks of misadventures before I spirit you away from this hellhole ... More or less as planned."

Her gaze traveled his body, attempting to assess how weak he was; how much time she had remaining in Redington. "What's tha'?" Maeve pointed to a sizeable mark of raised—maybe swollen—hairless flesh surrounded by patches of skin with small lumps on his left thigh.

"Oh—uh—that's a souvenir from my dinner a few weeks ago. Wild pigs are surprisingly adept at protecting themselves."

She frowned. "This isn't another coyote yarn, is it?"

Raising his prosthetic hand, Rafaele replied, "I swear it's the truth."

"Does it still hurt?"

"Nah."

Maeve delicately put her fingertips to it, finding the scar tissue harder than the surrounding skin. She pouted, longing for the ability to heal others as she could, herself.

"That feels so good. I wish you touched me more," he sighed.

She pressed her lips together in a pseudo-smile. "Tha' makes both of us. But someone never affords me the opportunity."

Their gazes met; he stared back with eyebrows raised and eyes wide.

"Clearly," he said, "that's been a terrible error in judgment. Thing is, I can never get enough time touching you. I kinda forget myself in the heat of the moment." Rafaele's gaze dropped as he stroked her thigh. She put her hand atop his.

"Maeve?" said Rafaele.

"Yea?"

"Why aren't you wearing your engagement ring?"

Maeve whispered, "Liam."

Frowning, he asked, "Liam?"

She shook her head and scolded herself for using his first name after everything he'd done to her. "Mr. O'Doherty stole it."

"O'Doherty!" Rafaele growled, jumping out of bed to dress. He yanked on his drawers and trousers then snatched his shirt.

She approached her mound of garments, pulling the skirts apart before she dressed. If the illusion of paradise was shattered, there was no harm in following up on a nagging thought: "Ye learnt tha' maneuver from an 'old trick,' did ye?"

He glanced at her warily, his arm in the shirt, his prosthesis still out of it. "Eh ..." he drawled. "When you're young and can only afford ten minutes of rented affection, you've gotta make each moment count; managing layers takes too long. Please ... Maeve. Don't hold me accountable for what I did before I met you."

"'N' were the shoe on the other foot?"

"What?"

Maeve turned her attention to putting on her combinations, supposing she should've taken the time to clean herself with a handkerchief first. "Never ye mind tha'." She clasped the busk of her corset, meeting Rafaele's gaze. "I'm gonna insist ye shave tha' awful thing."

"Awful?" Rafaele pouted, putting his fingertips to his mustache. "I thought it was dashing. You don't like it?"

If he were confronting Liam—assuming Liam was alive and recognizable —Maeve feared he'd figure out soon enough why she disliked it. "Ye look better without it. Please help me on with this."

Rafaele helped her dress and they emerged from the room, finding the Tiff and Tawny a good measure brighter than it was before they reunited; the flame of each oil lamp was robust, reaching well above the top of its glass enclosure.

He turned to her, whispering in her ear, "I did this?"

Despite herself, Maeve smiled, taking him by the arm. "No. *I* did this. Ye just ... lent a hand. 'N' lips ... 'n' tongue." She muttered, "... 'N' other things."

The party had, indeed, resumed without them, many people clearly drunker than they were when last Rafaele and Maeve saw them.

In the middle of it: Kököle, clearly the center of the Pack's attention, humiliated, and on the receiving end of eye daggers shot by Alexis from several feet away.

"This has never happened before," Kököle said, her eyes shimmering by lamplight. "Please—don't be scared of me!"

"You … you lied to me," Alexis countered. "You said you weren't like them. You're not what you claimed to be."

"You knew fully well what I am. Is it my fault you can't handle seeing it when it happens?"

"Excuse me." Rafaele gingerly pulled his arm from Maeve's and rushed to physically intervene. "Ladies. I need you to settle your differences another time." Directly to Alexis, he explained, "We have some pressing business to take care of."

What remained of Shadow Wolf Pack congregated in Redington's livery, illuminated by numerous oil lamps.

Maeve wrapped herself around Rafaele in the relative darkness, expecting complaint where none came. He slipped his right arm around her shoulders and squeezed her against himself as he addressed the group: "We've got a job to do at my place where I understand an unearthly entity has taken up residence." He raised his prosthetic arm with its gun extended in demonstration.

"I'll wait outside," Edison said sullenly. "I wouldn't want my convulsions impeding you."

Rafaele nodded. "I regret to say that's for the best. As none of us knows how to handle this thing, we need to be prepared and able to make a hasty retreat."

Kököle, Moencopi, and Alexis—who stood as far from Kököle as she could get while still being involved in this meeting—all turned pointed gazes on Maeve.

Her heart flew into her throat; now was not the time to spring this little talent on Rafaele and, besides, there was likely nothing she could do for Caitlyn. Any case, she regretted being open with Alexis about it. Not only had the information spread to the twins, but now they expected some miraculous abilities out of her. Based upon what, exactly? A few antagonistic single-sided conversations and a single dangerously amateurish out-of-body experience?

Under kinder times over the last few weeks, she'd scarcely been able to communicate with the poltergeist and with the way things were when Alexis pulled her from the cabin, she had no expectations of improved circumstances.

The three women looked displeased by Maeve's lack of response.

In the strained silence, Milton commented, "Wuh-we'll have to hope these weapons will protect us even if they c-can't do anything to whatever's in Wolf's place."

"That's the spirit," muttered Alexis, crossing her arms over her chest.

Despite her lack of enthusiasm, everyone else at least mustered tense chuckles over her pun.

Maeve couldn't fault Alexis her reluctance to return; she, herself wasn't eager to go back though she wasn't fearful of the otherworldly the way Alexis was. She couldn't fathom the terror Alexis had to be experiencing. *A giant scorpion made of scorpions 'n' spittin' flyin' scorpions at ye.*

Maybe she *could* understand it.

"Very well," Rafaele sighed. "No time like the present." He pulled his arm from around Maeve's shoulders and stepped away but Maeve's grip around his waist tightened.

Under everyone's expectant watch, Rafaele chuckled and dropped a kiss atop her head. With his lips against the hair at her crown, he murmured, "You're gonna have to let me go, Maeve."

She said nothing, her embrace growing fiercer yet.

"Much as I hate it, you should accompany us," he told her. "Probably serve us well to have more witches rather than fewer."

Maeve craned her head to meet his gaze with a frown. She was a consolation prize in this venture. Not Maeve, a Pack member, or Maeve, his future bride and partner, but Maeve, the witch. Maeve: additional body.

As they departed, Rafaele beckoned to the silent observer watching from an unlit corner of the livery. "Follow us. I suspect before long, we'll need you there, too."

It was after ten when Shadow Wolf Pack arrived at the door to Rafaele's eastern cabin, weapons deactivated but at the ready, their journey through the desert landscape lit by a handful of lamps.

Amid quiet shuffling in the dirt, Rafaele held the side of his finger to his lips, raised his pistol and pushed in the front door using his foot.

After peering inside, he shot a questioning glance at Alexis, then Maeve.

Rafaele stepped inside, his lamplight illuminating the last thing Maeve expected to see: nothing at all out of place.

"How can it be?" Alexis gasped. "I—the—the things—there was—" She shook her head.

They all filed in after Rafaele, including Edison, splitting up and lighting oil lamps as they came across them.

Maeve sidled close to Rafaele. "I don't understand it," she said, as baffled as Alexis sounded. "It's like nothin' ever happened. But when we left, it was … Pure chaos. Absolute terror."

Had both Maeve and Alexis hallucinated?

"Raf—" Alexis's strained voice came from the kitchen. "I think you oughtta get in here!"

Without a word, Rafaele took to the kitchen. Maeve, however, fell short, catching motion out of the corner of her eye as Moencopi and Kököle emerged from the bedroom and followed Rafaele to the kitchen.

She waited for them to go. "Cait?" whispered Maeve.

The misty disturbance passed without a word through the front door and Maeve followed.

"Miss Burke," Maeve hissed, squinting through the night. "Stop, please! I want to talk to ye." The form kept moving. "Oh, c'mon," she groaned, in hot pursuit. She raised her hands, allowing them to heat the air and illuminate her surroundings. "I need to talk to ye!"

The form stopped before drawing closer to her, enveloping her hands in a chill.

"Can ye not talk? I don't hear ye."

Tired. It was faint, a whisper lost to roaring winds: *Weak.*

Maeve swallowed. "What if … What if I came to yer plane? Will ye stay here so I can talk to ye?"

Fainter yet: *Yes.*

She'd kind of hoped for a 'no.'

Maeve turned to glance back at the cabin some distance away, flickering lamplight moving from window to window.

It was foolish to put herself in so vulnerable a position—rendering herself unconscious in the middle of the desert—but she owed it to Caitlyn. Broken promises hurt and she didn't want to be the cause of someone else's pain.

Maeve made herself comfortable on the ground surrounded by small prickly shrubs and focused on a spot of light in the distance.

Gradually, her body fell away as if she were falling into a wakeful sleep; so much easier to accomplish when she wasn't in physical agony.

"Maeve. This is a foolish thing you do for a dead woman."

"I needed to apologize; I'm so sorry I abandoned ye. Ye scared me witless in there! Tell me ..." Maeve got to her feet with the strange sense of freedom she felt when leaving behind her physical body. "What did ye do to Liam after I left?" She looked her over; Caitlyn was no longer the inky, vaguely feminine form she encountered in Rafaele's cabin, but a healthier version of the woman she remembered from their time together at the saloon.

Caitlyn turned to her with the familiar wicked grin she put on when she prepared to trap Maeve into saying something embarrassing during their vocabulary lessons. "I possessed him." She paused. "And I was surprised to find I hadn't been the first one there."

Maeve wanted to ask what she meant but there was something in Caitlyn's tone and expression that scared her too much to find out more. So instead, she said, "Ye saved me life, Miss Burke. Thank ye."

"You'd have done the same for me, I'm sure."

"I don't understand what changed. After everythin' ye said, everythin' ye touched 'n' destroyed ... Ye were obviously present on tha' plane. But when we came back to the cabin, I could barely see or hear ye."

"None of it was real. It was all for show, but it took all my strength; I was too weak afterward to make myself seen or heard anymore ... but I guess in doing it, I earned my freedom." She shrugged. "Whatever my freedom now gets me. I walk the earth in a place where nobody can ever know I exist. Nobody can ever hear me. Nobody can ever ... touch me." She regarded Maeve with shimmering eyes, her beautiful mouth pouting. "I can never experience physical affection again. Oh, my God." Tears breached her bottom lashes, her lower lip quivering. "I'm in hell."

Maeve set her jaw. "Not if I have anythin' to say about it."

"What do you mean? What can *you* do?"

Maeve stopped what was the noncorporeal equivalent of midstride. She studied their surroundings, what was a surreal blend of familiar and foreign. "I can escort ye to *Tír na nÓg*." She set her jaw. "I *am* escortin' ye to *Tír na nÓg*."

"The Otherworld?" gasped Caitlyn. "That's not myth?"

Maeve nodded. "The realm of health, joy, 'n' youth everlastin'."

"Can you … can you do that?"

"Yea, of course I can," said Maeve, because she was going to, anyway. "It's the least I can do considerin' I was the whole reason ye were trapped there. I'm so sorry. I only meant to help ye."

"I'm sure you didn't mean to trap me with him. I didn't want to have to say those awful things but … sometimes people need a little push in the right direction. And you! You, especially: you're so stubborn, you often need a big push." Caitlyn smiled at her. "But you have such a good heart." She hesitated. "Will I be allowed … in?"

"In?" Maeve continued walking. "In to *Tír na nÓg*?"

"Yea."

"I don't see why ye wouldn't. What matters is tha' I'm takin' ye away from tha' hell—'n' this one—to a far better place."

Caitlyn stopped her with a hand on her shoulder. "To be clear, I wasn't unhappy with my life. I was damn good at my job and I enjoyed what I did. I had the love of a good man. I have no regrets." She pulled her hand away. "I just don't relish being alone. And I'd be alone here."

Saying nothing, Maeve continued walking, guided by intuition, a feeling of being drawn home. She'd been there before; she used to go there regularly. Maybe she even loved there.

She dredged a song from the deepest part of her soul, halfway humming it, halfway singing what words she recalled as the landscape around them became thick with mist.

Between dense clouds of fog, the Arizona desert turned monotone, her surroundings rippling as if being viewed through moving water.

"And in the end," said Caitlyn, "I had the most remarkable, selfless friend a woman could hope for. I know she'll be OK without me."

"Will she?" Maeve swallowed hard. "How can ye be so sure?"

"She has the devotion of a good man." Caitlyn smiled. "Tell Forino he'll always have my heart."

The gloom of a desert floor shrouded in nighttime fog gave way to sunrise and before them stretched a shore: sand of crushed citrine, lapped by ocean waves the color of apatite. Further inland, a towered gateway of red and white limestone led to a path, and beyond that, hills swathed in dense green forest reached skyward, the roofs and towers of a stately city dotting the lush foliage.

Maeve led Caitlyn to the gateway but stopped abruptly there, though she couldn't put her finger on why. Was it Caitlyn's last request to relay a message of love to her intended, or the unsettling sensation of having her toes at the edge of an abyss?

She swallowed. "Welcome, Caitlyn, daughter of Muirne 'n' Finnegan, to the Land of Youth. No sorrow or pain shall find ye here."

"Thank you, Maeve. I wish you and your handsome rogue all the best." She paused, regarding Maeve with a peculiar expression before reaching out and caressing her face. "My dear, sweet nug."

"Don't—please. Ye'll make me cry."

Caitlyn smiled as she cupped Maeve's chin. "There is a beautiful place somewhere between rage enough to destroy half the world and standing idly by while people hurt and use you. Find that place. Live there and be joyful."

Maeve squeezed her eyes shut and exhaled through the fire searing her nostrils. "I don't want to say goodbye."

"Then don't."

Caitlyn pressed a kiss to her forehead and Maeve opened her eyes in time to watch her disappear through the gateway.

"Caitlyn, I wasn't ready. Wait—"

After a couple heartbeats, Maeve decided to pursue her, taking a step forward.

Blessed warmth engulfed her and her vision went white as if she were running head-long into a swoon. She called out: "Caitlyn!"

"No, no, no!" It was Caitlyn's voice, though she was nowhere to be seen. "You can't be here! Turn around, leave! Now! Before the Dallahan sees you!"

A mist barreled into Maeve like an icy locomotive and she tumbled backward through patches and flashes of the ethereal, unequaled beauty of the Otherworld and the harsh ugliness of the real one. She hadn't pulled back the veil between the worlds; she'd shredded it, shattering its surface as if being pitched through a stained-glass window, shards of color illuminated in flashes by *Tír na nÓg*, and then winking into darkness.

Through the distance as she tumbled, a pair of voices cried out: *"Maeve!"*

She collided with her body painfully, jolting conscious with a labored gasp.

Beneath her: unforgiving desert floor. Above her: black sky.

I remember this.

Prickly shrubs, a cloud-filled, moonless night.

I know where I am. I made it back.

"Oh, good lord, Maeve! Are you OK?"

Maeve blinked furiously, turning her head toward Kököle where she kneeled beside her, a lantern on the ground illuminating her face eerily from below.

"Yea," Maeve breathed; it was the loudest she could talk. "Yes, I am. I escorted Miss Burke to the Otherworld. Why do ye ask?"

Moencopi kneeled next to her sister, their equal faces etched with equal concern. It was Moencopi to whisper: "You were dead."

CHAPTER 20

afaele walked into the kitchen where Edison, Milton, and Alexis were gathered and watching a corner.

He followed their gazes, discovering who he guessed was Liam O'Doherty. Cowering in a fetal position with a badly broken leg, mumbling nonsense and weeping, he was hardly the picture of authority Rafaele had been envisioning all that time.

"Oh, dear," Milton whispered. "What do we d-d-do with him?"

"Whatever the hell was going on here left him fit for nothing but an institution," said Rafaele.

Edison put a shaking hand to Rafaele's prosthetic one. "Considering what you're suggesting, it would be a significant mercy to just kill him now."

He glanced at Edison as the older man pushed his white hair from his forehead, revealing the scar on his temple that served as a reminder of his past Rafaele didn't need.

Rafaele leaned in to get a better look at Liam, broken and bloody leg, descent into madness, and all. "Stilwell: Fetch Cummings from the front door."

"Do you think that's good enough?" Alexis whipped around to them, her eyes flashing. "No! None of it's good enough!" She charged for the shadow of a man in the corner, kicking him in the ribs. "Stand up."

"Alexis!" Rafaele barked.

She cast him an altogether scary stare before she regarded Liam. "That was for catching me off guard and making me feel like a helpless little girl." Alexis continued, one statement fuel for the next, and each punctuated with a kick: "That's for stealing Maeve's engagement ring. For selling something that wasn't rightfully yours. And for breaking the spirit of a beautiful woman!"

Alexis kicked Liam again, this time eliciting a noise from him that led Rafaele to believe there may have been a glimmer of consciousness left in the man.

She paused her assault as if mulling the noise over.

"Get up," Alexis hissed.

When Liam failed to promptly abide, she grabbed his shoulders and dragged him to his feet, slamming him against the wall. He groaned.

"And this is for forcing yourself on her!" Alexis punched him in the face, splitting his lip; blood streamed from his mouth and nose. She hissed in pain, pressing her fist to her stomach before noticing she'd gotten his blood on herself. She screamed and punched him in the face once more. "That's for hurting me for forcing me to punch you and for staining my best shirt, you sorry son-of-a-bitch!"

Alexis cocked her arm to punch him again when Milton intervened, struggling to restrain her.

Rafaele caught the glitter of tears in Alexis's eyes as he walked by her while approaching Liam.

He jammed the muzzle of his gun beneath Liam's chin and held it there.

Liam met his gaze. In it, Rafaele saw exhaustion, fear, resignation, and notes of recognition. He may have been on the descent into madness but there was still enough cognizance to be aware of what would be done to him at an institution. At least, that is, until they treated the remaining sanity out of him.

Under any other circumstance, Rafaele would've done to him as he'd done to Booker.

Liam, however, deserved worse for his indiscretions—to him, to Maeve, and to all the innocent people who'd gotten in the way of his crusade.

For those reasons and for the sheer spite of Liam's face, Rafaele lowered his weapon.

"Alex, Dandy: restrain the louse."

They relished his orders as Edison stepped back into the room accompanied by Marshal Cummings.

"Here's your villain," Rafaele told Cummings, motioning to Liam, "who sent Booker to destroy the train I was on, and then a posse to gun me down when he realized I survived. I imagine there's plenty of evidence at the remnants of the trestle showing Bocere tanks, among other things, same as at the Tiff." He hesitated. "Although I'm sure it doesn't mean much coming from me, Booker *did* confess to everything just before he died. I'm sure you can find their remains where I left them ... barring scavengers." Rafaele dug into his duster pocket and produced a small wad of papers he handed to the marshal. "They lured me onto the same train Booker's explosives sent to the bottom of a ravine. Every seat on it but mine was occupied—must've been a couple hundred he killed under O'Doherty's orders."

Guilt that he was at least a little at fault for so many deaths was going to eat Rafaele alive—if he allowed it. Better to shift blame to Liam, who was at least as responsible.

As Marshal Cummings leafed through and skimmed the telegrams, Rafaele commented, "I've little doubt Mr. Akbar will corroborate O'Doherty forced him to transmit those."

With a sour, far-away expression on his face, Cummings replied, "I'm already aware of O'Doherty's relationship with Akbar. I was an unfortunate firsthand witness."

"Angelino—however ambitious—only ever got ahead when allying himself with someone more powerful. He had the expertise, but not the leadership skills to plan any of this, himself. Esquivar, O'Doherty ... both could easily manipulate someone like Booker."

Cummings regarded Rafaele with narrowed eyes before clearing his throat. "The detective's insistence to pursue you turned him into the type of person he believed he was hunting." He smiled, warm as ever. "Always wondered why you never invited me along on our group's adventures. Why include me in this one?"

"Would've looked bad if a town marshal was active in its criminal element, don't you think?" Rafaele sighed. "I figured this time was OK since it's Shadow Wolf Pack's last ride. Not to mention you're the keeper of the straitjacket." He nodded to the garment in Cummings's hands. "The honor is all yours."

The marshal's warm smile turned wicked as he turned his gaze to Liam. "It sure is."

The twins let Maeve rest in silence for some time, a fact she was grateful for; there was much to consider between this new experience, and the things Caitlyn told her.

It was a distant voice to break the silence: "Maeve? Moencopi? ... Kököle?"

"We should return to the cabin," Moencopi said gently.

"Must we?" Kököle gave a pointed look to her sister.

Maeve was too tired to ask what else they were hiding and, besides, Alexis's cries for them were getting louder and more desperate.

"Let us see first what is happening."

Kököle took Maeve's hand to help her stand while Moencopi assisted her by taking her sleeve-covered elbow.

"Are you well enough to walk?" Moencopi asked.

Maeve nodded and the three set off toward Rafaele's cabin.

Several yards away they spotted Alexis, her worried face illuminated by a swinging lantern held by a shaking, outstretched arm. "Where the hell did you go?" she cried.

"She doesn't need to know the truth," Maeve whispered to her escorts. "It wouldn't help anythin'."

"I agree," said Moencopi.

"Where are the men?" Kököle asked Alexis upon their approach.

"They escorted O'Doherty back into town. He won't be bothering anyone anymore; they're detaining him at the jail overnight and sending him off to an asylum on the next train out."

"So ... It's just us here right now?" Kököle's voice lilted strangely hopeful.

"Where's the—um—" Alexis nodded toward the cabin. "The poltergeist?"

"Miss Burke is gone where she can't hurt anymore," Maeve assured her.

"Then yes, it's just us here right now," replied Alexis.

She and the Hopi women engaged in a brief, silent conversation.

Moencopi asked, "Who shall do the honors?"

"It was Alexis's idea," said Kököle. "She should."

Alexis sniffled, passing the lantern to Moencopi. She took Maeve's hands and squeezed them tightly before guiding her around the back of Rafaele's cabin.

She stopped a yard away from a small mound of dirt from which a small green sapling was emerging.

"What's this?" Maeve asked.

"It's a … memorial. You were so distraught at having nothing left of the baby you lost, so I thought symbolically, this way you'd have something … at least." Alexis gave her an uncertain smile.

Maeve's phlegm lodged in her throat.

"But …" Kököle put a hand on Maeve's shoulder. "You … You did. I mean, there *was* …"

Maeve met Kököle's gaze, trying to piece together what the woman was saying.

"Everything you lost over those first few hours …" Kököle bit her lip and exhaled, "I brought it here and committed it back to Earth Mother."

The words sank in as if ice water were being trickled down her body.

Trembling, Maeve crumpled to the ground with a whimper. She put a hand to her breast, the other going to the dirt of the tiny grave. Her fingertips sank in and raked it before she fell forward with a wail, pressing her forehead to the dirt.

Her body was wracked with sobs, a crushing ache in her chest making her nauseated and breathless.

"I'm so sorry," whispered Kököle.

"Me too." Alexis added in a tiny voice, "I truly thought you'd like it."

Moencopi kneeled beside her but refrained from touching her. "It was never our intention to cause you pain."

"N-no—" Maeve sobbed. She straightened, brusquely wiping her forehead and cheeks before pinching her eyes shut and taking shuddery breaths.

"It's OK to cry," Kököle said softly.

Maeve shook her head, choking on the words, "No, it's not. Milt told me cryin' doesn't bring people back from the grave. Lord knows if tha' was true, I'd have me baby back."

"Maybe … maybe it doesn't do that," replied Alexis, "but it *does* show they're missed."

"And that they mattered," the sisters said as one.

"Moreso on you than anyone else, Maeve," Moencopi added, "when your pain is literally etched into the skin on your cheeks. Tears from you do not fall lightly."

Maeve had no verbal reply, granting herself the freedom to weep, pain be damned.

Moencopi put an arm across her quaking shoulders. "I know it does nothing to know others have walked in your shoes … but I know this pain. I, too, had a daughter. She was taken by the sea."

Maeve turned to Moencopi and threw her arms around her, crying too hard to say anything more for a while. But when she did, her voice was weak and muffled by the fabric on Moencopi's shoulder: "I love it … I'm touched. But … I amn't ever goin' to get over this. Am I?"

Kököle said, "Some things are never meant to be gotten over. After all, you've lost a future you earned in loving—and being loved by—another. Honor the memory of what you made with him. Keep it close to your heart and remember it's OK to grieve. Forever, if necessary."

Alexis cleared her throat. "We've no guarantee how soon Raf will be returning and if you wanna keep this between us, we'd probably better finish out here."

Maeve sniffled with a nod, withdrawing from Moencopi and resituating herself to remove her left boot. She shook it over her open hand, then curled her fingers to her palm. She pressed her fist to her chest, gazing at the stars.

"Yer dadaí gave this to yer ma. 'N' now I give it to ye," said Maeve. Taking a shuddering breath, she wedged the ten-dollar gold eagle into the dirt at the base of the sapling growing from her daughter's grave. "May it keep ye safe in yer eternal rest."

A PERSONAL NOTE FROM THE AUTHOR

If you wept with Maeve over the loss of her pregnancy, you wept with me. The inclusion of these events was not just for the progression of Possession's plot—or to force change and growth upon Maeve (although both result from the experience). It was also written as therapy and catharsis for me to deal with the grief of my personal experience. Some of what I wrote was a page from my journal. Some was explaining away things I never got answers to when I suffered my miscarriage the day after Christmas in 2011.

If you have walked the journey with Maeve (and me) and wish to reach out and share stories, my social media accounts are open 24/7 and I'll consider it an honor to hear from you.

Please also consider visiting the following resources:

- http://facesofloss.com/
- https://www.seleni.org/advice-support/article/miscarriage-grief-is-real
- http://nationalshare.org/

KEEP READING FOR A PREVIEW OF THE NEXT
INSTALLMENT OF THE WITCHES' REDE

AVAILABLE NOW

Boot Hill, Redington, Arizona
March 1, 1884

Redington's cemetery wasn't much to look at, populated sparsely with older graves. Most were wooden markers, a few crosses, some nothing more than a rock with a name painted on it, long-since faded, their shadows leaning long and westward.

The newest grave marker was placed along the back of the fenced-off lot and had all of four words painted on it:

KATE LYNN
A WHORE

Maeve took a steadying breath. Nobody in town cared enough to spell Caitlyn's name properly. Perhaps whoever made the headstone didn't know any better.

She'd been told that the money for the marker was provided by her most dedicated patron and as much as she hated admitting it, she knew that referred to Rafaele.

Her soon-to-be husband, Rafaele.

If what they said was true, her fiancé likely told them how to spell—or in this case, misspell—her name.

Knowing the way Caitlyn felt about him, Maeve supposed she would have been crushed to see how little he knew her.

Good thing she'll never know.

Maeve had made certain of that.

The misspelled name was bothersome but as she stepped away from Caitlyn's grave, it was the words *"a whore"* that seared her like a burning lump of coal shoved beneath her skin.

What kind of tombstone would I have, she wondered, *had Frank or Liam gotten their ways with me? Somethin' similar to Cait's?*

More likely, she'd be occupying one of the unmarked plots in the back corner where the townsfolk dumped those who didn't matter.

If it's good enough for Mozart, it's more than I've earned.

Maeve reviewed the headstones of several men, each bearing his title, first and last names, and their accomplishments as though they had all done something remarkable—no matter how trivial they were in the grand scheme of things.

Several of those graves had smaller ones neighboring them, and on those markers were never more than three words: a first name, followed by *"his wife."* A couple only had those two words and no name.

These gravestones served as an unwanted reminder to Maeve of a woman's place in the world. Her place.

Wife.

Or whore.

Mother, if she were lucky enough. And so long as she had Dallahan chasing her, she was anything but.

Caitlyn, bless her soul, had given Maeve an option other women didn't have: to work as a psychopomp. It was something she could do that she was confident was rare; a career in which she'd have little to no competition.

Was it in demand?

Of that, Maeve was uncertain.

The only people to care about trapped souls needing release from this world, or guidance to the Otherworld were the souls, themselves; Lord knew the deceased didn't pay well.

It wouldn't be much of a living. Considering she'd be providing a service to the dead, that made a certain amount of sense.

Then again, conducting seances would've been a decent alternative—if she could make a name for herself as being the real deal as opposed to just another in a countless stream of frauds.

Contrary to what Maeve expected, there was not a soul in that graveyard when she arrived accompanied by Rafaele. He had wandered off to give her some time to pay her respects in private before—she assumed—he would do the same.

Another person arrived not long after, but she paid him no mind, consumed in her own grief.

It was a heartbeat, though, before he was behind her, his voice stopping her midstride. "Good mourning." He paused. "That's mourning with a 'u,' in case you failed to realize."

Without thinking, Maeve threw a punch somewhere in the vicinity of his awful face, but he caught her hand well before it connected with his chin.

She wrenched her fist from his grip.

"So," he sang with his breath on her ear, "how've you been, Miss MacKenna? Picking a spot for yourself already?"

Dallahan.

"Hi." He was chipper as a schoolgirl.

Maeve turned to look for Rafaele for her own security, realizing much too late how far from him she'd wandered while lost in thought. He seemed miles away.

She stiffly began walking toward Rafaele and replied to Dallahan with all the chill of an iceberg. "I think ye bloody-well-know how I've been. Ye do seem to know everythin'." *He knows bloody everythin'.*

"Yea, I do."

Her eyes went wide, and she glared at him. "It was ye! Ye told Brother Thurman about me baby before tha' sermon."

Dallahan—under his human and infinitely more attractive guise of Mr. Davidson—shrugged impishly. "Guilty as charged. But can you blame me? His dreams, after all, were so terribly easy to traverse. It was almost as if he put out a mat welcoming me. Mortal, you know. Easy little nut to crack, unlike you."

"I'll crack *yer* nu—"

"Maeve, Maeve, Maeve," chuckled Dallahan. "Propriety."

She hissed, "Do not ye dare use me first name."

"Oh, right. Before I forget, Maeve, you really should apologize to your friends for accusing them of telling the preacher you were expecting."

"I never did tha'!" *Out loud.*

"Oh, please. You were practically screaming it. Just like you did your sweet little prayer."

Since ye're so keen on listenin' in, I hope ye know how much I detest ye. She kept her eyes on the plots as she walked, trying not to draw Rafaele's attention to her or arouse his concerns.

Her limp, though, seemed to draw Dallahan's. "Leg still bothering you after that fall? You really shouldn't have fought him so. That was, by the way, my little gift to you."

"Me bum leg?" She thought sarcastically, *Thanks so much.*

"Sarcasm is unbecoming of you. No. I meant your old beau, of course. You seemed so lonely here."

"Ye orchestrated tha?"

"All the world's a chessboard and all the men merely pawns. I'm sure old Bill won't mind me paraphrasing; we do spend a great deal of time together. He was, in life, a fair bit infatuated with me. How often did he write about me?"

"Why do ye not leave me the hell alone?"

"Have I offended you?" Dallahan asked, quickening his pace despite his limp to come alongside her again. As he did, he pulled the little yellow flower from his lapel.

Maeve immediately recognized it as tansy.

He offered it to her. "Forgive me?"

She declined the flower, scowling at him spectacularly.

"How insensitive of me," he said with an apologetic smile that was insincere at best. "I suppose it's too soon to joke about that. Women," he said with a shake of his head. "Such confounding creatures. I rather thought that was funny."

"It'll never not be 'too soon' to joke about ye stealin' away me unborn daughter, ye wretched ghoul!"

"My little banshee, what a sweet pet name you've given me."

Maeve's breath caught in her throat. The words came out on a heated whisper: "How could ye take me baby away from me? She had a soul. She had a heartbeat!"

"Did she?"

That did nothing to quell her fury.

"This assumption coming from the woman who talks to ghosts—they are nothing but souls. Tell me: have you ever encountered a ghost with a heartbeat?"

Maeve scowled. "Is there no way to destroy ye?" She spat.

"Ah, see, there's another humorous thing you fail to appreciate. You *do* know how to destroy me." His eyes darkened considerably. "You've already done it."

Maeve slowed her pace enough to afford Dallahan a confused look.

"You know ... I think you delight in teasing me. How tired I am going around with you!" He made a grand gesture—not quite flail, nor exactly shrug—and smacked his thighs loudly with his palms. "You resist me, yet you always come back to me in the end."

"Surely I don't know what ye're carryin' on about."

"Of course you don't." He grabbed her by the upper arm, jerking her to a stop, facing him. "You were at my doorstep, Maeve," hissed Dallahan. "Twice! Hell, you've got one foot in the grave right now." He motioned toward her right shin currently hidden beneath full-length skirts. "Had your voluptuous friend not come to your rescue, you would've had that sweet little skull of yours cracked in twain by … that failure. That old friend of yours. Oh … what was his name again?"

"Liam," growled Maeve, yanking her arm from his grasp. "'N' do not ye think for one moment I don't realize ye turned him against me."

"Right, right. O'Doherty." Dallahan inhaled, glancing around the cemetery. "He was quite the cock-up. Surprising willpower and obnoxious ambition, though. But I digress. You walked that rental cunt right to my doorstep, of your own volition, to leave her with me. You crossed over. You were on my territory!"

She said nothing as they approached Rafaele at long last, and she slunk into his shadow to hide. He cast her a spectacularly morose look and hugged her fiercely.

"Forino," Dallahan greeted him.

"Ah, Mr. Davidson," Rafaele replied, to Maeve's dismay, without the slightest hint of animosity. From around her shoulders, he took Dallahan's hand with his left, shaking it heartily. "I haven't seen you in what feels like a lifetime. How's business?"

Maeve choked on a gasp.

"Can't complain. Still working on a major acquisition, though." Dallahan's eyes flickered to Maeve. "I'll get it, though. I always do."

"I'm sure you will," Rafaele replied with an encouraging smile.

Dallahan sighed, putting on a sad face while patting Rafaele's prosthetic arm. "I was so dreadfully sorry to hear of your loss. She was a great lay, that one, as you know." He spared a purposeful glance at Maeve, tossing the little yellow flower onto the otherwise undecorated mound of dirt where what remained of Caitlyn had been laid to rest. He tipped his hat with a flick of his wrist. "Good day to you, Forino. A pleasure, as always, Miss MacKenna. I'm sure our paths will cross again soon."

Maeve peered around Rafaele's arm to watch Dallahan leave.

As Dallahan walked, he curled his right hand into a fist and shook it, pausing to look back at Rafaele in disgust. His eyes shifted to meet hers before he turned again and vanished into the distance.

She leaned back, searching Rafaele's Death-marred eyes, praying she wouldn't notice a change in them. She didn't, but that didn't set her mind at ease, as she could never be sure what she was seeing in them.

"How many times …" She hesitated. *How to put this delicately?* "How many times have ye shaken tha' man's hand?"

He frowned. "Just once, just now. Why?"

"No reason," she mumbled, pulling Rafaele back into a hug. Her eyes fell upon Caitlyn's grave marker.

Kate Lynn.

"It's Maeve," she said. "M-A-E-V-E."

"Excuse me?"

"Me name. It's spelled M-A-E-V-E. Just in case ye ever need to make me one like this."

Rafaele frowned, his muscles tensing. "I thought we've already talked about this. Besides. God and I have an agreement that such things will never happen."

"What—?"

"Ladies!"

Maeve and Rafaele turned to see Alexis waving as she approached the graveyard fence.

"What're you doing here?" said Rafaele.

Alexis crossed into Redington's hallowed ground and her chipper expression went solemn. "I um … Actually came to visit an old friend."

"Zeke?"

She nodded.

"Ah." Rafaele shuffled his feet in the dirt. "We were just heading out. Maeve needs a break, and I have my own … *respects* … to pay to Rosenzweig."

ACKNOWLEDGMENTS

My undying gratitude to my alpha, beta, and proof readers across social media. Thank you so much for helping to make this book readable, and for your feedback on the cover copy. Your help is deeply appreciated!

ABOUT THE AUTHOR

Photo © Scott M. Leonard

JEWEL E. LEONARD lives in Arizona with her family. She is the author of the Witches' Rede series and the Rays of Sunshine erotic romance series. Visit her online at:

www.jewelwritesromance.com

facebook.com/Jewel.E.Leonard
twitter.com/JewelELeonard
instagram.com/jewel.e.leonard